CLOSING IN

Something wasn't right with the room. It had been bigger than this. There'd been a generous walk space around three sides of the bed. That was gone now. What's more, the ceiling was so low he realized he could reach up and touch it. Not that he wanted to.

Fisher didn't know why exactly…it was a gut instinct: the walls had become repulsive to him. They were no longer dry horizontal planes covered with a dull reddish paper. Though he couldn't actually see it, some quality of the wall was *suggestive* of being moist. They weren't vertical, either; they curved inward. And hardness gave way to a surface that might have been rubbery, or even muscular. Dust cascaded. He dragged his hand across his eyes so he could clear some of the muck that settled on his retinas. *The house is collapsing. Get to the door—get out.* But the door was no longer where it should be…

THE TOWER

SIMON CLARK

LEISURE BOOKS NEW YORK CITY

A LEISURE BOOK®

August 2005

Published by

Dorchester Publishing Co., Inc.
200 Madison Avenue
New York, NY 10016

ISBN 0-8439-5492-2

Visit us on the web at www.dorchesterpub.com.

THE TOWER

Prologue
Sounds off . . .

This was recorded fifteen years ago:

Did you hear that? Can you hear the noise? A kind of hiss . . . in and out, in and out . . . almost the sound of someone breathing. Only it's different, like . . .

No. It's gone again. Yeah, but you're like that, aren't you, house? You big old ugly pile of rock. First it's the sounds, you bang all the doors, and then it's the clock chimes. You're inventive with those, aren't you? But I'm not letting you get the better of me. I'm staying. Did you hear that, house? I'm staying. So, go on! Do your worst!

You're right. I should have kept my mouth shut. You should never goad anyone to do their worst. Not a drunk in a bar. Not a policeman. Not God. Not even this damned house. Because, the moment you make that challenge—*go on, do your worst*—that's exactly what they do. And sometimes it can be far worse than you imagine. Rather than sitting here shouting futile threats at the walls, I should be explaining what happened to me over the last three days.

OK, so I'll take it from the top. My name is Chris Blaxton. I'm twenty-three years old. I'm sitting here alone in a house called The Tower. And here I am in what was once an elegant ballroom with windows looking out over a garden that's now grown into this wild, wild jungle. Not that I can see much of it. It's nighttime. And, yeah, dear God, this is the worst part—when it grows dark. All dark and black and hidden, and the place is swamped by shadows that just ooze through the rooms like they're alive.

Enough. Once you begin brooding about how alone you are in this place and visualize what it's like in all those empty rooms, your imagination starts to eat you alive. Right. I'm sitting at a table that's big enough to seat twenty people. The tape deck is in front of me; the mic's in my hand. I'm going to make this record of what I did just in case I never get the chance to tell you in person. Three nights ago I left video cameras running in the ballroom, with more in the promenade and at the foot of the main stairs. What I saw on the tapes when I played them back was enough to . . . well . . . What I saw is going to be the starting point for this . . . document? Testament? Diary?

Oh? And didn't I tell you I'm now alone in the house? I did, didn't I?

I thought I was. But what you believe and what is true isn't always necessarily one and the same thing. There! Listen! I don't know if you heard that . . . I'm sure there's someone walking along the corridor to the ballroom. So . . . what do you do at a time like this? Run like hell and not look back? Or open the door? See who it is?

But this is The Tower. A house where its occupants don't always wear a human face.

Chapter One

"Go straight over it."

"No."

"It's dead, it—"

"No way!"

"—won't feel a thing."

"Fabian, no way in a million years will I ever drive over that dog."

"Deceased. A lifeless cadaver."

"How do you know?"

"If you don't scoot now we'll miss the ferry."

"So?"

"Miss that and we'll end up sleeping in this turd on wheels."

"Hey? You ungrateful—"

"Drive over the bloody dog or we'll miss the bloody ferry."

Ding, dong, ding, dong. Josanne and Fabian had been clashing with one another ever since London.

"Drive."

"No."

Fabian sat in the backseat like an English lord. But, then he did claim to have aristocratic blood. He was twenty-three, played keyboards, and wrote songs, but he acted like he was sixty-three. His blond fringe hung down in a soft hank that all but covered one blue eye. Josanne turned in the driver's seat to glare back at him. Her oval face with its normally flawless olive skin had been fired up with red blotches. Luckily she only had the steering wheel to hold. If it had been magically exchanged for a gun, she would have shot him. Bloody hell, she would have emptied the magazine into Fabian's arrogant face. That's true love for you.

These thoughts poured easily through John Fisher's head. There'd never been any question of him sharing the driving. Despite the grievous state of the car, Josanne loved it. She wouldn't let anyone behind the wheel. "It's a one woman car," she insisted when he'd offered. So he'd allowed himself three pints of Guinness at the pub. A warm glow surrounded him. For a while he was content to let the argument flow over him. Beer is Teflon coating for the nerves. Josanne's fiery temperament, Fabian's cool sarcasm—they all slid off John Fisher's sense of well-being without sticking. For the last hour of the five-hour journey, that is.

Now check this out. Darkness. Pouring rain. Muddy fields. Narrow lane. Last ferry leaving in fifteen minutes. Dead dog in road. Suddenly this couple's duel of tongues was beginning to stick in his craw.

Fabian declaimed, "We miss the ferry and we can kiss the job good-bye."

"What? Who the hell else are they going to find to house-sit for peanuts? Call that a job?"

"Josanne, drive over the bloody dog. If any of its

guts stick to your blessed car, Fisher here will clean them off for you."

"How do we know it's dead?"

"Just look at the thing. It's not moved a bloody hair in the last ten minutes we've been sitting here."

"It might just be hurt."

"Would you lie in the rain all night if you were still in the land of the living?"

"I'm not driving the car over it."

"Go round, then."

"Have you looked out of the window, Fabian? Have you seen how narrow the road is?"

Fisher's glow of well-being might as well have been a tiny defeated figure with a suitcase, the way it shuffled out of the car to disappear into the rain-sodden night. He groaned.

"Listen to that, Josanne. You've made Fisher unhappy now."

"If he thinks I'm going to crush a poor dog lying in the road, he's got another thing coming."

Fisher began to speak, but Fabian rode over his words in that cool, lordly way of his. "Trust me, Josanne. Pooch is in doggy heaven with all his canine ancestors. Now hurry along before someone rams into the back of us, there's a good girl."

"The road's deserted, Fabian. We haven't seen any traffic in the last half an hour. We're in the middle of a place called Nowhere."

"Then no one's going to see you flatten Fido."

"Didn't you hear me, Fabian? I'm not driving—"

"OK!" Fisher couldn't take any more. "I'll move the dog." He opened the passenger door. "Put the headlights on full so I can see."

Josanne clutched his arm as he started to climb out.

7

"I know it's dead . . . but you'll treat it with respect, won't you?"

Fabian smiled. "You'll lay it to rest with a twenty-one gun salute and a touching eulogy, won't you, old boy?"

"Fabian, drop dead."

"Quickly now, Fisher. You're letting the wet in."

The rain didn't fall in drops: it fell in chunks of ice-cold water that rolled down Fisher's neck. He could barely see ten paces ahead of him. It even obscured the animal in spray as the rain burst against the road. He hunched his shoulders in the forlorn hope that it would stem the rush of cold water through his shirt collar to soak his back. The car's headlights blazed their light into the silver cascade. Probably Josanne couldn't even see him now. Grimly he told himself, just grab the dog by the leg, drag it into the ditch, then get down to the river before the last ferry goes.

That morning he'd been spinning a fantasy of spending the next month rehearsing their music in a picturesque manor house in the tranquil English countryside. He saw himself strolling round the garden to admire the blossoms appearing on the trees. Not this. Not lumbering like the Hunchback of Notre Dame through the rain to haul a dog that was probably mangled to hell and back into the bushes, just so he could return to the car and listen to Josanne and Fabian bicker again.

Fisher muttered, "Where art thou, patron saint of bass players?" Then he answered himself sourly, "Probably being crapped on by the patron saint of lead vocalists." Fisher moved forward through the rain. Ahead, bathed in water droplets that were illuminated by the car's headlights, he saw the dark mound that was the dog. It lay on its side, its legs straight. The black button of a nose glistened. Its eyes were closed, something that Fisher was grateful for. He didn't relish having to meet the corpse's blank stare as he dragged it by its leg off the road and into the grass to rot.

Even so, he felt a stir of sympathy. "Poor devil. Who left you out here all alone, eh?"

The words were intended to prepare himself for seizing a wet hind limb. Only the moment he finished speaking, the dog's head jerked up, its eyelids lifted and Fisher found himself meeting the amber gaze of the dog. Its eyes were drowsy rather than pained.

Fisher paused. *If I grab it now it'll probably chew a lump out of my arm. Funny place to go to sleep, though.*

He clicked his tongue. "Come on, boy. Off the road. You'll get hurt if you stay here. . . . Great, I'm explaining road safety to a dog at ten o'clock at night in freezing rain." He raised his voice. "Move. Come on, boy. Move." He waved his arm to reinforce the command. The dog stared at him with those placid, drowsy eyes. "Oh, hell. You're not going to move, are you? What are you doing? Waiting for someone? Standing guard?" He shook his head. "Hell. Now I'm interrogating it." He gestured again in the forlorn hope the dog would move of its own accord. The dog simply lay there with its head raised while it looked Fisher in the face. "You're not hurt, are you?" He clicked his tongue in exasperation. "Damn silly question. It's not going to answer you, is it?"

"Fisher? Hey, Fisher?"

Fisher glanced back. Fabian had stuck his head through the passenger window. He shielded that neatly groomed blond hair against the rain with a magazine. "Hey, Fisher. What's the bloody holdup? Dump the mutt, then get back in the car. We've only five minutes before the damn ferry goes."

Fisher held up a finger. "Just give me a minute. OK?"

"I was only joking about the eulogy, you know?"

Fisher turned his back on Fabian. "OK," he told the dog gently. "I'm going to pick you up. It's for your own good. You're not going to bite me, are you?"

The dog didn't react to his words. It simply stared, its amber eyes glowing in the headlights. Fisher checked the dog over. It was a medium-sized mongrel with jet black fur. If anything, with its long pointed face, it resembled the jackal statues that guarded the tombs of the pharaohs. It didn't appear to be injured in any way. Maybe this really was its home territory that it was guarding. Not that there were any houses Fisher could see. There was nothing but flat agricultural land for miles around.

"Of course you're going to bite me," Fisher grunted as he squatted beside it. "Who wouldn't bite me if I picked him up and carried him around?"

Now he was too wet to bother about the rain trickling down his back. Making soothing noises, he extended his hands in a way that he hoped was nonthreatening, then gently scooped the dog up into his arms. It wasn't that heavy. Through the wet fur he could feel the movement of its bones as he lifted. The dog didn't so much as grunt. It simply continued to gaze into his face with drowsy eyes. A moment later Fisher set the dog down on the grassy bank at the side of the road.

From the car Fabian shouted. "At last! Now get yourself back here before we miss the ferry."

Fisher ran back to the car. Behind the splashing wipers he could see Josanne. She'd watched him anxiously as he moved the dog. Somewhere in the backseat Fabian would be impatiently drumming his fingers. Ferry, ferry, ferry; that'd be the refrain of his commentary. At the car door Fisher looked back. The dog still lay where he'd left it. For a moment it gazed at him, making eye contact. A moment later it lowered its head onto the grass.

I thought you were going to help me. But you're abandoning me, too.

Fisher hissed, "The dog isn't thinking that. You're only imagining what's going through its mind. It probably lives here. Lying in the road is probably what it does. There's no law against owning an eccentric dog." He opened the door.

Fisher sang out, "At last. Thought you were holding a full funeral service for the animal, old boy. What are you dawdling for? Jump in."

Josanne leaned across so she could make eye contact. "You did treat it with respect, didn't you? I'd hate to think you just—"

"It's alive." Fisher jerked his head back. "It doesn't look hurt."

Fabian shrugged. "Well, now everyone's happy, let's go."

Fisher shook his head so firmly that water flew from his soaked fringe. "I'm not leaving it here."

"Oh, Christ, Fisher. Leave the damn thing."

"No, Fabian. I'm not going to argue. I'm taking the dog."

"Fisher—"

Josanne rounded on Fabian. "We can't leave it here. Do you want it to die?"

"I want to catch the bloody ferry. Who gives a damn about some stupid dog?"

"We do." She opened her door. "Fisher, I'll give you a hand."

Seconds later they both crouched beside the dog. Once more it had raised its head to look at them.

Fisher examined the wet bundle of fur more closely. There was no visible sign of injury, but now he wondered if it was sick. "I'm not leaving it here," he said with feeling. "It won't survive the night."

"Don't worry, I'll wring Fabian's neck if he complains again."

"I'll pick him up. Can you open the back passenger door for me?"

"Sure."

The rain beat down harder. Once they'd moved to the side of the road, the car's lights didn't illuminate the ground, so Fisher found himself moving blindly with the dog in his arms. When he reached the car he saw a figure standing beside it.

"Fabian? Don't try and talk me out of it. I'm bringing the dog with us."

"I know you are, you sentimental idiot." He opened the door. "Here, wrap it in this."

Fisher looked up at Fabian. The man's blond hair formed a slick cap against his head as the rain soaked it through.

"That's your bath towel, Fisher. The dog's covered in mud."

"So I'll let you buy me another." Fabian smiled. "Now get yourself, and your furry friend, into the car where it's warm and dry."

Chapter Two

The patron saint of bass guitarists sprinkles what crumbs he can. Fisher opened the window as Josanne pulled up at the jetty. Moored there was the ferry; it was still boarding vehicles.

"We're in luck. It must have been held up." Josanne cranked her window down, too. The rain had stopped, but the cold night air gusted freely through the car.

"Can you at least shut one of the windows?" Fabian complained. "It's cold as Siberia in the back here. I'm sure the heater isn't working."

"We've made the ferry," she retorted. "Aren't you pleased?"

"Ecstatic. But my hairy friend and I are freezing."

"There's no pleasing some people," she muttered under her breath. The ticket seller came forward, so she was diverted away from an argument with Fabian by asking the price of the crossing.

Fisher looked back at the dog curled up on the backseat. Only the top of its head and eyes were visible in Fabian's luxuriously soft towel.

"Don't worry, old boy. Jak and I are the best of friends. We're looking after one another back here."

"Jak? Is that what you've decided to call him?"

"The only thing I've decided is to hand him in to the police at the earliest opportunity." Fabian pushed his damp fringe out of his eyes with distaste. "And no, I've not been getting all sentimental over our friend here. He's wearing a collar with the name Jak printed on it. Ergo, this is Jak the dog. My God, I hope there'll be hot water where we're going. I need a good long soak."

Fisher shook his head. Most of the time you entertain satisfying thoughts of socking Fabian on the jaw; then, every so often, such as when he wrapped the dog in his towel, he displays a tender side to his nature that leaves you disarmed. It won't last though, Fisher told himself as Josanne inched the car forward up the ramp onto the ferry. Soon you'll find yourself thinking murderous thoughts about him.

"My God," Fabian intoned from the back. "Look at this boat. It's nothing more than oil drums lashed to a frame."

"I think you'll find it's a little more sophisticated than that." It was a typical Josanne riposte for her boyfriend; yet Fisher had to agree that Fabian wasn't that far off target. The ferry was little more than a floating platform with a guardrail round the edge and something that resembled a small tool shed in one corner that served as a wheelhouse. It carried four cars and a couple of small trucks. It probably could have accommodated another car, but that would have been a full load. At 10:30, twenty minutes after it should have left, the engines rumbled. The lights of the jetty slid away. Through the windshield ahead he could make out the river. It resembled a mass of black jelly in the darkness. The rains had swollen it, and the engines of the ferry had to labor to make headway against the current.

Fabian laughed softly. "I hope everyone can swim."

"Shut up, Fabian." Josanne was uneasy.

Fabian enjoyed her fear. "Are you sure we're crossing a river in Yorkshire? Or are we really crossing the River Styx into the underworld?"

Fisher turned to the blond man reclining there in that lordly way of his. "Fabian. What on earth are talking about?"

"You know? The River Styx? The point of no return for the souls of the dead." He patted the dog. "Look, we have our very own Cerberus. Our hell dog. Of course, he's only got one head when it should be the three of legend."

"Christ, Fabian."

Josanne shot Fisher a grin. "You've got my permission to chuck him in the river if he keeps this up."

"Clearly Greek myth is lost on the pair of you."

"Well, Fabian, if we encounter Hades, he can have you with my compliments."

"Hades? God of the underworld. Josanne? I'm impressed." He chuckled. "I'm very much considering the possibility of allowing you to share my bed tonight."

How those two got into a relationship together, God alone knows, Fisher thought. Her parents worked in an industrial bakery. Fabian's father owned an import company. His mother was long gone, although Fabian mentioned that she kept a stable of racehorses. Fabian used these facts to overawe people he met. In reality, however, he had precious little money of his own, hence the ambition to make it big in music. And make the big money that went with it.

"Ah," Fabian cooed. "Just when I thought we'd drift the seven seas for eternity like a ghost ship."

The lights of the jetty on the far side resembled Christmas illuminations against the line of dark trees. If anything, the northern bank of the river appeared more remote from civilization than the one they'd just left.

Fisher pulled out a slip of yellow paper on which directions had been written. "It's not far now."

"Hallelujah." Fabian yawned.

"It says here to follow the road for eight miles until you cross an iron bridge."

"That will be the one over the Rubicon."

Fisher ignored him. "Once you've crossed the—"

"Rubicon."

"—bridge, the drive that leads to the house is on your right about a mile after that."

Within five minutes the ferry had docked. The ferrymen were eager to finish their shift and quickly waved the cars forward onto the jetty that led to a narrow road. All the other traffic peeled away onto a lane leading to a line of cottages that stood overlooking the river, leaving Josanne's car in sole possession of the road.

As Josanne pulled away she glanced back. "Fabian, how's Jak?"

"Oh? My new furry friend is fine. Sleeping, by the looks of him."

Fisher turned back to see the curled form beneath the towel. Only the tip of the black button nose showed. "He must have been exhausted."

"Him and me both," Fabian said with feeling.

Josanne accelerated along the road that led across a dead flat plain that seemed to consist of agricultural land dotted with copses of trees. She said, "Jak must have been abandoned. He'll be suffering from the cold."

"Then he needs what I need," Fabian announced. "Hot food and a nice warm bed for the night."

Fisher glanced back at Fabian lounging in the seat. "You do know there won't be maidservants waiting to serve you? We'll be the only people there."

"I'm sure Josanne can rustle something up for us."

"The only thing I'll be rustling up is nice selection of words that describe you."

"Only joking, dear heart."

The directions on the paper were accurate. After eight miles the car rumbled over the iron bridge. A mile after that, twin stone pillars flanked the entrance to the driveway. A sign nailed to a tree shone as the car turned into the driveway.

"That's pretty unequivocal," Fabian said, then began to read aloud. "Acquired by Ashmoore Associates for residential redevelopment. The Tower. Historic listed mansion with thirteenth century origins and former aircraft bomber base for . . . Ah, I've missed the rest because you've driven straight past it."

"See anything?" Josanne asked as she eased the car beneath the overhang of trees.

"Nothing yet." Fisher angled the paper toward the light thrown from the dashboard. "As far as I can tell we drive for another mile before we reach the house. But there's a warning."

Fabian leaned forward. "Warning? My, my, sounds ominous."

"It says keep to the driveway because there's marsh-land at either side of it."

"What, no mysterious figure in black with a hook for a hand and a taste for human entrails?"

"Ignore him, Fisher." Josanne peered through the windshield. The car's lights revealed a barrier of green bushes. Beyond that were shape-shifting shadows that could have been yet more bushes being tugged by the breeze. If anything, they could have reached the end of the world where solid land yielded to darkly empty tracts of infinity. Just when an unease began to creep through Fisher that the track would plunge away into boundless nothingness, a dozen lights suddenly blazed out into the night.

"Oh, wow. I hadn't expected anything this big." Josanne stopped the car in front of the house. "It's huge."

"Not bad." Fabian was impressed.

Fisher asked, "So who just switched on the lights?"

Lights burned in the massive windows, while lamps set at ground level amongst the shrubs shone up against the façade that had been turned black by the elements. Rising from the middle of the building like a prehistoric obelisk was the tall structure that gave the house its name. The tower stood five stories compared to the three-storied wings of the house that extended to the left and right. They were still staring at the house when the massive front door swung inward to reveal a figure.

"Ah," Fabian said. "Now we know who switched on the lights." He nodded at a man that raced across the gravel toward the car. "Marko beat us to it."

Fisher liked Marko, the band's drummer. Long ago Marko had convinced himself he was a reincarnation

18

of Keith Moon. He bounded up to the car to pummel the roof with both fists.

"Marko," Josanne said by way of greeting.

"Hey, what kept you guys? I've been here for hours. Did you like what I did with the lights? Hey, Fabbo . . . Fabian? Did you see what I did with the lights? I went round switching them all on, then switched them off at the mains, so when you came up the drive—" He made a sizzling sound. "Zap! All on together! Quite an effect, eh?"

Fisher climbed out of the car while Marko rushed round to grab suitcases from the trunk. Excitement switched his tongue into overdrive. "It's an amazing place," he enthused. "God knows how they kept the place clean. It needs an army of Hoovers. I'm glad you're here now, I don't know if I'd be happy living in a place like that myself. It's spooky once the winds are blowing. All the doors start opening and shutting by themselves. Here, Fisher, let me grab the other bass. Did you bring the Rickenbacker? Excellent, excellent. Hey, I didn't know you had a dog, Fabbo."

"I didn't and still don't. And my name's not Fabbo. We found this stray on the road. Fisher insisted we bring it along so it can crap all over the house."

"I love dogs. We had eight when I lived at my grandmother's."

"At least we've found our dog nurse."

"What's his name?"

Fabian sniffed. "Marko, Jak. Jak, Marko. There, introductions done. Where do I find a hot bath?"

"Take your pick. There must be fifty."

Fabian decamped from the car. "Does anyone know what this place was used as?"

"An old people's home. Posh one at that. You

should see the furniture." Marko stroked the dog's head as he talked. "There's the auctioneer's catalogues in entrance hall. It gives you a history of the place. During World War Two it was a bomber base. B-17s flew out of here to bomb Germany. There's supposed to be the remains of a runway, but I haven't found it yet."

Fisher picked up the dog. It was content to lie there in his arms. Or was it dying? Were these the final tranquil hours as it faded from the world?

"Come on," Marko said. "I'll find some food for Jak."

"What about us?" Fabian asked, pained. "Don't humans get hungry, too?"

But Marko hurried through the doors to be swallowed into the belly of the house.

Chapter Three

Marko bustled across the entrance hall. In his hands he gripped the black cases that housed Fisher's two bass guitars. He put the guitars down so he could cup both hands to his ears in an extravagant gesture of listening. "Hear that?"

Fisher entered, carrying the dog wrapped in the towel. It lay placidly in his arms, as drowsy as a new-born baby. "Clock chimes," he said.

"It'll strike eleven," Marko told them as he picked up the guitar cases again.

Josanne shook her head in bemusement. "So? It's eleven o'clock at night. It's supposed to strike eleven."

"Ah, its timing's perfect."

"So?" Fabian adopted his world-weary posture.

"It strikes the hours," Marko announced with a beaming grin. "But I haven't been able to find the clock."

"There'll be plenty of time for clock hunting,

Marko." Fabian's eyes roved around the hallway. "What I need to find is a bath."

"This way."

As the three followed Marko, Fisher absorbed details of the huge entrance hall. From the black and white tiles that formed a checkboard floor, a staircase rose with an elegant sweep to the upper floors. Above it rose a void that the walls of the tower enclosed. Hanging from the ceiling, maybe seventy feet above them, was a long cable that suspended a chandelier above the floor. The mass of cut glass teardrop pendants and geometric crystal pieces appeared to be lit by nearly a hundred light bulbs that cast a brilliant white light.

Fisher caught up with the others as they walked along the blue carpeted corridor. Above them, globe-shaped lampshades hung from the ceiling at intervals of a dozen paces. They managed to give the corridor, which couldn't have been longer than fifty yards, the appearance of stretching miles into the distance. Ahead of him walked Marko with the guitar cases, then Josanne lugging two suitcases, then Fabian carelessly carrying his coat over one shoulder with his finger hooked in the peg loop. In the other hand he carried an antique brown leather briefcase in which he kept the music manuscripts of his songs. Fabian appeared every inch the English lord returning to his ancestral home rather than a man of twenty-three who had just started a one-month stint of house-sitting. Of course he'd got them the job through family connections. Fabian's father played golf with the developer who'd bought the place. There were plans to convert the old mansion into elegant apartments. Fabian had been hired to guard the place against vandals. Fisher had to admit that Fabian had an eye for an opportunity. He sold the band the idea of using the month at The Tower as a place to rehearse before they recorded their demo at the beginning of May. "Just imagine," Fabian had told them all a week before as they sat crammed into the back room of his apartment, the same room they'd used for muted rehearsals since Christmas. "Just imagine, a month in a manor house in the country. We can set up the equipment and play as loud as we like for as long as we like."

Idea sold. After a winter of fog and rain in the city, a month in rural Yorkshire was as good as a month in paradise. Of course, the rain had stayed with them all the way up here. And any pleasant evocations of a sunlit stroll down a country lane to an old tavern where barmaids served foaming pints of ale were dispelled by a cursory examination of the map, which revealed that the nearest building to The Tower was a farmhouse three miles away. Even so . . . They could learn those songs of Fabian's that he promised would make them rich.

The corridor boasted paneling of dark antique oak to shoulder height; above that the walls were painted white. Set at intervals of ten paces were doors. Some were open to reveal entrances to bedrooms.

"They even left the televisions?" Fisher said as he paused to check a room.

"Everything's been left here." Marko kept walking. "It was an old people's home for a couple years; there's even clothes in some of the closets. Once The Tower had been sold, the previous owners didn't hang around."

Fabian wrinkled his nose. "But there are clean

sheets, right? We're not going to uncover any gooey surprises when we slip under the quilt?"

"According to guy who handed over the keys this morning, all the rooms on this floor have been cleaned, bed linen changed, bathrooms scrubbed—the works. All ready for us coming."

"Thank the Lord for that." Josanne spoke with feeling.

"And hot water?" Fabian asked.

"Don't worry, Fabbo. It's all sorted. This floor is on a separate heating system. All these room have hot water. Take your pick."

"When do we get to eat?"

"We use this kitchen." Marko pushed against a door marked "Staff." "There's a freezer full of microwave meals."

Fisher smiled. "At least you won't starve."

"Microwave meals? My taste buds are going to suffer."

"You'll survive, Fabian." Josanne set the suitcases down with a relieved sigh.

Marko held the door open. "I brought a tubful of steaks with me. A drummer's got to have his protein, you know."

Fabian cheered up. "Well done, that man. Josanne, didn't we bring that case of red wine along. The Bombero?" He looked at her expectantly.

"You know we did." Then her expression became pained. "You mean you want me to bring it from the car?"

"I need to go through these songs before tomorrow."

Marko shook his head. "Don't worry, Fabbo. Once I get the steaks on, I'll fetch the wine. You go wash behind your ears, or whatever you wanted to freshen up."

"Magnificent. Remind me to keep you on the pay-roll, old boy."

That's a typical Fabian joke, Fisher thought. A joke that isn't a joke. It's a reminder of Fabian's status. His band, his songs. He's in charge. *What did I tell you about murderous thoughts?*

Marko put down one of the guitar cases so he could tug his forelock. "Thank you, Mister Fabbo, sir." Then to Fisher, "There's plenty of blankets, Fisher. We'll make Jak up a bed by the radiator where it's warm. When I've done that, I'll chop up a couple of beef fillets for him."

Fabian tutted. "Watch it, Jak, old boy, those two will end up killing you with kindness." He opened a door and marched through it with a shout of, "And stop calling me Fabbo."

Josanne paused in the doorway. She appeared awkward. Fisher knew she would have preferred to play her part in looking after the dog, but . . . *Loyalty to Fabian stops her joining the regular guys.* Marko must have been cloning Fisher's thoughts, because he asked, "Fancy a beer, Josanne?"

"No, thanks, I'll . . ." She nodded toward the door that Fabian had swept his elegant self through. "You know. He might want to talk to me about the songs."

Or to run his bath . . . ouch . . . that's uncharitable of you, Fisher.

"OK, give me time to fetch the wine and get the steaks on—and see to Jak here, of course."

"Thanks, Marko."

"Just shout if you need anything."

Marko shot me a meaningful look, then said, "Take Jak through. Let's see if we can get him firing on all cylinders."

The staff kitchen looked out over the grounds. Not that Fisher could see much apart from bare branches. Compared with the luxurious furnishings of the bedrooms, this spoke of utilitarian necessities. A large freezer in the corner, a refrigerator. A pair of microwave ovens on a shelf. A stainless steel sink beside an electric stove.

Marko nodded, "Through the door is the staff recreation area. There's chairs and stuff. Oh, and a dartboard. I'll pull one of the mattresses in, then I can sleep close to the dog." He looked at Fisher with a sudden anxiety in his eyes. "That is, if you don't think I'm muscling in?"

"No, not at all. You know more about them than I do."

"My grandmother used to collect strays. Mostly what abandoned dogs really need is to form a bond with the person caring for them. If they know someone loves them, that's worth more than injections and pills." He paused. "Only I didn't say all this in front of Fabian."

"I know what he's like. I'd do the same."

Fisher had known Marko from the old days, when they played in a four-piece band that toured the local clubs and bars at weekends. Fisher and he were good friends right from the start, despite Marko's temptation to loon around like he was the reincarnation of Keith Moon. Of course, back then they played for free beer and little more than loose change. That was before they were "discovered" by Fabian. One night he bought them drinks, then spun seductive words about how talented they were, that he had the contacts to get them noticed by record companies. All they had to do was let him play keyboards and write the songs. Ever hear the story about the Trojan Horse? How invaders get inside the fortified city by hiding in a wooden horse. Once they're on the inside, they attack.

That was what Fabian did. By Christmas Fabian had forced Zak (vocals and guitar) out of the band. On New Year's Eve Zak had been replaced by Adam Ambrose, some kind of protégé of Fabian's. The music was changing, too. Zak always said they played blue-collar rock and blues. Fabian had a more cerebral approach. Fisher couldn't help replaying a lot of what happened in the past four months as he and Marko built a bed out of blankets round the base of the warm radiator. Jak remained in the towel as they worked.

The moment Marko said, "OK, Jak, what do you think?" the dog stood up, shook himself out of the towel, then walked onto the bed, turned round three times and lay down. Once more Fisher was struck by how the animal resembled the jackal god that sat watchfully at the tombs of pharaohs. Those animals guarded their masters from attack by demon and human for all eternity. As a boy the story made an impression on him. He liked to imagine the dog statue coming to life to tear out the throats of the tomb robbers.

"Hey, hey." A warming glow of satisfaction spread through Fisher's body. "That's the first time I've seen him walk."

"Hey, high five, bud." Marko slapped Fisher's palm. "You know, he was probably just cold. When their body temperature drops they shut down. He'll probably be right as rain in the morning."

"Really?"

"Sure."

"Of course, how's all this going to play when we write our autobiography?" Fisher couldn't stop grinning now the dog appeared to be recovering. "Shouldn't we be munching pills and screwing around between playing stadiums full of screaming fans?"

Marko bent down to pat the dog's head. A pink tongue slipped out to touch Marko's finger tip. "Nah, that's next year. This year we get to take care of stray dogs and rehearse Fabbo's songs in a big old house."

"Are we doing the right thing, Marko?"

"It's our one chance." As he stood up he held his hands apart as if measuring a huge object. "Our one big chance at fame, fortune and the rest of it. We've got to take a shot, haven't we?"

"I guess so."

Marko crossed to the stove, where he started chopping steak for the dog. As he used a carving knife to slice it, he said, "You know, I gave notice at the workshop? It's this or nothing now."

"Yeah, we're so rock-and-roll, aren't we? I walked out of the office. It only hit me the next morning when I woke and I sat there with my head in my hands saying, 'My God, what have I done?'"

"Now that is rock and roll, Fisher." He added water to the steak in the saucepan, then put it on the electric ring to heat.

"Marko, just imagine what Fabian would say. You're cooking the dog's food before his."

"Fabbo? He can go swivel on a rusty pole. You know what my grandmother said about the dogs she took in?" He stirred the meat in the pan. "She looked into the dogs' eyes and she swore that she could recognize members of our family who had died."

"You mean reincarnation?"

"Something like that. Help yourself to a beer. They're in the refrigerator. You can get me one, too. Cheers." He paused as he cast his mind back. "To her, each dog she cared for had something in it, some character trait, that resembled a dead uncle or aunt. You know, the way they'd look at you when you talked to them? Is that weird to you?"

"We had a dog when I was growing up, but it was always Mack. I didn't see it resembling anyone I knew who'd died."

Marko shrugged as I handed him a bottle of beer. "It's one of the reasons she took such good care of them. It was as if she'd been given a second chance to love someone again she'd lost." He filled a bowl with cold water, then put it against the wall close to Jak. "Your dinner won't be long now, boy." He returned to stirring the chopped beef. "I'll simmer this for five minutes, then leave it to cool. Fisher, how long is it since your father died?"

"Ten weeks." Fisher thought for a second. "Yeah, ten weeks today."

Marko nodded at Jak. "Look who you found on the road today. My grandmother would have said that was too much of a coincidence." He stirred the pan again. "Would you keep any eye on that? I'm going to do the master's bidding and bring the wine from the car."

"It's in a white box. You can't miss it."

"Cheers."

Marko left Fisher to stand at the stove. He gazed at the pale brown liquid bubbling so it jostled at the strips of beef. Even eleven weeks before it would have seemed crazy to stand up at his desk, throw down his pen, announce he was leaving and wouldn't be coming back, then just walk out of the office building. After his father died he did just that. It was as if all the world's boundaries had changed. All the realities in life that seem fixed suddenly became fluid. He'd watched a kind man who always put his family first evaporate before his eyes as the cancer tore through him during the course of sixteen weeks. When it boiled down to the reality of it all, the doctors who'd troop into the hospital ward to stand by his bed could do nothing for him. Dad would smile and nod at them. They'd ask, was he comfortable? Was he in pain? Dad would smile back and reassure them that he wasn't suffering in the slightest. Good man. Good caring man, who never wanted to give anyone any trouble or cause for concern. But the scene could have been played out fifty thousand years before by a campfire. Stone Age men and women as they crouched there with their spears and flint axes could have done nothing for this man. These doctors with all their years of training and computer driven scanners and smart drugs couldn't do any more than their prehistoric ancestors.

So all anyone could do was watch the once-towering figure get thinner as he lay in the hospital bed. There he patiently watched the sun rise over the trees and set again. Time was the aggressive warrior that allied itself with the cancer. Every day time and the tumor—that axis of evil—ranged their weaponry of hours and minutes and rogue cells to blast away the muscle from his skeleton, until his bones pushed through his emaciated face. Yet still the kind eyes shone out.

Fisher turned away from the stove. The dog lay in bed with its head raised. Its amber eyes met his.

"Hello, Dad," Fisher said. The dog didn't react to the words. Instead it continued to meet his gaze in that placid way of his. Fisher gave a savage shake of his head. *What a stupid thing to say, there's no reincarnation, there's nothing!* Now he felt a fool for saying the words: As if he'd see something in the dog's eyes to hint that Marko's grandmother had been right.

A moment later Marko backed his way through the door with the case of wine. "Hell, Fabbo does it style. I expected half a dozen bottles. There's twenty in here. Bombero? Is that good stuff?" He set the case down on the table. "No sign of the others yet?"

"No, Fabian'll still be soaking himself. Can't you just see him lying back in a lace shower cap with slices of cucumber over his eyes?"

"The scary thing is I can picture exactly that. Ready for another beer?"

"Yup."

"Coming right up. If you put the pan on the window ledge to cool, I'll fry the steaks."

Like a film that had somehow burned itself into his brain, Fisher replayed scenes of driving to the hospital the night the nurse called with the news, then more repeats of the funeral. The arrival of the hearse. The way just the sight of the casket in back had been a physical shock that made him gulp for breath. It all replayed through his head, but he helped fry the steaks, he poured the wine, he made small talk with Marko. Still, there was that sense of unreality, as if ten weeks ago, he'd parted company with the world and still hadn't found the return path. Now he'd got these four weeks here with the band. He was determined to make it work. *Or die trying.* Flippant thoughts were his self-defense mechanism these days. Even so, the words ran a chill down his spine.

"Listen," Marko said. "The clock's striking midnight."

Chimes shimmered through the air. The twelfth note appeared to echo back from great distances beneath the house with a shimmering sustain that ghosted through the kitchen for a full minute before decaying to a whisper and finally dying away.

Chapter Four

At one o'clock the unseen clock chimed a single time. Josanne lay in bed waiting for Fabian to join her. He sat at the table where the light shone on his papers. He silently mouthed the lyrics of a song he wanted to practice tomorrow.

Rather than disturb the dog, Marko had dragged a mattress from one of the rooms so he could sleep close by in the rest area of the staff quarters.

Fisher had chosen a room two doors down from Josanne's and Fabian's. After changing into a T-shirt and shorts, he lay in a king-size bed with the lights out. Even though the building had been a retirement home for the elderly, it more closely resembled a country house hotel. Every room Fisher had seen so far had been scrupulously cleaned; the furniture was all good quality. Outside, a breeze sighed through the trees. Clicks sounded from the ceiling. It would be easy to imagine feet moving about upstairs, but he knew that they were alone in the house they were to stand guard over for the next twenty-eight days. He'd hoped he'd fall asleep quickly. He was pleasantly warm; his appetite had been satisfied by the steak. The red wine Fabian had brought with him was powerful stuff. Although he'd been drowsy enough as he climbed into bed, his waking self didn't yield to sleep just yet. He hovered in that lazy borderland between waking and sleeping. His senses possessed a drowsy fluidity where sounds seem to merge with the first ghostly dreams that began to emerge from the unconscious. Fisher imagined what it would be like to walk through the house at night. Alone. Without switching on lights. What if he should become a floating breath of atoms that could easily pass into the fabric of the building to run like electricity through the walls? Why stop with the walls? He could sink down through the floorboards, down through the cellars, into the earth beneath. There he'd find foundations of medieval buildings that had stood on the same tract of land before the manor house. What mixture of rotting timbers and human bones would he encounter there? What lay beneath that layer? Hearth stones from the Dark Ages? A Roman cemetery containing the bones of centurions two thousand years dead? To sink deeper would reveal flint arrowheads embedded in the skulls of mammoths that roamed this place when it was tundra ten thousand years ago.

As easily as you can allow your imagination to roam through the building, or down through the foundations into the soil, you can let your mind drift back through time. Before The Tower was an old people's home, it was a base for the U.S. Air Force. They flew B-17's out of here to attack the heavy industry of the

Ruhr Valley. The Tower would have been home to air crews who were far from home. This remote corner of Yorkshire must have seemed a bleakly alien place to them. There are no towns or villages nearby. Their world would dwindle to this big old house, and what? A concrete runway and a couple of aircraft hangars? The only life they'd know away from the seclusion of the house would be in those dangerous skies above Germany when the air would turn black around them from the smoke of antiaircraft fire and the Nazi interceptors would come screaming at them with their guns blazing death.

Outside the breeze rose, then fell. A respiratory sound. The creaks of settling timbers intruded through his half-sleeping, half-waking state as he imagined uniformed men sitting in this very room playing cards in a blue haze of cigarette smoke as they waited for their next mission.

This house has seen a lot of death. How many airmen were delivered back here as corpses to lie in the morgue until their funerals? Come to that, from when this house was built, how many people had died within its black walls? This house must have an appetite for death now. It must be hungry for souls. . . . Drowsy thoughts slipped through him. There was something lubricious about the images now. As if they were poured into his head from some external source. In a house the dust is the sloughed skin of its inhabitants. How old was this skin dust he smelt now? Was it the skin of the old people, or the pilots and bombardiers and gun crews from the wartime bombers? Or did it go further back, when this place was what? A TB sanatorium? A lunatic asylum? Back to when it was a family house? All that human dust. He was inhaling it. He could taste it on his tongue. . . . It dried the back of his throat.

Thud. One of his guitars falling. After the thud he could hear the deep bass hum of the strings as they vibrated. Damn . . . He shouldn't have propped it up against the wall. It should have been laid down flat on the floor. Fisher opened his eyes. Immediately he blinked as something irritated them. He blinked again but could see nothing in the darkness. He turned his head to see the pale oblong that was the drapes drawn across the window. Clicks, squeaks, a creaking like wood being flexed. Could there someone be walking upstairs? And what about my damn eyes? What's wrong with them? The room was unfamiliar but he had an idea where the light switch was above the bed. In the dark he reached upward. Smooth wall, then the hard line of the switch plate. A second later he had the row of switches under his finger. He pushed it. A light sprang out from above the dressing table.

Fisher blinked as he looked up. The pricking of his eyes told him particles had settled on his eyeball. But what the hell had happened to the ceiling? It was no longer flat but bulged downward. In the light of the lamp he saw that dust fell from the ceiling in a yellowish blizzard of particles. What occurred to him first was that a water pipe had ruptured upstairs, allowing water to pool above the ceiling boards. Now the weight of the accumulating water caused the ceiling to bulge downward in the middle. He opened his mouth to shout to Marko, but the dust fall sent particles swirling across his tongue to hit the sensitive skin at the back of his throat. He coughed to clear it before shouting again. Only . . .

Only something wasn't right with the room. It had been bigger than this. There'd been a generous walk space around three sides of the bed. That was gone now. The ceiling was so low he realized he could reach up and touch it. Not that he wanted to.

Fisher didn't know why exactly: it was a gut instinct. The walls had become repulsive to him. They were no longer dry horizontal planes covered with a dull reddish paper. Though he couldn't actually see it, some quality of the wall was suggestive of being moist. They weren't vertical either; they curved inward. And hardness gave way to a surface that might have been rubbery, or even muscular. Dust cascaded. He dragged his hand across his eyes so he could clear some of the muck that settled on his retinas. *The house is collapsing. Get to the door—get out.* But the door was no longer where it should be. It appeared to press against the foot of his bed; worse, it dragged the wall with it, so the entire end of the room puckered. Fisher pushed back the sheet to scramble from the bed. He held his free hand up to his eyes to shield them from the dust fall. Yet his hand was no higher than his forehead when it struck the ceiling lamp. Fisher scraped his knuckles across his eyes again to clear them. The ceiling bulged downward. The light shade that hung from it was of a reddish brown glass in the shape of globe. He saw it now press down against his chest. The wire had been as thick as a little finger, now it became engorged as some fluid appeared to pump from the ceiling into it. Even the light bulb swam with a luminous green liquid as it crushed down on him. He tried to slide sideways across the mattress to escape it. Only now the walls flowed inward over the bed to enclose him. The once-smooth surfaces were dimpled. Moisture seeped through the red wallpaper to stand in beads on the material. Everything became distorted, enlarged . . . morbidly enlarged. He could see the weave in the paper. Falling dust particles were the size of salt grains. The light bulb inflated. The metal collar that attached the glass vessel with its element had swollen. It pressed against Fisher's upper chest. He could even read the name of the manufacturer stamped there, only the letters bulged sickeningly from the metal like diseased fingers that had inflated to grotesque dimensions. AXXLYTE. He couldn't take his eyes from the word. Not that there was choice now. He couldn't move his head. The walls of the room pressed inward, crushing him. The pain in his chest was unbearable. He longed to cry out. As much in disgust at the wall with its mucouslike sheen. *I'm going to die.* The thought seared him like a lightning flash. *I'm going to die now. And I can't make anyone hear me.* The walls were touching his face when he realized this was his last chance. He couldn't take a lungful of air, but he knew he had to shout, if only to express rage at having his life crushed from him like a wood louse ground under the heel of a boot. This time he ignored the burning presence of the dust in his throat. With the last few cubic inches of air in his lungs he yelled. The effect was like yelling into a box full of blankets, the sound absorbed the moment it escaped his mouth.

He knew he had to try again, only this time the pressure was too extreme to inflate his lungs. Tears ran down his face. What light reached him from through the engulfing folds of the wall began to die. Darkness poured into the tiny void occupied by his head. A dwindling void at that. The clock chimes rang out. A pulse of brassy sound. Then . . . a rushing, swirling sensation. An impression of a huge physical presence retreating with such speed that currents of air raced to fill the vacuum. Light hit him with the suddenness of a slap in the face.

"Fisher! What's the matter?"

Gasping for air, rubbing the dust from his eyes with the sheet, Fisher struggled into a sitting position. He sucked air into his lungs as though he'd been sitting at the bottom of a swimming pool for the past five minutes.

"Fisher? Are you OK?" A figure stepped through the dazzling light toward him.

"Marko?"

"What on earth's wrong?"

"It's the walls . . . the house . . ." He gasped for air. "It was falling on me."

"Falling?" Marko chuckled. "You've been having a bad dream."

"No!" The force behind the word was enough to make Marko flinch. "It wasn't a dream."

"Whatever you say, mate."

"It started with the dust," Fisher panted. "Then the walls fell . . . only they changed when they fell . . . they were wet. Look, if you don't believe me. Can't you see the dust on the pillow? Look! There's more on the blanket."

"Dust? Yeah. It's an old house, Fisher. Dust's everywhere."

"But when the walls came down on me, everything became swollen, like . . . you know, like it was deformed. The light up there was pressed against my chest. I could even see the manufacturer's mark on the metal collar of the light bulb. It's made by a company I haven't heard of before. Axxlyte. That's what's stamped on the light bulb. Axxlyte."

"Fisher, look, why don't—"

"Marko. Get up here." Fisher slapped the mattress with his hand. The movement was panicky. "Marko. Stand here and tell me what it says on the light bulb."

Marko looked as if he'd argue against it, but with a shrug changed his mind. Barefoot, he jumped up onto the mattress.

"Marko? It says Axxlyte, doesn't it?"

"Hang on, the letters are so small I can't make it out." He stretched as far as he could up toward the light.

Fisher hissed, "What does it say?"

"Axx . . ." He strained to make himself taller. "Axxlyte. Yeah, Axxlyte."

"Axxlyte, I told you. The whole ceiling pressed down on me. It was crushing me. The light grew like it was swelling. How would I have seen the maker's name on the bulb otherwise?"

Marko shrugged. There was an expression of genuine sympathy on his face. "The ceiling looks all right."

"Oh, God." Fisher's chest hurt when he breathed in, but now that he'd got some air into his lungs, his racing heart started to slow down. "Sorry, Marko. Hell . . . I must have sounded as if I'd gone crazy."

"It was the dog that woke me. He started barking. When he stopped I could hear you making . . ." He shook his head. "Making groaning sounds." He smiled to break the tension. "Didn't sound like groans of fun, mate. I thought I'd better investigate."

"Sorry, Marko."

"Sorry? What for?"

"For waking you. I must have been dreaming."

"No problem. You're an old pal. We look out for one another."

"Thanks, Marko." Fisher briskly rubbed his face, then shook himself as if shaking himself awake. "Give Jak a pat on the head for me when you go back."

"Will do." Marko sniffed at the air as he looked around the walls. "It's stuffy in here. Want me to open a window?"

"Heck, don't you go treating me like an invalid. I'll do it."

"Fair enough. See you tomorrow."

When Marko had left the room Fisher didn't go to the window straight away. Instead he crossed the floor to the mirror. There he paused and glanced back at the ceiling light that was housed in its glass globe. Then he lifted his T-shirt. On his chest was a large round bruise. A new one.

Chapter Five

Bruise or no bruise, Fisher was up by nine. He found he'd already missed the arrival of the others. He stood in the corridor rubbing his sore chest through his T-shirt as Adam Ambrose swept along the corridor with his harem. A brunette and the blonde. Yeah, trust Adam Ambrose to have two girlfriends. They were new. Fisher didn't even know their names.

"Ciao, Fisher. Nice boxers, man. Catch you later."

Teeth and hair. That's how Fisher always thought of Adam. Teeth and hair. Not so much a man but walking golden hair that framed a mass of teeth. Fabian had appointed Adam as lead guitarist and lead singer. There'd no been discussion or democratic vote in the band. One afternoon Fisher and Marko had turned up for rehearsal to be told by Fabian that Zak had left. His replacement was the golden-haired Adam Ambrose. That was that.

Marko walked along the corridor from the direction of the main entrance. Jak trotted alongside him. The dog looked up placidly at Fisher, his tail swishing.

"So they arrived," Fisher said. His ribs ached when he spoke.

"Been here about an hour. Fabian's been showing them round the place like it's his own personal estate."

"Last night I was thinking we'd wake up this morning to find the dog had died. He looked pretty ropey yesterday."

"He'd probably lost so much body heat it made him lethargic."

"He seems fine now."

"Yeah, I gave him some milk and cornflakes, then took him out for a run in the woods. You don't mind, do you?"

"Why should I mind?"

"You found him?"

"That doesn't make me his owner." Fisher spoke good-naturedly. In fact, he found himself smiling at the look of concern on Marko's face. "It's not as if you're stealing my girlfriend."

"So, you've no problems with me feeding him?"

"Feed him, walk him, throw Fisbees—be my guest."

"Thanks, Fisher."

There was something about Marko's affection for the dog that was touching. Yeah, Marko would loon around doing the Keith Moon mad drummer bit. But the glow of pleasure on Marko's face because he had the company of the dog was nothing less than heartwarming.

Marko said, "When you're ready, there's cereal, milk, coffee and stuff in the kitchen."

"Thanks. Is everyone here now?"

"Yeah, they got the first ferry over this morning. We've already started setting the gear up in a big room at the back of the house."

43

"I best get some clothes on, then."

"It's cold in there, so it'd be a good idea."

"Has Fabian said what time he wants to start?"

"Wait, you'll love this. He wants us to assemble at ten thirty sharp, as he puts it. But not to rehearse—he's going to make a speech."

"A speech? Why? Is he making a declaration of war or something?"

Marko grinned as he bent down to pat the dog's head. "Fabian's planned to say something inspirational, I bet. Or tell us we're locked up here until we're note-perfect."

A speech? Wasn't that typical of the guy? Oddly, the amusing prospect of Fabian standing up to make his pompous pronouncement vanished the moment Fisher stepped back into his room. Sure, the bed was how it should be, with the covers rucked after a night's sleep. The drapes were part open to reveal a gray morning. Beyond the glass, overgrown bushes clustered around the window. Steam still settled in the bathroom from where he'd just showered. He even caught the faint mint smell of his toothpaste. But it was those walls . . . he remembered how they crowded in on him. He rubbed his sore chest through the T-shirt. The bruise there was a big dark one. Round as a dinner plate, too. He glanced up at the globe lampshade. At that moment he didn't want to think about what happened last night. The incident—the nightmare?—had too much emotional weight involved, much like the death of his father ten weeks before. He hadn't figured out what that meant to him yet. So trying to deal with what the room did to him would be too much like emotional overload.

"Get out, just get out," he muttered to himself as he

grabbed his jeans from the back of the chair. The place exerted a claustrophobic pressure. In fact, breakfast could wait; he needed fresh air.

The Tower by daylight. Well, almost daylight. Even by nine thirty, the light struggled to make it through the gray cloud that pressed down on this remote part of Yorkshire. Fisher stood on the driveway that had brought them to the house. He looked at the building, rising out of the bushes that crept up to it in a tide of spiky, leafless branches. There was a kind of megalithic simplicity in its architectural design. A horizontal slab that formed the bulk of the house consisted of three floors built from sandstone that had turned black from hundreds of years of violent rain and snowstorms. A vertical block formed the tower. That rose to five stories with two oblong windows per floor. The entire structure had been roofed in pantile that would have once been a terracotta red. Exposure to Yorkshire's harsh elements had transmuted the red into a dirt brown. From where he stood beneath the trees, which dripped water and groaned in the breeze, he judged that the house was perhaps eighty yards in width. The oblong windows, of which there were dozens, had all the appeal of dead eyes. Set deep into the black sandstone walls, they had a glistening gray quality. For some weird reason he wanted them to blink, anything to break that lifeless stare. The developers had their work cut out to transform this mausoleum into an alluring residence. Even the setting lacked picturesque appeal. The Tower sat on a flat agricultural landscape punctuated by copses of leafless trees; there were no other houses to be seen. The flatness created a massive gray sky that Fisher found oppressive. It was as if the huge hand of some eternally angry god pressed its palm down on the land, crushing the spirit out of every living thing. Sure, those trees would burst into leaf in a month or so; Fisher knew that intellectually; but, emotionally, he sensed that this was a place that winter left grudgingly. Even then, something of the cold frosty spirit would remain lurking in the shadows.

Morbid thoughts again, Fisher told himself. Stop it. It's too easy to start thinking about what happened to Dad. And about what happened last night. Hell . . . Why did the room collapse in on me? Is this how a nervous breakdown starts?

Before he could stop himself, random helter-skelter images dashed into his mind. The hearse arriving at the house for the funeral. Just sight of his father's coffin had knocked the air from his lungs. The way the ceiling appeared to descend to crush him. If it was a hallucination, why did he have a bruise on his chest? He remembered the force of the light fitting pressing down on his ribs. The rescue of the dog from the road in the downpour of rain. Once more he remembered Marko talking about his grandmother's passion for saving stray dogs, and her belief that the dogs assumed the characteristics of dead members of her family.

I should have brought Jak with me, Fisher told himself. He'd distract me from raking up the past. I could have thrown sticks for him. Anything to take my mind off what happened to Dad. Sixty years old? These days, that's young. It shouldn't—

Fisher shook his head. No, don't go there. . . . Walk round, get some fresh air, then go listen to what Fabian has to say. He kicked a stone as he walked.

When he kicked stones like that in the past it was playful, just a habit from childhood. Now he injected fury into the kick. That's unresolved grief, he told himself. He passed the band's vehicles parked by the front door: then he pushed himself to walk faster to dispel the gloom-laden thoughts. To reach the rear he had to weave through hawthorn bushes that surrounded The Tower. The building looked like a dirty tomb poking up through the mass of spiky branches. For a while he even lost sight of the hulking presence of the house due to the wild, untrammeled growth of hawthorn taking root in every square yard of soil around the place. It wasn't even the kind of ornamental bush you'd have in a garden. It was a feral plant.

So, House, you plan to keep visitors away, don't you? Fisher intended the thought as a flippant distraction from his preoccupations, but the proximity and the density of the hawthorn really did seem evidence of a protective thicket around the building to prevent the uninvited getting too close. Every so often he had a glimpse of the dark stone flank of the house with its patches of green moss. At least he was moving in the right direction if he was to find the rear of the property. Gusts of wind tugged at the black hawthorn. The overgrown branches were whip thin. Fisher had to jerk his head back when a branch lashed at him with its weaponry of sharp thorns. He turned his mind to the U.S. Air Force bomber crews stationed here. This bleak setting would do nothing for morale. He could imagine the men falling into moods of fatal gloom as they waited in that bleak pile of stone for orders to fly out over hostile territory to bomb cities and factories. How long before the crews found themselves brooding over images of the men, women and children their bombs had killed? How they might advance across those fields as an army of vengeful ghosts?

My God. That's what this place does to you. It insinuates strange ideas. This is a house where you can imagine anything happening. A room where its walls deform, where they creep in to hold you like an alligator can hold a rat inside its mouth before crushing it. You could stare out of those bleak, dead-eye windows and picture the phantoms of mutilated people creeping in a dark tide toward you.

Fisher found that he'd been walking with his head down, his hands pushed into his pockets as his mind entangled itself in morbid ideas. When he looked up, he suddenly realized he was free of the hawthorn bushes. Here at the back of the house the bushes yielded to an expanse of knee-deep grass that ran down a gentle slope to what appeared to be a straight concrete road. This has to be the runway, he told himself. Surely they'd have ripped it up years ago. But then some were kept mothballed, just in case more runway space was needed by the military at short notice. Straightaway, he noticed a bunker at the side of the runway. Now the morbid thoughts slipped from Fisher's mind as he waded through the damp grass toward the runway. So this is where the huge glittering bombers would sit with their propellers spinning in the dawn light before lumbering into the air eastward. From their bedrooms in the house, flight crews would be able to watch mechanics working on the wing-mounted engines of the B-17's. When they'd finished another team would hoist high explosive ordnance into the belly of the aircraft to be anchored in the bomb bay.

THE TOWER

Some distance from the runway Fisher paused. A strange thing had happened to the thirty-yard-wide strip of concrete that ran for perhaps a thousand yards across the landscape. Weirdly, it was surrounded on both sides by a shallow lake. The runway itself stood just an inch or so above the water's surface. The whole area is reverting to swamp, he told himself. Drainage ditches in the area must be so neglected that the ground water is rising.

Evidence of this came in the shape of dead trees that presented their forlorn skeletal forms against the gray sky, while the bases of their trunks stood in stagnant water. A few years before, this would have been pasture that flanked the concrete landing strip. Fisher moved closer to what had become a narrow concrete island standing in what looked like about a hundred acres of water. He pictured himself strolling along it while frogs leapt off the sides back into the safety of the lake. He'd enjoy the exercise. It would dispel the residue of morbid thoughts that had followed him like a black cloud this morning. Only at that moment he heard chimes shimmer on the cold breeze. That was Marko's phantom clock. How on earth could the sound of a clock striking ten in the house reach him down here? Another of The Tower's secrets in need of an answer, he told himself. If it was ten o'clock, he should be heading back. Fabian would be making his speech at ten thirty. Being late would only piss the guy off. Still, he had a few minutes yet. . . . There were no hangars that he could see. Then, they'd have been flimsy structures of corrugated iron. Nowhere as rugged as the bunker built from concrete blocks and topped with a concrete slab roof. Clearly, they'd made sure it would not only be strong enough to withstand the fearsome northern weather but also bear the brunt of strafing attacks by marauding enemy fighters. This thought prompted him to check the building. He pushed on through the long grass, aware that his feet were soaked from the wet vegetation, but not in the least bothered. He was glad something had taken his mind off the morbid introspection. There were nothing that could be described as windows apart from half a dozen glazed slits set about ten feet above Fisher's head. They might have been intended to admit daylight into the bunker. He walked round the building, which he judged to be about twenty-five feet in height. Iron ties that helped bond the structure together now bled rust red stains down the dark gray walls. On the side that faced open countryside there were around about a dozen pockmarks that might have been made by machine gun rounds from a German fighter. Fisher tested the depth of the bullet holes with his finger. They hadn't gone all the way through. The bunker's occupants had strolled safely away from that attack at least. After walking completely around the building, which was in the region of ten by fifteen paces, he'd discovered the only entrance was a steel door that was solidly locked. He put his eye to the keyhole. All he could make out in the gloom were a flight of concrete steps that still bore traces of paint that could only be described as a drab military green. The odor oozing through the keyhole didn't make him linger. It smelt as if some animal had crept in there to die. With a cough to drive the foul air from his lungs, he stepped back. Time to call off explorations for now. He glanced at his watch. He had fifteen minutes before Fabian launched into his speech. If the man had any grand plan for the band's future, Fisher should be there to hear it. He turned his back on the bunker that squatted beside the runway and walked back toward the house.

Chapter Six

The man watched the new arrival through one of the window slits in the bunker. The stranger had emerged from the hawthorn at the side of the house to walk down through the long grass to the edge of the runway. There he'd examined the bunker before returning to the house. As the man watched the stranger ford his way through the grass, leaving a line of broken stalks, he picked a rat out of the mesh cage. The rodent twisted its head, fixed fierce eyes that glinted like beads of black glass in its head onto the man's thumb, then thrust its jaws forward to bite. The man didn't flinch. His heavy-duty canvas gloves didn't allow the teeth to penetrate. In his unhurried way, borne of years of practice, the man positioned the rat over a vertical metal rod that was no thicker than a pencil. The rod ran from elbow height down to where the other end was fixed into a balk of timber that rested on the floor. Once the rat's belly rested against the filed point of the rod, the man exerted a steady pressure downward against the rat's back. The animal writhed; it arched its spine in agony; its jaws jerked wide open as its enraged squeaking rose into a high-pitched shriek. More pressure. The rat spasmed in his hand; its tail lashed—a naked snakelike member that curled around his wrist. Pressed harder, and . . . *in.* The spike passed through the rodent's skin, through its gut to pierce internal organs, then its spine with an audible crunch. This was routine. Efficiently the man threaded the body onto the metal rod. He slid it smoothly downward, its passage made easier by the creature's own blood that lubricated the metal. When the rat couldn't descend any further because of the fifteen skewered rodent bodies beneath it, the man stepped back to check his work. The apparatus resembled an abacus. The bodies of rats and birds on ten more steel rods that jutted vertically from the timber could have been the abacus beads. The upper parts of the rods were vacant as they awaited more animals. The bottom halves of the rods were sheathed in decaying animals. Dried blood formed sticky patches on the concrete floor. The weakly squirming rat with the rod penetrating its body added more oozing rivulets of crimson to the mess.

Satisfied with what he saw, the man nodded. In fact, the satisfaction came as a surge of relief that made his neck muscles relax. He'd begun to wonder if he'd left it too long. Maybe he should have added another rat or bird to the poles; otherwise things might have gotten a whole lot worse. No, he wouldn't leave it as long next time. But he hadn't anticipated the arrival of the bunch of young men and women yesterday.

When the old people left at the end of last year, he thought he'd have the ancient house with its sandstone tower to himself forever and ever—amen!

Strangers unsettled him. They'd no right to be here. Ideas of talking to them filled him with deep unease. What if they were inquisitive? However, a more powerful instinct told him to learn why they were here. Those kind of pressures on him to converse with people after all this time, coupled with a fear that they might invade the private world he'd built for himself, made him increasingly edgy. One rat wasn't enough, was it? Best catch another soon, or a magpie maybe. If only he still had the motorcycle he could ride into a nearby town and pick up a cat. He slipped off his canvas gloves. These he pushed into the pockets of his leather jacket. Before he left he crouched down to put his face so close to the rat on the rod that his nose almost touched it. Its pink mouth was partly open, he could see the moist tongue; it had blanched from pink to white. The mouth would soon go like that, too. The animal didn't move. The limbs were still; the tail hung limp. He blew on it. The force of his breath ruffled its brown fur. He blew again. No movement. Not a flicker.

"You're dead, old son," he told the rat with satisfaction. Still nodding, he picked up the wire cage and headed for the door. As he fished the key from his pocket, he worked out what he should do that day. Bait the cage. Shave away the stubble from his face so as not to make the strangers suspicious if they should see him. He opened the steel door in the bunker just an inch so he could check there was no one about. From this side of the building no one in the house could see him leave. A second later he exited the door. After locking it behind him, he stood at the edge of the runway. The cold March air felt good on his skin. As well as refreshing his blood, it cleansed him like a stream of fast-flowing water. He gazed out along the runway that ran like a causeway through the lake. Although it was no more than ankle-deep in places he knew there were submerged hollows and ditches. If you didn't watch your step, you could easily plunge out of sight. That was exactly what happened to an old man who had wandered from the house when it was a nursing home. It had been one summer when the swamp water had turned bright green with algae blooms. He'd watched the old man walk out along the runway. The man had waved his arms as if beckoning to an invisible aircraft to land. After that he'd begun wading through the shallow water. He'd gone about thirty paces, a shrunken figure with an untidy shock of white hair, then . . . *Ffftt!* He'd simply dropped out of sight as the submarine ditch had swallowed him from view. The man's hands had broken the surface as if he were trying to stir the air above the water. Then the hands had slowly sunk beneath green scum. It took the staff in the home the best part of a week to find the old boy. The state of his face proved to everyone that one animal that wasn't scarce round here was king rat.

The man checked the cage. Soon it would perform its duty again. With a glance back at the brooding presence of the house he followed the path to his home in the woods.

Chapter Seven

Fabian made his speech. Topics: work ethic, rehearsal schedule, band name change, musical aesthetic, the targeted approach as opposed to hoping to attain success on a wing and a prayer, and . . . and . . .

. . . and Fisher wondered if he should be taking notes. Sitting here in the ballroom at the back of the house, with Fabian standing in a lordly manner on a plastic crate beside Marko's drum kit. Behind Fabian the ceiling to floor windows revealed the expanse of grass that Fisher had walked through to the runway that stretched out like a finger of concrete into the marsh. The speech had begun fifteen minutes ago. Fabian was, it seemed, only just getting into his flow.

"Being a success isn't achieved by the quality of the music alone." Fabian made a fey movement of his hand to push his lank, blond fringe from his eyes. "Yes, we have the songs." He pointed to his leather briefcase that lay on the electronic keyboard. "They're excellent songs . . . *excellent.* I've been honing them for the last twelve months. But as well as having great material we need a great name."

"What's wrong with Cuspidor?" Marko sat on the floor with his back to an amplifier.

"You know what a Cuspidor is?"

"Sure. A pot for spitting in."

"Then a spittoon isn't a great name for a rock band, is it?"

"The Beatles were named after an insect. They did all right. And look at REM, they—"

"Marko . . . Marko. I'll open this up for discussion at the end. I'm wanting to present the band's manifesto here."

"Manifesto?"

"Hey, Marko." This was Mr. Teeth & Hair, Adam Ambrose. "Let the man finish speaking, OK?"

Marko assented with a shrug. He adopted a bored expression that challenged Fabian to continue. Fabian didn't seem to notice.

So this is how it's shaping up, Fisher told himself. Fabian and Adam have junked Cuspidor. They're only recycling elements that are useful to them. Now they're putting together a new band. He glanced at Marko. The guy was probably thinking the same thing. Cuspidor had started as a bunch of friends playing the music they loved. Now it had become a commercial enterprise. Forget the music; it's about the product.

Fisher let his gaze drift round the ballroom (at least, that was the name on the door). When The Tower was a nursing home, this would have been a communal lounge. It was thickly carpeted, with walls painted in warm shades of orange. Someone had pushed all the armchairs back against the walls to create a big open area where the band's equipment now sat. There were half a dozen amplifiers that were as big as refrigerators. They were all painted black and stood in line like tombstones in a cemetery. Marko's drums were in place. The gleaming cymbals appeared to hover like a squadron of golden flying saucers on their stands above an array of drums. Fabian's keyboard stack faced where the rest of the band would play, so he could assume the role of conductor rather than fellow band member. The guitars were still in their cases. Even in rehearsals it was so easy for them to be knocked over or trampled on as people moved around or flounced out if they felt offended for any reason. And these were the very people that he'd be holed up with in a remote country house for the next month. Fisher counted them. Seven men and women. Not one over the age of twenty-five. As his mind drifted away from what Fabian was saying he found himself listing them:

Adam Ambrose, lead guitar, vocals. A willowy man with hair and teeth that somehow seemed to outshine the rest of his body. Age twenty-one (and if you believe that, then keep watching the skies for flying pork chops; Fisher guessed the man was much, much closer to thirty, but whaddya know, this is showbiz). Adam sat in a wooden straight-backed chair which, the more Fisher thought about it, resembled a throne. Adam's two girlfriends sat on the floor at his feet. Apart from their names, Belle and Kym, Fisher didn't know much about them. They were exotic beauties who moved with the grace of catwalk models.

Marko. Drums and percussion (and bullhorn/harmonica fusion that had to be heard to be believed). A compact, muscular guy of twenty-two with curly, light brown hair which had already started to recede at the temples. He had been raised by his grandmother. Father absent prior to birth; mother working the cruise ships as a waitress. Not spectacular wages, Marko would say, but she couldn't bear being in the same place for more than forty-eight hours.

Sterling Pound, rhythm guitar and saxophone, aged twenty-five. Shaven-headed with a black goatee. Fisher had endured the same school he had. Although Sterling had been three years Fisher's senior, they played in the school's weird orchestra, Ad Hoc. It consisted of fifteen lead guitarists, including Fisher; two drummers, four keyboard players, and an odd-looking kid who played a dented tuba in between sucking lollipops. Fisher had seen a way of improving his status in the band by switching to bass guitar. So he did. Good move, too. The plethora of wannabe guitar heroes were dispensable, but with Fisher as the sole bass player, the music teacher always made sure that he had privileged treatment. This meant he managed to escape hated mathematics lessons for band practice. He and Sterling became good friends. Back than, Sterling had been known by his real name, John Smith. When they'd formed Cuspidor in their midteens and got as far as writing their own songs, John insisted that he be credited as Sterling Pound. Surprisingly, the name stuck. Sterling was easily the most placid, centered member of the band. He sat patiently through all those "musical differences" arguments; then, when the others had run out of points to wrangle over, he'd ask in a laid-back way, "Shall we play some music now?" His role in life seemed to be as a form of human glue. Sterling's presence became the adhesive that kept the band members bonded together. Fisher didn't know if the man could still keep them cemented in place. The old band members of the now-defunct Cuspidor had little in common with newcomers Fabian and Adam Ambrose, other than the ambition to have hit records. Whether that was enough to create a viable rock group was debatable.

Fabian, age twenty-three, there on the plastic crate declaiming his musical manifesto. Maybe he wasn't joking when he'd told them he had aristocratic blood. His blond hair framed a face with fine-boned features. Body language? Yeah, if you imagine the way an English lord walks—with a tendency to look down his nose—his gestures were a sort of blend of louche and elegantly casual. That was Fabian to a T. His wealthy family background reinforced the impression of aristocracy. The times he began one of his loquacious anecdotes with the words, "When we wintered in San Tropez . . ." No doubt about it: Fabian was the architect of the band. He was its songwriter, its driving force. He'd told them right from the start that he'd decide musical direction. He'd produce the recordings for the album. He would be controlling all the levers.

Josanne, twenty-four years old. Fabian's lover, or should it be factotum? As Fabian talked, she didn't listen as the rest did. She checked points on a clipboard. Several times she handed him color photocopies of album covers by other bands to demonstrate examples of a particular image concept. When she wasn't doing those things, she took photographs with a classy digital camera. Fisher experienced what he could only describe as a flash-forward. He thought: In ten years' time there's going to be a big glossy coffee table book with "by Fabian" on the cover. Those photographs are going to be in the first pages. Under what heading? *Genesis of a rock band. Our first steps.* Fabian had sold Josanne the same dream of success. So now they'd all subscribed to his Faustian pact. *We've all surrendered a chunk of personal integrity for the promise of being famous and very, very rich. So, what other price do we have to pay for that?* Flash forward. Another chapter in the book, titled "Fisher speaks! My months of rehab hell." *No, the price won't be paid in ten years' time. There's a price to pay now. Right here in The Tower.* The first flippant musing was suddenly shouldered aside by the revelation that they'd have to confront a menace within these walls.

Yeah, right. That was another attempt to be flippant, but it didn't have the muscle to suppress a conviction that he'd have to face dangers here in The Tower. Was it so melodramatic? He remembered only too forcefully what happened last night when the room had seemed to collapse inward to crush him. Was that a hallucination brought on by unresolved grief over his father's death? Was it the result of an abrupt departure from his old life? Walking out on his day job? Then suddenly finding himself here on the threshold of a new chapter? Changes were taking place at breakneck speed; it didn't take a psychiatrist to explain that this must be traumatic.

Fisher had completed the list of the people he'd be sharing his life with here, in an old country house miles from anywhere. That would be test of nerve in its own right. Wait . . . there was one person he'd missed from the list. He looked round the ballroom until he found him. Yup, there he was. Dark hair, with black eyebrows arching over eyes that were thoughtful enough to suggest that their owner had something on his mind. *There he is: John Fisher, bassist, age twenty-two.* Fisher gazed at his reflection in the window. The Fisher caught in the windowpane gazed back at him. *Hello, Fisher. You've sold your soul for a chance of fame, haven't you?* Flippant thought, part one million and one. The reflection had his father's eyes. It had his father's of tilting his head a little to one side with a far-away expression when lost in thought. At that moment the clock chimed. Shimmering notes ghosted through the ballroom. The dog began to bark. Fisher hadn't realized it was anywhere near the ballroom. For a moment his own eyes reflected by the windowpane held his attention with a mesmeric power. The reflection smiled back at him; its eyes hardened into a penetrating stare. The explosive barks, the chimes. Fabian stopped speaking; the sheaf of papers slipped out of his fingers to fall to the ground. The smile on Fisher's reflected face grew wider. Fisher's hands darted to his face to explore his lips.

I'm not smiling, he thought, stunned. I'm not smiling. But my reflection is.

Chapter Eight

"For crying out loud!" Fabian's lordly poise had vanished. "That bloody clock! Is there any way of stopping it making that damn awful noise?"

Marko shrugged. "I told you. I can't even find the clock, never mind stop it."

As Josanne rushed to pick up Fabian's fallen papers, he continued to rage. "And shut that blasted dog up!"

Fisher moved as if he were in a dream. Seeing his reflection smile like that when he wasn't smiling produced that same sense of internal chaos he'd experienced when the walls of the room had lost their cohesion and closed in on him the previous night. When something you take for granted—such as, rooms generally possess immovable walls, and reflections don't behave independently of the object they reflect—when those physical laws are demolished, then your image of the world explodes. *Dear God.* Fisher had covered the lower half of his face with his hands when he'd checked if he was smiling insanely to himself. No, he wasn't smiling. What's more, a mirror image of his hands should have appeared in the windowpane. They hadn't. There'd only been a reflection of his entire face wearing a smile that morphed into a leer. Something else had generated the image.

"Fisher, are you going to shut up that dog or what?"

"OK, OK, I'm going." He reached the doorway to find Jak standing in the center of the corridor with his hackles standing upright on his neck. Without letup, he barked explosively.

"There's nothing there, Jak," Fisher told the animal as he looked along the corridor in the direction of the main entrance door. Immediately the dog stopped barking, shook himself, then sat down with his amber eyes fixed on the entrance hall, some thirty yards away.

"Are you coming in here?" Fisher stepped back to allow him into the ballroom. Jak was calm again, but instead of moving into the room, he remained sitting. "So, you want to stand guard? Is that it, boy?" The dog resolutely watched the corridor as if he expected the arrival of a visitor at any moment. "There's a good boy, you keep watching out for us, eh?" The conviction that Jak was standing guard against an intruder wouldn't leave Fisher as he returned to the others.

Fabian stood with his hands on his hips. "I thought you were taking that stray to the police?"

"Why not hang onto him?"

"Whatever for?"

"He'll come in useful as a guard dog."

"A guard dog?" Fabian acted as if he didn't believe he was hearing this.

"Why not?" Marko asked. "Look at all this equipment. It only needs someone to break in and we're screwed."

"Yeah, keep him," Sterling said. "I like dogs. We'll be able to have a laugh with him."

"OK, OK ... Only do something to stop that bloody clock from chiming. We'll be recording these rehearsals—the last thing we need is ding-fucking-dong all the way through the damn music."

"As I said," Marko told him patiently, "I couldn't find the clock."

"It must be somewhere. It's not a ghost clock, is it? It's not invisible."

Fisher found his attention being drawn back to his reflection in the glass. Yeah, this time it was just a reflection. Just an everyday, regular, run-of-the-mill reflection. When he rubbed his jaw, the mirror image man copied. Only a niggling fear remained that the Fisher trapped in the atoms of the windowpane might suddenly rebel again to smash the laws of physics.

"I'll tell you what," he said as he made an effort to look away from the window. "Marko and me will find the clock this afternoon."

Fabian appeared relieved. "Fair enough. Only don't break it. Or they'll dock our wages, and we need all the cash we can get to buy studio time. Just unplug it or tie your ruddy sock around the striker. OK?"

"Fine."

"All right, everybody." Fabian checked his notes again. "Can I finish this before we break for lunch?"

This time when Fabian started speaking, Fisher made sure that he couldn't see his reflection in the glass.

* * *

They made lunch a fast one in order to give them time to find the hidden clock. Later in the afternoon Fabian intended to play recordings of his solo demos. So the clock was the main topic of conversation over microwaved enchiladas and coffee. There was beer in the kitchen, but already Fabian had taped a timetable onto the kitchen door. In prominent letters at the top of the sheet were the words NO BOOZE UNTIL 8PM. WORK FIRST. PLAY LATER. As they ate, the hidden clock struck a lone chime to mark the passing of one o'clock.

"Sound like a cue if ever I heard one," Marko said. "You ready?"

Fisher drained his coffee cup. "As I ever will be."

When they had left the others eating cake around the table, and were in the relative privacy of the corridor, Marko said, "If you hate these songs of Fabian's, are you going to leave?"

Fisher felt the dry smile tug the muscles of his mouth. "So we've been thinking the same thing?"

"I'm not going to stay in a band if I don't like its music. Life's too short."

Fisher strolled along beside Marko. Outside, blustery weather threw rain at the window.

Marko shook his head at the rattle of raindrops. "Jesus, could Fabian have picked anywhere bleaker on earth?"

"It's deliberate. He wanted to isolate us here. So we wouldn't slope off to the clubs."

"He found the right place, then. There isn't so much as a farmhouse for miles. And have you seen that swamp at the back of the house? It just about turns this place into an island."

Fisher spoke with feeling, "Yeah, but if we decide to get out of here, Sterling can drive us out in the van."

"Knowing Fabian he'll have thought of that, too. He's probably got all the car keys hidden under his bed."

The talk had been flippant, but when they both paused to look at each other, Fisher found himself thinking: Maybe that's closer to the truth than we think.

When they reached the entrance hall with the twin doors to their right and the elegant staircase sweeping upwards to their left, they stopped again.

Fisher asked, "OK, Marko, any ideas where the mystery clock's hiding itself?"

"Your guess is as good as mine. The chimes come from everywhere."

"Hell, you can even hear them outside."

Marko grinned. "So it's a phantom clock. Let's tell Fabian that and forget about it."

"Yeah, just imagine the look on his face."

"Wait, I'll grab one of these. It might tell us something." Marko pulled one of the glossy brochures from the boxes stacked by the entrance. They were the sales particulars for the auction of the house. From the date on the cover, beneath a photograph of The Tower in sunlight, the auction had taken place six months before.

Marko flipped thought he pages. "Dimensions, specifications, services. Heck, there's pages of it."

"There might be something in the introduction."

Marko flipped back the pages, then began to read. "'The Tower. A substantial property of largely eighteenth-century construction with a medieval core, comprising a thirteenth-century façade of a dwelling house of astonishing preservation . . . ' That goes on to talk about its construction and architectural what-not. Hey, listen to this. 'Extensive grounds of woodland, open pasture . . . and water-based habitat—' "

"That'll be the swamp."

" 'There is a serviceable runway of World War Two vintage with civil aviation authority for use by light aircraft. However, military authorities have reserved the right to requisition the facility if required in the unlikely event of national emergency.' "

"That means World War Three, and the bombers will come back. Any mention of the clock?"

"Hold your horses, Fisher. But look at this. 'In 1944, a German fighter plane machine-gunned an outbuilding before being hit by ground fire. The aircraft plunged into the east wing of the property, killing eight servicemen in their second-floor dormitory.' Hey, listen to this: 'But such is the durable construction of the house that even though the blast wave resulted in loss of life, damage to the property was limited to a broken window. Its stone structure escaped unscathed.' Isn't that weird? To include details of an explosion that kills eight men in the house you're trying to sell?"

"Any developer who buys it won't care; they're not going to be living here, are they?" Fisher regarded the staircase that curved upward to vanish into the dark body of the tower above them. He sensed the weight of all that stonework sitting on the buttresses hidden within the walls. "It'll add to the romance of the place."

"Yeah, as romantic as Frankenstein's castle."

"Mind if I join you, gentlemen?"

Fisher turned to see one of Adam Ambrose's girlfriends, the one with short dark hair. She wore a tightly fitting sweater and jeans that were tucked into shiny licorice-black boots. Her astonishingly slim waist flexed in a lithe way as she walked. Kym or Belle? he asked himself. I can never remember which one is which. But I think this is the Eastern European one.

"So is it alright if I walk with you? To find the clock that is the bane of Mr. Fabian's life?"

He was right. Her Eastern European accent had a delicate exotic quality.

With effort, Marko stopped staring at her. "Yeah, fine, OK, sure." Blushing, he smiled like a tongue-tied fourteen year old.

"Be our guest," Fisher told her. "I don't know how exciting it will be."

"But Mr. Fabian must have his clock made silent, is that not so?"

"That's right, uhm . . ."

"I'm the one called Kym. Belle is blonde. You'll remember now?"

"Yes, thanks." Now Fisher found his blood warming as he began to fully appreciate her combination of looks, poise, accent and gentle charm.

"You're part of the band?"

"Yes," Fisher said. "I'm Fisher. This is Marko."

"Fisher? Like a man who catches fish?"

"That's just my name. I play bass."

"I'm joking. Perhaps Czech humor isn't to your taste?"

Fisher smiled. "It's fine by me. And welcome to The Tower, by the way."

"It's one to creep the nerve, isn't it." She mimed a shiver and rubbed her slender arms. "When I look at it, it makes my body cold."

Marko was staring again.

Fisher said, "Marko? *Marko*." Marko snapped out of it. Fisher continued, "We best find the clock; otherwise Fabian will go and sulk in his room."

Marko beamed his boyish smile again. "Mr. Fabian to you, Fisher."

Kym put her hand to her lips as she laughed. "I'm sorry. I teased you. I always think the gentleman wishes that we should call him *Mr.* Fabian."

Fisher still smiled; only he wasn't at all confident where this woman's loyalties lay. "Any luck with the catalogue, Marko?"

"Uhm?"

"The clock."

"What are you using there?" she asked as she reached out slender fingers to lift the document so that she could see the cover.

"It's the sale particulars put together by the auctioneer. We hoped it might mention the clock."

Marko still had a propensity for the shy grin. "We can find out about the history of the place, but nothing about the secret clock."

"Check in the appendices," she told him. "There will be a section on mechanical installations and plumbing. There's no need to stare at me, gentlemen, we have education in Prague, you know? I didn't grow up milking goats in a peasant shack."

Marko fumbled the pages. After some flicking forward with a lost expression on his face, his eyes suddenly opened wide. "Ah, here. 'A blind clock built by Joshua Melpesson, installed in 1898. Converted to imperial standard alternating current in 1929. Spring chime sounds hours.' A blind clock? What—" For a moment he seemed to debate whether to use more vibrant language in front of Kym. "What the dickens is a blind clock?"

Fisher shrugged.

Kym explained, "A type of clock where you can't see the face."

"What's the use in that?"

"You're not supposed to see it, Marko," she said. "You hear it. Don't you see? In a big house like this, it would have been expensive and inconvenient to provide a clock for every room and passageway. However, it would be necessary for inhabitants and domestic staff to keep track of time. So the owner installs a blind clock. It chimes on the hour and everyone here knows the time. See?" She folded her arms. "Don't keep looking at me like that, gentlemen. I do know what I'm talking about. Such timepieces can be found in the big houses of Eastern Europe, too."

"But how can you hear it all over the house?"

As they climbed the stairs she scanned the walls, then pointed. "See the air vents set in the walls? They are also sound conduits, you know? Like the old speaking tubes on ships. The tubes conduct the sound of the chimes from the clock. If those are the outlets for the sound, there will also be a box, perhaps made of tin, that will act as a resonator to amplify the sound, much like your Marshall amplifiers."

Fisher nodded. "Well, I'm convinced. The only question now is, where did they hide the clock?"

"Ah," she said. "That is the salient question. Where? It is a clock that need not be displayed, so it might be buried in the walls."

Marko grunted. "Then we might not find the damn thing anyway."

She began to climb the stairs at a faster pace, "Oh,

there will be an inspection hatch. Its mechanism will require periodic maintenance. Yes?"

At the first floor she struck off along the corridor. She was so eager to find the hidden clock she didn't bother with the lights.

"Ah, gentlemen," she called out. "Quickly! Come and see what I've found!"

Chapter Nine

Kym stood with her palms resting on top of the balustrade. Marko and Fisher followed behind along the corridor. She thought: They're surprised at what I know. They think that, because I am one third of that triangular relationship of Adam's, I'm some kind of idiot. But they are nice men. I like them. They are unpretentious. Unlike Fabian. He's a cold fish of a man.

Now she delighted in revealing what she'd found. "You have to press that strip on the wall. See, it switches on the lights. They're on a timer." Along the wall ran a narrow strip of metal at waist height. "Go on, press it, Fisher. It won't bite you."

He was good-natured enough to know that she was teasing in a friendly way. He touched the silvery strip. Immediately light sprang from globes set in the ceiling.

"Now come see what I've found. Be quick. The lights are governed by a timer. They'll probably go out in a moment."

They joined her at the balustrade. If anything, it resembled a balcony that didn't look out, but instead looked in. She enjoyed the surprise on their faces when they stared downward to see a wall of rough stone; it was the color of sun-bleached bone. Set in the wall were a row of five windows on the second floor. On the first floor was a low oblong doorway that even a child would have to stoop to pass through. At either side of that dwarfish aperture were two more sets of windows. They were framed by slabs of black stone that also formed the lintel to support the wall of roughly hewn stones. Above the front door was the weathered carving of what might have been a bird or dragon. Wings were visible, along with a long, curving neck that terminated in a head with wide-open jaws.

Fisher said, "I take it that's what they describe as the medieval core of the house."

"Oh? It says so in the book?" she asked.

He nodded. "It's called the Good Heart."

Marko whistled. "So why have they built one house inside another house?"

Kym shook her head. "No, the other way round. What you're seeing is the front of the house that was here many centuries ago. It had ancestral importance, you know? Like a family heirloom? So, rather than demolish the old house when they built The Tower in the eighteenth century, they constructed it so the new structure enveloped the old house. Now you have a building within a building, like those Russian dolls that contain a smaller figure within the body." They were impressed. "In fact, within that older house, you might even find the remains of a yet more ancient dwelling."

At that moment the lights went out, plunging them

into darkness. With the fire doors shut to the staircase, not a glimmer of light penetrated the gloom.

"You can find that strip on the wall again?"

"Got it." That was Fisher's voice. A second later the ceiling lamps came on to throw their light onto the pale stone. Simultaneously the hidden clock struck two. The shimmering chimes ghosted through the air. They hung suspended for a moment in a sustained hum before dying away.

"Fabian will be expecting us back to hear his songs."

"Ah, Marko. Mr. Fabian is cracking his ringmaster's whip?"

"We're committed to making this work," Fisher told her. "That's why we've taken the trouble to come here."

"Then I best silence the clock, so you can work in peace." She held out her hand to Marko. "If I can have the book." Quickly she fanned through the pages. "Surveyors should be professional, therefore, they need to have stated the location of the clock mechanism. Ah, here . . . I suspected so. The medieval core of the house is situated in its center. Leading to it is the ornamental walkway known as the Promenade. Therefore the tower extends directly above the Good Heart, so it becomes the ideal location for the clock mechanism. Yes. The service hatch is located in a buttress just within that doorway down there."

"You can't go down there."

Kym looked at Marko in surprise. "Why ever not?"

"There's no power in that part of the house. They shut down everything except the power to the ground floor in the wing we're using."

Fisher frowned. "Well, the lights work up here."

Kym shrugged. "An oversight, or they're on the same circuit as the emergency lighting."

"But they might not work down there."

"I know," she told them brightly. "You two gentlemen remain up here in the gallery. Whenever the lights go out, reactivate them. I can see switches down there at the end of the façade. Once I've switched on those, I can find the clock mechanism and make Fabian happy with the quiet we'll bring. You're OK with that?"

Fisher said, "You're confident you can take care of the clock?"

"Take care? Oh, I see. Take care of the clock, meaning killing it. Well, I won't hurt it. I'll simply remove the fuse so it doesn't work. I can replace the fuse when we leave. See, you're looking at me as if I've grown three heads. Yes, the workings of the clock don't concern me. My university degree is in engineering, for the study of locomotion by electrical means. I wrote dissertations on Volta and the linear motor. I don't think an electrical clock should present difficulties, do you?"

The two men shook their heads. Fisher asked, "And you don't want us to come down with you?"

"You'll have noticed I'm a big girl now, Mr. Fisher. Stay here with Marko to work the light, so I can see. I'll be back here in five minutes."

The lights went out. She heard the tap of a hand on the light switch. A second later, radiance flooded them to spill over the balustrade. It illuminated the front of the ancient farmhouse that until two hundred years before had stood foursquare to the brutal elements of this northern land.

THE TOWER

Fisher waited by the balustrade, while Marko hung back near the corridor wall where the strip switch ran along its length. Kym would have to walk downstairs, then enter the walkway beneath him through a door in the entrance hall. The light switches were set in the wall right at the end of the preserved shell. He'd never seen anything quite like this before. Years ago he'd visited a hotel that had been built on the site of a monastery. The first floor of the monastery had over the years sunk underground. The hotel utilized the ancient subterranean level as its wine cellar. This, however, had been lovingly—obsessively?—preserved. The bone gray walls stretched up two full stories in front of him, a height of perhaps twenty-five feet. He looked directly into the glazed windows that were so small and deep-set that they were nothing like modern windows. They radiated an aura of something alien rather than antique. The little panes supported by an intricate web of lead strips glinted with a dark violet hue, as if that house within a house had filled itself with liquid shadow to conceal whatever might reside there. Just to look at the structure with its bowed walls and misshapen windows invited notions that the entire structure had at various times become soft as warm plastic—which resulted in its dimensions losing their symmetry. Its appearance also reinforced the notion that this house didn't obey the normal rules of the universe. Only too pungently he recalled the way his room had imploded last night, until it had felt as if his body were being crushed by the jaws of a monster. Semiconsciously his hand rubbed the sore bruise on his chest. Then there was the reflection in the glass this morning. Strange times, Fisher, he told himself. Strange, strange times.

"Can you see her yet, Fisher?" Marko leaned forward over the balustrade to look down into the Promenade, which formed a chasm some twenty feet wide and thirty feet high in the center of the building.

"Marko, you're supposed to stay near the switch in case the . . . There, it's proved my point."

The sixty-second timer killed the lights again. Darkness was instantaneous.

"No sweat, Fisher, I'll find it."

It took Marko seconds to cross the corridor. Fisher imagined him feeling his way across the wall until . . .

"Got it." A second later the lights burned again.

"Gentlemen. I thought you'd left me alone here in the dark."

Fisher looked down to see Kym standing there in her patent leather boots. She returned his gaze from a stone walkway a good fifteen feet below him. Kym smiled up at him and he found a reciprocating smile come to his face. *Why does she have to be tied up with Adam Ambrose? Even the way she calls Marko and me "gentlemen" is erotic. OK, OK, concentrate on the job in hand.*

"I thought you were going to use those lights." He nodded at the switches just paces from her.

"Marko's right," she responded. "The power supply has been cut down here."

"Wait there until I can find a flashlight."

"No need. Keep the lights burning up there. I should be able to see. It's only a question of removing the fuse."

She stepped forward with that swaying walk of hers. Her boots clicked against the stone floor.

"Be careful," he told her. She smiled back. Was that gratitude for his concern or an "oh, I can take care of myself, little boy" smile? *Hell. She's beautiful. I could watch her walk all day.*

She stopped at the doorway. It formed a roughly squared opening. Its black slab of a lintel bore the weight of the stonework above it. She would have to dip that lovely head of glossy black hair to enter the medieval core of The Tower. Kym paused to glance back at Fisher. Her brown eyes met his unflinchingly.

The lights went out. Darkness rushed in.

When she spoke, her Eastern European accent was beautifully modulated. There wasn't even a hint of panic. "Switch them back on again, gentlemen. No fooling about, do you hear?"

"Marko," Fisher hissed. "The light switch."

"I can't find it. It's crazy, I put my hand straight on it the last couple of times, now I can't . . . Hell, Fisher. What can have happened to it?"

"Guys? Did you hear me? I can't see a thing down here."

Fisher called out into the darkness. "Don't worry, we'll have them back on for you in a minute." Then to Marko, "Hurry up."

"I'm trying!"

"Gentlemen. This is not funny anymore."

"Marko?"

"Shit! Wait . . . wait . . . got it. There!"

"So why aren't the lights coming on, Marko?"

"I don't know. I pressed the strip. I know I did."

For seconds the darkness weighed on them as if an invisible gargantuan foot ground them down. Fisher found it hard to breathe, as if that weight had settled on his ribs.

"Bingo!" Marko exclaimed.

The lights burned as brightly as before.

"Just a glitch," Marko said. "I told you I'd pressed the switch."

Fisher leant over the balustrade to reassure Kym. When his eyes scanned left and right for a second time, he had to admit to himself: She's no longer there. He looked down at the empty walkway. Stone slabs gleamed dully.

"Kym. Where are you?" The dead stones, in the face of that house within a house, drained the sound of his voice from the air.

Chapter Ten

Kym thought, I don't want to wait any longer. By the time they find the light switch again, I can be inside the medieval core. She extended her hand through the darkness. Her fingers found the stone lintel. It was cold. Like handling raw meat straight from the refrigerator. Strange; for a second it seemed as if the stonework twitched beneath her fingertips.

With the doorway being so low, she had to duck as she moved from the Promenade into what had once been an ancient dwelling in its own right. The quality of the sound was different, the air much cooler. She caught a faint scent of sandalwood. Instinctively, her eyes scanned what would be the interior; only it was so perfectly dark that she couldn't make out so much as a silhouette or glimmer of light.

"Gentlemen, this is not funny anymore." *So I've said the words once already, but they're worth repeating. What are those two playing at? Are they deliberately trying to frighten me?* "Can we have the lights please?" No reply.

Surely they can hear? For heaven sakes, they're only in the gallery twenty feet away. "Lights please. Otherwise I shall be angry with you."

Maybe it is their idea of fun to leave the Czech girl alone in the dark. They might have already returned to the ballroom to laugh about their prank with the others. Idiots. She liked Fisher. She'd even started to imagine herself spending time with him. Why had he played this trick on her? She extended her hand to feel for a wall. *I might have to find my way out of her by touch,* she told herself. *This is a cruel trick to play on anyone.* Her fingers didn't make contact with anything solid. Cool air wrapped itself around her wrists. Another current of cold stroked her naked arms. When she took a step, her foot scraped on the floor. The sound returned to her as a flock of echoes from the darkness. She took another step. The echoes grew louder. For all the world it sounded as if someone unseen had taken a step close by.

"Is anyone there?" she whispered.

Echoes ghosted down at her. *"Is anyone there? Is anyone there? Is anyone there?"*

"Please . . ."

"Please, please, please . . ."

"Don't do this."

"Don't do this, don't do this, don't do this, don't do this-sssss . . ."

The echo became a hiss that continued until it decayed into what seemed to be a whispering, as if there were invisible intruders close by who she couldn't see. Meanwhile her imagination became a menacing, predatory monster in its own right as it transformed the echo into a hiss of sinister voices: *Look how she stands with her arms by her sides. I could put my hands around her throat before she even knew I was there. She doesn't know she's standing at the edge of the old well. Push her down. Imagine how she'd scream as realized she was falling to her death? Why not creep up behind her? She'd never see us in the dark. We could set fire to her hair. Can't you just see her dance with her head blazing?*

"Stop it," she told herself. The voices weren't there. It was just imagination.

"Stop it, stop it . . ." mocked the echoes.

"There's no one there."

". . . no one there, there, there, no one, no one . . ."

That flock of echoes ghosted on the air as if they'd roamed some cosmic distance before their return. In that time they'd become distorted, corrupted—reformed into new sentences that held dark promises for the woman standing alone in utter darkness. *"No one . . . stop it. No one stop it, no one . . . No one. . . . No one . . ."* The hiss of the echo sank on her, as dry as the dust of bones floating through the still air of a tomb. . . . The darkness leaned over her; she felt its greedy presence here. A vampire darkness that would suck the light of her soul from her body. Kym clenched her fists as a surge of panic rose in her chest. Her throat was shrinking. The dry walls of her larynx constricted. She couldn't shout now. She could barely breathe. She struggled to draw air into her lungs. Her heart thundered in her chest. With a wild effort she struggled to open her eyes wider in case they could capture the meanest glimmer of light. Crimson spots bloomed into blood red stains in the darkness as her optic nerves fought to capture even a glimpse of what haunted this cold, lightless room. Then . . .

Dear God.

White light streamed through the doorway. More light slanted in rays through the leaded windows, too. At last. What had kept those guys? With illumination came a sense of relief. Suddenly she could breathe again. Inhaling deeply, she looked around the inner core of the building—this house within a house. The angle of the light only revealed her surroundings from the stone slabs of the floor up to waist height. There were no furnishings other than a large table in the center of the room—a billiard table, maybe? Above her, shadows formed a black pool of surreal intensity. She realized that when the builders of the later house had enveloped this medieval dwelling with their new structure, they'd removed all the inner rooms, the ceilings, and its roof, to leave a box-shaped husk. Not enough light was reflected upward to be certain, but she guessed that this formed part of the base of the eighteenth-century tower. Now she stood looking up into the shadowed heart of it. If only she could find the lights. That would be an awesome view. Only . . .

Only she didn't relish the prospect of the light dying again. The lights in the upper passageway that Fisher and Marko activated (if they hadn't scooted) tripped out every sixty seconds. *Do what you came to do. Find the clock mechanism. Unplug it. Get out. It's as simple as that.* Restricted by the meager light, she scanned what she could of the whitewashed walls.

How long now before the timer cuts the light? Forty seconds? Thirty? I should have kept track of the time.

At least those malevolent voices she'd imagined had evaporated. And no, there was no pit yawning in the floor. To one side of her, where a wall ran at right angles from the medieval façade, was a bulky chimney of deep red brick that housed a fireplace big enough to roast a whole ox. Set in the whitewashed wall beside the chimney was a small wooden door about two feet by four. Bingo, as Marko was fond of saying. That could be the electric clock's inspection door. Quickly she crossed the floor.

"Please don't be locked," she murmured. "I just want to get out of here now."

There's something wrong with this place. She didn't put that sentence into words. She knew the truth of the statement nonetheless. Who would build their mansion round an evil-looking house, anyway? Talk about the imp of the perverse.

Bingo again. There was no lock on the door. She grabbed the brass knob and pulled it open. Of course it was dark in the mechanism housing. If only she had brought a flashlight after all. Now she had to crouch to be eye-level with a shadowed lump of something inside the recess. It was too gloomy to see much detail apart from the body of the blind clock, which was rounded rather than squared. If anything, an organic shape. Like a large black cat crouching there. A surreal image, she knew, yet an apt one. The curving feline shape sat on a bed of stone which must have been carved from the medieval wall when the clock was installed over a hundred years ago. She could make out cables, then shadowy vertical lines behind the housing of the clock. That could be the hollow tube that transmitted the sound of the chimes through the entire building. Now, there should be a switch to break the current so the engineer could service the mechanism. At least the recess appeared clean. Not even a cobweb. Still crouching by the miniature doorway she inserted her hand into the void. Although it was deeply shadowed, she'd made out a square object the size of a cigarette carton fixed to the wall. A cable snaked in one side and out the other.

The switch box, if I'm not mistaken, she thought. She leaned into the recess, her hand stretching out toward the inner wall. That was the moment the clock started to chime. *Damn.*

One . . . two . . . three . . .

Three chimes. It's not three o'clock.

Four . . . five . . .

The chimes continued, a shimmering sound that evoked a shimmering bell given voice by a muffled striker.

Six . . . seven . . .

Wait, she thought, there's something wrong with the timing. I haven't disturbed the mechanism. Yet the chimes continued. They appeared to grow in volume. The shimmering sound flew outwards only to rush back at her as echoes that had become grossly mutant. The stone surfaces of walls and floors disfigured the purity of the chime. They appeared to grow louder, harsher, more insistent—more like the scream of an alarm warning of approaching danger. Kym turned her head as instinct urged her to look back over her shoulder. A man approached through the gloom from the center of the room. The angle of the light falling through the windows meant she couldn't see above his waist. But she saw his pale hands dangling by his sides, his dark trousers, a leather belt around his waist.

"Fisher? Have you brought a flashlight? Fisher . . ." Her voice died in her throat.

His feet? The man didn't wear shoes. The bare feet

were gray in that light; dark patches mottled the skin. The toes were blackened with dirt.

The chimes didn't stop. They grew louder. More insistent. Now it seemed they screamed inside her head. The savage noise tore at her nerves. As she flinched, shocked by the sight of the approaching stranger with his top half concealed by shadow, her hand found the geometric shape of the switch box on the wall. That was when the lights went out.

"Fisher!" she yelled. "Fisher! Switch them back on!" The chimes pulsed their furious sound from the clock. Fisher wouldn't hear her call. Now she was alone with that barefooted stranger who approached across the stone slabs. There was absolute dark. She could see nothing. *Kill the noise.* It made sense to switch off the clock chimes so at least she had a chance of hearing how close that sinister figure was. She reached further into the recess as she searched for the switch.

There! She knew what her fingers had found in the darkness. Two metal prongs—they formed the contacts that held the main's wire in place. Why she had time to identify what she'd found before it struck she couldn't tell. But she knew she'd just pressed her fingertips against the naked electrical contacts. The voltage snapped up her arm into her body with such force that she felt as if she'd been struck by a car. It knocked the air from her lungs. A blue fire flickered in the inspection chamber. It illuminated the interior with such a vivid light that she saw the rounded shape of the clock's housing, while all the time it seemed to her that sharp teeth had erupted from the wall to gnaw at her fingers as the electricity blazed from the terminals into her skin. Convulsions tore through her body. Her head snapped sideways as the figure extended a pallid hand toward her throat.

Kym opened her eyes. She lay on her back on a hard surface.

Electric shock, she told herself as her mind swam back into focus. *Like a fool I touched bare electrical contacts.*

Sounds returned as she regained consciousness. *Those chimes. Why don't they stop?* Now the chimes tolled with a heavy leaden sound. They were slower, too. She smelt a musty, organic smell. Like an animal's nest found under boxes in a potting shed.

Switch on the light, Fisher.

Only the shock had robbed Kym of her ability to speak. She blinked. Above her was a piece of timber. A ceiling beam? No. She didn't remember any of those. But there, directly above her as she lay on her back, was a balk of timber about a foot wide and maybe six feet long. The chimes rose in volume. There was an urgency in that shimmering quality. Kym sensed a figure nearby. She turned her head. She saw a torso that vanished into shadow. The head and arms were hidden by darkness. She turned her head to look down. Bare feet. The same gray bare feet she'd seen before. Panic snapped through her body with the same kind of force as that jolt of electricity. She tried to raise herself from where she lay. Then she realized she'd been tied to a tabletop. Leather straps fastened her wrists to the wooden surface.

"What are you doing?"

A gaunt face with blotched skin and a stubbled jaw appeared to float out of the darkness. On his forehead a scar formed a moon-shaped crescent. He looked down at her. He nodded, satisfied. The chimes began to clamor in a single throbbing note. Movement from above. She sensed it first, then saw it. The timber descended smoothly toward her. That didn't make sense. A ceiling beam couldn't be lowered like that. Only then it did make sense. Terrible sense. Monstrous sense. An iron spike protruded down from the center of the beam. The spike was perhaps three feet long and little thicker than a pencil. She lifted her head to watch its descent. Her eyes bulged. She wanted to scream. All she could do was pant.

And the chimes rose into a phantom scream. The iron point approached the center of her chest. Two feet away. A foot away. Eight inches. Five. Four. Three. Two.

"NO!"

One.

The point settled onto her chest. Its point pressed into her flesh. The fabric of her sweater pulled tight.

And the agony. Kym had never experienced pain like this before. With a manic sense of disappointment she saw that the point of the shaft was really quite blunt. That's intentional, she thought. He wants me to suffer.

With a fatal fascination she raised her head as high as she could so she could see the iron point pressing against her ribs. Agony tore through her in withering blasts.

But it's too blunt. It can't puncture my skin. It can't kill me. Only the downward movement hadn't been stopped yet. Some mechanism applied more pressure.

A *pop!* audible even above the mad cacophony of chimes. The iron spike broke through the barrier of skin. Unimpeded it slid smoothly into Kym. The iron shaft was so cold as it entered her lungs. She watched with a horror-stricken fascination as blood released through the puncture wound jetted upwards. There was only one lungful of air left in her body now. She used it in the only way she could. She lifted her head from the table and opened her mouth until her lips stretched in a huge agonized O. Then Kym screamed. Oh, how she screamed . . .

Chapter Eleven

Light flooded the floor, slabs polished smooth by centuries of feet. Servants. Footmen. Maids. Lords. Ladies. Even knights in armor. An image rose before her mind's eye. Men clad in silver metal, with feathered plumes rising from the crest of their helmets. One breaks the leg off a roast rabbit to toss it to a black dog that sits in front of the crackling fire. . . .

Wakefulness filled her head in a rush. Suddenly she could see properly. She could hear. She knew the stupid thing she'd done.

Kym opened her mouth; her tongue seemed too big for its cavity; she did her best. "Bnn . . . Stupid idiot . . . I'm stupid . . . I've given myself an electric shock, haven't I? Then dreamt I was skewered by a man in bare feet, while that thing kept on chiming. What on earth is wrong with it?"

Fisher stood watching her with concern on his face. "Are you sure you can walk alright? Would you like to sit down?"

Kym blinked in surprise. "I didn't even know I was standing."

"When I came in here you were there by the fireplace. You say you suffered an electric shock?"

"Yes, I touched the terminals. Don't worry." She managed a smile. "It's low voltage. Perhaps made my hair stand on end a little bit."

Fisher smiled. "Your hair's fine.

"I should see to the clock. Those chimes were going crazy. Bong, bong, bong."

"Really? We couldn't hear anything."

"So you and Marko didn't leave me?"

"No, we wouldn't do anything like that. We stayed up in the gallery. Marko hit the light switch every time they went out. I kept watch to make sure you were OK."

His concern touched her; she felt a sudden glow of affection for the man. "Thank you."

"Only when the light went out and we couldn't switch it back on for a few seconds, we saw that you'd gone."

"Oh, I found my way through the façade by touch. I didn't want to waste time."

"The moment you vanished I came down here. Though I had to wait out in the walkway area when the lights went out. The switch is crap. It must be faulty. It takes a minute or so to reactivate."

"So you didn't see the man in bare feet? Or hear the chimes go crazy?"

From the way Fisher smiled, Kym realized he thought she was pulling his leg. "Chimes? Bare feet? I don't get it."

"No, neither do I now, Fisher." She sighed. "You know something? I must have blacked out when I was fooling around with the bare wires. I think the shock got reality and dreams all mixed up inside my head."

"Are you sure you're OK? You don't want to sit down?"

"I want to get out of here before the lights go again. But if you will allow me to take your arm?"

His smile was a warm one. "By all means. Let me know if you need to rest."

"I will, Fisher. Thank you."

Fisher made it to the doors of the entrance hall, with Kym linking her arm with his, before the timer tripped the light out again. He paused in the doorway as the Promenade that ran beneath the frowning façade of the medieval house was plunged into darkness once more.

"Oh!" she exclaimed.

"What's wrong?"

"I forgot to switch off the clock. Those chimes will drive everyone crazy."

"Don't worry," he told her. "I ripped the power cable out of the junction box. It's dead."

Fisher felt her palm through his shirt as she lightly touched his chest. Her dark eyes caught the daylight falling through the hallway windows. "Thank you again." Her smile and her Eastern European accent captivated him. "I think you have saved my life today."

Fisher had feared she'd been dying there by the fireplace in that weird house within a house. Her eyes were dull. Her chest had been jerking in convulsive starts as she choked for breath. What he didn't tell her was that she'd been sobbing, a heartbreaking sound of sheer grief.

Marko ran lightly down the stairs. "What ho, captain," he called cheerfully. "Got it done?"

Kym answered for him. "He has. And he rescued me, too."

"Did you need rescuing?" Marko asked in surprise.

"Yes. Fisher, my hero, rescued me. I don't know what to do to repay him."

Fisher quelled with a glare any comment Marko might have planned to make.

"I guess Fabian will be expecting us to report back," Fisher told her.

"OK. I'm going back to my room to rest. Gentlemen." She nodded at them. "I'll see you later."

As she walked away, Fisher saw that her balance had returned.

Marko winked. "When you going to collect payment from her, Fisher?"

Grinning, Fisher put his arm around the man and pressed his fist against his face. "Go play your drums, Marko, and don't say another word."

Marko grinned back. "Yeah, but you don't know what I'm thinking, don't you?"

"Behave, you strange little man."

Marko's grin grew even wider. "I'm imagining you. And I'm imagining Kym. She's wearing a silk robe as she glides toward you." He adopted an Eastern European accent. "Oh, Mr. Fisher. Thank you for saving my life. Take what you want. Only be gentle with—"

"OK, I warned you."

Marko bolted down the corridor in the direction of the ballroom. Fisher followed, trying to shout threats, but his laughter made the words come out all wrong.

In the ballroom Fabian stood at the keyboard. He shuffled pages of music. With barely a glance up he asked, "What kept the pair of you?" Then the hidden clock chimed three times. Annoyed he stabbed his finger into the air. "And weren't you going to put a stop to that?"

Chapter Twelve

Fisher sat on the end of his bed to pull off his shoes.

"OK, room." Fisher adopted schoolteacher tones of authority. "You're going to behave yourself to-night, aren't you?"

The art of flippancy, he thought. Kill a sense of foreboding with a lighthearted comment. Does it work every time? Does it, hell.

The time was 11:15. Around him the house creaked as it settled itself into the cold witching hours until dawn. Hawthorn bushes squirmed outside his window in the breeze. They were like shaggy beasts with coats of spikes that constantly shook themselves in a state of barely suppressed agitation as cold air currents rushed at them from the swamp. He imagined what it would be like to walk through that swarm of bushes with their stabbing thorns. . . .

"Stop it. You're brooding," he told himself. "Get some sleep. Fabian's going to be on your back if you're not up by seven. Obey the master. His every whim is your command." *Flippant comment number two. Yeah, but check out Fabian's rules: Bed before twelve. Rise at seven. No heavy duty liquor (that's wine and beer only, then only in moderation, and, hell knows you could use those golden shots of whisky tonight; you don't know what the house will pull on you next—hey, Fisher, what's that you said about brooding?). What's worse? That Fabian imposed all these rules? Or that you, Marko and Sterling agreed to go along with them? Of course . . . it's that promise of money flooding into your bank account, of seeing your face on the cover of music magazines.* Fabian had sold them the dream. They'd bought it. Now they were prepared to go along with the guy.

The wind blew harder. It drew a single note that became a rising cry in the night before subsiding to a sobbing sound. For a second he believed it really was someone in distress. Only the blast of air currents came again to swirl around the carved stonework and draw out yet another cry that seemed to combine human emotion with a quality that was deeply inhuman, as if the architecture of the house colluded with the cold north wind to mimic a human being—one with all the frailties and the fears that beset every living man and woman. The cry came again. It forced currents of ice through Fisher's veins. The cry grew louder. It was the north wind shaped by the stone lips of the house, only it throbbed with human emotion. Fisher sat hypnotized by the sound. The grief he felt for his own father that lurked just below the surface of his joking, what-the-hell-let's-party disguise threatened to spill over and seize hold of him. And here he was: alone in The Tower—a house that contained a grim, forbidding inner house. Loneliness poured in as relentlessly as the cold jets of air whistling through gaps in the window frames. *I'm alone. There's no one to talk with.* As solitude threatened to crush him, wild thoughts flooded his head—of searching for whisky, or just racing out of the house to run through the woods and fields until exhaustion annihilated this volcano of grief inside of him. As all that weighed down on his spirits with all the suffocating pressure of grave soil being mounded over a coffin, the house with its ally the north wind subtly altered the sound of the air currents gusting across the grim masonry. The cry rose again, this time into a screaming sound that was twice as loud as before. Branches rattled at the glass windowpanes—stiff, dead fingers frantically tapping. Now, as the scream decayed, the sobbing sound wasn't repeated. This time that pulse of throaty notes didn't imitate an expression of grief; it was a chuckle. It delighted in the effect it had on the twenty-two-year-old sitting on the bed with his head in his hands. It mocked his misery. This grief of his; this was something it could feed on. . . .

Fisher ran his hands through his hair. "Stop it." Did he tell the gales to stop? Or did he tell himself to stop these brooding thoughts that were drowning him? At that moment he couldn't tell. He only wanted out. . . . *And, dear God, at this moment any exit will do.* . . .

The sound didn't register at first. Then it came again. Someone lightly tapped at his door.

If I open it, who's gong to stand there? What's going to stand there? Dad? As dead as nails? Or something without a human face? Flippancy became malignant now. His comments didn't protect him. They burrowed into his soul to rot it from the inside out. *Tap, tap, tap . . .*

"Fisher?"

He came out of it. For moment his heart beat hard. He blinked. He realized he'd been in some place that wasn't quite this room, or quite this time. He'd been in a dark place that desperate people find themselves trapped in. A dangerous place where you're vulnerable. Now he was out. He'd escaped.

"Fisher . . ."

"OK." He crossed the bedroom to the door.

"Fisher, hurry up."

Those Eastern European accents. "Kym," he said opening the door, "you'll piss off Fabian, breaking the curfew. You know what he—"

Kym rushed at him with all the speed and fury of a whirlwind. She grabbed hold of his head with her hands to kiss him full on the mouth. The force of the kiss made him take a step back; immediately she used the heel of her foot to shut the door. The kiss caught him by surprise, although he kissed her right back, placing his hands on either side of her waist that moved so in such a supple way. Her furious kisses went on. Each time he expected her to break away, a renewed surge rose inside of her. Soft lips pressed against his. Her hands slipped down his head as at last she broke the kiss to stand back. There she stared at him with nothing less than defiance.

"Kym?" he managed to say.

"People use too many words," she told him, still locking her eyes on him. "I say act first, so we know where we stand."

"Stand?" Fisher's heart beat hard. This wasn't unwelcome, but . . . "What about Adam?"

"You wouldn't understand the nature of our relationship."

"I wouldn't?"

"I like you." She tossed her head. "Do you like me?"

"Yes?"

"Then we should make love."

Is this the Czech way? He doubted it. This was Kym being Kym. Everything about her breathed a powerful eroticism. The swaying walk. Her short dark hair that was glossy as silk. Her clothes; those licorice black boots that hugged her beautiful calves. Ebony eyes that sent a shiver across his skin every time she looked at him. These thoughts flitted through his head. But to strip her naked? Make love to her? This whirlwind speed took him by surprise.

"Well, Fisher. Do you want me? Or would you like me to leave your room?"

In the end the answer didn't come from him. The cold breeze droned around iron fall pipes. It roused the bushes to strike their sticks of bristling thorns at the window pane. A night of this alone in this room . . . in this house . . .

"Stay," he told her.

"You want me, Fisher?"

"Yes."

"But whatever we do, whatever our experience when we fuck, we don't talk about it. OK?"

"No. It's just between you and me."

"And in the morning I'll be with Adam. So we act as if there is nothing between us."

"But if you think you're cheating on Adam—"

"Who said anything about cheating?" Her expression radiated cold waves.

"It's just that—"

"Just nothing. As I said, you don't understand our relationship. It's not what you think."

"OK."

"You want me to go?"

Here's your choice. The solitude of this room? A room that collapsed in on you? Or human company? To distract you from brooding thoughts?

Fisher lunged at her. She drew in a gasp of air, perhaps afraid he'd decided to attack her. But he hugged her against him, crushing her body against his as he kissed her on the mouth. The tension melted from her muscles. She became pliant again. A warm, healthy, supple-torsoed woman. Her fingers pushed through his hair. Her mouth had a cool freshness as if she'd been drinking ice cold spring water. The passionate surges returned to her body. They were met by his.

Now there was no marsh being ripped by biting northerlies. He didn't hear the tap of branches on the window or the whine of air currents wrapping invisible limbs about the house. He kissed her with so much passion that the sheer heat of it all drove away the brooding thoughts that had nearly suffocated him a moment before.

This time when she broke the contact, mouth on mouth, she smoothly slipped her sweater off to reveal her small, firm breasts. She kissed him on the face, then lay back on the bed. As she pushed her thumbs into tight-fitting ski pants, she looked him in the eye and said, "Help me with these."

That moment of afterglow. He'd just lain down beside her on the bed. The cool air touched his bare skin. For the past half hour he'd not been aware of it or of anything else, for that matter, apart from the delicious sensation of locking limbs with Kym. Now their breathing began to slow as the heat of their passion passed. Kym turned her head to look into his eyes, her face no more than six inches from his.

"Nice," she told him in the softly accented voice. "We made the right decision."

"I believe we did." Fisher smiled. "I know we did."

"I had to get out of the house," she explained.

"Hmm?"

"I knew I couldn't leave this rotten house and go away. But I had to leave it for a little while. Like this. Do you understand?"

"I guess I do."

"Don't make a sad face. I like you. This wasn't a . . . how you say it? A clinical fuck. It was two warm-hearted friends fucking. Isn't that nice with you?"

Fisher felt the smile return to his face. "Nice? Awesome. Fucking awesome."

She kissed him on the lips, then used her fingertip to trace a line around his face. All the time her eyes roved over his features as if embedding them deep in her mind, so she'd remember them.

"You'll stay the full month?" she asked.

"I guess so."

"A girlfriend waiting back home?"

"No girlfriend. No day job."

She gave a soft laugh. "Ah, no girlfriend. I wondered why you seemed so pent up. Like so full of inner pressure. Volcano, it goes—" she tweaked his nose "—boom."

"I broke up with a girl a few weeks ago. We realized it had run its course."

"Ah, failure to commit. Classic case. Now . . . Here it comes again."

She sat up as the chimes shimmered their ghost

music through the air again. Solemnly she sat there looking up at the ceiling. When it finished striking twelve, she shivered. Fisher saw goose bumps rise on her skin.

Kym shrugged. "And to think I electrocuted myself today trying to disable the mechanism. And it's still damn well chiming."

He frowned. "I must have pulled out some obsolete wiring. The power feed might run into it from a different direction."

"Next time we take plenty of flashlights. I don't intend to be stranded in darkness again. That old medieval house inside this one . . . pah, it's weird. Whoever built this place must have been, you know? Lost in the head."

"You want to leave?"

"Ah, I'm made of strong nerves, Fisher. My husband tried to shoot me when I told him I was leaving. Now he's in jail in Prague. I'm not easy to frighten."

Fisher wasn't sure how to ask this without sounding crass. Nevertheless . . . "Your relationship with Adam?"

"Oh, what a bruise on your ribs. It's enormous. What happened?"

"It's nothing. You and Adam. And Belle?"

Thoughtfully she stroked the bruise on his chest with a lightness he couldn't have believed was possible.. "You are curious, aren't you? Belle has her own reasons. For me? It is necessary to embed myself in your culture and your society. Even with my university degree I'd be a chambermaid in one of your hotels or carrying food to restaurant tables. Only I am determined to fast-track myself into a position where I have earning power and status. There, you know enough for now. Is what I do wrong?"

"It's ambitious."

"Then aren't we cut from the same cloth? You obey all of Fabian's little rules and sit like oh-so polite children listening to his music."

"Like children?"

"Don't kid yourself, Fisher. We're the same. We've made our principles elastic so we can get what we want from life." She turned so she could kiss his bare chest. "Hmm, salty. And don't look hurt again. I love salt more than sugar. I put salt on chopped apple. Try it some time." She kissed him again. This time on his stomach. "Salt on raw onion, too. Tastes wonderful." She ran her tongue across his midriff. "Nice and tangy. Hmm, do you know that our blood is virtually the same composition as seawater? We evolved. We left the oceans. But we still have the remains of gills inside our ears. And we have brought the sea with us. Our bodies manufacture salt water." She kissed him again, then licked her lips. Then, kissing quickly with a velvety softness, she tracked her lips down across his stomach. Fisher had to clench his fists when he felt the delicious tickling sensation on his loins.

Then . . . a single chime. A rogue chime. Frowning, he glanced at his watch on the bedside table. Nine minutes after midnight. So why the chime?

Kym lifted her head; her eyes scanned the ceiling as if the chimes might appear like glowing orbs of energy through the plasterwork.

"So what's the blind clock saying, Fisher? 'I'm still here'? 'I'm still working despite all your efforts'? 'Don't you dare forget me'? Hmm?"

Go back to what you were doing before, he thought. Forget the chime.

She knelt on the bed. "You know when that electric shock knocked me clean off my feet? I had such a vivid dream. I dreamt that I lay on a table. From above a long metal spike came down." She mimed a stab to her stomach; her clenched fist pressed against her skin just below her dark-tipped breasts. "It penetrated me. Went right through. There was so much blood. Blood all gushing out. I believed it was real. I saw the man. He was barefoot. His face was very thin, like a skull. He had bristles on his jaw." She shivered. The faraway look in her eye revealed that the nightmare had genuinely disturbed her. "And he had a scar here." She ran her finger from her bangs to her right eyebrow. "A shape like a crescent moon. Even pale yellow like a moon. As if a flap of skin had been torn back from his forehead, then hadn't healed well." Another shiver shook her so much that Fisher felt the bed tremble beneath him. "Ah . . . darling Fisher. It's getting late. I need to go to bed."

"You can stay."

"We're being discreet, my darling." She gave a gentle smile. "You ask me, will I come back here again?"

"Will you?"

"I am seriously thinking about it. Now . . ." She kissed his stomach. "I dress." Her smile broadened. "And, if you like, you can watch." Quickly, she pulled on her sweater. "Remember not to mention this to anyone. Don't let your body language betray you either. This is secret."

Then she left as she'd arrived. A whirlwind in reverse. It took scant seconds for her to dress. She moved to the door, opened it, checked that no one was there.

Fisher climbed out of bed. *I want to tell her about*

what happened to me in this room. How its walls seemed to fall on me. I want to tell her all that. And I want to kiss her again before she goes. Only she was closing the door behind her. Through the gap she shot a dark-eyed glance. A whispered, "Bye." Then gone.

Chapter Thirteen

Her skin burned with the heat of the lovemaking. Her face would be flushed, she knew. Adam and Belle would figure out how she'd spent the past hour. What they'd say didn't concern her, if they said anything at all. Only she intended that particular triangular relationship to retain its present equilibrium. So Kym didn't return to her room. Instead she padded along the corridor to the entrance hall and crossed the checkerboard-patterned tiles to the front doors. Carefully she eased one open. She didn't want hinge squeaks to attract her housemates' attention. Nor had she switched on the entrance hall lights. The illumination spilling from the corridor was enough. Kym could stand here for a moment to enjoy the breeze that would chill her skin and chase away the pink flush from her cheeks.

There were no lights in the distance. The trees that formed a haphazard line along the drive swayed in the night air. There were no stars; clouds covered the entire sky tonight. Scents of moist earth reached her nose. All she could hear was the hiss of air currents streaming through the branches.

A hand touched Kym's shoulder.

"Fisher. You shouldn't have followed me." Kym spoke the words as she turned back toward the door where the silhouette of a man stood against the backdrop of light. "Fisher?"

The blow knocked her sideways. Then there was a sense of falling.

A spasm ran through her body as she clenched her fists. The side of her head was numb. Her right eye felt stiff. Kym was worldly enough to know when she had a bruised face. When she opened her eyes she realized she lay on her back on something smooth and unyielding. *No, I don't want to dream this dream again.* Only that same smell returned. A musty, organic smell. The scent of a rodent's nest found under boxes in a potting shell. A muskiness of animal bodies curled up in their nest. Above her, the room was a dome of pure darkness.

Switch on the light, Fisher. That's what she'd thought in her dream after the jolt of electricity had knocked the wits out of her. Then she'd collapsed onto the floor of the house within a house. After that, the nightmare had crept through her unconscious mind. Now this dream again. Wait . . . She remembered her time in bed with Fisher. That searing heat as he climaxed. Later, she'd stepped outside into the night air to cool the glow in her skin.

Oh, but my head . . . This feels like a real ache. . . .

Kym gazed up into the darkness. Why were her arms and legs so heavy? A restlessness gripped her. She needed to make herself comfortable but all she could do was lie on her back. Rolling her head to one side, she saw a gray line running up vertically from the floor ten feet or so. Was that an aperture revealing a sliver of outside? Suddenly a light blazed to reveal twin doors like those of a barn. They were open just a couple of inches. Through the gap she glimpsed the profile of the tower against the night sky. A deep gray against deep black. She groaned as she searched for the source of the light. That pain in her head. It throbbed like part of her skull had been torn away. At best she could only rotate her head from right to left; her aching skull rolled against a hard surface. Then Kym looked above her.

That's a vehicle hoist, she told herself. The kind they use in garages to lift your car so the mechanic can change the muffler. She lay directly between the steel channels that the car would pass along to mount the hoist. These were perhaps five feet above her. Now with a rising surge of panic she searched for what she knew would be there.

As her eyes searched, she heard the sound. A chime. A resonant shimmering tone on the air. Then another. The same chimes that sounded in the house. Then she made out the cross-member of a balk of timber spanning the steel beams of the hoist. The wooden cross-section was perhaps eight feet long by a foot wide. The chime sounded again, then another. Faster. More urgent. A harshness brushed aside the shimmering hum. *But how can I hear them now? Why in this garage? And, for God's sake, why am I lying on a table beneath the hoist?*

It's the dream. . . . it's the same dream. . . . However, panic crackled inside of her. Her heart thudded. And yet with the brutal clarity of a wide-awake mind she saw the iron spike protrude down from the timber. It was painted black except for its point, which glittered with the silvery hue of naked metal.

Oh, God . . . She tried to rise from the table. Leather straps held her ankles and wrists. Tearing her eyes away from the steel shaft that pointed at her stomach, she twisted her head to the left. Floating out of the shadows was a gaunt face with blotched skin. Kym saw the stubbled jaw again. On his forehead was the sickly yellow scar in the shape of a crescent moon. He gazed at her with gray, watery eyes. Then he nodded. He was satisfied. He moved back toward the shadowed wall. With an effort, Kym lifted her head so she could see his feet.

The floor had been painted white; it had the appearance of surgical room, a place where cleanliness came first. And of course he had bare feet. He wouldn't want his footwear to soil the pristine white of the floor. So there he was with neither shoes or socks.

"What are you doing!"

He didn't answer. The chimes grew faster, harsher, they clamored in a single note that throbbed, a heartbeat of brass.

She turned her head to see the house looming from the darkness. It appeared to crowd the door, a mass of masonry and black windows that softened as they distorted—a fish-eye view of a face peering in at her. A stone face. A face within a face; a house within a house. For a second she saw the bulging front of the eighteenth-century house; then it turned inside out in a single fluid movement to reveal the alien visage of the medieval façade. Back and forth. The exterior. Then the medieval core, looming with fish-eye distortion. The chimes were thunder tearing through her brain.

"No! Go away!" Kym screamed at the house. "Go away. . . . I don't want you to watch!"

Watch? Of course you want to watch. You must watch. You made this happen, didn't you? Because the truth in all its searing intensity struck her. *I've dreamed about this before. Now it's really happening . . .*

The chimes throbbed louder. They synchronized themselves with the throb of the motor that lowered the car hoist. Her eyes bulged as she looked up at the balk of timber that grew in size as the hoist smoothly and slowly descended. She couldn't take her eyes from the point of the iron spike. Like her dream of just eight hours before, it was blunt. Only she knew it wasn't *that* blunt. Not so blunt it couldn't penetrate her sweater and then her flesh beneath.

The point settled on her stomach.

This was no dream agony. This was real. Her eyes bulged as the point dug deeper into her body. It formed a depression there that creased the fabric of her sweater. Her eyes hurt as they strained from her face. She wanted to scream. Yet all she could do was pant. And the chimes rose into a phantom clamor; the sound drove through her ears to enter her flesh where they harrowed her nerves like a plow blade.

The motors of the hoist rose, labored with the shriek of slipping drive belts to bring the balk down further with its protruding iron spike. Agony tore through her in withering blasts.

Then that audible *pop!* The pencil-thin spike that resembled a huge iron thorn broke through the weave of her sweater. A second later it was through the skin of her stomach. Unimpeded, it slid smoothly into her body. The iron shaft was so bitingly cold as it entered her gut. She watched in dread as blood, released through the puncture wound, jetted from her in a crimson fountain. With it came heat that steamed the air white.

Kym had held onto her last lungful of air for as long as possible. There wouldn't be another. With the chimes raging in her ears and the iron spike sliding through her body to break out the other side, she opened her mouth until her lips stretched into an agonized O. Then Kym screamed.

This was a full-blooded scream of someone dying in agony. The scream of someone who knows perfectly well this is no dream.

Chapter Fourteen

"Has anyone seen Kym?" Josanne had a worried expression on her face when she asked the question at noon. The shrugging replies didn't help at all.

Fabian displayed irritation. "She told me she'd be here to time the songs. Josanne will have to do it now."

Josanne didn't respond to the new allocation of duty, instead she stood on a chair in the ballroom and clapped her hands together. "Everyone? Hello? Can I have everyone's attention? Who can tell me when they saw Kym last?"

From behind the drum kit, Marko said, "About ten last night, when we finished supper. She said she'd take a couple of apple pies out of the freezer to defrost." Jak sat on the rug beside the drums. With those serene eyes of his, he watched the face of each person who spoke. The dog's nose twitched slightly, as if he could even catch a scent of something on their words—just like old country people will tell you

that a dog can catch scent of the first snow of winter
hours before it arrives.

Adam Ambrose sat against the wall alongside Belle.
She draped her arm around his neck. They seemed to
live in their private world; only reluctantly they
emerged to talk to the others, and then mainly only
Fabian.

So much for band camaraderie, Fisher thought.

Josanne pursued her questioning, "Adam? Adam?"

He broke off from an intimate tête-à-tête with
Belle.

"Adam? When did you see Kym last?"

He conferred with Belle. She answered for him,
flicking back her long blond hair as she did so. Her
cut-glass accent was redolent of polo matches and
hunt balls. "Adam and I remained in our room all
evening. We last saw Kym about seven last night."

As if to contribute to the conversation, the hidden
clock in the medieval core of the house struck midday.
The chimes haunted the room with their shimmering
presence. They were enough to make everyone pause
as if they were no longer comfortable talking over
them. As the last chime died on the air, Fabian clicked
his tongue. "Will someone make the effort to kill that
bloody thing? This afternoon we're learning the intro
to the first song."

"Fabian?" Josanne wasn't going to be distracted.

"Oh? Kym? Same as Marko. I watched her open the
apple pie boxes. You know that, Josanne. We left the
kitchen area together at ten. We came back here for a
few minutes with Marko to work on the tension of the
bass drum."

Fisher's skin crawled. At first no one had been par-
ticularly concerned about Kym not showing for

breakfast. Adam and Belle hadn't appeared, and seeing as Kym was a component of the trio, everyone
drew their own conclusions. At ten that morning
Adam and Belle had sauntered in. Fisher and Marko
had been practicing the rhythm section of the song
with Sterling patiently making suggestions to help
them improve it. Adam immediately wanted to de-
velop his guitar intro. Fabian decided they should
work with Adam so his glissando opening wouldn't be
swamped by the other three instruments. Everyone
had been too preoccupied with the music to wonder
about no-show Kym. Everyone, that is, but Josanne.
Now she even had to push Fabian into backing her
on the question of whether Adam, Belle and Kym all
shared the same room. No, Adam had replied as if
the question was beneath him. They had three separate rooms right at the end of the corridor. Although
Belle had shared his room last night. So, no Kym.
Josanne had started to become anxious.

Now she stepped down from the chair. "What
about you, Sterling?"

"I hadn't slept in forty-eight hours. By eight last
night I was zonked. . . . So, hmm . . . I must have seen
Kym at around sevenish. Wait a minute, I thought I
heard voices in the corridor around midnight. Yeah,
she has like a Russian accent, doesn't she? I'm sure it
was her."

"Where's your room?"

"Next to Fisher's."

Everyone looked at Fisher. Immediately his heart
lurched in his chest. *Hell, what now? I promised Kym not
to mention anything about us getting together. If I do and
she walks through that door in ten minutes, that proves to
Kym I'm a shit, pure and simple.*

"Yeah," Fisher said, thinking hard. "I'd been to the kitchen to take a look at the dog."

"At Jak? What on Earth for?"

"I'd heard him whining. So I left my room around twelve to check on him. As I came out I saw Kym."

"What did she say to you?"

"You're beginning to sound like a detective, Josanne."

"I'm beginning to sound worried. Kym appears to have disappeared. We should make sure she's alright."

"Oh, she'll have gone out for a walk," Fabian said dismissively.

"In this fog?"

"Why not? There isn't a law against it, is there?" He returned to his keyboard so he could begin making notes on a sheet of music.

"Fisher? Simple question," she said. "What did Kym say to you?"

Fabian adopted a rich Transylvanian accent. "Enter my lair, I vont to drink your blood."

"Isn't funny, Fabian."

"Good God. She'll be out for a stroll."

"Fisher?" Anger hardened Josanne's mouth. "She did say something, didn't she?"

"Well . . . she asked if I couldn't sleep. I said I was fine and had just been checking on the dog because I could hear him whining. Then we said goodnight, see you in the morning, that kind of thing."

"Then what?"

"Josanne? What do you mean, then what?"

Fabian gave a bark of a laugh. "Own up, man. The question she's really asking is: Where did you bury the body?"

Josanne exhaled a lungful of air in exasperation.

"Hey, you people. Am I the only one taking this seriously? Fisher, in which direction did she walk after you said goodnight to her? Back to her room? Or to the entrance hall?"

Adam spoke up before Fisher could reply. "I'll tell you what happened to Kym."

Fisher clenched his fists. *Does he know that Kym was in my room?*

"Gone, dear heart. Kym's flown the nest. Scooted home. She was bored here."

"How? All the cars are parked outside."

Adam shrugged as Belle toyed with his long hair. "Taxi?"

"We've no working phones. Cell phones don't pick up a signal out here. How does Kym call a cab?"

"I don't know, do I? Fabian?"

Fabian's role appeared to include protecting his star of the band. "There must be buses," he told them. "If she's left, she'll have caught a bus at the end of the drive to York, or back to the ferry."

"Without telling anyone?" Josanne held him with her glare.

"Why cross-examine me? I don't know. How about shamefaced for not seeing her commitment through? Angry for some reason? Allergic to Yorkshire pudding?"

"This isn't a laughing matter."

"Hey, maybe she's decided to punish us by sneaking out so we waste half the bloody day, arguing about her oh-so mysterious vanishing trick when we should be working on our ruddy music."

"Fabian—"

"Jesus Christ, we're not playing at this, you know? It's for real. We've got twenty-eight days to rehearse and bond as a group, so in six weeks' time we can walk into a recording studio and lay down ten tracks that are not only note-perfect but wonderful, fucking wonderful! And win ourselves a recording contract that—hey, Josanne. Where the hell are you going?"

"I'm going to check Kym's room, of course. Belle? What number is it?"

"Eighteen." Belle looked bored, but that could have been affectation; maybe she was relieved that Kym had gone. Now she had Adam Ambrose to herself.

Guilt stirred in Fisher. He unplugged the bass guitar, then lifted the strap over his head. If Kym turns up, fine. If not? He'd lied about what really happened last night, how she'd come to his room for sex.

As he set the guitar down on its stand he called to Josanne, "I'll give you a hand."

"Dear God." Fabian held out his arms to the others. "I don't believe this. It's like being back at school again. Someone jiggers off, so two more people go look for them." He threw the pen aside in disgust. "Marko? Are you going, too? Sterling? Want to help them look under the bed?"

They didn't have to search Kym's room. They stood side by side at the foot of the neatly made bed.

Then Josanne turned to Fisher. "She'd not packed, then. All her stuff's here. Money. Her purse. I'm not happy about this, Fisher. Where can she have gone?"

Confide in her, he thought, tell Josanne what really happened. But what if Kym breezed in after a long walk? Things were tense enough with their fledgling band. To confess an erotic liaison with Kym would do nothing to engender harmony.

Instead, Fisher shrugged. "OK, she's not packed up and left."

Josanne was grim faced. "So much for Adam's conclusions."

"In that case she's either in the house—and there's a lot of house—or she's out in the grounds." He looked through the window. Thick fog pressed up close to the glass. "Whether that's likely or not, I don't know."

"Damn," Josanne hissed. With that, she ran from the room.

Fisher followed her down the corridor back to the ballroom. From there came the sounds of choppy notes on an electric piano with Fabian singing *lah-lah-lah*. He wasn't wasting any more rehearsal time. Josanne didn't stop running. She pelted through the doors.

When Fisher reached them, she was calling out, "Stop . . . stop! Kym's not in her room. All her money and clothes are there. She's missing."

Sterling and Marko exchanged glances. Clearly they were uneasy now. Fabian's reaction was one of irritation. He slammed his hand down on the keyboard. Adam looked up from the guitar he was tuning. His expression was one of bemused innocence. He couldn't figure out what the fuss was about. Fisher thought, come down from your cloud, Adam, and walk amongst us regular mortals for a while.

When all Fabian did was stare at Josanne, her concern for Kym cranked into anger. "Fabian, don't you see the problem? We can't find Kym. No one's seen her since midnight. This dump is in the middle of nowhere; she can hardly have strolled to the nearest café."

"Josanne. Take a dose of perspective. It's only just midday. Kym's off somewhere reading a book or admiring the countryside."

"Have you seen how thick the fog is? She might have got lost out there."

"Dear Lord, this is Yorkshire, not the upper reaches of the Zambezi. She's hardly going to encounter headhunters or be devoured by crocodiles."

"I'm calling the police."

"How, sweetheart?" Belle asked. "There's no way you can get a signal on your cell phone. I've been trying for bloody hours."

"I'll drive back to the ferry crossing. There'll be a pay phone, or I'll ask at one of the houses in the village."

Adam gave a languorous stretch. "Knowing Kym, she'll have gone looking for magic mushrooms or tree bark. She's into those kind of natural highs. When she comes back, she'll be off her head."

"No, I'm not buying that," Josanne said. "OK, she might have gone for a walk, but not for three hours in that fog."

Fabian massaged his temples with his fingertips. "You know, guys, we should be rehearsing. The last thing we need are cops dancing all over the place in their ruddy great boots."

Fisher chipped in, "I'm sure we don't need to call the police."

Josanne glared at him. "Fisher, I thought you were worried about her, too?"

"Look," he said, "We just need to make a search of the place. I'm sure we'll find her."

Fabian shook his head in disbelief. "Why don't we sit here and count to a hundred while you two go off and fucking hide yourselves. Why bother learning these songs when we can play stupid games all day?"

Belle walked forward. "Oh, you've got all your sexy keyboards, Fabian. You can stay here and play with yourself."

Josanne appeared surprised. "You're going to help?"

"Of course I'll help, sweetheart. You coming, Adam?"

He flashed his glittering smile. "Why not."

"Great, just great." Fabian glared as if he were the victim of a sadistic conspiracy.

Sterling set down his guitar on its stand. "Count me in."

"And me." Marko stepped out from behind his drum kit. The dog stood up, too, sensing people were on the move.

"So that's everyone going to play hide-and-seek." Fabian sighed.

Fisher became irritated by the guy's attitude. "Kym might be hurt, Fabian. We can't carry on here like nothing's happened."

"Alright, alright. Go find her. But I'll time how long it takes, then we'll add that time onto the rehearsal this afternoon."

As if to remind them of the passage of hours the blind clock struck one from its lair. The chime echoed in the room as they filed out into the corridor.

Chapter Fifteen

Oh, she's dead alright. Dead as those rats on the spikes.
Now he knelt on the concrete floor of the workshop
to gaze up at the prize he'd offered to The Tower.
He'd elevated the car hoist to its maximum height
and dragged away the table to the far end of the
building. Blood's difficult to shift. It changes from
liquid to congealing jelly to a sticky, tarry mass over
the course of an hour. What he wouldn't give for a
high-pressure steam hose. He'd been compelled to
rely on a brush, cloths and pure muscle power to
scrub the floor clean. Now, even though the concrete
hadn't yet dried properly, more drops of blood patted down on the floor. *Pitter, patter, pitter, patter.* Each
drop burst in a miniature explosion of red. He didn't
mind. This act would bring him a reward, he was sure
of it. His life would be better from now on. The pains
had already left his face, and this morning he'd been
able to sleep a full three hours without those nightmares of falling. At last, he lifted his eyes. When the
spike had passed through the woman's torso, it had

122

exited through her back without touching the spine. The point of the steel spike had bent over when it encountered the oak table. Now it resembled the barb of a fish hook. When he'd raised the hoist, the spike hadn't retracted through the body. Instead, it carried the woman with it. She hung, suspended by the skewer that penetrated her stomach, six feet above the concrete. Her back arched, her head hung down so her upside-down face pointed at the wall, the open eyes staring sightlessly. Her short dark hair had ruffled into points. Her legs bent at the knees so her feet dangled down. As did her arms, the fingers curled inward like claws. He didn't know if this was postmortem shrinkage of the muscles or if they had stayed like that from when she clenched her fists in agony. She was very pretty. He regretted there'd be no way to preserve her looks. Of course, she couldn't stay here. When it was dark, he'd hide the body. Best would be to drop it into the swamp. The lady vanishes . . . as simple as that.

A thin pain ran through his left eye. No, it wasn't starting again so soon, was it? He'd given the house its best prize yet. Surely it could reward him with a least a few days free of pain? He pressed his palm to his eye with a cry. "What does it take to stop this hurting?" Currents of agony ran up his back. He moved his hand from the eye to the back of his neck as pain invaded the muscle there. He glared at the woman hanging beneath the hoist, so consummately punctured, then he turned to cry to The Tower, "What is it? Isn't she enough? Do you want another one?"

Instantly the pain dissolved into pools of numbness. He sighed as muscles that had tensed in response to the surge of agony relaxed.

The Tower had spoken.

"So you do need another one. You can have them all. All I want, please . . . all I want, *please,* is that you take the pain away." For a moment he thought the house called to him. He heard a faint voice.

"Hello . . . Hello . . . Kym?"

No, not the house. Strangers. Quickly he ran to the far end of the building where he'd left his boots. Without bothering with the laces, he pushed his bare feet into them, then he opened the door and stepped outside so he could lock it behind him. For a moment he stood beneath the dripping trees. The fog was so thick he couldn't see the house. In fact, even this cluster of World War II service buildings that housed stores and the workshops were just muzzy shapes in the mist.

"Hello . . . Kym?" The fog robbed the voices of expression, too. The sound had a flattened quality.

Kym? So they were looking for the girl. *That must be Kym in the workshop.* Had to be. Knowing strangers were so close gave him an itchy feeling. He wanted to get back to his hut where he could lock himself in.

"Kym? Shout if you can hear us." The voice came from the rise that lead to The Tower. "Kym?"

He stood with his back to the garage door as he angled his head, trying to force his eyes to penetrate the mist. A jab of pain returned to his face to remind him what the house needed from him.

"This time it's a deal," he whispered. "It's a contract. I'll give you another one if you stop the pain."

Ghosting from the distance came the chime of the clock that was hidden in the center of the house.

Yes.

The house had answered. He bit his lip. "We got a

deal then. I'll give you another. I want this to stop hurting. If you take the pain away, I can be normal. I'll be human again."

"Hello?"

He started at the closeness of the voice. Images whirled through his head of the dead woman sliding down from the metal spike to walk to the door and murmur the greeting through its boards.

"Hello. I'm sorry. I didn't mean to startle you."

He turned to see a young woman with striking golden brown skin. "I didn't see you there." He made it sound like an accusation.

"My name's Josanne. I'm staying up at the house."

"Oh?"

"I didn't realize there was someone else on the estate."

"I keep an eye on the grounds. If the ditches aren't kept clear, the swamp will take the rest of the gardens."

"That's something I'd not taken into consideration, Mr.—?"

"Cantley."

"Mr. Cantley."

"No. Just Cantley."

His blood turned hot in his veins. Excited, he thought, If I can stand close and get her to look away, she won't know what hit her. I can offer her to the house. This one will be enough. I've got a deal with The Tower. One more gift, then I'll suffer no more pain. Keep her talking. Quick, she's going. . . . she's going! His hand slipped into his coat pocket to find the wrench he'd used on the other woman.

The woman smiled. It was a wary one, the kind he took for granted now when a stranger talked to him. "I best get back to my friends," she said.

"Kym. Shout back if you can hear us!"

He heard their calls but he couldn't see them in the fog.

"Any trouble, miss?" he asked.

"Nothing much. One of our friends has gone for a walk somewhere. I'm sure she'll be back soon."

"Kym."

"Have you met her?"

"Yes." So the dead woman *was* called Kym. He was thinking quickly. "Yes, I saw her about an hour ago."

"Are you sure?"

"She was walking down that way . . . through the trees."

"I don't think it could have been Kym."

"Yes, it was. I saw her like I'm seeing you now. She introduced herself just like you. Said she was staying here."

The woman was interested. Still wary, though. She glanced back in the direction of the house. No doubt she wanted her friends so she wouldn't have to talk to the strange disheveled man alone. *Christ knows, little miss bitch, how'd you look after you were born hurting and grew up in agony every day of your fucking life. That's real pain. A whole world of pain and you live in it. Shitting, eating, looking, sitting, walking, breathing, blinking—every single thing causes hurting. More pain in one minute of my life than ten years of yours. It gets where I only get respite if I make pain for something else. But me and The Tower have a deal now. I'm getting rid of this pain for good.*

Cantley took a breath, mindful his words could easily become a gibber. "She walked down there after talking to me here in the yard. She had short dark hair and brown eyes. Very pretty. Like you, miss."

"Thanks." Again that wary smile. "I'll fetch my friends."

"No . . ."

At this raising of his voice, she shot him a startled look. He slowed the words so they didn't spit from his mouth. "No . . . ah . . . I mean, I need to show you where she went. There's paths all over the place here. If you don't get the right one, you could wind up lost. If you end up in the swamp, it'll be dangerous. Ah . . . a sad case last year. Really sad case. Ah . . . old man from up at The Tower wandered off into the swamp and drowned." He realized his words were running away from him.

"If you could just show me which path she went down, then?"

"Yes, miss. The one by the stream. If you come with me to the stile, I can show you where it goes. Then you know you're following the right one. It doesn't take you into the swamp. . . . You'll be safe." Cantley's fingers closed around the cold metal wrench in his pocket. He saw the woman didn't relish the idea of being in his company for a moment longer; yet she need to find her friend. He guessed she'd negotiated with herself, balancing dislike, even fear of him, with the need for information that would reunite her with Kym. Of course, little did she know . . .

As Cantley pointed the way, so she'd walk with him the few paces to where three different paths radiated from a stile, he could guess what she was thinking. *OK. I'll go with him just as far as the stile, find out which path Kym took, then leave with a perfunctory thank you.*

As they crossed the yard, his hand returned to his coat pocket. She deliberately kept her distance from him as they approached the stile. But he mentally rehearsed the words to make her turn away from him: *Look through the trees, miss. Isn't that your friend coming this way now?* He'd practiced the line a second time and had begun to shape the words with his lips when a blurring object raced into the yard. Instantly there was a furious barking.

He flinched. "Blasted dog!"

It advanced toward him, then braced itself with its front legs rigid so it could unleash a torrent of angry barks at him. The woman reacted with embarrassment.

"I'm sorry about this."

"Dogs aren't allowed to run loose here. You should keep it locked up!"

"I didn't know he was out."

Sweating now, he backed away from the black dog. It barked in that vicious way that showed off its pointed teeth. He sensed the animal's hatred of him. If it should attack him, he'd kick the life out of it. So help him, God that's what he'd do. He'd ram his boot into the dog's mouth, break those sharp teeth!

"No dogs allowed here," he shouted while still backing from it.

"I'm sorry. He's not normally like this." She bent over so she could grab the dog by the collar. Blood and Christ, it would be so easy now! She wasn't looking at him. He could strike her head with the wrench if it weren't for the dog. Only sure as jiggery, if he lunged forward, the fucking thing would rip his hand off. He continued to back away as the woman restrained the snarling beast. He'd reached the edge of the yard where a path ran down to the swamp. Still the animal barked, its eyes flashing.

"You should keep it tied up! Do you hear?"

As he shouted a man ran up. "Josanne, are you alright?"

"Fine. Jak's decided to misbehave, though." She shushed the dog. Then she lifted her head. "Sir? Mr. Cantley? Can you tell me which path my friend took this morning? Wait a minute, please. I won't let the dog hurt you. Sir?"

But he hurried down to the swamp, where he knew there was a path that would take him safely away through its muddy lagoons, to a place where even the dog couldn't reach him.

Chapter Sixteen

Fisher said, "What do you make of Prince Charming? A real bundle of laughs, isn't he?"

Josanne shrugged. "He probably just doesn't like dogs. Jak scared the crap out of him."

"Couldn't have happened to a nicer human being." Fisher bent down to stroke the dog's head. "Good work, Jak." The dog's tail swished the grass.

"Not so good, Fisher. Cantley told me that he talked to Kym this morning. He was about to show me which path she'd walked along."

"Uh, damn. Sorry, Josanne."

"Not your fault. But I'm worried about Kym now. The man told me that some of the paths run out through the marsh. Not only is it easy to get lost, it's dangerous, too. Last year one of the residents from the house drowned."

"Hell. We've got to keep looking, then."

"If Fabian would listen to me, I'd call in the police. These grounds go on for miles. There's only seven of us to search."

"You think this guy Cantley would help?"

"He could be useful. He's some kind of groundskeeper. Although he seemed a bit—" she bored her finger against her temple "—in the head to me."

"Then he might have lied about seeing Kym."

"He's seen her alright. He could describe her."

"Do you know if Cantley lives here in the grounds?"

"He didn't say."

"Kym, hello . . . hello." That was Marko's voice somewhere off in the mist.

"This fog isn't helping, either." Josanne rubbed her arm as the cold penetrated her clothing. "Kym could be standing twenty yards from us and we wouldn't see her."

She'd hear, though, Fisher told himself. If she can't, that means something bad's happened to her, and the nearest hospital's a long way away. He left the thought unvoiced. Josanne was deeply worried. Fabian's entire strategy for rehearsing here appeared to be in danger of unraveling in a tragic way.

"Kym, can you hear me? Knock once for yes, twice for no."

"So Fabian hasn't lost his sense of humor," Fisher muttered. "Uh, sorry, Josanne. I keep forgetting you and him are . . . you know . . ."

"An item? Fabian can be brusque at times. But he's alright. Once you get to know him, you'll realize you can trust him with your life. Right, candid revelation over. I'll find the others and tell them what Cantley told me."

"OK, I'll head down to the runway. That's the only way to get into the center of the marsh without getting your feet wet, as far as I know."

For a moment, Fisher crouched to pat the short

black fur on the dog's back. Both man and canine watched Josanne as she walked back in the direction of the house. The path took her through unkempt grassland into the all-encompassing mist. In a moment she became an ill-defined shape, as if her body were evaporating into the cold, damp air. A moment later she'd vanished.

A plaintive call drifted through the gray fog. *"Kym . . . Kym . . . Just give us a shout if you can hear. . . ."* That was Sterling's voice. Now that's a guy you can trust with your life, Fisher thought. I'm not as sure as Josanne that Fabian could be depended on in the same way. For a moment, Fisher remained crouched as he patted the dog. Jak's amber eyes watched his face expectantly.

"You know we've important work to do, don't you? We've got to make sure that Kym's safe." He murmured the words softly as he scanned what landscape was revealed in the murk of swirling water vapor. Diffuse silhouettes of trees. A stretch of overgrown lawn. A clump of spiky hawthorn. Hell, who'd willingly live here so close to a swamp? The poor bastards sent here by their families wouldn't have had much choice. They were probably elderly parents who'd become temperamental if not downright insane. Yeah . . . out of sight, out of mind. Pun intended.

Fisher rubbed Jak's head. "But then, ours isn't to reason why, is it?"

The dog gave a small "yip" in the back of his throat.

"So you agree with me? You know, Jak, I think we're going to be friends. Come on."

Fisher guessed the direction of the swamp even though he couldn't see it. Just keep heading downhill, he told himself. Follow your nose, too. You can smell it. Jak followed as if he'd known Fisher for years. They fell into the same stride. Even paused together when they heard an unfamiliar noise. Apart from the others calling Kym, the only sounds appeared to be the cry of water fowl. Although the house rose up massively just a hundred yards or so away, Fisher couldn't see even its outline. This murk drowned everything but a few square yards of damp sod and the trees around him.

The smell of stagnant water grew stronger as the shallow incline leveled off. Sure enough, within seconds the vertical oblong of the old bunker resolved its grim presence from the vapor. Fisher decided it reminded him of a prehistoric monument, carved with pagan runes and the scratched outlines of eviscerated men and severed heads. *Hell, this chill seeps through your clothes all the way into your bones.* Meanwhile, Jak walked alongside, sometimes circling round, but always keeping in a kind of holding orbit no more than twenty paces from Fisher.

"You like it down here as much as I do, don't you?" Fisher said to the dog. "And that isn't much."

A narrow trackway of rough grass linked the runway with dry land. As far as he could tell, the rest of this strip of concrete was surrounded by liquid mud and interconnecting pools of water. Thrusting up from the water were hundreds of grass-topped tussocks. They appeared like great heads covered by shaggy hair in the misted gloom. He could have been watching aquatic phantoms rising from the swamp.

Fisher walked out onto the airstrip with the words, "Jak, this is the kind of place where your imagination

can run away with you. Hell, it can run away with you
to a place where no one can hear you scream, then
rip your arms and head off." His grim chuckle caused
the dog to look at him. "See what I mean?"

Thirty yards wide, straight as a rule, the apron of
flat concrete ran ahead until it vanished in the mist.
He walked for perhaps a hundred yards. At either
side of him, the swamp lay just two or three inches below the lip of concrete so it awarded him the impression of strolling along a long island, one that was as
flat as a tabletop. From the distance came the sound
of three ringing tones. Chimes from that blind clock
in the heart of the old house had stalked out across
the marsh to find him here. *That's some clock . . . some
damned weird clock . . .*

As he walked along the edge of the runway, he
peered into what stretches of the swamp he could see.
Its glistening black pools appeared more viscous than
water. Liquid appeared to have a different consistency
here. There was a thickness like blood. Methane bub-
bled to the surface from decaying vegetable matter. At
intervals a bulge would deform the surface, then it
would rupture with a popping sound to release the
marsh gas. More than once he heard an object swirl,
as if a fin had broken the surface, or even a scaled
leg. . . . After it had happened a dozen times just beyond the cordon of visibility, his imagination supplied
images of green tentacles emerging from one of the
lagoons to writhe in the air. All it needed was for him
to wander within striking distance . . .

"See what I meant about runaway imaginations,
Jak?" The dog sniffed at the air. *What do the tentacles of
swamp monsters smell like?* Fisher felt the tug of a smile

on his lips. *What a place. What a weird, unfriendly, inhospitable sinkhole of a place. Would Kym willingly have strolled down here in the mist? You don't do that for fun. You would only come here for some compelling reason. Perhaps to drown yourself in the swamp. Jesus, that muck would suck you down in seconds.*

He cupped his mouth with his hands. "Kym . . . Kym!" No echo. His voice left his mouth to die in the swamp. "Kym!" Then he paused. "She wouldn't have killed herself, would she?" But, then, did he know anything about her? Only that she was from the Czech Republic; she was well educated; she was ambitious. She hadn't appeared depressed when he'd seen her last night. Maybe a little on edge. As if she needed company. Jak sat down again, so he squatted beside the dog. It felt good to be in the animal's company. It was like enhancing your own senses, so you were more aware of the world around you. In a constant state of readiness, the dog's eyes flicked in the direction of every sound, no matter how faint.

Yeah, even hearing the big green tentacles that his own imagination had wickedly supplied.

"Something's not right here," he murmured to the dog.

It gave an answering yip as if it agreed wholeheartedly with the human's observation.

When Fisher reached into his pocket he felt a hard square wrapped in foil. He pulled it out. Chocolate? He'd forgotten all about that. It must have been kicking around with the loose change, lint and old train tickets for the past couple of weeks. When he peeled the silver wrapping away, a line of thought started in his head. Kym had seemed unsettled. She had every reason. Yesterday afternoon she'd gotten an electric shock from the clock. When he'd spoken to her later, she'd told him the jolt had knocked her cold. She'd also become troubled when she recalled a dream she'd had while unconscious. In the dream she said she'd been stabbed—skewered, she'd described it— by a barefooted man with an emaciated face. She'd also recalled another detail: the man's forehead had been scarred. The injury was the shape of a crescent moon; it had even been pale yellow in color.

The strangeness of it all was enough to prompt him to say the words aloud. "Now that's odd. Cantley's forehead had a scar. It was a crescent shape." He frowned. How could Kym dream yesterday that she was murdered by a stranger, then today he and Josanne encounter a thin-faced guy with what appeared to be an identically shaped scar on his forehead? *That's not coincidence. So?*

"So Kym's seen Cantley before she suffers the electric shock. She must have seen him yesterday, because she only arrived yesterday morning. Then why didn't she mention that she dreamt about a stranger she'd seen yesterday? Instead, she talked about the man in the dream being someone she'd never met before." Fisher turned round. A sensation that someone stared at him made his back itch. In the murk he could make out a dozen rabbits hopping to and fro. They were perhaps ten yards away. For some reason they weren't fazed by the presence of a dog. Come to that, Jak watched them with a detached interest, as if noting they were there but having no interest in chasing them.

"What to do, Jak, old boy?" Absently he broke the chocolate in half. One chunk he held out for the dog, who gently mouthed it out of his hand. Fisher ate the other piece. Melting chocolate flooded his mouth with sweetness. Maybe it was the kid in him, but he still loved chocolate. Only this afternoon he was too preoccupied to appreciate it. So what happened to Kym? Now he began to attach more importance to her dream from that zap of voltage yesterday afternoon. *Can an electric shock scramble your brain so much that you act out of character? Maybe even wander off with amnesia?*

"Nothing for it, Jak." He patted the dog as he stood up. "I'm going to have to come clean about Kym turning up at my room last night."

With Jak at his side, he headed back in the direction of the house. This time the rabbits scattered, a dozen dwarfish forms that fled from the concrete raft of the runway to hop from tussock to tussock before vanishing into the silent wastes of the marsh.

Chapter Seventeen

Josanne stepped into the shower stall. The cold fog had seeped through her clothes to leave her skin damp after being out on the grounds. Fabian and Adam had drifted back to the kitchen for hot coffee. That left Marko, Belle, Sterling and Fisher searching— not to ignore Jak, of course. If anything, the dog was the most effective component of the search party. Jak had found her when she'd been walking by that cluster of buildings with Cantley. She hadn't liked the man one bit. Jak's arrival had been a relief.

Jets of hot water pummeled Josanne's skin. It flooded through her hair to chase away the chill left by the mist. Oh, this felt good. Erotically good. Sexy. She loved the heat of a hot shower. It was an infusion of body heat. As if a giant living being breathed new life into her. After soaking her body under the embracing heat of a shower, she could fearlessly face the world again. She soaped her neck. Stiff muscles began to relax. The scent of soap banished the wet earth smells that had filled her nostrils during the

search. And as for Kym? They were deluding themselves, weren't they? Surely no one imagined that the
woman would cheerfully stride into the house with a
"hello" in her Czech accent, then declare that she'd
enjoyed a marvelous walk. Josanne lifted her face to
relish the prick of focused water jets. The simple rit-
ual of bathing cleared her mind. *We can't search the entire grounds; even the house is big enough to hide a gang of
escaped convicts. Weird Mr. Cantley isn't going to help; he's
probably huddled over his fire in a cave somewhere grilling
water voles for supper, or whatever he does here. So what's
the answer, Josanne?*

She spoke the words aloud into clouds of steam.
"Fetch the police." With that sense of urgency pushing her, she turned off the shower, then stepped out
onto the mat. Steam billowed in the bathroom as
densely as the fog outside the windows. But this was a
luxurious warmth. It cleared her mind. She knew
what she'd tell Fabian as soon as she was dressed. "I
know we can't telephone the police from here, so I'll
drive to the nearest village. No buts. I'm going to report Kym as missing."

Josanne wrapped a soft towel around her head,
then a big white towel around her body so it ran
down from beneath her arms to her knees. She used
another small towel to dab her face.

Uh, here they come again. The chimes pealed through
her room. Josanne glanced up at the walls, searching
for an opening that admitted the sound. She saw
nothing. Yet the chimes came through clearly. One,
two, three. So, three o'clock. If she dressed quickly,
she could be driving away inside ten minutes. How
long to reach York? An hour? It couldn't be much farther than that. Her clothes were still damp, not to say

muddy from scrambling over fences. Not ladylike, she thought as she gathered the clothes into a ball and threw them in a corner, but, as the saying goes, time's of the essence. It would be dark by the time the police arrived anyway. If Kym lay out there hurt, she'd be in danger of exposure. Quickly Josanne went to her closet. There she pulled out a sweater and a pair of black trousers that she laid carefully on the bed. She was about to unwrap the towel from her body but noticed the drapes were wide open. Although she could see nothing but the hawthorn and the stifling gray wall of fog, she didn't relish glancing up from slipping on her underwear to see Cantley's face pressed to the glass. With a sweep of her hands, she closed the drapes. Then she returned to the dressing table where her hairdryer lay in front of the mirror. Today there'd be no time for makeup. Sitting on the plush stool, she pushed her cosmetic bag aside as she picked up the hairdryer and clicked it on. When she pulled the towel from her head, she shook out her hair to unstick a little from her scalp. Now she was face-to-face with her mirror image. It matched her movements as she adjusted the temperature of the hairdryer, then raised it to play the stream of warm air over her head. Her olive skin still glowed despite the concern that had begun to eat into her. The sooner she learned Kym was safe, the better. Before she picked up the comb, she pushed the black curls on her head with her fingertips so the rush of air from the dryer could evaporate the clinging remnants of moisture.

What stopped her she didn't know. In the mirror her reflection turned as her eyes lifted toward the ceiling. Her movement was driven by instinct. Surely she'd heard nothing. But what was that? A sense of arrival almost, as if she expected to hear a knock on the door. Or the window. Or . . . She thumbed the button on the hairdryer. Its motor slowed; the rush dropped to a whisper, then faded to silence. What was it? There was such a disconcerting sense of imminence. Of an event about to happen. It even made her teeth tingle. The inside of her ears itched. Her heartbeat quickened. With exquisite sensitivity she was aware of her blood pulsing through her arteries.

He's sitting on the bed behind me.

Who? Cantley? She half expected to see that burning stare of his. No. She was alone in her room, so there was no way that—

It started. A soft sound at first. Almost something sensed rather than heard. A pulse of white noise; a shimmering sound that ghosted through the air. Like the hum of a tuning fork without the percussive tap that caused it to ring.

"It's the clock," Josanne said aloud. "The thing's chiming again." She glanced at her watch. Twenty past three. No way the clock should be chiming again.

But listen to it. It's a surreal chime. A vibration of the bell rather than a simple strike. The phantom note shimmered. It swelled in volume, then receded before swelling again. A moment later the note decayed into a mutant glissando. Then the blind clock in the house within a house—the strangely named Good Heart—sounded the chime with confidence. The chime rang clearly through Josanne's room. It was sharper than usual—louder, too.

"Stupid thing," she breathed. "You're the only clock I know who can't tell the time."

Chimes pulsed through the air. One, two, three,

four . . . They were insistent. A forceful expression. As if they issued a statement. Five, six, seven . . .

She hissed, "Damn clock. Someone should rip out your wires and shut you up for good." Eight, nine, ten. "Shut up, you idiot," she said more loudly. Then, dismissing the recalcitrant timepiece, she switched on the hairdryer. Immediately, however, she switched it off again. There was a soft hissing. Frowning, she looked round the room. A hiss like escaping air . . . or water.

Surely I haven't left the shower running, she thought.

The chimes didn't stop. They grew faster. More insistent. They were a pulse of brassy sound now that began to rag on her nerves. She swiveled on the stool to look in the direction of the bathroom door. Damn . . . No mistaking that, girl. You idiot. You've left the shower running.

Water pressed through the gap beneath the closed door. It darkened the carpet.

Damn. All she wanted now was to drive to York to report Kym's disappearance. The last thing she wanted to do was spend half an hour mopping this water.

"And you can shut up," she told the chimes. They pulsed faster now. Their sound grew harsher, a metallic jarring note. She hated them; they jangled against her head with so much force they hurt her ears. As if in harmony with the raucous chimes, the table light flickered. For a second, darkness swamped her room. Then the lights brightened again. The fluctuation in power did nothing to interrupt the chimes. They must have struck a hundred times by now. Gritting her teeth, she strode across the room to the bathroom door. Now she could hear the hiss of the shower above the chimes. Damn thing must be at full power. The plumbing had turned rogue, just like the clock. She reached the door. There, she put her hand on the handle. It vibrated, whether with the force of the shower or the volume of the chimes she didn't know.

Josanne turned the knob, but the door held as if pushed from the other side. She shoved harder. The chimes rose into a savage clanging. Taking a deep breath, she shoved even harder at the door. The resistance increased for a moment, then vanished. She almost fell as the door swung open. Water streamed over the tub. It had been dammed by the door, so now a wave ran at ankle height over the carpet. This water was cold. It smelt of the stagnant morass of ditches in winter. The shower curtain billowed with the force of water jetting into the tub. *Turn it off, then get help to clean this mess up.* The thought ran through her head as she stepped forward. The chimes grew faster . . . louder. A pulse of sound that became a furious bellow. At that moment, water erupted from the toilet bowl. She stared at it, her eyes so wide with shock that the skin stung at their corners. Water wasn't simply overflowing; this was a geyser of black water filled with noxious decayed matter. The force of it staggered her. The fountain struck the ceiling so hard a liquid that stank of marshland pools sprayed her face. Black splotches violated the towel she'd wrapped around her.

Now the force of the inundation drove her back. The flood reached her knees. Panicking, she turned to scramble for the room door. She grabbed at the handle. Desperately she tried to open it. Only the force of the water held it shut. In disbelief she looked down. The filthy swamp water now reached her waist. Clots of green slime floated there.

"Fabian . . . Fabian . . . Anyone!" Josanne hammered at the door. *"For God's sake! Can anyone hear me?"*

The influx of that body of water drove the air before it. Winds tore at her hair. The chimes rose into a mad pulsing beat against her skull. When she turned back to the bathroom, she saw a torrent of coffee-colored water roaring out between its doorframe to swirl around the room. Chairs, bedding, clothes, scent bottles, aerosols buffeted against her.

Thoughts crowded—first, to tell her this was impossible. Then came the overriding imperative. *Get out. Save yourself!* Only the influx was nothing less than an explosion. Its shocking cold robbed her of her breath. When she gagged, foul-tasting spray invaded her mouth. The currents tore away her towel. Streaks of green weed wrapped themselves around her naked body. For a moment Josanne struggled to wade across to the window. Break the glass. Get out! Then she realized her feet no longer touched the carpet. Desperately she tried to swim, only the vortex spun her around the room. Foam splashed at the top of the walls. Another surge pressed her against the far side of the room; a painting of a seascape was torn from the wall to rush at her with enough force to cut her bare shoulder as the glass shattered on impact. Now her blood joined those streaks of green weed, shoes, clothes and pillows that whirled ever faster. When she reached the windows the curtains had been torn away by the whirlpool. Briefly she glimpsed the calm exterior of the house. Dark clumps of hawthorn bushes. Fog-bound lawns. Her head struck the lampshade as the evil tide dragged her backwards. She had time to take one lungful of stagnant-smelling air before the surface of the water rushed up to meet the ceiling. With her head underwater, the roar of the flood vanished. When she opened her eyes, she saw she hung suspended in a brown aether. Silver bubbles rose. She made out the window, revealed as a dim oblong.

Break it. Escape!

The chimes returned. Now they were ghostly, shimmering peals. The sound of a bell in a church tower that had been inundated by flood. The currents moved her so that Josanne flew like a naked angel through this aquatic universe. For a moment, it seemed that she drifted into the Good Heart. The medieval façade expanded in front of her as she glided through a tiny window. All the people who had ever died here were waiting; they swayed as though they'd been weighted at their feet so they floated upright. Strangers. Then Kym floating there with her eyes wide open in shock.

The chimes grew louder. The air burnt in Josanne's chest. She couldn't hold it in her lungs a moment longer. It vented from her mouth in a rumble of bubbles. The chimes became thunder. The Tower pulsed to their rhythm. Windows bulged to the beat. The sound shook the universe. Distant tombs collapsed inward under the pressure of the sound. Coffins imploded. Around the world televisions echoed a single rogue chime.

Yet no one will ever know chime signaled my death, she thought. What a way to die . . .

Josanne didn't fight now. She didn't breathe. If she could have moved her limbs and had pressed her hand to her chest, she wouldn't have found a heart-beat. As her mind faded out for the final time she seemed to see herself floating there in the water-filled room. Her mouth yawned wide as if to bite down a lungful of air. That opportunity had gone. Instead of air, water with clots of green algae streamed down her throat into her lungs. Her eyes were wide open, too. But if there was anything else to see, Josanne was past caring.

Chapter Eighteen

When Fisher returned from the search with Jak, he went straight to Josanne's room. Marko had boiled frozen hamburger for the dog. It smelt amazingly disgusting, but Jak wolfed it down. Now Fisher stood knocking at Josanne's door feeling like a kid who'd come to confess a sad litany of misdeeds. He knew he had to explain that Kym had come to his room the last night. Also there was this mixed up dream she'd experienced, where a man resembling Cantley had murdered her. It was probably nothing, but . . . Oh well, here goes. He knocked on the door again. Marko paused at the kitchen doorway to watch Jak eat. When he was satisfied that his cuisine for canine tastes hadn't let him down, he stepped into the corridor.

"Fisher?"

"Yeah?"

"When Josanne came back she said, she'd go for a shower first. We're all meeting up in the ballroom at half past three to decide what we do about Kym."

"Alright . . . thanks, Marko." Fisher glanced at the

door. Now that Marko mentioned it, he could hear the faint sound of running water. OK, so he would postpone telling Josanne what happened between him and Kym, but he'd confess at the earliest opportunity. The rest of the band? What would they say? Come to that, how would Adam Ambrose react? After all, Kym was his girlfriend. Along with Belle. Hell, he saw a whole knot of problems coming his way.

A gloom-filled ballroom waited for him. Clearly he was the first. He switched on the lights. Outside, dusk crept in early as the fog grew thicker. Through the windows he glimpsed hawthorn bushes with their spiky limbs reaching out to the glass, as if exploring for some gap in the window that would let them in.

"Fuck you!" He quickened his pace toward where he'd left his bass guitar. "Who the hell's done this?" He was the only one to hear his words. Not that he gave a damn. Anger boiled up inside of him. His four-thousand-dollar Rickenbacker bass lay facedown on the carpet. Someone had pushed it—or worse, kicked it—off its stand. He saw a curling line of silver winding from the neck. *Damn, one of the strings snapped. If anyone's damaged my guitar . . .*

He picked up the instrument to examine it.

"I take it no one's got any news about Kym?" He glanced up as Marko and Sterling walked in. Sterling sipped from a massive cup.

"Now there's man in love with the mighty Rickenbacker," Sterling observed in that easygoing way of his.

"Huh?" Fisher searched its red body for scratches.

"I said it must be true love. You only put new strings on yesterday."

Fisher turned the instrument over to examine its

glossy red back. "Check your kit. Someone's been in here."

"They've what?" Sterling picked up his guitar. He brushed the strings. "Jesus. Someone's detuned it. Marko?"

Marko tapped the drums. The sound they made had the flatness of someone striking a cardboard box. "There's no tension in the skins. Looks as if we're being jerked around."

"At last." Fabian sounded relieved as he entered to see everyone with their instruments. "So we're ready to play at long last?"

Fisher said, "Check your keyboards, Fabian."

"Pardon?"

"Just check them."

Fabian obliged by pressing a key. A chime boomed from the speaker. It was a clone of the sound they heard every hour from the hidden clock. "Very funny, guys. Who sampled the clock?" Rather than smiling, he glared at them. "Of course, it now means I'm going to have to spend twenty minutes reprogramming the synth. I had presets in there to underpin the harmonies." He scowled as he pressed another key. The cloned chime burst from the speaker with the force of an armor-piercing shell. "Thanks a bunch . . . you bastards."

Marko spoke up from behind the drum kit. "It was nothing to do with us, Fabian."

"Who, then?"

Sterling brushed the slack strings of his guitar again. Instead of the rippling notes of a chord, it made a lackluster thud. "Detuned. Marko's drums have had the same done to them. Fisher's bass has been kicked across the room."

"Jesus Christ." This news really did shake Fabian. "Any lasting damage?"

"A broken string," Fisher said. "Some scuff marks on the body. I guess you could say I've been lucky."

"So we've had visitors?" Fisher's eyes roved over the assembly of amplifiers. "Anything missing?"

"Not that I can tell," Fisher said.

"What about Adam's guitar?" Marko asked.

Fabian was earnestly checking through his pages of precious songs as he answered. "Took it with him . . . When we went out to hunt for Kym he locked it in his room."

Sterling nodded. "1966 Fender Strat. Who wouldn't?"

"Where are Belle and Ambrose now?"

Fabian still leafed through his music. "Gone to clean up. They wandered into the bloody swamp. Mud up to their knees . . . *Thank God!* At least all these are here." He held up the songs before carefully sliding them into his briefcase. "These stay with me all the time now."

Fisher said, "We need to keep this room locked while we're out. We're lucky that nothing got wrecked."

Marko began work on tightening the drum skins. "Who the hell would do this anyway?"

"None of us," Sterling spoke with conviction.

Fabian tutted. "There's no one for miles. Who's likely to wander in by chance, then go to the trouble of reprogramming my keyboard?"

"There is someone else on the estate," Fisher told him. "A guy called Cantley. He's says he's a groundskeeper, but for all we know he could just be here to steal what he can get his hands on."

Sterling frowned. "Yeah, I could see some drifter

nicking a guitar. Though are you going to tell me he'd reprogram a synth so it plays the same chimes as the house? And why detune the guitar and drums?"

The house is afraid of the sounds we make. It's fighting back. . . . The thought came out of nowhere; it could have been the flippant aside that Fisher's mind generated all the time—whether he wanted it or not. But it had all the resonance of a revelation. He looked up at the ceiling. *Are you listening to what we're saying, house? Can you understand us?*

The chime came with startling suddenness.

Marko flinched. "OK, Fabian, we know what the sample sounds like. Do you have to keep hitting us with it?"

Fabian shrugged, mystified. "That wasn't me. I never touched a thing."

"It's that fucking clock," Sterling growled. "What do you say to finding the wire cutters and shutting it up for good?"

Hey, house, did you hear that threat? We're going to kill your clock. Fisher's skin tingled. For a second he believed the house would respond. Recollections of the room imploding to crush his body, Kym suffering the electric shock, the weird guy with the scar on his forehead—they all rushed at him. Shit, there was something venomous about the place.

"Listen!"

They all turned to the doorway. Josanne stood there. Her entire body had stiffened with tension; her shoulders were bunched up toward her ears as if she was in pain. Her eyes were wide as she glanced from face to face.

Fisher noticed that she'd struggled to dress herself. With her blue jeans she wore a T-shirt that had been roughly dragged on as an afterthought. Her feet were bare. Tremors ran through her body.

"Listen to me! Can you see me? Am I really here?"

Fisher recognized terror in her eyes. "Of course we can see you, Josanne." He looked more closely. "Josanne? What's wrong?" He rushed forward as she took a single staggering step forward and fell to her knees. Gently he helped the woman to her feet, then guided her to a chair. "Here, sit down."

Fabian hurried to crouch beside her. "Josanne, sweetheart, what's happened to you?"

"I'm warm, aren't I? I mean . . . I mean I'm not dead, am I?"

"You're shaking."

"But I'm not dead?"

"Of course you're not dead."

Fisher crouched down, too, so he could see into her brown eyes that were on fire with terror. "What made you say that?"

"I . . . I . . ." She clenched her fists, the took a deep breath. "I showered. I went to dry my . . ." She touched her hair. "It's dry. . . . How can it be dry after that?"

Fisher squeezed her hand. "Something happened to you, didn't it?"

She nodded.

"What was it, Josanne?"

"What's wrong?" Fabian asked. "Has someone attacked her? Fisher? What do you know about this?"

"Shh, Fabian. Let her speak. . . . Josanne. What was it?"

"It seemed real. It *was* real!" She took another deep breath as tremors shuddered through her body. "I sat down to dry my hair. I realized I'd left the shower running. Water was trickling under the door. I opened the door, and . . . *BANG*. This wall of water—dirty water with weed and filth—all this just hit me. It filled the room. I was swimming . . . then it was over my head. I couldn't breathe. Oh God, Fabian, I drowned . . . I knew I drowned."

"Hey, sweetheart . . ." He spoke gently. "That's not possible, is it? Look at yourself. Dry as bone."

"Kym told me. . . ." Fisher's voice trailed.

Fabian appeared suddenly suspicious. "She told you what, Fisher?"

"It was when she got that jolt from the clock yesterday. She blacked out for a moment. Later she told me that she'd had a nightmare."

Josanne's eyes suddenly came back into focus. "What happened in the nightmare?"

"Nothing?"

"Fisher, tell me."

"You know, just a nightmare."

"Tell me what she dreamt."

"Look, it was just a nightmare, but . . ." After concealing his liaison with Kym he knew he'd have to tell the truth now. "Kym told me she'd dreamt that someone killed her."

"How?"

This made Fisher uncomfortable. "That's the weird thing. He used some kind of machine to stab her. . . . Look, I told you, it was a dream."

"Well, I've just had the most vivid dream of my life. I dreamt I drowned in my own room." Josanne had snapped out of the confused state now. Her eyes were clear. Self-confidence returned to her voice. "It's getting dark. No one's seen Kym since last night."

Marko said, "There's just no way we can search this place alone."

"I know," she told them, suddenly businesslike. "I'm going to drive to the nearest telephone, then I'm calling the police. They're going to have to bring fucking dogs and helicopters, but they've got to find Kym."

"I'll come with you," Fisher told her.

"No, stay here. One of you keep checking the rooms she's likely to use. The rest split up—search the rest of the house and the grounds. There are flashlights in the kitchen."

Fisher glanced at Fabian. If there was one man here to disagree with Josanne, he'd be the one.

Fabian stood up. "You get some shoes on. I'll have the car running for you by the time you get there." Josanne allowed him to help her to her feet.

"Just one more thing." Fisher shrugged. "It doesn't seem much compared with Kym vanishing, but someone came in here and messed around with our kit."

Marko shook his head. "Hell, Fisher, this isn't the time—"

"It *is* the time. What happened to Kym might be related to whoever came in here while we were out."

"So? You want us to stand guard?"

"No, but you've got a video camera, haven't you, Josanne?"

"Yes. Is it important?"

"Before we look for Kym again I think we should leave the camera running; it'll film this area where the instruments are."

Sterling whistled. "And catch anyone who monkeys around with them?"

Fabian rubbed his jaw. "Sounds a fair idea to me."

"OK," Josanne said. "If it helps. I'll get the camera." She paused. "Fabian, instead of starting the car for me?" She gave a tired smile. "I don't fancy the idea of going back to the room alone."

"Sure, I'll come." He put his arm round her as they left the ballroom.

Marko pursed his lips, then spoke so Josanne and Fabian wouldn't hear, "Just when I was beginning to think that.in place of a heart Fabian had big, cold lump of naked ambition . . ."

Sterling nodded. "Goes to show. He's not as bad as we thought."

Fisher didn't comment. He was thinking about Kym's vivid description of her death by the man with the scar. Bumping alongside that were images his imagination supplied of Josanne choking to death as a deluge of water filled the room.

Yeah, as if you could be killed by a bad dream.

Deep in the house the blind clock struck four. The three men paused as the chimes resonated through the room before dying back into its ancient walls.

Chapter Nineteen

Josanne returned to the ballroom five minutes later, alert and focused. She wore her sneakers, jeans and a white fur-trimmed jacket with a hood. Josanne had a mission: to bring the cops to search for Kym.

When she handed Fisher the video camera, she spoke briskly. "There's a blank tape ready in the camera; the batteries are fully charged."

"How do I—"

"Everything's automatic. Just press the button on the side to shoot. When you want to stop recording, press the button again."

"Thanks."

Fabian stood in the doorway. "You really think whoever jerked around with our instruments is going to come back?"

"They might. At least with this running we've a chance of seeing who it was."

Josanne said, "My money's on Cantley."

"He looked weird enough." Fisher checked the

controls on the camera. "I'm going to set this on the table over there and just leave it running."

"They'll have to show up quickly. There's only an hour's recording time."

"It's worth a shot."

"Right," she said, "wish me luck."

"Make it quick," Fabian told her. "It's getting dark."

"I shouldn't be more than an hour."

"Are you sure you don't want me to come along with you?"

In that businesslike way she shook her head. "I'd prefer it if you join the others looking for Kym. I keep picturing her lying hurt somewhere. And if we don't find her soon . . ." She shrugged, leaving the words unsaid.

"Don't worry," Fabian told her. "We'll keep looking."

"OK, I'm ready."

Fisher glanced at her. Anxiety made her smile appear forced.

Fabian picked up on the emotional tension, too. "I'll walk you to the car. And be sure to keep your doors locked when you're out on the road."

"I will." She kissed him.

"Are you set, Fisher?" Fabian paused by the door. "The others have already gone out to search the grounds. We can go through the house again."

"Sure. I'll just leave this running." Fisher thumbed the button on the compact video camera, then placed it on the table with the lens pointing in the direction of their instruments.

Fabian nodded at the bass guitar on its stand. "You're not going to lock the Rickenbacker in your room?"

Fisher shook his head, "Bait," he told him, then followed the pair out of the ballroom.

Josanne switched on the car's headlights as she accelerated along the driveway to the road. Even though it wasn't yet five in the afternoon, low cloud and mist collaborated on drawing the dusk down early to engulf the countryside in gloom. She glanced back through the rearview mirror. Fabian stood in front of The Tower. The massive building of black stone dwarfed him. The tower that gave the old mansion its name reared above her boyfriend. For a second the tower held her attention. A tombstone-shaped monstrosity looming against a dull gray sky.

The hiss of tires running off the asphalt into soft mud snatched her attention back to the driveway in front. *Dear God, the last thing I need now is to crash the car. Stay focused. Kym needs you.* Josanne shivered. A weight had settled on her shoulders in the last few hours. She worried about what happened to Kym. The drowning nightmare preyed on her mind. *Sure, just a wacky nightmare. That's all.* But it had been brutally vivid. When she'd woken in her room she found herself lying facedown on the floor. Weird choking sounds had been coming from her throat. Her ribs had ached, she'd breathed so deeply. I want out of that house, she told herself. I want to get away. Never go back. The place made her skin crawl.

At the gateway Josanne realized she'd made a right turn instead of a left. A left would have taken her to the houses near the ferry terminus. She knew there she'd find a telephone, only . . . only . . . I want to see bright lights, she told herself. Back that way is a country road that leads to middle-of-nowhere houses. York lies in this direction. Even if I don't make it to the city, I'll probably reach a small town in twenty minutes.

Just a couple of days in The Tower had begun to seem like weeks of internment. Even a rural town would be a bustling metropolis in comparison. She could find a gas station, make that all-important telephone call. Then maybe take the others back some freshly baked pizza. After hunting through fog-bound grounds they'd welcome some hot food. It shouldn't take the police long to reach The Tower, either. With those thoughts Josanne began to relax a little. If anything it was good to be away from the brooding presence of the house. Those long bleak corridors were so damn depressing. Even driving along this deserted road was vastly more pleasing than that grim pile of rock back there. Josanne loved the car like it was home anyway. Sometimes she wondered if she was afflicted by a perverse sense of pleasure, but often she'd drive for miles for the sake of it. Its seats were more comfortable than an armchair. Inside it she felt as snug as a kitten curled up in front of a log fire. As miles of countryside slid by, she gave a sigh as she sank deeper into the driver's seat. Tension left her muscles. Her body softened as her spine relaxed into the shape of the cushioned backrest. *Don't go back, Josanne. Just keep driving. Leave Fabian and the rest at the house. They'd welcome the lack of distractions anyway.* The thought took her by surprise. Hell, the notion of never going back to the sullen building was tempting. Just telephone the police, tell them about Kym, then hit the road to York.

Yeah, now that was an alluring proposition. She glanced at the clock on the dash. She'd been driving thirty minutes. In all that time there'd been no sign of human habitation. No houses. No garages. No welcoming wayside tavern. In the misty dusk all she'd seen were dark sentinels of trees lining a deserted road. No cars either. Not one passed her by.

Josanne murmured, "This road does go somewhere, doesn't it?" When she reached a crossroads she paused for a moment, the engine idling. "So which way now?" She leaned forward with her chin touching the steering wheel so she could look left, then right. Nothing but wet roads vanishing into the mist. "Great. Just great. No road signs either." Josanne frowned. "OK. Left? Right? Straight on?"

A sharp rap sounded on the car body. She lurched in the seat. "Who's there!"

The doors . . . I did lock them, didn't I? The rap sounded again over the purr of the motor. Her heart hammered against her chest as she jabbed her fingers at the central locking control. When the click of door locks sounded all around her, she sighed with relief. At the same moment an object struck the hood of the car. Again the loud tap.

"Idiot. It's only drops of water falling off a tree."

Even though she'd identified the source of the phantom rapping, she didn't hang around. Without thinking about it further, she chose left at random, then accelerated away. *Damn tree, dripping water like that onto the car.* In her head the water drops striking the hood had begun to adopt the resonance of clock chimes.

Fisher found himself in the center of the manor house, back in the Promenade. On the musty air rode the faint scent of sandalwood. There was something faded about the smell. As if whatever exuded it had been walled up centuries ago. He swept the light across the high walls that formed a kind of interior chasm about twenty feet wide by thirty feet deep. To one side there was nothing but featureless white-washed stone which extended up to a walkway. Only yesterday he, Marko and Kym had stood gazing in astonishment at what lay opposite them. Now he turned the flashlight onto the façade of the ancient house-within-a-house. Why someone had chosen to name that mutant slab of a building the Good Heart heaven alone knew.

"Hell," he murmured at the structure. "You've not grown any prettier since I saw you last."

Fisher had searched the ground floor. Fabian had elected to check upstairs. By now the chance of finding Kym had become remote. Fisher's search had brought him to the Good Heart. The place had all the allure of a funeral home. Once more his eyes took in the gray stone. The color of bleached bones, they were uneven blocks of all different sizes, ranging from rounded lumps the size of a bunched fist to craggy boulders. Directly in front of him lay the doorway. Like the tiny windows it was framed with slabs of smooth black stone. Eight hundred years before, men and women had used that dwarfish doorway to enter the house. Maybe then it was a home of astonishing modernity. After all, it boasted glazed windows. In an attempt to make it classier they'd set the carving of the animal above the front door. From its tapering tail, he figured it must be a dragon. Although the carved stone had weathered for centuries before being enveloped by the structure of the later mansion, he could make out veined membranous wings. From its shoulders extended a neck that resembled the body of a serpent. The neck terminated in a reptilian head with a set of jaws that stretched wide open as if about to chew a lump from its prey. He could imagine naughty children being brought to see the carved monster while a parent wagged a finger and said, "If you don't behave yourself, that there beastie will find you and eat you up." *Sweet dreams, children.* Flippant thoughts stole into Fisher's mind again. They always did: a safeguard against troubling ideas. God damn it, he'd even compared this artifact—this preserved façade of an ancient farmhouse—to a funeral home. He'd done that because there wasn't a day went by that he didn't recall walking up to the funeral home with its black door and black-painted window frames, the funeral home where his father lay in his coffin. That memory slithered like a viper from under a log to strike at him every time he let his guard down.

"Come on," he told himself. "Let's see what you're hiding in there."

He stooped so he could pass under the doorway into the weird house-within-a-house. Immediately he had the sensation of entering an alien dwelling. The ceiling had long ago being removed to afford views of a hollow section of the tower above him. A lofty void of somehow troubling spaces. An irrational impression perhaps, but there you go. Thick walls had been covered over the centuries with so many coats of whitewash there were no corners as such, only softly curving transitions from one vertical plane to another. The stone floors had been polished by generations of feet. There was something slick about them, as if they'd been brushed with oil. Damn it, it was cooler in here, too. Scratch "cool." Cold. He exhaled to prove the point. White vapor billowed from his mouth. A sweep with the flashlight revealed that only a table re-mained to furnish the room, while the fireplace had more in keeping with the entrance to a tomb than a home to a welcoming fire. The cavelike opening oozed shadow. Again, an irrational impression, but this wasn't a place where rational ideas would find comfort. A shiver plucked his skin into goose bumps. The Good Heart? It has a smugness about it, he thought. It excretes smug waves like a man sweats salt water from his skin. It's smug about its longevity. It watches young people move around inside of it. Its stones enjoy the spectacle of its occupants aging. Time is its weapon. Hours its bullets. Years its bombs. Time remorselessly bombards those young bodies.

Unchanging, immobile, coldly detached—the house watches as silver begins to salt dark hair; wrinkles form around eyes. Immune to the corrosive power of age, the house sees its occupants change and decay. In seem-ingly no time at all, young lovers with flashing smiles and sparkling eyes become shuffling hunched things—little more than shells that only vaguely resemble their younger selves. Then one day it's over. The funeral cortege pulls away from that front door. Soon another young family enters with a spring in their step. And don't you just know it? The short-lived dance begins all over again. Smug house. Smug bastard house.

No doors led off from this room in the so-called Good Heart. So to dispel the morbid drag of thoughts, he turned to walk briskly through the stunted doorway and out into the Promenade with its stale odor of sandalwood. At that moment the blind clock began to chime.

"Stupid clock," he snapped back over his shoulder. "It's not six o'clock yet."

Yeah, like the house is ever going to take your word for it.

The chimes ghosted through the doorway. A sound that mocked him, and mocked anyone who entered The Tower. A gloating that resonated inside his head long after he ran for the door.

"Come on. Some music. Happy music. Cheer up, Josanne."

The straight road cut through mist-shrouded countryside. The speedometer quivered on sixty. Civilization seemed half a world away. Surely she should have reached a village by now? After driving for the best part of an hour, she needed the company of the car radio. Only the presets were locked onto local radio stations in the London area. Static rushed from the speakers. A surge of distorted classical music drifted through the car, then spluttered into crackles again. Josanne's eyes flicked from the deserted road to the radio. In the subtle orange glow of the LED, she saw frequency numbers scrolling forward as the radio's circuits struggled to lock on to a new station. Anything with upbeat music, she thought. The LED screen flickered. With the pulsing of the orange glow, it found a strong transmission.

"Hell . . . you *are* joking?"

To the same rhythm of the flashing light came a pulsing sound from the car's speakers.

"Chimes?"

She stared at the pulsing orange light on the illuminated display. A row of zeros blinked where the radio station ID should have been. The chimes rose in volume. A hard brassy note. An angry sound. One, two, three, four, five, six . . .

Josanne tore her eyes away from the radio just in time to see the road curve sharply to the right. In front of her, bushes formed a spiky wall in the lights of the car. Before she could even take her foot off the gas, the car slashed through them in an explosion of branches. With a cry she stomped on the brake with all her strength. Beyond the windshield more branches whipped out of the fog to strike the car.

Don't roll over, she begged, please don't roll over. Even though the car's wheels had locked, they skidded across wet grass as if it were ice. An obstacle struck the side of the car with a crash that turned into a scream as it gouged the metalwork. Grass spewed out of the darkness in front of her. A bush loomed from the mist to vanish in splinters against the hood. A torrent of grass flowed at her as the car slid. Then a brown boundary of naked mud. Then a glistening plain of . . .

Water! The word exploded inside her head. Her mind flashed back to the nightmare. Water inundated her room. It filled it. She'd struggled through stagnant liquid clotted with green weed.

Now the lake filled her field of vision. The car's nose bucked up until all she saw were twin cones of light boring into the mist. A moment later the nose dropped as the car bellied down onto the lake with a splash that sounded like thunder.

Chapter Twenty

Water sounds. Like dozens of sucking mouths. A slurping, gluttonous noise. Josanne kept her eyes closed. The chimes were silent now. All she heard above the water sucking at the car's body was a sizzle of static from the speakers. Cold air filled the car. At any moment she expected the water to gush in as it sank down toward the lake bed. The car tilted slightly as it settled deeper.

Josanne opened her eyes. The headlights still burned. She blinked at what she saw. Fog. That same fog as before. Afraid of upsetting the delicate equilibrium, she turned her head very slowly to the side window. Rivulets of water still ran down the glass from where the car had explosively made its entrance into the lake. From what she could see in the headlights, the lake's surface had the appearance of dirty chrome. By now the waves from the splash had subsided to ripples; even those were smoothing out. Could the car really stay afloat? Slowly Josanne turned her face back to the windshield. She was afraid any sudden movement on her part would capsize the car. Then the lake would burst in through the windows with the same savagery as the stagnant water had burst into her room. She bit her lip. That nightmare of just a few hours before bore all the resonance of reality. She couldn't help but recall the influx that had swirled her around and around until her head reached the ceiling. The flood level had risen until the air gap had gone; when she'd gagged for air, water gushed down her throat into her lungs. In the nightmare I drowned, she told herself. The water poured in and it killed me. And what about Kym? She'd told Fisher that she'd dreamt she'd been murdered. Now Kym's vanished. Cold tides of unease washed through Josanne. Shivering from scalp to toes, she peered out through the car windows. Water surrounded her. Moving as cautiously as she could, she eased the wiper switch so it would make a single pass across the windshield. The rubber blades swept by, scraping away beads of water and strands of weed. At least she could see a little more. The lake stretched in front of her. The headlights illuminated perhaps forty yards of it until the fog swamped the light beams. In fact, all she could see beyond the car was water. She couldn't make out any banks. Was it a lake? Or could it be the river that they'd crossed on the ferry. That was a menacing expanse of water. Swollen by rain, the river would carry her out to sea. The sudden surge of panic choked off her breath. For a moment she had to struggle to control her fear so she could breathe again.

No, you've not sunk yet. The water's still. It isn't the river. Even so, if this is a lake. . . . Josanne pictured the car sliding beneath the surface to tumble in slow motion down a hundred feet to the lake bed. Bubbles would vent in silver clouds from the windows. There at the lake bottom, huge black eels would worm through a jungle of weed. She imagined them sliding hungrily through the vehicle's broken windows to where she sat strapped into the seat.

Carefully Josanne gripped the door's lever, pulled it until the mechanism clunked, then eased open the door. No inrush of water. The car remained stable. The surface of the lake met the car's bodywork just two or three inches below the sill of the door. When nothing calamitous happened, Josanne unbuckled her seat belt, then reached into the back where Fabian had left his black umbrella. It was the kind used by business executives to prevent rain from touching their expensive hand-tailored suits. To avoid rocking the car, she moved in slow motion. She lifted the umbrella over the passenger seat and transferred it to her other hand, then as she held it by the cane handle, she inserted the steel point into the water. Gently she lowered the umbrella so the surface of the lake swallowed the gleaming steel. Deeper. The fabric began to disappear. When a foot of the umbrella had been consumed, it stopped. Josanne pushed harder. There was the sensation of penetrating a couple of inches into soft mud; then that, too, stopped. Josanne let go of the umbrella. It remained standing upright in the lake. She laughed. A sound of sheer emotional relief rather than amusement.

"Oh God . . . it's only a foot deep." With a sigh Josanne rested her head back against the head restraint. "You'll never drown in that. Not in a hundred years . . ."

Chapter Twenty-one

Fisher met Fabian at the bottom of the stairs.

Fabian held out his hands. "Not a sign of her. You?"

"Nothing." Fisher switched off the flashlight.

"My guess is that Kym fell out with Adam and Belle. So she decided to pull this stunt."

"You think she's just sulking somewhere?"

"I've seen worse."

"You've got to be joking, Fabian. You mean she's been hiding for hours on end without food?"

"Something of the like." He spoke dismissively. "Now I'm going to fix myself a hot drink."

"You're out of your mind, Fabian. This is serious."

"OK, wait till the police get here. Then Kym will flounce in and we'll look like bunch of idiots, not—I repeat, *not*—a group of professional musicians who're trying to get their act together!"

"Fuck you, Fabian."

"And fuck all of you! You're a bunch of amateurs. When you're forty you'll still be playing in bars for beer."

Fabian hurled the flashlight at the wall where it shattered. With that, he marched down the corridor while his voice rose into something close to a scream: "And when the cops get here they can take away that bloody dog!"

Josanne realized she'd been sitting in the marooned vehicle for an hour. *Could I try driving out? What if the car's balancing on a ledge? If it slips forward into deeper water?*

"Then I'll be sunk. Literally." *I could wade. The water won't come above my knees.* "Just make sure those conger eels don't bite. . . ." She sighed. "But if I wade out of the lake, where am I going to walk to? I'm miles from anywhere." Her eyes roved across her bleak surroundings. Although she'd switched off the lights to preserve what was left of the battery, she could just make out her surroundings in the darkness. There wasn't much to write home about. A few hundred square yards of cold, cold water. Above that, ghostly wraiths of mist drifted toward the car. She stared at them anxiously, half expecting them to resolve themselves into demon faces. Mist, she told herself, only droplets of water floating in the air.

So what to do? Try starting the motor? Then reversing out? In her mind's eye she saw the car slithering into an underwater abyss. Josanne would drown in her seat.

Josanne grunted. "Don't be stupid. You're only twenty-four. Heaven isn't ready for you yet."

Her beloved automobile wouldn't be swallowed by the lake in a twinkling of an eye, and that was a fact. The downside was that she'd have to wait until daybreak. With luck, the fog would have lifted. Then she could get towed out of the water. And call the police.

With Fabian sulking in the kitchen, Fisher decided to return to the ballroom. He'd had a bellyful of the lordly Fabian grouching about the band's failure to rehearse. What did he expect? That everyone continue like nothing had happened? Kym had vanished. There were no houses for miles that she could decamp to. They might as well be stranded on a desert island or even the dark side of the fucking moon. For a moment he paused outside the ballroom door. Tempting to return to the kitchen after all and knock Fabian on the jaw. It would serve the arrogant bastard right.

   Instead, he took a deep breath, then pushed open the ballroom doors. Straightaway he checked his guitar. The Rickenbacker stood where he'd left it on its purpose built stand. He'd sweated blood to save to buy that bass. The music store described it as a "professional entry instrument"—that meant its sound quality was sufficient for a working musician, but for Fisher the Rickenbacker was lightning in a bottle. This was the instrument great bassists lusted after. The guitar was an inspiration. With it, he found he could play better than ever before. All he had to do was plug it in. Then it seemed to whisper to him, "Play me." Fisher decided to take it back to his room, then carefully stow it in its hard case. After that, it could stay locked away until he needed it again. Although whether that would be here was debatable. Already he saw signs that the fledgling band was disintegrating.

Through the windows he glimpsed a pair of moving lights. Marko and Sterling—they were crossing the lawn to the house. Jak wove between them as he sniffed at scent trails in the grass. So they'd had no luck in finding Kym either. He glanced at his watch. Six thirty. "Hurry back, Josanne," he murmured. "We're going to need those cops." Standing there with the bass securely grasped in his hand, he glanced round the room. The drums appeared undisturbed, as did the keyboards. Of course, Fabian had locked away his briefcase full of songs. Fisher imagined the guy slept with them under his pillow. Hell, he probably even handcuffed himself to them. As Fisher shook his head at the mental image he headed back to the door. Then he remembered . . .

"Camera." He crossed the room to the table. The tiny light on top of the camera had switched from green to red. It revealed the tape had run through to the end. Nothing in the ballroom appeared to have been touched. Even so, he decided to return to his room to check the tape. He'd be able to replay it on his TV. With the bass in one hand and the camera in the other, he left the ballroom and headed along the corridor. As he opened his room door, Fabian appeared behind him. The man stared.

Was this some kind of challenge? Would Fabian pick up the row where they'd left off? Shit, Fisher didn't need this now.

Fabian announced, "Josanne's not back yet."

Fisher expected some sarcastic comment about the tardiness of his girlfriend. Yet to Fisher's surprise he saw a glint of anxiety in Fabian's eyes. The guy bit his lip as he added, "Shouldn't she be back by now?"

* * *

Cantley watched the two men from The Tower. They walked through the woods at dusk with their dog. *The thing's a menace.* Cantley wanted the black mutt dead. Although he'd been confident the pair wouldn't see him, their blasted dog had started barking in his direction. Oh yes, the beast had known a stranger had his eye on them. When the dog's barking grew increasingly vicious, the men had headed in the direction the dog had been staring. *Damn them.* Cantley had to retreat along his secret pathways. That mutt had become an obstacle to his plans. It had to go.

What was it now? Josanne'd promised she'd be back at The Tower within the hour. Now more than two hours had elapsed. And here she was, still in the lake. Her car had become a little metal island with a sole inhabitant. Josanne had done what she could to make herself comfortable. She'd closed the door, pulled on her coat, then sat sideways with her knees drawn up so her feet rested on the passenger seat. Heaven knew what damage she'd wrought as she crashed through the hedge. *Oh well, that's a bridge to cross when I come to it.* Briefly her spirits soared when she realized her cell phone was in her pocket. She tried to call the police, but there was no signal. The entire tract of water-logged land must have been bereft of transmitters. Then, there were no houses here; only fields with the rare intrusion of a road now and again. For a while she'd peered through the rear window in the direction of the road she'd so dramatically exited. Even with it being foggy, she was sure she'd see the lights of passing traffic. None passed. Roads in Outer Mongolia would be busier than this hidden corner of Yorkshire. She hugged herself to try and stay warm. But the cold, damp air managed to slither its way into the car. To save the battery she'd switched off all the lights. At last, however, she conceded she needed company of sorts. She switched on the radio. The first channel she found played doom-laden organ music. Ominous sounding chords lumbered. A funeral march for dead gods.

"Not on your life," Josanne muttered. "This is creepy enough." After working through more radio bands, she settled on a station playing classic pop. As the Beach Boys launched into "Wouldn't It Be Nice," she muttered grimly to herself, staring at the body of cold water, "Yeah, wouldn't it be nice . . . huh." She clicked her tongue in disgust. "You're telling me."

Fisher ran the lead from the video camera to the input at the back of the TV. Once he'd done that, he returned to lie on his bed. It had become habit now to glance at the ceiling. "Stay where you are, ceiling. No tricks, OK?" Back to the flippancy, he told himself wearily. But clues had begun to stack up. The night he arrived here, he'd experienced some kind of hallucination—hell, it had to be hallucination, hadn't it?—OK, he'd had this nightmare—or hallucination—that the walls and ceiling of the room had rolled in to try and crush him. Later, Kym suffered an electric shock in the medieval structure called the Good Heart. In a nightmare she'd witnessed herself being stabbed through the chest by a spiked mechanism. Now Kym was gone. Earlier in the day, Josanne had appeared at the ballroom in a state of glassy-eyed shock. She'd muttered something about being drowned in her room when it had filled with water. OK, another bad dream. But why was everyone having bad dreams? Josanne should have been back an hour ago. Despite the trade-mark arrogance Fabian did appear concerned. The last Fisher saw of him was Fabian walking down the driveway to wait at the gate for Josanne. Once more Fisher's eyes rolled round the walls and the ceiling.

"Perfidious room," he murmured to himself. The chimes from the hidden clock began to strike. This time the number of strikes matched the time of his wristwatch. Seven o'clock. Through the windowpane he saw darkness had descended. Wisps of fog wandered through the light cast from his room. Fisher switched on the TV. Tuned to a dead channel, it showed nothing but a blizzard effect of white dots; static hissed from the set. Fisher pressed the "play" button on the camera. More pixilated snowflakes. Of course: he'd have to rewind the tape. He wasn't familiar with the controls, so it took a moment to check he was pressing the right buttons on the tiny control panel. He touched one marked with a backward pointing arrow. An image snapped up on screen. It revealed a figure walking backwards away from the camera. For a gloomy barn of a place, light levels in the ballroom were better than he anticipated. He recognized the figure as himself. One John Fisher, age twenty-twenty-two, bass player with a yet-unnamed band. The tape must have run out just before he'd picked up the camera. For a moment he watched his on-screen self move in reverse, first to hold the bass guitar, then put it on the stand before walking backwards to the door. Fisher tapped the "stop" button before touching the miniscule "rewind" button on the camera's plastic shell. With a faint hum the tape respooled itself to the start.

A clicking from the ceiling make him glance up.

His eyes scanned the smooth expanse of white. He was wary that at any second it would rush down at him again. A faint tapping started. It spread from one side of the room to the other, then slowly faded. *Someone's running a hot water faucet. That's all.* Even so, he watched the ceiling with an unblinking fascination. *Just in case . . .* When the clicks subsided, he pressed the play button, then shuffled back to the bed to watch what appeared on-screen.

A dark mass moved away from the lens to reveal a video image of himself. He'd just leaned forward so he could switch the camera to record. The shot was a longish one of the amplifier stacks, the drum kit, and Fabian's keyboards, with Fisher's bass guitar standing upright in the center of the shot. He could no longer see Fabian and Josanne: they'd be standing near the ballroom entrance. However, he could see himself giving the room one last look over.

"You need to shave more," he murmured to his video image. The dark shadow on his jaw was plain to see.

Off-camera he heard Fabian's voice as he addressed the video-image Fisher: "You're not going to lock the Rickenbacker in your room?"

On TV he saw himself shake his head. "Bait."

Fisher yawned. He dragged a pillow toward him, then beat a hollow in it for his elbow. Once he'd made himself comfortable, he turned back to the TV. No sounds came from the speaker. The screen revealed a crisp shot of the bass guitar resting vertically on its stand; its four strings gleamed with a silvery light. Behind the instrument were the drums, keyboards, plus a wall of oblong amplifiers. Snaking across the carpeted floor were glossy black cables running to a central power board, which contained circuit breakers. Fisher stared at the cables. For a moment their significance didn't quite click. Then he sat upright on the bed to stare at the screen. A tingle ran up the back of his neck. The camera shot was static. The camera sat on the table. It filmed anything that happened to occupy a given space in front of its lens. Fisher had not noticed any movement. Yet the camera had moved. It must have. Because when he began reviewing the footage, he couldn't see the cables.

"So what the hell have you done?" he murmured.

Instead of being around three feet from the floor, the height of the table the camera rested on, Fisher figured it had ascended to around six feet. Its position had been subtly angled so the red bass guitar remained in the center of the screen. Now, however, it revealed several square feet of ballroom carpet with black cables running across it. Then the camera began to move. A slow pan . . . very slow. The bass guitar slipped from the center. Fisher leaned forward to lock his concentration on the TV. The camera image rotated with such smoothness that surely it must have been mounted on a tripod. The amplifiers with the windows behind them slipped offscreen to show the wall at the far end of the ballroom. Then faster. The camera turned to reveal the ballroom doors yawning wide open (*but I closed them as I went out*). With a burst of speed, the camera darted forward. Effortlessly it flew through the doorway, then swung left. Its velocity was so great that the walls of the corridor became a brown blur. The brightly illuminated area of the entrance hall expanded. The camera banked, then hurtled through the doorway into the Promenade. Once there, it stopped outside the ancient façade of the farmhouse that was enclosed within the mansion. The camera revealed crisp details of the gray wall, the deep-set windows with their latticework of lead strips that held antique glass panes in place. The camera slowly retreated from that strange building-within-a-building. Like a wild animal back-stepping in a furtive way—as if to escape? Or to lie in wait for its prey?

From the blind clock, the chimes started. Were they chimes recorded by the camera? Or had they started now? They shimmered on the still air, a phantom resonance that worked its way into his head. He hated the sound now. Their timbre irritated his ears. On-screen the camera revealed a view of that stunted doorway. The chimes grew louder. Now he could make out a splash of light moving round behind the façade. The chimes quickened. An urgent pulsing sound. Metal against metal. A brassy heartbeat.

Then the camera lunged forward. It sped as if he were looking through the eyes of a tiger bounding after its prey. The doorway expanded to swallow the camera into the Good Heart. Fine name for such a miserable conjunction of stones.

The light moved in the shadows. Suddenly he was seeing himself, his video image, shining the flashlight round that low-ceilinged room.

Bingo! He understood. "You bastards. You bloody, tormenting bastards."

As he watched himself playing the flashlight over the fireplace, he realized what had happened. Marko . . . Hell, it had to be practical joker Marko. . . . He'd sneaked back in to grab the video camera to play this trick. What stupid, irresponsible timing . . .

"I'll break your legs for this, Marko. I'll rip you in . . ."

Fisher's words petered out as the view of himself shifted. The camera must have been rising, maybe a full five feet above him. Yet all the time its unseen operator angled it downward so that he, Fisher, was in the center of the screen. But how could Marko do that? He must have stood on furniture to film from that high angle. He saw the top of his own head. A truncated image of his face with the light catching his forehead. His shoulders hid the rest of his body from this angle. He only caught a glimpse of the pointed boots on his feet.

But why didn't I notice Marko there with the camera? It must have been obvious there was someone else in the room. I can't have been so dense as not to see the guy standing over me.

The sound of the chimes had receded. Now they returned. They came tumbling from the walls. An avalanche of notes. A frenzied clanging of a dead fist beating the door of the tomb. Their volume was nothing less than savage. In life, the flesh-and-blood man on the bed grimaced as he clamped his hands to his ears. On-screen the video image of himself did the same. With a surge of chimes that sounded like entire worlds exploding, the camera lunged down at the videotaped Fisher. Wounds broke open on his face as if invisible masonry had fallen from the tower above him. Blood filled his mouth. The skin above his eyebrows opened in a jagged crack. Depression wounds mottled his cheeks. An invisible force pushed the eyeballs back into his head so deeply that his eye sockets became two vast craters. For a moment they yawned as hollow voids. Then blood rushed from internal hemorrhaging to fill the twin craters with pools of liquid crimson. The mouth opened to scream. It remained locked wide open as the face stopped moving. There was absolute stillness on-screen. Just that stark image of the corpse face in close-up. No sound now.

On the bed, Fisher ran his hands over his eyes. Nausea jetted from his stomach into his throat. When he could at last bring himself to look at the screen again, he saw the bass guitar in the center of the TV. Behind it the amplifiers and drum kit. There was no movement. The image was still. Outside a gentle breeze tugged at the hawthorn bush. Its branches tapped on the other side of the glass—the sound of someone trying to attract his attention. An individual with important news to share with the damned.

Chapter Twenty-two

Fresh air. That's what I need. Fisher yanked aside the drapes so he could reach the window catch. For one vertiginous moment he'd been ready to seize the TV and hurl it through the glass. What did it mean that he'd seen himself being crushed by an invisible force on the video tape? He must have fallen asleep. A nightmare . . .

"No," he panted as he hoisted the sash window. "I was awake. I know I was." He thrust out his head. Instantly cold air washed over it. The shocking suddenness of it was as acute as being dowsed by iced water. He sucked in the air with a stuttering moan. Oxygen poured down his throat into his lungs. A tingling supernova of a sensation. Fisher breathed deeply. His heart beat with wanton fury against his ribs. If it had exploded from his chest there and then, he wouldn't have been surprised. Not after he'd witnessed his own death on TV. But could he make sense of it? He'd left the camera running early that evening as he searched the building for Kym. The camera had dutifully recorded a view of his bass guitar, the amps, drums, keyboards. Yet the camera had appeared to move. Who picked it up? How had they run to the Good Heart to find him? An invisible avalanche had appeared to mangle his face. Jesus Christ. How can anyone fake that? He remembered the details so clearly. The shocked expression as the camera lunged into close-up. He'd even glimpsed the sharp pointed boots he'd been wearing. . . .

This thought caught him like a stinging slap. Fisher turned from the window to look into the room. The pointed black leather boots sat against the far wall.

I wasn't even wearing those boots tonight, he told himself as he looked down at his feet. I'm wearing sneakers!

The night was going to be a long one. The clock on the dash told Josannne it was coming up to eight thirty. She gloomily regarded the world of mist and cold, dark water. Great, she thought, just great. I'm going to have to sit this out until first light. To beat back the graveyard silence, she nudged up the radio volume. Lou Reed intoned details of his perfect day.

For a moment Fisher didn't even realize what he was doing. He wandered about the room in a daze, first going to the pointed leather shoes. He picked one up and bent it in his hands. *If I destroy the shoes . . . what I saw can't happen to me.*

Dear God. Insane thoughts. Rock and roll isn't about the music, someone once wrote, it's about the drugs. Hell, he'd not touched drugs in years. Drugs made bad guys rich. He refused to be part of that. So he enjoyed a beer, occasionally wine. . . . I'm rambling, he thought. He returned to the window for more of that cold, cold air. Even so, he gave the TV plenty of space between himself and its dead screen. Right now it seemed perfectly logical for a pair of corpse arms to thrust out from the set, grab hold of him, then haul him into some TV never world that lies between the wave bands.

"Oh, God. Give me air," he grunted. Once more he leaned forward, rest his weight on the sill and pushing his head out into the night. The bushes whispered as a slight breeze stirred them. It pushed the fog away, too. Above him the silver disk of the moon shone fuzzily through strands of mist. Now he could see down the slope to where the water stretched away in a myriad of glistening pools. The gray finger of concrete that was the runway stretched into the marsh.

Fisher tensed. That was the moment he saw the figure standing out there in the gloom.

"Kym!" Fisher ran out of the room. He shouted the words but didn't know if anyone heard him. "It's Kym!" He ran to the kitchen. No one there. He grabbed one of the flashlights from where it had been left on the table. "Kym's down on the old runway!" Hell, was anyone else even in the building? No one answered his shouts. Never mind, he thought, I can bring her back myself. For some reason the figure had stood unmoving in the center of that slab of concrete, staring in the direction of the house.

"Kym's outside," he shouted down the corridor. "She must be hurt. . . ." Still no reply. *Oh, blow them.* He ran down the corridor to the entrance hall; from there he exited through the main doors. Outside the moon revealed the gaunt forms of trees.

"Fisher!"

He turned to see Fabian running up the drive. In one hand he held a flashlight that blazed into Fisher's face. Shielding his eyes against its glare, he saw that for some reason Fabian carried a white electric guitar by the neck.

"Hey, isn't that Sterling's guitar? What are you doing with it out here?"

The man panted as he thrust the guitar out at Fisher. "Take this."

"What the hell for?"

"I . . ." He took deep lungful of air to catch his breath. "I found it against a tree down there near the road."

"But what—"

"How the hell do I know who it got there. Take the bloody thing before I break it over your head!"

"What the hell's wrong with you?"

"Josanne hasn't come back yet." Fabian appeared agitated. He shot anxious glances along the driveway.

"Fabian. No, wait. I've got to tell you something. . . . That video camera I left running in the ballroom. It recorded. . . . Wait. Fabian! I've got tell you this!"

"Tell me later. I'm waiting down at the road for Josanne!"

"Fabian? Fabian! There's another thing. It's Kym. She's on the old runway. Fabian! I've seen Kym. Aw, for Christ's sake . . ." Fisher knew he was wasting his breath as Fabian ran along the driveway to the road. Fisher looked at the guitar. Its cream-colored body glowed in the moonlight, a luminous glow as if the light seeped from its core. The chrome pickups gleamed. The steel strings were six parallel lines of silver radiance. Found against a tree? No one in their right mind would leave a musical instrument like this outside in the damp. But did Fabian seem in his right mind? What had the guy seen to make him so jumpy?

Fisher cast his mind back twenty minutes to when he'd watched the video that appeared to show him being crushed to death. How his eyeballs had sunk into his head as if sucked inward by a vacuum. They'd left two craters. He'd watched in horror as the twin holes in his face filled with blood. He gritted his teeth. Had Fabian experienced a vision of himself? Or of Josanne? One which revealed a bloody death? He knew that Kym had witnessed herself being stabbed in a nightmare.

"Kym?" *She might still be out there on the runway. What if she's ill or injured?* He glanced down at the guitar in his hand. It would take too long to return it to the house. If he met Sterling on the way, it would mean trying to explain how his precious Gibson came to be outside in the first place. The thing would have to come with him. Kym was the number one priority.

Keeping a grip on the guitar's neck, Fisher ran to the house where the hawthorn clustered. He had to weave round the bushes while holding the flashlight high enough to see their slender branches that extended out across the path at head height. Each branch bristled thorns that were needle-sharp. He imagined the pain of such a thorn puncturing an eye. When he rounded the massive stone bulk of the house, he saw the gentle slope running downward. A hundred yards away stood the old World War II bunker. A grim tomb of a place in the moonlight. Beyond it stretched the runway. A slab of flat concrete flanked by stagnant pools of water and mud, it ran away into the distance to eventually dissolve into invisibility in the mist. And there . . . he saw the figure just as he glimpsed it from his window. Kym stood as thin and as straight as a gatepost in the center of the runway. She was perhaps a hundred yards further away. More than once he thought about putting the guitar down. His arm ached carrying the instrument. Its body was carved from maple; the pickups, machine heads and bridge were all made of metal. Ten pounds of prime electric guitar. *Leave it here, then pick it up on the way back. But who the hell would leave their friend's guitar lying in wet grass? Damp would seep into the electrics. The neck might warp. That's one sure way to destroy the thing.* Fisher panted with exertion; his breath came in gusts that misted white in the cold air. In a moment he hooked the leather guitar strap over his shoulder, carrying it on his back as a soldier carries a rifle. That done, he pushed himself to run faster. Ahead of him the runway stretched out, a ghostly pier of concrete that ran into the marsh. Within seconds he had passed by the silent bunker. Down here the smell of stagnant water oozed into his nostrils. A flavor of pond slime even left its mark on his tongue. Damp seeped through his clothes to touch his skin. Above him the moon burnt with a cold ghost light that imbued the shifting wraiths of fog with a weird half-life, as if the mist carried out maneuvers governed by its own mysterious agenda. Humped forms shaped out of the luminous water vapor crept across the runway in front of him. They passed between himself and the figure standing just fifty yards ahead. The figure remained perfectly still, a watchful presence rather than a human being.

"Kym!" he called. "Kym? Are you all right?" Fisher

slowed his pace as the figure resolved itself from the murk. "Kym, I saw you from . . ." His voice died in his throat. "Sorry . . . I thought you were someone I . . ." Once more his words petered out.

No, it wasn't Kym, the beautiful Czech girl. Instead he saw a man. He was as tall and as thin as the woman Fisher had taken into his bed the night before. Only this stranger was older, forties probably. The man didn't even appear to notice Fisher. From a thin face, a pair of pale blue eyes gazed up at the silhouette of The Tower in the moonlight. Not only did Fisher ask himself why the man chose to visit a remote quagmire at this time of night, but why on earth was the guy dressed like that? He stood there in the cold air dressed in a cream-colored sweatshirt and sweatpants, and his feet were clad in sandals, the kind a business executive would wear on a vacation at the beach. Come to think of it, even in the light of the flashlight, the man's thin face wore a tan.

The flashlight didn't distract the guy. He stared up at the outline of The Tower. His eyes roved over what details he could make out in the gloom. The tombstone shaped windows. The bushes clustering about its base. Then, at last, he did notice Fisher. The man raised his hand so the glare didn't strike him in the eyes.

"Sorry. I didn't mean to dazzle you." Fisher lowered the light. Out in the swamp a frog croaked; the pools of liquid mud sucked away the amphibian's voice to replace it with silence.

The man's blue eyes focused on Fisher. His expression suggested someone slowly rousing themselves from a trance.

"You're carrying a guitar." The man didn't ask a

question. It was a statement—a grim statement at that. "It has a white body."

The guitar's slung across my back. How can he see what color it is? Of all the subjects to start a conversation out here at night it seemed a weird one. *But it's weirder to stand on a disused runway in near-freezing temperatures dressed in clothes a vacationer might wear to lounge by a pool on a summer's day.*

"You've come to see this?" Fisher turned back to nod at The Tower. The man flinched when he fastened that unblinking stare onto the white electric guitar. Then the man tore his gaze away from the instrument to direct it The Tower. To do so required willpower on his part. His body language was that of a man forced to look at the worst thing in a morgue.

Fisher nodded toward the mansion as he repeated, "You've come to see this?"

"I guess you could say it's what I'm looking at now."

Odd answer. Fisher glanced back at the cream-colored lounging suit. Inside the sandals, the man's toes had turned gray with cold.

"I might have startled you," Fisher began. "But I thought you were someone I knew."

"Uh?"

"Are you OK?"

The man ran his tongue over his lips. They must have seemed dust dry to him. His eyes gleamed with mutant mix of wonder and absolute fear.

"No. I'm not OK . . . not now that I've seen you. Or that pile of bloody rock up there."

"Have you parked nearby?"

"Parked?" He laughed. It was as cold-blooded as the frog's croak of just moments ago. "No, I'm not parked nearby." He glanced down at himself. "I'm not dressed for this night jaunt, am I?" He shook his head. "I didn't expect it."

"Do you want to come up to the house? It'll be warmer."

"No . . . not on your life. I'm not going back there."

Hell, what now? Fisher guessed the guy had wandered away from some kind of hospital. He clearly wasn't firing on all pistons. Not appearing like this in lightweight clothes in these temperatures. Then Fisher realized it must appear odd that he himself was jogging round the grounds with only an electric guitar for company.

"My name's Blaxton." The man spoke faster now, as if he had information to impart but time was running out. "And you are?"

"John Fisher."

"Well, John Fisher. Do you live in that viper's nest?"

"The Tower? Just for the time being."

"Alone?"

Blaxton's questions were suspiciously intrusive. "Who wants to know?" Fisher asked adopting a defensive tone.

"You want to know, John Fisher. You want to know everything—if you know what's good for you."

"Hey, is that a threat?"

"I repeat, are you living there alone?"

"No. With friends. Not that it's any—"

"Fifteen years ago I stayed there for a week. I was there with friends, too. I was the only one to come out alive."

Fisher stared at him. Red splotches flamed in the man's cheeks. He spoke with fervor. The cloud of confusion had lifted from him. Fisher's urge to walk away from the guy was shunted out by the instinct to hear what he had to say.

Fisher tried not to—this he didn't need to hear, not after the events of the past twenty-four hours—but he did it anyway. He found himself uttering the fatal words: "Why? What happened?"

Chapter Twenty-three

Out on the concrete runway that had launched B-17 aircraft on bombing missions over Germany, two men talked. Both were incongruous. In the moonlight, with mist drifting in from the marsh, Fisher stood with the white electric guitar slung over his back by its leather strap, while the man called Blaxton, clad in his sweatshirt and sweatpants, blew into his cold hands.

The man's words spoken seconds ago resonated in Fisher's head: *"Fifteen years ago I stayed there for a week. I was there with friends, too. I was the only one to come out alive."*

Blaxton gazed at the house as though looking into the face of an oozing corpse. "There won't be enough time to tell you everything. Huh, I don't suppose you'll believe me for a moment." He shrugged. "I can't help that."

"You said you were the only one to come out alive?"

"That's right. The only one." Blaxton's face was grim as he turned to Fisher. "Has it started on you yet? Have any of your friends been hurt? Anyone wished they'd never been born?" His voice grew increasingly bitter.

"Tell me what happened, then."

"You're an impatient one, Mr. Fisher, aren't you? Or is it an instinct for self-preservation? Good God, let's hope it's the latter." He rubbed his arms as the cold sliced through the thin fabric of his sweatshirt. "Your guitar?"

Fisher shook his head. "A friend's."

To ask why Fisher had chosen to lug a guitar round the countryside would have been a natural question, but the man was no longer in a mood to digress. "We arrived here fifteen years ago. It was early spring. I remember there was still snow on the ground. There were five of us. All under thirty. The house hadn't been used in months. Before that it had been a conference center which had gone bust. I'd formed a production company with people I'd worked with at the BBC. We didn't have much money but pooled what we had. So we rolled up here in an old van with a camera, tape stock and more ambition than was healthy. We'd decided to make a program that would generate the most publicity, which would then lead to a series commission. All clear cut. Well planned. Research done. Everything." He looked at me. "We were on a ghost hunt." He blew into his hands. Tendrils of white vapor bled out between his fingers. "And we'd got The Tower to ourselves. A huge haunted house. We had automatic cameras, tape machines to leave running in empty rooms. . . ."

I left the video camera in the ballroom. I saw what happened to me. . . . Already Fisher had decided to invite Blaxton to see what he'd recorded a couple of hours ago.

Blaxton talked faster as if sensing the clock ticking away the seconds. A countdown . . . but a countdown to what? "We set up the camera. I filmed talking head shots of our presenter. 'Tonight ladies and gentlemen, we find ourselves in a mansion in a remote corner of Yorkshire. The Tower. The most haunted house in Britain . . . ' You know the sort of thing, Mr. Fisher. You'll have seen plenty like it. Only this was turning out to be different from what we expected. Have you taken a look round inside the place?"

Fisher nodded.

Blaxton continued, "You've seen the walkway called the Promenade?"

"And the Good Heart."

"Yeah, the Good Heart. An innocuous name for the most diabolical . . . evil . . . bit of stonework on this planet." He suddenly appeared uncomfortable at speaking the name. He glanced back as if he expected to see an eavesdropper. The mist had thickened again now. All Fisher could make out were a few square yards of concrete flanked by pools of stagnant water. Again a frog croaked in the darkness. "Ugly place, isn't it, Fisher? You know, it's all sinking into the mire. Best place for it. Yeah, well . . . we set up a tape recorder in the Good Heart and left it running. Research told us that the Good Heart was a medieval farmhouse built in the thirteenth century. Originally it was called the God Heart, but later owners changed it. Maybe they thought the God Heart was blasphemous. Of course, whoever built the ugly pile wouldn't have been referring to the Christian God, anyway. It would have been the temple site of one of the pagan honchos. A historian we interviewed even speculated that this was the burial site of the heart of a pagan god. You've seen the carving over the door? That's a carving from the original temple that stood here. It'll have been incorporated into the newer stonework to act as a kind of talisman. Maybe owners of the farmhouse that would become known as the Good Heart hoped it would bring good luck." His eyes strayed back to The Tower. "It brought anything but good luck. Parish records show that when the county was hit by the plague, lots of people from the area retreated to the house, where they thought they'd be safe. A year later when the king sent his army back into the areas that had been decimated by disease, they found all that was left in the house were dozens of skeletons. Vermin had picked them clean. So you'll be asking yourself, why wasn't the Good Heart ripped down when The Tower was built on the same site? People can be superstitious. In Britain nearly every church is built on the site of a pagan temple. Some even recycled stone carvings from the temples into the fabric of Christian churches. When the new priests had their churches built, they believed that the old magic hadn't vanished. That it was still humming away there in the ground—all primed and ready to go. And they could draw on the old supernatural powers. Maybe it was with the best of intentions. You know, that it would bring them luck, keep away the devil, fill the churches with the faithful every Sunday. Same goes for the guy who built The Tower. Maybe he walked into the ruined old farmhouse before he brought the wreckers in and he thought, 'Whoa. Just feel this vibe. I want some of that.' So, not only did he leave the façade standing, he enveloped it with his own house. He wanted to capture lightning in a bottle. What did he do when The Tower was finished? I don't know. Maybe he sat naked on a huge throne in the Good Heart and crafted schemes of world conquest." He glanced at his watch. "That's it for the history. We're almost out of time." Blaxton's voice adopted an air of finality. The kind of tones a prisoner might use when the guard on death row told him it was almost time for that last walk. Even though Fisher only stood ten paces from the man, a mist drifted between them. It blurred his face until it resembled a skull hovering there above the ground. A frog called. A splash sounded from the swamp. A sense of foreboding knotted Fisher's stomach. *Time is on collision course with the inevitable.* That understanding didn't come in words but in painful clenches inside his body. Nerve endings flared in alarm. The man's face now appeared as a melting skull in the mist. Surely, it was an effect of moonlight conspiring with drifting droplets of water vapor. Only . . .

Only Fisher recalled the video he'd watched of himself. And those nightmares . . . Kym and Josanne had them, too.

Fisher spoke. "Blaxton. How long was it before your friends started having the bad dreams?"

"Bad dreams?" He gave a bitter laugh. "Don't you wish they were only bad dreams?" Once more Blaxton checked his watch. This time he grunted as if he experienced a stab of pain. "Mr. Fisher. I'm sorry. There isn't time to tell you what you need to know."

"Why?"

"Don't ask why. Don't interrupt. I'll keep speaking for as long as I can. What you do with the information is up to you. OK, you and your friends have been having bad dreams. My friends did, too. And here it is without sugarcoating. They experienced visions of their own deaths. Within hours or days of that vision they died. Sorry to be brutal with the truth. But there it is, my friend. Ssh, no questions. There isn't time. The first to die dreamt he fell from The Tower. When he woke up he told me about it. His hands were shaking with fear. In the nightmare he'd been walking on the roof. He heard the chimes. . . . Oh, yes, you've heard the chimes, I know you have. . . . He heard the chimes from that clock in the Good Heart. Anyway . . . the roof is flat. It's designed for walking on. Only, as he heard the chimes in his dream, it tipped up. He dreamt he slid off of it like meat from a chopping board. Bang. Fell down on the driveway. My friend had tears in my eyes as he told me he felt his bones break. That he knew he was dead. Yeah, right. Just a nightmare. We took the piss. We laughed at him."

"Then it happened."

"Hell, yes. Then it happened, Mr. Fisher." Blaxton spoke with renewed urgency. "The guy went up on the roof with the camera. He planned to set up a shot of the grounds. I guess the nightmare still scared the crap out of him, but we'd taunted him so mercilessly he didn't want to be seen as a coward." Blaxton shrugged. "My friend screamed. I saw him fall all the way to the ground. Just like he told me." Now he looked too cold to shiver. "The next day it was the same. Carol-Anne told me that she'd dreamt her car burst into flames. She said as she burned she could still hear the chimes of the clock. Those blasted chimes, eh, Mr. Fisher?"

"What about the rest?"

"What do you think? I don't have to spell it out, do I?" He glanced at his watch. "Not that there's time anyway. But they all dreamt their own deaths. They all heard chimes. They all died. If you've had similar nightmares then it's time to get the hell out—and fast. You follow?"

Fisher nodded. A grim coldness spread through his veins.

Blaxton fastened his stare on his watch yet again. "I make it to nine. But I know this watch is a few seconds fast."

"Why? What's so important about the time?"

"Nine o'clock? If you're crazy enough to stay here you'd best find some answers. When I left, I didn't stop to pick up my stuff. But I'd already stored some audio tapes in the cellar. I tied them in a plastic sack—a big red one. If it's still there, you can't miss it. They might be useful."

"After fifteen years?

"The tapes are probably exactly where I left them. Believe me, not many people visit the cellar. They're the original medieval vaults of the Good Heart. The epicenter."

"I'll find them."

"Good. But even better if you drive away from here tonight."

"We're looking for our friend. She hasn't been seen all day."

"Then God help her." Blaxton became agitated. His eyes darted from Fisher's face to The Tower. He took a step backward. The mist crept over his face again, blurring the edges. His features became distorted. The eyes were suddenly not eyes, but circular voids in his head.

"Blaxton?"

"You should think about saving yourself, Mr. Fisher."

Simon Clark

"Blaxton? When you saw me for the first time, you knew I'd be carrying a guitar, didn't you?"

"Yes! Yes, I did!" Fear ran through Blaxton's voice.

"And the guitar would have a white body. How did you know that?"

"You idiot. Don't you get it?"

"Get what?"

"You haven't understood what I've told you. That's not my fault. God help me, I tried!"

"Blaxton? How did you know I'd be carrying a white guitar?"

Suddenly he lunged forward out of the fog. His eyes blazed. "Because fifteen years ago I lay in bed in that house and I dreamt exactly this. I dreamt I'd stand here on this concrete again while a man walked out of the fog with a white guitar! This is my nightmare—my death dream! Do you understand now? In the dream I saw myself standing here at night. Then you approached me. We talked. I told you what I know about that damned house. Then the house killed me." His eyes grew wild as terror gripped him. "Do you understand? *I died, Fisher! I died!*"

Chimes drifted through the air. They were possessed by a metallic coldness that sent shivers down his spine.

Blaxton whirled round. Panic gripped him. Cries spurted from the back of his throat.

"Blaxton. If you knew what the house could do, why did you come back here?"

"I didn't!" He still backed away as if fearing attack. "I was at home. I opened my eyes—and that's when I found myself here. Did you hear that, Fisher! *The house brought me back!*"

The chimes continued. To Fisher's ears they were

faint as they counted the hours from one to nine. Yet to Blaxton they seemed to peal with such volume that he flinched with every strike. Grimacing, he pressed his palms to the side of his head.

"Blaxton. Wait here. I'll bring a car down. I'll drive you away to—"

Fisher's plan exploded to nothing as Blaxton ran into the fog. For a second Fisher saw the man racing across the expanse of concrete. Then he vanished as the mist swallowed him.

"Blaxton. Come back!"

Then came splashes; they faded away as the man ran through shallow water. Then came the screams.

"God help me . . . please . . . Fisher . . . Fisher! I can't climb out! I'm going under . . . I'm going—"

Then the screams vanished. Silence rushed in like air rushing to fill a vacuum. Fisher ran to the place he thought he heard the screams came from. He shone the flashlight into the mist. Only it grew thicker. Visibility dwindled to no more than twenty yards. What was there to see? He could make out nothing but pools of still water. They didn't look as if they'd been disturbed in five years . . . ten years . . . fifteen years. . . .

Chapter Twenty-four

Jak stood in the main entrance of the house as Fisher returned with the white guitar slung across his back. The dog stepped forward to greet Fisher, who plodded toward the animal with a tired word of greeting. All the time he sensed the oppressive mass of The Tower rising above him. It carried the same violent promise as a raised fist.

This is where Blaxton's friend fell to his death. Fisher's plodding feet crunched on the driveway gravel. What noise would the impact of a one-hundred-eighty-pound body make after plunging six stories?

Jak fell into step alongside him as they crossed the entrance hallway. Above them the staircase curved upwards into the stone carcass of the tower. *This is where Blaxton walked when he came on his ghost hunt.* Fifteen years before, a bunch of young people had come here with optimistic plans. One by one they had that "death dream." Then they died one by one. *This is where I walked when I first entered the house. A couple of hours later I had my death dream, too.*

THE TOWER

So where is Blaxton now, in his cream-colored sweatpants and sweatshirt? He's at the bottom of the swamp. The house brought him back here. His death dream became reality when he saw the man with a white guitar. Then Blaxton heard the chimes. Panicked. Ran into the swamp. Dead. End of story for Blaxton. He'll lie there in his grave of stagnant slime for all eternity. But what about us? What about the living?

A breeze blew outside. It sent drafts whispering through the hallway. Unseen doors creaked: the sound of ancient tombs opening. The drafts raised a chorus of sighing through the banister posts. The dog's ears pointed as he picked up all the noises that Fisher couldn't hear. He noticed the way Jak looked up the stairs as if he knew something stirred up there.

Fisher sensed the weight of the tower above him. Shadows appeared to creep down the steps. He was sure it was darker up there than it had been a moment ago. Jak gave a tiny bark in the back of his throat. Short black hairs bristled on his back.

"You know it, too, don't you, boy?" Ice slid in Fisher's veins. "This house. It's only just started to work on us, hasn't it?" He shivered.

Jak dog gave that "yip" sound in the back of his throat again. He held eye contact with Fisher for a moment before turning his head back to the stairs. Here the lights burned in the hallway, up there the power had been cut by the developer. The big staircase rose in a long curve to the next floor and then the next. Above the second story was nothing but a realm of shadows. Fisher glanced at Jak. The animal's amber eyes appeared fixed on an object that no human could divine.

He breathed, "There's something up there, isn't there?

Again Jak made the faint sound in the back of his

throat. The amber eyes flicked between the stairs and back to Fisher. There was an expression of expectancy. In fact, Jak's entire body trembled as his muscles quivered in response to the flood of adrenaline that triggered the "fight or flight" response. Fisher moved so he had a view of the corridor. No one else about. He hoped he'd catch sight of Marko or Sterling. No doubt Fabian still conducted his vigil down by the road.

Gently Fisher stood the guitar in the corner of the hallway, then he raised the flashlight. He would switch it on at the last second. If this was an intruder, he preferred at least an element of surprise. A dazzling shot of light might catch them off guard. "OK, Jak," he whispered. "Let's see what we've got here."

Instinctively the dog stayed close by him as they climbed the first flight of steps. There were ten or so risers before the curve of the staircase took the next ten out of view. With the dog shadowing him, he silently climbed the ten steps. As the staircase turned to the right, Fisher saw that the risers were concealed in shadow. Cold drafts ghosted down at him. They were strong enough to force tendrils of air through his fringe to crawl across his scalp. He raised the flashlight until he held it like a pistol. His thumb was on the button, ready to switch it on the moment he saw a figure. He ascended three more risers, then stopped. A black shape squatted there in the center of the stairs. As Fisher stared at it, a pair of glistening eyes flicked open from the shadowed head.

With his heart giving a furious lurch, he crushed the button with his thumb. The dog let out a bark that sounded like a scream. Light dashed from the flashlight to strike the hunched figure on the stair.

Fisher saw a stark face, wide eyes, a glint of teeth behind parted lips.

Air exploded from his lips as he made the leap of recognition. "Josanne?"

Cantley watched the man at the drive's gateway. Like a rogue toothache that had no respect for territory, the pain that had started in Cantley's jaw earlier in the day spread into his cheekbones, then into his eyes before burrowing like a spiny-backed worm into his forehead. When he'd killed the one called Kym, the house was pleased. It had quelled the pain in Cantley's body. Only a brief respite, though. The house had an appetite for more sacrifice. It was hungry for another gift. A bloody gift. A bloody, writhing, twisting, screaming gift. Cantley grinned in the darkness.

Fisher ran up the staircase to where Josanne sat in the shadows just four steps from the next floor. Jak ran partway, then stopped short of her. The dog froze into an odd stillness as he stared at the seated woman. Fisher paused just a few steps below her. Josanne sat with her knees forward and her arms limply hanging down at either side of her, her palms resting flat against the step. Her face was usually an olive brown, but now it appeared a bloodless gray. She stared forward with no expression. The glare of the flashlight didn't appear to intrude on her thoughts at all. The woman appeared to be locked inside a daydream.

"Josanne?" Fisher took another step toward her. "Are you alright?"

Slowly she emerged from the dreamy stare. "I'm back, aren't I?" Her voice was hoarse.

The bare meaning of the words should have

seemed sarcastic. To Fisher's ears, however, she uttered the words in a dazed way, like an accident victim realizing that something both unexpected and shocking had happened.

"Yes," he said gently. "You're back at the house."

"Oh . . ."

"Did you find a telephone?"

"Hmm?" She gazed up into the shadows above her. Her body language spoke of someone in a state of deep confusion.

"Josanne. Did you telephone the police?"

She looked back at him. "Fisher?"

"Yes, it's me . . . Fisher." He shone the flashlight at himself. "And here's Jak . . . the dog we found," he added when she looked blankly at the animal, who still refused to approach her.

She closed her eyes for a moment, then opened them. This time she appeared a little more focused. "Fisher? How did I get here?"

"What's wrong, Josanne?"

The words came quickly. "I crashed the car into a lake. It wasn't deep. But I knew I was stuck. I'd have to wait there until morning. I know I tried to sleep." A breeze rose. Air currents droned across the window frames. A sharp tapping started as a black rain began to fall. She flinched at the sound, then turned to hold Fisher with a wide-eyed stare. "Why aren't I still in the car?"

A cold prickle ran down his spine. He knew what had happened. For some reason he couldn't yield to the truth. Not yet. If he could deny it to himself, then there was a remote chance he could hold this curse at bay. "Josanne. You must have managed to drive the car out of the lake, then back here."

Slowly she shook her head. "The car was stuck in the water. Fisher?" A note of panic crept into her voice. "Fisher, I sat in the car, I closed my eyes. When I opened them again, I was back here."

"Oh, God." Blaxton's words came back to him. *"I was at home. I opened my eyes—and that's when I found myself here. Did you hear that, Fisher! The house brought me back!"*

She gave tiny heartbroken laugh. "It's alright, Fisher. You can tell me I've gone insane. I can take it. Did they find me gibbering at the roadside? Did you drag me into the van and drive me back here?"

"No, Josanne," he said as gently as he could. "But we've got to get everyone together. It's important we talk."

"Kym?"

"She's . . ." *Dead.* Realization cut through him, but without missing a beat he said, ". . . Not been found yet."

"She'll get wet. . . . Have you seen the rain?"

"Can you stand? That's OK, Josanne. Put your weight on my arm." Hell . . . so that's why Jak keeps his distance from her. The moment he steadied her as she climbed unsteadily to her feet, a penetrating cold slammed through the bones in his hands. They ached so much he had to clamp his teeth together. *She's got the essence of the house in her. It must have infected her when it brought her back here.* At that moment he recalled an old phrase a priest would have used to describe her condition. *She's become one of the damned.* Jak smelt it on her. He backed away with his ears and tail down.

As Fisher guided her down to the hallway, Sterling appeared. First he looked up at the pair descending the stairs. Then he saw his guitar propped in the corner.

"Fisher, what's going on here? What are you doing with my guitar? I've been looking all over for that."

"Fabian found it outside."

"Outside?"

"Look, Sterling, we've got to get everyone together."

"What the hell was it doing outside?"

"Sterling. You'll find Fabian down at the main road. Bring him back here."

"What's wrong with Josanne? Have you seen her face? It's gray."

"Sterling, please, man. Bring Fabian. We'll be in the kitchen."

Jak slunk along the edge of the walls to keep his distance from Josanne; then he raced along the corridor to where Marko stood outside the kitchen door. Sterling couldn't tear his eyes from Josanne's face. It was as if he'd noticed a disfiguring scar for the first time.

"Sterling."

"OK, I'm moving."

"You best have this." He tossed the flashlight to him. "I'll take the guitar with me. Now hurry! I've got something to tell you."

Chapter Twenty-five

"No, I'm against it. Dead against it," Adam told them as they all sat in the kitchen. "Why the hell do we need to search the bloody cellar at this time of night?"

"It's only just gone nine." Fisher didn't believe he was hearing this.

Belle added, "Fisher, look, darling. You're over-wrought. Have a glass of wine."

"I'm not overwrought. Listen. I saw a guy down on the old runway. He was dressed in lightweight clothes and sandals. He said he—"

"Wine, Fisher. Have couple of bottles of red and you'll sleep like a cadaver." That was Adam Ambrose's typically oddball contribution as he sat at the kitchen table. Belle stood behind him massaging his neck.

So Mr. Teeth and Hair doesn't believe me anyway. Fisher chewed his lip. "What about Josanne? Her car was stuck in a lake. How did she find her way back here?"

"We dealt with that ten minutes ago, Fisher." With a shake of his head Fabian adopted tones of someone with limited patience explaining the damned obvious to children. "Joanne's car is on the drive. She must have driven it back here."

"Without realizing she was in the car, steering it, pushing the pedals?"

"Josanne suffered from shock. She was nearly killed out there when she came off the road."

Belle added, "And if Josanne ran the car into a lake, how do you explain that it's dry inside? There's no sign of silt or pond weed on the bodywork."

"She told us the lake wasn't deep enough to flood the car. As for mud, it's been raining," Sterling told her. Thank God, Fisher thought, an ally at last. "That downpour was so hard it would have blasted every scrap of mud off the paintwork."

The argument paused. The dog approached Josanne. She sat with a thick fleece jacket round her shoulders. For the first time since her return, she smiled. She held out her hand toward the dog so he'd come to her. Jak appeared in two minds about it. He wagged his tail, but held back.

"Come on, boy. . . . It's OK."

Jak dipped his head a couple of times. The tail wagged faster. Then he walked up to her to snuffle his nose into her fingers. She patted his head before stroking his back. He sat close up so he could lean against her leg. Fisher thought, so whatever had clung to her when she appeared back here has gone. Jak knows she's no longer tainted.

Dogs everywhere have a knack of doing what Jak was doing right now: lightening atmosphere in a tense situation. Moments before, everyone in the kitchen appeared to be locking hostile glances. Now nearly everyone watched Josanne stroking the dog as he wagged his tail with pleasure. Fisher took the moment to glance round the room. Adam, Fabian and Josanne sat at the table in the center of the kitchen. Belle stood behind Adam. Her fingers worked his neck muscles. He closed his eyes, but it didn't stop him from trashing whatever Fisher had to say. Meanwhile, Fisher, Marko and Sterling stood with their backs to the kitchen counter. Sterling needed to be there because he was the guy with the golden heart; he insisted on warming a pan of chicken soup for Josanne. Of course, what was really happening was obvious to anyone with a shred of understanding of human behavior: battle lines were being drawn. The men and women in the room had demonstrated their allegiance to their leader by physically moving to be near him. Fabian had his old friends close. What was left of the old group, Cuspidor, had rallied around Fisher by the kitchen sink. Fabian's brave vision of this stay at The Tower being an exercise in forging disparate individuals into a united group of musicians wasn't working yet. After they'd assembled here, with Fabian drying his hair after the soaking in the rain and Josanne looking so gray she might as well have been dragged off a mortuary slab, Fisher had begun to tell them about his encounter with Blaxton. He'd almost managed to explain the need to search the cellar for the audio tapes that Blaxton had abandoned fifteen years before when he fled this forbidding heap of rock. No dice. Fabian, Adam and Belle were having none of it. Josanne sat with them, but she was still so dazed by her ordeal that she took no part in the subsequent discussion. At least now the olive hue had returned to her skin. Jak sensed that whatever had gripped her had evaporated.

So they'd drunk hot coffee. They'd discussed what happened. That discussion degenerated into argument. Fisher glanced through the window. Rain drops slid down the glass. Beyond that there was only unfathomable darkness. Sterling pulled a bowl from a shelf, cut slices of bread from a loaf, then returned to the stove to watch over the soup.

What now? Does Adam expect us all to hit the wine bottle and drink our way out of the dilemma? Fisher couldn't stay silent. "What about Kym?"

"You think we're not anxious about her?" Fabian rolled his eyes. "Have you got a bloody monopoly on compassion? Of course we're all worried about her, Fisher."

"So, what do we do about her?" Marko asked.

"Quiz your pal about that," Adam said. "He's all set to rummage through the fucking cellar for God knows what."

Fisher grunted in frustration. "What's down there might help us understand what we're facing here."

"The cellar can wait." Belle scowled. "Adam and I are going to drive to a telephone."

"We've tried that once," Fisher's voice rose. "Did it help? Look what happened to Josanne."

"It was thick fog then. Now it's only raining."

"Tell them, Josanne." Fisher gestured with his hands. "Tell Adam and Belle it won't let them go."

"What won't?" Belle was bemused.

"The house, of course."

Adam chuckled. "Are you sure you've not been knocking back the vino already?"

"I wish I had been. It might kill the pain of trying to make you understand what's damn well obvious."

Sterling set the bowl of steaming soup in front of

Josanne. "Don't mind the squabbling children, Josanne. Start eating. You need it."

"Thanks."

Fisher felt stung. "Sterling. I'm not squabbling. I'm just trying to—"

"Tell us the house is haunted. We know, dear boy." Adam closed his eyes again as Belle rubbed his neck. "You keep playing the same old tune."

Belle nodded. "Adam and I will go find a house or a garage. We'll call the police and tell them about Kym."

"Don't. It's not safe."

"Dear God in heaven." Fabian rolled his eyes. "Here we go again."

Sterling took the coffee jug, then began refilling everyone's cup. "OK, we agree to differ on this, but—"

Fisher broke in. "If you'd only talked to this guy Blaxton. He would have—"

"Fisher. *Fisher.* Do you mind not fucking well interrupting me?"

Fisher yielded the floor with a sigh.

Sterling continued, "Thank you. If you let me have my say, this is what I suggest. Fabian stays here with Josanne. Belle and Adam find a telephone—Fisher, if you dare interrupt, I'll throw this coffee over you—I know I saw a payphone back at the ferry. Meanwhile, you, Marko and me will search the cellar. Does that satisfy everyone?"

Marko grinned. "Sterling, old buddy. You should have been a diplomat."

Josanne sat still for the course of the argument. The words washed over her without touching her mind. If she'd been questioned later, she wouldn't have been able to recall what was said. Cold held her in an icy blue grip. Fabian's thick fleece jacket didn't seem to be helping much. At that moment Josanne's attention wasn't there in the kitchen but locked onto a memory loop that played itself over and over in her brain.

In the car . . . the lake all around. Thick fog. Songs on the radio. She'd told herself, *I'm going to have to make myself comfortable. I'm going to be stuck here all night.* Even so, it's difficult to relax in a car that's up to the sills in water. Suddenly you're Robinson Crusoe on a little man-made island of steel, a wheel at each corner. Every so often she'd sat up so she could look through the back window. The fog obscured the lake bank and the field that led back to the road. If that gray murk lifted, no doubt she'd have seen the muddy ruts in the grass gouged by the car's tires as it sped down here. Marooned. Wasn't that a great start to what should have been a mercy mission? This didn't help find Kym one little bit. Josanne had turned the radio off for a moment. There was a chance she'd hear traffic passing on the road. The second the radio died, silence flooded the car. That silence appeared to bring a wave of cold that made her breath ghost-white. She shivered. A change had taken place in the air. It felt different against her skin, almost heavier, as if it had gradually increased in pressure. Along with that subtle transformation the quality of the silence underwent a change, too. Her mind supplied graphics of the car slipping into a subterranean tunnel. Colder air. Altered sound. The dynamic of the space around her was altering, too. Maybe water had begun to seep into the car's passenger cabin?

Even the seat had lost its upholstered softness. As Josanne turned round to sit up, she put her hands palm-down. No soft fabric now, only a hard, cold surface. A light shone in her face. Ice formed in her heart. That was the sensation. Her center was ice, it pumped freezing slush through her veins.

When did the transition take place? She couldn't say. One minute she sat in the car. The next she sat on the stairs in The Tower. Someone shone a light, but her senses were too detached from her body to react. At least not at first. Only then she saw Jak. The dog shrank back as if afraid of her. Then Fisher was there with a flashlight in his hands.

"Josanne . . ." His voice had seemed far away. A ghosting shell of sound with no substance. It didn't pass through the air to her, but through some other substance. Six feet of grave soil . . .

"Josanne . . . Josanne?"

"Hmm?" She realized Fabian spoke her name. She blinked. Back in the marooned car? In a room filled with water? On the staircase in the dark? In a coffin underground? For a moment she could have been in any of those places. . . .

"Josanne."

She blinked again. Suddenly it was the kitchen that laid claim to reality. The bowl in front of her was empty. She licked her lips and tasted chicken soup. She'd eaten without realizing it.

"Josanne." Fabian smiled at her. "Look, I know you're not feeling well."

"I'm fine," she said, but didn't mean it.

"Can I get you anything else?"

"No, I'm OK. Honestly."

"Belle and Adam have gone to find a telephone.

They're only driving as far as the ferry, so they shouldn't be long."

"Oh . . . Where are the others?"

"Fisher and company? Huh. They've gone on some bloody expedition to the cellar. Tell me, is everyone losing their mind round here?"

"OK." Marko stood in the corridor with his flashlight. "I'm with you on searching the cellar. Does anyone have any idea where the cellar is?"

Sterling shrugged.

Fisher nodded along the corridor. "It'll have been near the original kitchen where the domestic staff could have access to stores. Blaxton said that they were the original cellars to the medieval house." Fisher noticed the way the two caught each other's eye. "Are you siding with Fabian?"

"What do you mean?"

"He thinks I imagined meeting the guy out there on the runway?"

Sterling responded in his typical calm way. "Fisher, if you say you saw a guy called Blaxton, then that's good enough for me."

Marko grinned. "Yeah, me, too. You haven't got the imagination to conjure up a pretend friend."

"Thanks." He found himself smiling. "I'll take that as proof of your everlasting trust in me."

"By the way," Sterling said as they began to walk along the corridor, "what happened to Blaxton?"

"He went to the bottom of the swamp."

"Are you sure?"

"Me? I'm not sure of anything anymore. This is it." He shouldered open the door.

This kitchen had been designed to feed residents

on an industrial scale. The kitchen they'd left behind a few moments before had merely served as a staff lounge where they could cook up snacks or grab coffee on the run. This was a lofty barn of a room with tall windows that glistened with rain. Strips of lights brilliantly lit the place so they didn't need the flashlights yet. Most of the appliances had gone. What was left must have been worthless junk that had been left behind by the vendor.

Marko whistled. "Hey, you could feed a whole battalion here. Look at the size of those walk-in freezers."

"Anything look like a cellar door to anyone?"

"Nope."

"It's not going to be far away. Try at the far end."

They passed by vast sinks that would have been used to wash produce. There were gaps in the counters, revealing expanses of tiled wall where hoses and cables protruded. Probably for the ranks of dishwashers, stoves, plate warmers, mechanical potato peelers—you name it. One old stove remained with enough gas burners for at least a dozen pans. At the end of the kitchen three black doors were set in the wall.

Marko pushed open one with his foot. "The larder from the look of all those shelves."

Sterling pushed another one open. "Hell." He stepped back.

"You've found the cellar?"

"I think it found me. Just come stand here. No, closer. Feel it."

Fisher shuddered. "You've just found the expressway to the North Pole."

"You think there's some refrigeration down there?" White vapor billowed from Marko's mouth.

Fisher gave a grim smile. "Here's a newsflash, gentlemen. Hell's just frozen over."

A crusted old light switch clung to the wall like some diseased mollusk. Half expecting the thing to electrocute him, Fisher beat the switch down with the side of his hand. In the void below, four naked light bulbs offered what light they could muster.

Fisher led the way. At the bottom of the stone steps was a line of upright vacuum cleaners that had been dumped here when they'd outlived their usefulness. Lining the walls were stone shelves. These contained bundles covered with powdery deposits where paint had flaked away from the ceiling.

Sterling pulled a face. "I don't know how long this wiring's going to hold out. Look at it, some of the cable's bare metal. The rubber's rotted off."

"Yeah," Fisher agreed. "Just don't touch anything. It might be live."

"Don't inhale if you can help it either," Marko masked his nostrils with a hand. "Shit . . . I think someone buried a pig down here."

Fisher grimaced. The place stank of rot. "Come on, sooner we're gone the better."

"What are we looking for exactly?"

"A red plastic sack. Blaxton said he dumped a load of audio tapes down here fifteen years ago."

"Sure it'll still be here?"

Marko coughed as the smell settled in his throat. "From the look of it, I don't think anyone's bothered to take out the trash for the last couple of centuries."

As they reached the cellar floor they clicked on their flashlights. Fisher ran the beams over the walls. He didn't look too closely, but he swore he saw a rub-

ber flying mask lying on top of an Air Force uniform.
Or the decomposing remains of one.

"Give me a heads-up if you see rats," Marko called
as he crossed the oozing floor. "I hate rats."

"Fisher? Red sack."

"You've found it?"

"There on the shelf by the stairs. It's been left in a
hurry. It looks as if Blaxton just leaned over the stair
rail and dropped it down onto a pile of old blankets."

For a moment it appeared as a black mound on
mold-covered blankets. However, when Fisher shone
the flashlight on it, he saw a gleam of red as the light
pierced the encrustation of filth.

"OK. Everyone out. I'll grab it."

Marko and Sterling didn't need any more telling.
They quickly climbed the stone steps to the doorway.
Fisher gripped the sack where it had been tied shut
with wire. The contents shifted with a clicking sound.
He thought, I'm probably the first person to touch
the sack since Blaxton dumped it here before he left
fifteen years ago. Hell, left? From what he was saying
he ran like the devil had gotten scent of him.

Within three minutes they'd made it back to the ballroom. They still rubbed their arms where the cellar's
chill clung to their skin like a shroud.

Fisher called to Sterling, "Have you still got that
tape player? The little handheld one?"

"Yeah, but it doesn't kick out much sound."

"No problem. I'll run it through my bass amp.
Marko? Can you bring Fabian? If these tapes still
work, he should be one of the first to hear them."

Marko nodded.

217

Fisher crossed the ballroom. Outside, the darkness was filled with swirling rain. He wished he'd been able to persuade Adam and Belle not to go hunting for a telephone. At least not until daylight. But now he should have persuasive evidence. He dumped the bag on the table, then he pulled out his pocketknife. The plastic had been coated in a crust of dirt that must have dripped from the ceiling. In places, it had built up peaks of some white deposit as if stalagmites had begun to form. It didn't prove to be a hindrance, though. Fisher's sharp blade zipped through the plastic. He upended the bag. Cassettes tumbled out. He ran his fingers over them. All dry. Blaxton had done good work sealing the bag so thoroughly.

"Got it." Sterling returned with a tape deck that was no bigger than a paperback book. He used it mainly to record Marko's drum work so he could practice his own rhythm parts at home. Sterling gazed down at the table. His eyes went wide. "There really were tapes in the sack."

"Yup. Something I couldn't have known if Blaxton hadn't told me."

"I'm not doubting you saw someone who claimed he was called Blaxton." Fabian had arrived. "But whether he manifested himself in a puff of smoke? That's another matter entirely."

"OK, Fabian. Take a seat." Fisher glanced at Sterling. "You've hooked that up to my bass amp before?"

"Sure."

"Use the lead that's already in. You'll need the adapter for the jack plug. There's one in the box with my guitar picks."

"Got it." Sterling went to work, plugging in the

minitape player to the closet-sized amp. He flicked a power button. Speakers in the amp began to hum.

Josanne shadowed Fabian. She looked more herself now, apart from a reluctance to stray too far from her lover. Noticing the activity, she asked, "What's happening?"

Fabian answered with a lordly wave of his hand, "Fisher's putting on a show for us. Isn't that right, Fisher, old boy?"

"Wait and hear it for yourself."

"Adam will be back with battalions of police before you've done fiddling with those tapes."

Fisher merely grunted. Suddenly time seemed too valuable to waste it arguing with Fabian. Blaxton had methodically written details on the boxed tapes that had been used in the ghost hunt of fifteen years before. There were locations within the house, dates, times, whether the tape machine had been left to record alone or with people present. For a moment Fisher turned over the tape cassettes as if he were sorting dominos. *OK, which one do I play first? The answer's obvious. They're all numbered.*

A moment later he turned up tape number one. "Alright." He held it up. "Here goes."

Fabian assented with a nod. "I'll give you five minutes, then I'm opening a bottle of wine."

Marko came in with a mug of coffee.

Fisher glanced across at him. "Any sign of Adam and Belle?"

"Not back yet." Accompanying Marko was the dog. He was sticking close to people, too. There was something about this place that didn't encourage solitary wandering.

Fisher handed the tape to Sterling, who clicked it into the deck. "Hit 'play' whenever you're ready, Sterling."

"Three, two, one. Go." Sterling thumbed the "play" button. The bass amp hummed. Clicks followed by a scraping noise came from the speakers. It could have been the amplified sound of someone positioning a microphone stand.

Fisher nodded. "This was recorded here fifteen years ago." With rain tapping at the windows they listened to the whispered voice.

Did you hear that? Can you hear the noise? A kind of hiss . . . in and out, in and out . . . almost the sound of someone breathing. Only it's different, like . . .

No. It's gone again. Yeah, but you're like that, aren't you, house? You big old ugly pile of rock. First it's the sounds, you bang all the doors, and then it's the clock chimes. You're inventive with those, aren't you? But I'm not letting you get the better of me. I'm staying. Did you hear that, house? I'm staying. So, go on! Do your worst!

You're right. I should have kept my mouth shut. You should never goad anyone to do their worst. Not a drunk in a bar. Not a policeman. Not God. Not even this damned house. Because, the moment you make that challenge—go on, do your worst—that's exactly what they do. And sometimes it can be far worse than you imagine. Rather than sitting here shouting futile threats at the walls, I should be explaining what happened to me over the last three days.

OK, so I'll take it from the top. My name is Chris Blaxton. I'm twenty-three years old. I'm sitting here alone in a house called The Tower. And here I am in what was once an elegant ballroom with windows looking out over a garden that's now grown into this wild, wild jungle. Not that I can see much of it. It's nighttime. And, yeah, dear God, this is the worst part—when it grows dark. All dark and black and hidden, and the place is swamped by shadows that just ooze through the rooms like they're alive.

Enough. Once you begin brooding about how alone you are in this place and visualize what it's like in all those empty rooms, your imagination starts to eat you alive. Right. I'm sitting at a table that's big enough to seat twenty people. The tape deck is in front of me; the mic's in my hand. I'm going to make this record of what I did just in case I never get the chance to tell you in person. Three nights ago I left video cameras running in the ballroom, with more in the Promenade and at the foot of the main stairs. What I saw on the tapes when I played them back was enough to . . . well . . . What I saw is going to be the starting point for this . . . document? Testament? Diary?

Oh? And didn't I tell you I'm now alone in the house? I did, didn't I?

I thought I was. But what you believe and what is true isn't always necessarily one and the same thing. There! Listen! I don't know if you heard that. . . . I'm sure there's someone walking along the corridor to the ballroom. So . . . what do you do at a time like this? Run like hell and not look back? Or open the door? See who it is?

But this is The Tower. A house where its occupants don't always wear a human face.

Chapter Twenty-six

Josanne listened to the recorded voice rumble through the amplifier. In the spaces between words the hiss of static sounded like bone ash being poured into an urn.

And here we sit in a solitary house, she thought. The five of us listening to the tape. The Tower's a lonely pile of black rock in the middle of nowhere. All around are clumps of miserable trees. Does the sun ever shine here? I can't imagine for a moment it does. Rain, swamp, fields of mud. She shivered. The house had all the morbid ugliness of a skull picked clean of skin and hair. Even the concrete runway resembled the gray spine of some primeval beast. A sense of detachment sidled through her. This part of the world could have broken away to drift into some dark abyss. Morbid thoughts. Dear God, they were morbid thoughts. But just as some houses have walls that draw damp from the cold wet earth, so morbid thoughts might seep through the stonework before migrating through the dank air to settle on her skin.

She shivered again. Her eyes were drawn to her watch. The time was ten forty-five. In another fifteen minutes the chimes would sound again. They rang out as punctually as death. . . .

Josanne rubbed her cold arms. *See what I mean by morbid thoughts. . . .*

Now the grave voice of the stranger emerged from the speaker. There was no echo. The walls of the ballroom hungrily devoured every syllable. *"Listen, house, you're not going to make me crack. I can take it. Do you hear me? I can take anything you throw at me. . . ."* The voice ended there, but the tape continued. Josanne heard the respiration of the man. The pronounced rasp as his lungs drew the stale air of the house into his lungs, then expelled it again. As if there was precious little oxygen in the atmosphere, he appeared to breathe harder. The cycle of respiration grew quicker. In her mind's eye she saw Blaxton, then a young man of twenty-three, sitting here in The Tower. He'd issued his challenge to the tomb of a building. He'd invited it to do its worst. Attack me or leave me alone, he seemed to be saying. Blaxton goaded it to put up or shut up. So this unseen thing that approached him as he sat in the ballroom? Did Blaxton wait for it to reveal itself? Or did his nerve break? Did he close his eyes and bury his face in his hands, and wait until it had gone? Josanne found her eyes drawn to the amplifier. The foot-wide round speaker in its center gripped her attention. She had to wait here, listening to the sound of that amplified breathing recorded fifteen years ago. She braced herself. Any second now the man would shout out what he saw. Josanne clenched her fists. She bit down against her teeth so hard her jaw ached. An involuntary need to stare at the open mouth of the speaker kept her eyelids pulled back. In her reflection in the window she saw her frozen face. Her eyes stared in a horror of anticipation. The sound of respiration grew louder. Then: *click!* The recording ended. It left that drizzle sound, as if hard, dry particles pittered down onto an equally hard surface.

Fisher nodded to Sterling, who switched off the tape recorder. All that remained was the faint hum of the amp.

"OK." Fabian nodded. "You have the tapes. You met a guy on the old runway."

"You believe me now?"

"I can accept I've just listened to a tape made by someone called Blaxton. But what has all this got to do with us? We're putting a band together here."

"It is important, Fabian. Hell, that guy explained what happened to him and his friends when they came here to make a TV program fifteen years ago."

Fabian reacted with a prickly defensiveness. "Fifteen years ago? Who the hell cares?"

Sterling spoke calmly but he put some force into the words, "Fabian, listen to what Fisher has to say."

Marko added, "For crying out loud, man, you know something's been happening here. I mean, where's Kym, for God's sake?"

"Alright. Tell us everything, Fisher." Fabian sat back down with his arms folded. "Because in the next twenty-four hours we've got to decide whether to continue working here or cancel everything. And I mean everything. The rehearsal, the recording studio—because when we turn up there, you lot won't know the fucking songs."

Rain tapped at the window. For a moment Josanne

anticipated that Fisher would simply walk out. Instead he took a deep breath. The guy was angry, but he'd made up his mind to see this through.

"OK, I'll tell you what Blaxton told me. If you've got any questions, wait until I've finished. Even then I won't have answers. Blaxton ran out of time." He looked round at the others. Josanne managed a nod. She didn't want to hear this, but she had to. God knew she had to. For a second she saw herself twisting in the maelstrom of floodwater, her mouth open to admit a rush of water into her lungs. Marko and Sterling nodded, too, their expressions serious. Jak went to Marko to rest his head on his knee. Fabian gave one of his "OK, whatever" shrugs.

Fisher spoke matter-of-factly. From the disquiet burning in his eyes, Josanne knew he told the truth. "When Blaxton arrived here fifteen years ago with the production team, they were a lot like us. In their twenties, ambitious. They were alone here in the house. Like us. The bottom line is, they experienced dreams. . . . Only they were more than dreams: to them it seemed like real experience. And to give it to you all straight: they experienced their own deaths. They were violent deaths. It happened like this: As they saw the vision of their own death, they heard the chimes of the clock. We've all heard them. We know what they sound like. Blaxton's friends heard the same. One saw himself falling from the roof of The Tower. A few hours later it happened. Blaxton witnessed it. A girl told him she'd dreamt she wrecked her car and was trapped in it when it caught fire. As it burned with her in it, she could hear the chimes of the clock. The day after that she tried to drive away." He shrugged. "She never made it." Fisher looked into their faces. "Blaxton told me he dreamt he died out there in the marsh. The last I saw of him he was running into the mist. After that I heard him screaming." Fisher rubbed his face as if muscle tension had locked him up tight. "Nothing more to tell, guys. It happens as simply as that. Blaxton described the vision as a 'death dream.' You have the dream. You hear the chimes. A few hours later you hear the chimes again. Then you die."

"Wait," Sterling said. "You said Blaxton made the recording fifteen years ago?"

"Sure."

"But then he didn't die within hours of having this death dream?"

"Like I said, Sterling. I won't have answers. I don't know the mechanics of it."

Fabian stood up to run his hands through his hair. "You realize what you're saying, Fisher? That people who come to this house suffer some kind of curse. Then once they're hexed, they die."

"OK. You want theory, Fabian? How about this? Ten thousand years ago a pagan temple stood here! The local inhabitants got pissed off with their god, somehow they trapped him and cut out his heart, and then they buried it right here. Then ten thousand years later, some crazy son of a bitch built a house slap bang on top of it. You're shaking your head, Fabian? Don't you believe me? OK, how about the God-fearing people burned a witch here, and she curses the lord of the manor with her dying breath. No, not good enough for you?"

"Fisher—"

"How about this for a theory—Fabian, sit down and listen! You wanted fucking theories. Theory number three is that this was a burial site for plague victims. No? Is that too much a throwaway TV horror movie for you? Stay there, Fabian. I'll spin you more theories. This house was a U.S. Air Force base in World War Two. How about the Nazi secret weapon theory? This is a doozy. Hitler and Goebbels are Satanists. They're into all this black magic shit. So they open up their Big Bad Book of Spells and put a hex on the place. Everyone who walks through the fucking door, gets a fucking curse on their head. One of the indelible kind. You can shower all fucking day in holy water and you'll never scrub it off. Fabian . . . Fabian?"

Fabian walked to the door. "I'm not listening to this, Fisher. You're a jerk." He turned to jab his finger at him. "In fact, consider yourself sacked from the band."

Sterling spoke up. "Hey, calm it down, guys."

"Tell it to Fisher. You saw him. He was taking the bloody piss."

"I wasn't." Fisher's voice rose in frustration. "I'm trying to warn you. There aren't any glib theories to explain it. There's no old burial ground or voodoo curse. It's what happens here."

"Josanne." Fabian spoke coldly. "Are you coming back to the room with me?"

"Ignore theory," Fisher demanded. "Stick to the facts. I dreamt, or hallucinated—whatever you want to call it—that the building collapsed on me. I believed it killed me. Last night, Kym came to my room—and you might as well know this, we fucked around—but afterwards she told me that when the electric shock knocked her out, she saw herself being stabbed to death. She even described the guy who murdered her. He was weird and scruffy looking with a scar here." He touched his forehead. "Now Kym's missing, and the guy she described is the same as the guy in the woods, Cantley."

Marko and Sterling exchanged uneasy glances. Fabian stood perfectly still. A tic had started at the corner of his mouth.

Fisher sounded exhausted now. "We've been through this before, Josanne. But tell Fabian what you dreamt when you were alone in your room."

Josanne stiffened. Memories of that violent inrush of water still possessed a savage presence in her consciousness. Even as she opened her mouth to speak, her lungs felt suddenly stifled, as if there wasn't enough air in them to give voice to the recollection. Worse, there didn't seem enough air in them to feed her body with oxygen. She looked at their faces as they waited. They expected her to speak. She glanced at Fabian. Whatever she said now would determine their future together.

"God almighty, you can forget leaving!"

Everyone snapped their heads in the direction of the piercing voice. A hooded figure strode into the room. A hand gripped the hood to pull it back, while a free arm shook away drops of water. Belle's haughty face appeared. It was unsmiling.

"I've never seen rain like it," she thundered. "It's bouncing so hard against the ground you can't even see the road." She noticed the charged atmosphere of the room. "What's wrong? Am I interrupting an orgy?"

Sterling asked, "Did you find the phone?"

"Did we find a phone?" Adam breezed in. He'd grabbed a towel to dry his hair. "Did we find a phone?

We couldn't even find the damn road to the ferry. The blasted rain's so heavy, you can't see twenty feet in front of you."

"Besides, the one road we did try had been flooded out. If the others are like that, we need to paddle out of here in canoes. Dear heaven! Look at my shoes. My mother bought me these from Harvey Nicks. She'd go crackerjack if she saw the state of them, absolutely bloody crackerjack."

Josanne said in a flat voice, "We're trapped."

Belle harrumphed. "Don't bank on popping out for cocktails while this lot is teeming down."

Adam finished rubbing his hair. "This place is low-lying; just keep your fingers crossed it doesn't flood." On the word "flood," the hidden clock struck eleven. Its chimes shimmered out of secret channels buried in the walls that carried the sound from the Good Heart. The metallic resonance pressed down from the stale air, tolling promises of ominous intent. As the final chime clung to the void of the ballroom as if reluctant to decay and die as a chime should, Belle gave a visible shudder.

"That reminds me," she said. "You know, we were in the car for so long, I fell asleep. I had the most god-awful dream.

Adam clucked his tongue. "Tell me about it. She screamed so loud I nearly rammed the car up a tree."

Belle continued, "I dreamt that this evil-smelling man stabbed me. It was awful. I could really feel the blade being pushed through my skin." She gestured at the ceiling. "And as he killed me all I could hear were those damn chimes." Belle stared back at the people in the room. "Why is everyone looking at me like that? What have I said?"

Chapter Twenty-seven

Eleven o'clock came and went. The chimes didn't fail to remind them all that another hour had pushed them sixty minutes closer to the grave. Fisher repeated to Adam and Belle what he'd told Fabian and the others: all about Blaxton, about what the man had called the "death dream." And the fact that when Blaxton heard the chimes, he panicked, that he ran into the marsh. Fisher didn't doubt that the man had heard those same doom-laden chimes thundering inside his head as he was sucked down into the mud to drown. Now there was a sense of free-fall, as if they'd fallen from the top of a skyscraper. This was the uncanny in-between time, between parting company from the safety of the building and the shattering collision with the earth.

So there's seven of us left, he told himself. And until the rain eases we're trapped here in The Tower.

Outside, the spring rain had turned to sleet. Even though it was dark, Fisher could make out lawns with a crusting of white. It wasn't the pristine fresh whiteness of snow, but a grayish dirty white. More like the off-white of mold growing on a decaying tree trunk. For a while, Fisher and the rest shifted between kitchen and ballroom. The moment you arrived at the ballroom, the kitchen seemed a better place to be. Only the instant you walked through the kitchen door, the ballroom became a preferable destination. Fisher told himself, it's going to be a long, long night. . . .

By half past eleven Fisher mooched back to the ballroom. He'd picked up his bass guitar from his room first. He didn't have a plan in mind. However, to walk with the guitar in his hand recaptured a little of that childhood comfort of climbing the stairs to bed while gripping a teddy bear. He found the ballroom to be empty. The others were probably opening wine bottles in the kitchen. They were trying to find their own safe platform over the fathomless abyss that appeared to be widening beneath their feet. As he plugged the lead into the bass, he recapped what Belle had told them. She'd fallen asleep in the car. Then came a nightmare: hearing the chimes as she watched a stranger plunge a blade into her flesh. Belle's eyes had widened as she described the agony. And all the time, those damn chimes.

Fisher pulled a wooden chair toward him. Instead of sitting on it, he rested his foot on it so his knee was raised. Lovingly, he sat the female-shaped body of the Rickenbacker on his lap. The fingers of his left hand pressed taut steel strings to the frets. Then with his right hand he thumbed a string. The deep sound thudded from the speaker. It didn't so much enter his ears as nudge his stomach in a way that was nothing less than muscular. He sighed. This felt like a release from the madness. With the guitar in his hands he sensed he could take control of his life again. He ran through old bluesy bass lines. The ordered progression of notes stroked his nerves. They soothed him. Tense muscles unknotted in his shoulders. Fisher filled the room with velvety notes. They ran through the air like heartbeats, an antidote to the metallic hardness of the clock chimes. The bass notes were so deep that he felt them in his chest and stomach. He allowed his eyes to close as his own heart opened up to the mellow sound. When he opened his eyes again, he saw Marko watching him from the door. Fisher didn't stop playing. The music dampened down anxieties. The structure of the notes shaped his own thoughts; they imposed order where there had been disorder. There was something beautifully sane about the simple melody he played. He'd never even noticed Marko move, but when he heard the tap of the stick against the hi-hat, he glanced back. Marko sat on the stool behind the drum kit. He tapped a simple rhythm to compliment Fisher's bass line. Marko smiled and nodded. They were back in the saddle again, they were doing what they loved.

What's that saying? Fisher asked himself. A band of musicians is greater than the total sum of its parts. His and Marko's old kinship reasserted itself. Every so often they made eye contact, maybe exchanged a nod. They were flying in formation now. A moment later Sterling appeared. Instead of the guitar, he carried his sax. When the spirit moved him, he could play that shining instrument of sculpted brass with such soul that Fisher had seen people shed a tear. Now that the three were playing together, Fisher could sense their power impose itself on their world.

This felt so good. He experienced the melting sense of release that came when he played without consciously directing his fingers.

Sterling used a light touch on the finger keys. Gentle notes sighed from the flared horn of the saxophone. Next Adam drifted in with his electric guitar. He plugged in, switched on. If he harbored ambitions to be the band's shining star, he didn't reveal them now. Tonight he was content to sit on the floor against the amplifier and play muted chords on the guitar. Adam didn't dictate the pace or the mood of the music. He fell in step with the other three to play an introspective improvisation around Fisher's bass line. As they played, Belle and Josanne drifted in. They sat on the sofa to listen to the music. Their expressions were calm; the melody had the power to soothe jangled nerves. Even Jak curled up on the rug beside the sofa. Those amber eyes were relaxed as he watched the musicians play. This was his pack now. He belonged to it; he felt at ease.

Fisher glanced up to see Fabian standing in the doorway. Fabian watched for a long time before he made a move. At last he stepped up to his keyboards. He said nothing. For once he buried his ego out of sight. Setting the volume low, he played gentle runs on the piano. The sound conjured images of drops of water falling from melting icicles. The music filled a room with positive, life-enhancing energy. It empowered musicians and audience of two alike. This was tapping into a primal force. For thousands of years music had forged bonds between individuals. It lifts hearts. It energizes. Fisher closed his eyes. The instruments magically combined to create a living being of pure sound. That was how it felt to him. A vital entity that had its own rhythmic heartbeat enclosed by a body of musical notes. Feel the energy. This entity has its own melodic voice. That was why he wanted to be a musician. When he wasn't playing, he was simply going through the motions until he could play his bass again and revel in the life force that sizzled through his veins.

The chimes that mourned the passing of twelve o'clock must have sounded. This time Fisher didn't hear them. Neither did anyone else.

By midnight, the hail rode the north wind. White, twisting veils emerged from the darkness to strike the windows. Fortunately, the heating system kicked out plenty of warm air, so the ballroom was a comfortable place to be. The music they played together had been a welcome respite. Now they were relaxed enough to wind the day to a close.

As they switched off the amps, Sterling said, "We might be able to make better sense of all this in the morning."

Adam nodded. "In the cool light of day. Yeah, I'm all for that." He headed for the door with the guitar in one hand, while Belle linked arms with him. "Good night, one and all," he said in that faux gentleman way of his.

Fabian gave a thumbs-up. "Sweet dreams."

Marko sauntered away with his drumsticks under his arm. He waved a good-night. Jak followed him out of the room.

Fabian pulled the covers over his keyboards. Josanne unplugged the amps at the mains. Everyone had developed a safety-first mentality over the past forty-eight hours.

"Fisher?" The expression on Fabian's face was nowhere near as hostile as it had been. "I guess what you've told us, and played for us—" he nodded at the tapes on the table "—have given us all food for thought."

"That's a classic example of understatement," Josanne said with feeling.

Fabian sniffed. "Well, my good people, as the ever trustworthy Sterling Pound so rightly declared: perhaps we can all make better sense of death dreams, curses, hexes and the like in the morning."

"You still don't believe me, do you, Fabian?"

"Look Fisher. We've had a difficult day. Everyone's dog tired . . . Josanne?" He held out his hand to her. "Oh, Fisher? Consider yourself unsacked by the way. I was being unforgivably tetchy."

Again that lordly manner reasserted itself. Fisher felt as if he were being tossed a favor by a passing nobleman. Fabian continued in cut-glass English accents, "Might as well turn in now, old boy."

"You want more proof?"

"What I don't want is to beat this particular dead horse."

Josanne was curious. "What have you got?"

"And I'm not listening to any more of those old audio tapes tonight." Fabian waved a dismissive hand. "Anyone could have faked those."

"No. What if I said . . ." Fisher turned from one to the other. "What if I said you could watch a video recording that proved everything?"

Josanne gripped Fabian's hand. "Please, Fabian. I need to see it."

He nodded. "OK, Fisher. Show us your proof."

Chapter Twenty-eight

"Make yourselves comfortable." Fisher nodded at the bed. Fabian and Josanne sat down side by side. The tick-tick of sleet hitting the window was the only other sound apart from their muted voices. Fisher switched on the TV. It fizzed white sparkles on a dead channel. He pulled the video tape out of its case. "Remember when I asked to borrow the camera earlier today, Josanne?"

She nodded.

Fabian asked, "Didn't you have plans to catch whoever jerked around with our instruments this morning?"

"That was the plan. But watch this." He slotted the tape into camera, then thumbed "play" on the control panel. "I hope you don't mind, Josanne. I'm using your camera as a player."

She shook her head. With a tense expression, she asked, "What did you film?"

"See for yourself."

Just as when he'd watched before, the image appeared of the ballroom with the amplifiers lined up in a wall of upright oblongs. Standing in the center was his bass guitar. There were fleeting glances of Fisher as he finished setting up the camera to run, then Fabian asking off-camera, "You're not going to lock the Rickenbacker in your room?" Then Fisher's reply, "Bait."

They sat for twenty minutes. The image held steady on the bass guitar standing in front of the amps. No sound came from the TV speaker. There wasn't so much as flicker of movement.

So, he asked himself, what happened to the camera rushing down the corridor to find me in the Good Heart? What happened to the scene of me being crushed by something invisible?

Fabian yawned, then check his watch. "Well, Fisher?"

"I don't understand."

Josanne's eyes held his. They were trusting. She believed. "There was something on the tape? I mean, something more than what we're seeing now?"

Fisher nodded. "A hell of a lot more."

"So?" Fabian prompted.

"So it's not there now. It's gone!" Fisher slammed his hand against the wall. "It's this house. It's tricked us. It's always tricking us!"

He saw Fabian exchange glances with Josanne. Meanwhile sleet made the tap-tap sound against the pane as it floated out of the night sky to make contact with The Tower.

After Josanne and Fabian had returned to their own room, Fisher replayed the tape. There was a perfect view of his Rickenbacker bass in its livery of warm yellow melting into an orange surround. He could even make out the subtle grain of the rosewood fingerboard. Only there was this problem: the view remained static. It didn't present the same turbulent images that Fisher had seen the first time around. No wild flight down the corridor to the medieval core of the building. Neither was there the high-level shot looking down on Fisher when an invisible mass smashed down to destroy his face in a crimson burst of blood. When the tape ended, Fisher sat on the bed to brood. Perfidious tape. Treacherous tape. The Tower had made a fool of him in front of Fabian and Josanne. The atmosphere of the room was charged. He was aware of the tons of masonry above him. The crossed beams of the timbers helped it all defy gravity, yet there was a sense of all that accumulated downward pressure. Even the air locked away in all those silent rooms above him added to the ominous mass. The darkness, too. Darkness to the house was like blood to the human body. It ran thick in those arteries of the building, its corridors. It pooled blackly in the cellar. When a light was extinguished, it flooded into the cavity. Darkness oozed through the building. He glared at the walls. He defied the house to hurt him. But he knew it was waiting now. For the right moment . . .

Marko made Jak's bed out of a hill of pillows in the corner of the room. He saw how Jak turned round three times before lying down. If by chance the dog made contact with the wall, he flinched away from it as if its touch was unpleasant. Marko pulled back the covers of his own bed and climbed in.

"Don't worry, boy," he told the dog. "We'll soon be away from here."

Jak fixed his eyes on the man.

"We'll sleep now, then we'll tell Fabian we're packing up in the morning and going home."

The dog wagged his tail.

"Are you coming home with me, old feller?"

The dog gave a single bark as he wagged his tail even harder.

"That's the answer that I wanted to hear." Marko grinned. "Hear that house, you ugly heap of crap? We're leaving you tomorrow. You can rot in peace." Marko switched off the light. "Good night, Jak." He lay there in the dark. It's something about this house, he thought, even the darkness is heavy. I can feel it pressing against my eyelids. Feels like fingertips . . .

In the next room, Fabian made love to Josanne. She continually marveled how he could compartmentalize situations. It was as if the today's events had never happened. For her, however, memory nagged. A few hours before, she had been marooned in the lake. Then she opened her eyes to find herself sitting on the central staircase in the house. Kym had vanished. Fisher had played them the tape recorded by the Blaxton guy. Then there was talk about this hex.

"Lift your legs higher," Fabian ordered. "That's it." He pushed into her. She looked up at his throat as it reddened with exertion. Veins stood out from the skin. The Adam's apple moved like some bulbous animal through its burrow. She wasn't in the mood, but Fabian was different. He'd been brought up in the African city of Khartoum, the son of wealthy expats.

Fabian had lived among a coterie of English noble-men who continued to live on in Africa as if the British Empire had never withered away. Fabian had grown up with the same lordly manner that mani-fested itself as reserve at best and arrogant disdain at worst. As he thrust his hips against her body she thought, that's my curse. I'm attracted to those char-acteristics. They're indicators of power. And power over people is erotic. I wish I didn't find his manner enticing, but there you go. I do. And there isn't a thing I can do about it.

Fabian squeezed her breast. This gave him enough pleasure to make him sigh. Still he didn't look down into her eyes as he thrust into her. He stared at the wall in front of him, his eyes blazing at it as though it was the most fascinating thing in the world.

Look at me, Fabian. I want you to look at me.

He jerked hard enough to shake the bed and grunted as his respiration quickened. At that mo-ment the clock struck one. The chime pealed through the room.

Fabian paused. She watched his head turn as he lis-tened to the metallic reverberation slowly fade back into the walls. "My God. It's time someone killed that bloody clock."

The interruption piqued him enough to discharge his anger into Josanne with a dozen hard thrusts into her that knocked the air out of her lungs.

Adam drank the glass of red wine as Belle sat naked in front of the mirror to brush her hair. As they heard the single chime of one o'clock, they paused to look up. In The Tower, it was easy to imagine the metallic note manifesting itself in the air above their bed.

When the reverberations died away, Belle examined the reflection of Adam. He flicked back his long hair with his fingers before taking another sip from the glass.

"You shouldn't be drinking red, you know?" Belle told him. "It stains the teeth."

"Hell, I need something to make me sleep."

"Do you want out of here?"

Fabian shrugged. "I liked those demos that Fabian played me. They've got commercial potential, you know?"

"You think so?" Belle studied the man in the mirror. He was good-looking, but she suspected those fine features might be fleeting. And, make no bones about it, show business is the profession where your face really is your fortune.

Adam drained the glass, then poured himself another from the bottle on the nightstand. "But from that look in your eye, Belle, I can see you think otherwise."

"The songs have potential. A good producer will smooth out the rough parts. . . ."

"But?"

"Do you really think Fabian's got the killer instinct?"

"Killer instinct?"

"He must get the rest of those musicians working hard all day and every day before they play like a band."

"A lot of shit hit the fan today, Belle."

"You know what Napoleon asked people when he was thinking of promoting a general?"

"You do love your history books, Belle." He grinned as he raised the glass to his lips. "What did Napoleon ask, dear formidable old Belle?"

"Before Napoleon put a general in charge of fighting a battle he never wanted to know about the man's qualifications. The only thing he asked was, 'Is he lucky?' "

"Lucky? You're becoming profound in your old age, dear thing."

"Adam, I don't think Fabian is lucky."

Adam took a deep swallow of wine. "After what's happened since we arrived here, you might well be right."

She walked across to Adam as he lay there half-asleep on the bed. Deliberately she allowed her hips to sway so they caught his eye. And as he sipped wine from the glass, she gently stroked his head. "I'll brush your hair before you sleep. I don't want this lousy damp to dull it." She eased herself onto the bed beside him so that her bare breast pressed against his shoulder. Slowly she inhaled deeply to increase the pressure of her body against his. A subtle move. It worked, though. Adam moved his hand so it rested against her inner thigh.

"You know, Adam?"

"Hmm?"

"When we reach a phone, it might be worth giving your agent a call. He mentioned there's a band needing a genius on guitar and vocals."

Adam shrugged. "They're just wanting some bloody metro-gnome to play rhythm. I play lead. Amazing lead. I'm not chugging chords for any fucker."

"I know, darling." She kissed his forehead. "But I can help them decide what they really need is the best guitarist in the world." She kissed him again. "You." She stroked his hair. "Besides, they've already had a top-twenty album. Fabian's still to get his feet wet in the top one hundred."

Drowsily he murmured, "I'll think about it."

Her voice grew husky as she whispered between kisses. "A little, hmm . . . phone . . . call . . . can't hurt . . . can it?" Gently she eased the covers from his body with one hand while her lips touched his nose, chin and throat as they worked their way down to his chest.

Sterling Pound sat with his back to the wall of his room. He played the saxophone so quietly that the gentle notes sounded more like a breathy voice. He told himself to stop playing. But he'd drifted into a near-comatose state. He couldn't stop if he tried. The phrasing of the instrument became the channel for an alien tongue that muttered from the glittering horn. The origin of the sound no longer came from Sterling's lips and through the reed in the mouthpiece. Instead it came ghosting from a cavity beneath the earth where a monstrous hatred for all things human remorselessly increased in pressure until it would erupt in a fury of hatred and destruction. And when the blind clock in the Good Heart struck twice, something of that toxic passion sank into the body of the metallic note. It deformed its tone. The vibration reached such an intensity of pitch that everyone who heard it in the house covered their ears. They grimaced as the sound jagged at their nerves with the same kind of pain a dentist's drill causes when it rips into the nerve of the root canal. Then the chime's echo rolled through the stale air toward The Tower's medieval core. The echo that had all the harsh finality of a tomb door slamming shut refused to fade. It rushed through the dark hollows of the house in a thickening pulse of sound. No walls blocked it. The furnishings did nothing to dampen its guttural resonance.

The black dog sitting upright on his bed snapped his teeth at the sound as it passed by. If only Jak could talk. He knew the signs of approaching danger. . . .

Chapter Twenty-nine

"You haven't been listening, have you?"

He spoke without turning from his file of oh-so-precious song lyrics—*those lyrics*—that were going to earn Fabian a fortune.

Josanne sighed. "Haven't been listening to what?"

"I told you to keep out of the cellar."

"The cellar?" Frowning, she shook her head. "Fabian, I've been nowhere near the cellar."

"No?" He stroked the song sheets as if they were some bloody pet. "Are you sure?

Irritated, she glared out the window. "Of course I'm sure." The setting sun channelled blood reds over the marsh. Its trees were all twisted man-shapes with clutching hands.

"Oh, Josanne, Josanne, Josanne . . ." Fabian spoke in such a gloating way that she shivered. "What are we going to do with a girl like you?"

"Fabian, what the hell's wrong with you? I've been nowhere near the bloody cellar."

"No?"

"No!"

"So where do you think you are right now?"

Josanne turned away from the window, ready to chew Fabian out. But instead of seeing Fabian fondling his beloved songs, she saw the festering brickwork of ancient vaults. The place was dimly lit by four naked lightbulbs hanging by cords from the ceiling. For a century this grim, damp cellar full of shadows had been a dumping ground for unwanted property. On stone shelves were moldering airmen's uniforms. Ones that Josanne somehow knew had never been collected because the crews hadn't made it back from their bombing missions alive. Old upright vacuum cleaners stood against one wall beneath white shrouds of spiderweb. There was something pitiful and shrunken about the abandoned Hoovers. And now in the uncertain light of the cellar they looked less like electrical appliances than dwarfish creatures standing mummified there in the gloom.

Get out of here, Josanne, get out. . . . That voice in her head was as insistent as the one that asked how she'd got down here. She'd been talking to Fabian in the bedroom when all of a sudden she'd been—

What? Transported here?

How? By magic? Give me a break. . . . *Or sleepwalking? That must be it. After what happened today, is it surprising I'm sleepwalking? And I'm wearing pajamas, so that explains how I got down here.*

But the cellar? Why sleepwalk down into the cellar?

OK, so get out. That thought had come sharply enough. She started to move back along through the tunnel-like vault, her heart thumping. God, it was so cold down here; she could see her breath spurting in white clouds from her mouth. And that smell . . . It made her think of meat that was long past its best. She breathed through her mouth to divert the air from her nostrils. . . . Hell, that's worse. She could taste the decay now. Moving faster, she headed for the cellar steps. Josanne needed company right now. Being down here was scaring the wits out of her. Nearly there. She saw the end of the cellar. Ahead was the mold-covered wall. So that's where the stairs would have to be . . . where they should be. She stopped dead, her heart beating painfully and her frightened breathing surging in her ears.

"Oh no . . ." The words fell from her lips. This was the first time she'd been down into this grim subterranean vault. What she thought was the route to the stairs and back into the house was in reality the path deeper into the cellar. There were no stairs here, no welcoming doorway to the kitchen. She'd have to turn round and walk back the other way. Instantly her skin became gooseflesh beneath her nightclothes. A cold, wet tongue of air licked around her bare ankles.

I'm not going to make it back, she told herself as a sense of dread oozed into her. I'm not going to get out of here. For a moment she stood as still as stone. Her heart pounded against her ribs, a doom-laden rhythm that went throbbing through her stomach to continue down into the rock slabs beneath her feet. She imagined the huge beat of terror spreading out through the floor that seemed to feed on the electric lights, draining their radiance away into the roots of the house. The lightbulbs flickered as if struggling to make up for the loss of illumination—but this damp, shadow-haunted vault was winning the fight. Josanne shivered to the pit of her bones.

Josanne thought, the house knows I'm down here.

It can hear my heartbeat. She reached out to touch a wall that wept moisture from the nearby swamp. For a moment she believed she felt the heartbeat of the house flutter beneath the brickwork. *The Tower is alive. It knows where I am. Just like a viper knows when a child is close . . . Get out of here, get out, get out. . . .* In her head the words flashed like lightning. She had to escape. Now! But as she ran through the vaulted passageways back to where she hoped the stairs would be, she realized she was too late.

One by one, the electric light bulbs dimmed and then slowly died.

She didn't stop. She blundered forward through the dark, her crabbed hands feeling along the cold, wet brick. God willing, in a few moments her fingers would close around the stair rail. Her toes might slam against the bottom step. *But who cares, who gives a damn!* She'd climb the stairs in five seconds flat, then she'd be free of this suffocating grave of a place. And why stop at the kitchen? She'd grab her car keys and drive home. Once she was a hundred miles from The Tower, she'd feel safe again.

With the darkness as deep as that of any grave pressing against her eyes, she lurched through the icy wash of air. The only sound was the thud of her heart and the hiss of her own breathing. Nearly there, surely she must be nearly there, please God. This cellar couldn't run underground forever, could it? Any second now she must—

There! Her hand struck something hard. The spindle of the banister. She must have found the staircase. Running her fingertips up the spindle she found the stair rail and began to climb.

Chapter Thirty

The mood Adam was in, he'd drink what was left of the red wine when he woke up in the morning. With the time nudging toward three, she decided to return it to the kitchen. Belle was mindful that Adam shouldn't coarsen his voice by downing too much liquor. What's more, there was the problem of wine staining his teeth. Teeth and hair were Adam's assets as much as his strong singing voice. Belle knew the combination was enough to make them rich and catapult them into the media spotlight—something they both craved. She was pragmatic enough to recognize that need; he thought he worked for the integrity of the music, but he loved the attention of fans as much as anyone. Maybe it ran in the family, she thought with a flash of cynicism. After all, Adam's father was an Anglican bishop.

Adam would be annoyed if she simply tipped the bottle down the sink, so that short trip to the kitchen was a necessity after all. She donned her red silk robe—it was cold as chilled water against her skin—then trotted barefoot out of the room to the kitchen. It lay just twenty paces down the corridor to the right. Cool air washed around her bare calves. The lights burned dimly tonight. Then again, it was a bloody miracle that electricity made it through the power lines to this Godforsaken backwater anyway. A yawn overtook her. She was three-quarters asleep. Way down at the end of the corridor, the entrance hall was a clump of shadows that hid the staircase to the tower.

I wonder what it's like up there, she asked herself as she opened the kitchen door. Just picture it. A big gloomy, ghostly tower. Morbid stairs. Dolorous windows. A balustrade of stone ribs. No doubt a human skull over every bedroom door. Perfect scare territory. But not tonight, my dear. Time for your beauty sleep.

When she hit the light switch, the fluorescents flickered on with a brilliance that made her narrow her eyes. She crossed the kitchen floor to open the refrigerator and pushed the bottle to the back of the shelf, then piled blocks of cheese in front of it to conceal it from Adam. OK, so he wasn't a lush. But boys would be boys.

Chilled air from the refrigerator encircled her thighs. The red silk dressing gown didn't have the thickness to keep out the cold. A shiver rippled down her spine. *For heaven's sake, girl, get to back to bed where it's warm.* The thought prompted her to move faster. After closing the refrigerator door, her bare feet carried her back across to the kitchen. When she opened the door she was surprised to see that the lights in the corridor were extinguished. Utter darkness engulfed it.

"Bloody power supply," she muttered. "No, it can't be that. The kitchen lights are working." She glanced back at the brilliantly illuminated interior. "I could just go for it, I suppose." The light flooding from the kitchen revealed the dark oblong of her door. She reasoned, I could cross to the wall, then work my way along by touch alone. First is Marko's door, then Sterling's, then ours. The third is the one to open. "Don't be a bloody fool," she told herself. "Like anyone'd want to go strolling round this heap in complete darkness."

Belle opened the kitchen door wider so more light fell into the corridor. That's more like it, she told herself, you only have to find the bloody light switch. The brass switch was set directly in front of her. Turn on the corridor lights, then bed—preferably before that rotten clock strikes three. She hated the sound of those chimes. They had all the charm of monotone notes being played on the ribcage of a skeleton.

"Uh, that's my first mistake," Belle whispered as she stepped into the corridor. The kitchen door swung shut behind her. It must have been on a spring closer, but she'd never noticed before. Now she was plunged into darkness. She couldn't see a thing. She froze. A stir of icy air crawled up her bare legs beneath the robe. Don't be such a coward, she scolded. The light switch is just a couple of steps away. Walk forward with your hands straight in front of you. You'll find it with your fingers. Switch on, then get to the room. Run to the room. That was what she wanted to do now. Her heart drummed. Her breath came in short gasps. This darkness pressed down on her, its presence suffocating. She wanted light. Wanted it now! She took one decisive step forward, her arms stretched in front of her, fingers splayed out, sensitive skin at the fingertips feeling the play of cold air currents. Another step forward. Then a third.

Her fingers found the light switch. At least they should have found it. A swelling button of something soft. A protrusion. Not the cold brass switch. She gasped.

A nose. *I'm touching a nose.* Beneath her fingers she detected skin, then the rounded swelling of what could only be eyes, the bristle of eyebrows . . .

Belle jerked back with explosive speed. Her back slammed into the kitchen door, knocking it open. The light flooded out. In front of her, a figure appeared in the splash of radiance. A disheveled figure. A tangled nest of hair. A scarred forehead. A partly open mouth that revealed yellow ruins of teeth. A pair of watery eyes . . . She held the stark image. It burned itself deep into her brain as the figure lunged forward, dragged her away from the kitchen door so that it closed, plunging her in darkness again. Before she could cry out, a solid mass struck the side of her head.

I should be shouting for help. . . . Belle tried as she fell; not even a whisper escaped her lips.

In the cellar just three feet beneath where Belle struck the corridor floor, Josanne fumbled up the flight of steps in total darkness. The iron stair rail she clung to was by turns either covered in cold slime as if gigantic slugs had tracked over it, or it was so corroded that flakes of rust pricked her fingertips.

Get out of here—get out, get out, get out! If I can just reach the top of the steps, there'll be a door . . . When Josanne found the light switch by touch alone, it was like finding a casket of gold. It took a hard pull to flick the old switch downward. Contacts scraped after years of damp; its mechanism must have been all but rotted away. But at least the thing worked. Light blossomed in the cellar once more. In this section of the vault, three filthy lightbulbs hung on mildewed cables. But to hell with it, it was light. Light was all that mattered. What it revealed made Josanne groan. This staircase led nowhere. Years before, it provided a convenient exit. Now she was confronted by a wall of concrete blocks which filled an archway of ancient brickwork that would have once allowed access to the body of the house.

"OK, this isn't a problem," she told herself. "You've got the light. Just go down the steps, through the cellar, and leave by the other stairs." Grimacing, she glanced at her hands. They were streaked a brownish yellow from the slime on the stair rail. This entire place had succumbed to growths of subterranean fungi. Meanwhile every nerve in her body flashed a sense of urgency—a searing imperative to quit this place as fast as possible. By now she'd reached the bottom of the stairs. Beneath her feet, this section of floor consisted of dark woven brick. The tunnel-like vault ran forward twenty paces before it narrowed to an archway. Beyond that it opened up into the cellar she'd found herself in ten minutes ago. White clouds of vapor gusted from her mouth as she crossed the floor. Running alongside her were shelves fixed to the walls. A fungus spread its sickly yellow rash across them. It had even extended its toxic fingers over bundles of old aircrew uniforms as if claiming them for its own. Halfway along the vault, three massive pipes as thick as tree trunks ran from the ceiling, down through a gap in the shelves, and then plunged vertically into the floor. That same crust of yellow fungus had begun to invade those, too. She imagined the toxic spores could infiltrate through the iron tubes to contaminate the water. The idea of drinking water that flowed through those loathsome conduits was enough to send a wave of nausea through her. As she regarded that trio of water pipes, she heard a clang. Was that an airlock in one of them? Had someone taken a bath and now a cistern was refilling itself, drawing clean water through those filth-encrusted tubes? The bang came again, the sound of a steel bar striking against a pipe. Oddly, it could have been some mutant progeny of the chimes issued by the blind clock. It possessed that same metallic note. The bang sounded yet again. This time it was massive enough to enough to stop Josanne dead. A moment later, when the echoes had died, the chimes did come. They pulsed through the air. A sound of ancient metal. A monotonous series of notes that invaded the still air around her. Each note subtly altered: sometimes the after-echo deepened to shake the muscles in her belly; sometimes they rose in pitch to gnaw at the sensitive skin deep inside her ears. She wanted to thrust her nails into her ears to block out the noise that irritated her beyond belief.

It must be three o'clock. One, two, three . . . yet the chimes continued. They rose into brittle notes that set her teeth on edge, then deepened into the tolling of a bell to shake the bones of her skull. The sound mutated again. This time the chimes appeared to come from the pipe. She turned to stare at them with an "oh my God" distorting the shape of her mouth. Before there was any visible sign, she knew. The chimes imitated the groan of metal being subjected to irresistible force. *The house warned me. It showed me what would happen . . .*

The pipes ruptured. Hunks of metal simply peeled away. With them came a blast of water. This wasn't fresh water from the dams. This stank of pond weed and the silt where dead things lay in darkness to rot. She flinched back as the displaced air gusted at her before the inrush of water. Light bulbs swung. Shadows lunged crazily across the walls. Then she reeled as the wave that was already knee-high struck her. When she turned to run, the black tide carrying pale rafts of scum had already covered the cellar floor. Behind her the flood thundered from ruptured pipes. Cold water swirled round her legs. Her pajamas clung to her as spray soaked them. And underwater, soft things folded around her bare ankles. In her mind's eye she saw slick black eels carried in with the cascade of foul-smelling liquid. She imagined sharp teeth sinking into the flesh of her calves. Or the creature's head, set with glittering eyes, would strike at her face from the water.

Worse . . . much worse than that . . . Josanne remembered the vision of how she drowned. The water smelt the same. Her panic was the same. The chimes sounded the same. She'd die the same.

Fisher woke when he heard the chimes that signed away three o' clock. Outside, hail tapped at the window. Another four hours until daybreak. He now knew that they had to leave this place. Maybe they'd have a better chance in the daylight?

At night, the fastest way to reach morning is to

sleep. Only Fisher realized he didn't feel even remotely drowsy. He resisted the temptation to switch on the light that would dispel this oppressive darkness. Even so, he reached out his hands to either side of him, then stretched his arms directly upward. He'd had his "death dream," as Blaxton called it. The walls and ceiling had rolled in to crush him. For the moment his hands swam through the dark; nothing solid struck his fingertips.

I believe, Fisher told himself without any sense of surprise. I believe what Blaxton told me. That the house shows you a vision of your own death. So why the chimes? Is that the source of its power; or merely the device that gives voice to its own version of mocking laugher? Kym saw herself being stabbed to death. Belle had the same vision. Josanne dreamt she was drowning. But other than drowning in a bath, how do you drown inside a house? So, house, how long have you been doing this to people? You know what I'm talking about. Before you murder them, you shove that dream into their heads of them dying. That's when you play them a little of your death music, too.

The house goes way, way back. Did the farmers who lived here in the medieval house dream that they were rotting with leprosy? Then, later, they noticed the patch of dead white skin on their hands? Maybe the leper bell they rang to warn people they were infected was the ancestor of the morbid chiming that haunted The Tower. Later they'd walk through the house ringing their handbell as their skin fell away by the fistful.

What of the airmen stationed here in World War II?

Fisher closed his eyes while his mind's eye played the scene in vivid detail.

The crew walks out in the early morning mist to the B-17 waiting on the runway. The propellers are whirling. The four motors housed in the wing nacelles throb. The aircraft are loaded with bombs ready for the attack on Nazi munitions factories. The tail gunner tells the ball turret gunner, "Heck, Joe, I had a hell of a dream last night. We were all playing cards in my room back at the house when a Focke Wulf flew through the window and fried our asses to a crisp."

"Yeah, and I dreamed I lived on a desert island with Joan Crawford. They've both got the same chance as coming true as us sprouting big feathered wings and shitting incendiary all over Hitler's head."

But Joe doesn't mention that as he lay in bed in The Tower last night, he had the same dream. Only there's another detail. Just seconds before the nose of the fighter slammed through the window, he heard chimes. Dozens of fucking chimes. That got louder and louder . . .

Fast-forward sixteen hours. The aircrew returns safely. They've gathered in the tail gunner's room to blow off steam. They're sitting on his bed as they slap down the playing cards. They're hitting whisky hard enough to send a buzz through to their nerve endings; Glenn Miller's on a windup gramophone. The mood's upbeat. Another mission done. They're closer to going home. Joe's found letters from the tail gunner's girl. He's laughing as he reads aloud, "Dear Hank, I'm writing this as I lay here in bed so I can think about you. I'm totally, totally naked . . . apart from those pink socks my grandma knitted for my birthday. As I write this, darling Hank, I slip my hand down so I can touch my—"

"Hey, it doesn't say that. And give it back, you dirty fink."

"A dirty what? Fink?"

The rest of the buddies laugh at the sight of Hank's blushes. The pilot shuffles the deck of cards and flicks out the ace of spades. The navigator cranks the gramophone as trombones run down into a slurring dirge. A gunner pours them all another splash of scotch.

"What the hell's wrong with that clock?" asks Joe. "It's ten o'clock, so why's the damn thing chiming twelve?"

And the chimes don't stop there. The chimes grow louder. They quicken. They become a pulse of sound, an ominous string of notes that mutate into a ringing cacophony that chews into their skulls so that they grimace, shake their heads, cover their ears. Hank recalls the dream of them gathering here in his room to play cards. Joe remembers the part of the dream where the chimes started. How they grew louder. How they became a metallic thunder that battered his eardrums. As they remember, they suddenly lock eyes with each other.

From the night sky, the single-engine Focke-Wulf dives at the airfield with all the predatory menace of a hawk. The pilot sees the bunker in the moonlight. He strafes it with cannon fire. The shells explode against the concrete wall in balls of yellow flame. From the ground antiaircraft gunners fire white hot tracer at the plane. One shell tears away the wing. The plane spins in a screaming roll directly into the front of the house.

In Hank's room, the chimes reach a frenzied pitch. Men curse. They clamp their hands over their ears. That's when the steel nose of the plane smashes through the window. Remnants of the whirling propeller hack Joe into bloody chunks. As the gore strikes the walls, the aviation fuel spewing into the room from ruptured tanks ignites. In the killing furnace the room has become, Hank's last thought is: That dream . . . It came true. . . .

A knock sounded.

The walls . . . With a grunt, Fisher searched for the switch by the bed. The moment light banished the darkness, his eyes searched the walls for the first sign of them bulging in at him. The knock sounded again. With a sigh of relief, he realized someone was at the door.

He opened it to find Marko standing there fully dressed. His friend wore a worried expression. "Fisher? Can you hear running water?"

Chapter Thirty-one

At the same moment Marko uttered the words, "Fisher? Can you hear running water?" Josanne was fighting for her life. She had to battle to keep upright as the water swirled around her. Now it reached the top of her thighs. The stuff was like liquid ice. And still it thundered into the cellar.

Josanne struggled across the vault to where it led into the main part of the cellar. The force of the flood compressed the air in the confined space so that it hurt her ears. At the end of their moldy tethers, lightbulbs swung wildly; shadows became living things that dashed crazily across the cellar walls. And constantly the chimes hammered away at her skull. It could have been the tolling of a cathedral bell. The sound was huge, overwhelming. Nothing less than a sonic assault on her ears.

I've got to get out. . . . If I don't, I'm going to die within the next ten minutes. She forced herself against the black tide. The water stank. When it splashed on her lips, she thought she'd vomit. Her pajamas were drenched. Objects carried underwater by the vortex thumped against her shins—an old chair, maybe, or one of the jars from the shelves. Even old airmen's uniforms floated on the surface, the fabric limbs moving in some weird dance.

The water rose with breathtaking speed. Moments before, it crept up her thighs. Now it crossed her hips with a surge of liquid ice that made her shout a stuttering, "Oh, God!" When she didn't think it could get any worse, it did. The turbulent waters formed waves of bursting spray. Not only did the evil smelling liquid splash into her eyes, but it hit the exposed light bulbs. For a moment her eyes alighted on one as droplets struck the hot glass. They sizzled off in steaming spits of white. Then a larger splash soaked the bulb. It popped. Instantly it was gloomier. Yet the shadows from the remaining bulbs were no less frenzied. A monstered version of Josanne cavorted across the walls. When she raised her arms at either side of her head to balance herself, the shadow version of thrashed the air with its upper limbs.

"Come on, damn you," she hissed to herself. "Get out of here. Get out. . . ."

Spray burst as the mounds of water clashed. Droplets hit another bulb. It shattered with the sound of a gunshot. The third—and last—light bulb in this section of the cellar simply faded out with a sizzling sound. Now the only light came from the bulbs in the main part of the cellar. There, light was forced through the narrow archway in the brickwork in front of her. Apart from a strip of water five feet wide she could see nothing of this vault. For all she knew, figures might be lifting their heads up from the surface to gloat over her misfortune.

As the current bore Josanne toward the next flooded section of cellar, the lights there died in a blue flash as water overtook the light switch. Now she was plunged into total darkness. For a moment she froze there, not daring to move. Objects carried on the tidal wave hit her in bruising impacts. A bone-aching cold tortured her from head to toe. Mushroom odors of fungus now forged a foul-smelling alliance with the stink of pond slime. The chimes continued, a vicious pulsing sound. The metallic noise disoriented her. Its ever-mutating harmonics hurt her head.

Please . . . I want to see. Don't let me drown here in the dark.

The darkness was absolute. When at last she lost her footing, the water level had reached her shoulders.

Engine oil. Lubricants. Greased metal. The smell told her where she was before she opened her eyes. I'm in a garage, Belle told herself. But how did I come to lie in a garage? I'm in the house. I must be in bed with Adam. That's it, I'm dreaming. I'm in The Tower. . . .

The hum of an electric motor buzzing into life told her that was where she *wasn't*.

At last Belle managed to open her eyes. Her head ached like fury. When she blinked, her vision snapped into focus. She saw she lay on her back in a repair shop. An old one, at that, with whitewashed brick walls. The roof was unusually low. Then she saw why. The dark mass above her slowly descended. A glance to her side revealed everything. She lay beneath the heavy-duty wheel runners of a car hoist. The electric motor lowered it toward her. The dark mass was the underside of a car. The chassis, with the rusty pipe of a muffler running from fore to aft, filled her area of vision. Another five seconds and it would come down on her.

So why am I lying here?

Then she saw something else to freeze her nervous system. She gagged. A timber cross member, lashed so it ran from one wheel runner to the other, lay directly above her chest. Extending downward from it was a steep spike. The point had been filed to a silvery sharpness. The shaft, however, had been smeared with some sticky brown substance. In a second she identified it: blood. She could see it clearly. God damn, she could even smell it. This time instinct kicked in fast. She realized she was lying on a wooden table. By now the steel point was no more than two feet above her chest. Another three seconds and it would nail her by the ribs to the table top. She rolled sideways.

"No!" The guy lunged from the shadows. In a split second she took in the wild mane of hair, the disheveled clothes, the moon-shaped scar on his forehead. Same guy who knocked me cold in the corridor. *The same guy who murdered me in my nightmare.* He flung himself on her. Belle smelt his musty body odor. More animal than man—this creature lived in a lair rather than a home.

As he used his own body weight to force her against the table, he squealed, "No! You've got to lie flat. It won't work if you don't lie flat!"

Belle glanced at the descending spike. "OK! But you're staying here with me!"

She threw her own arms around him in a desperate hug that held his upper body over her own. Grunting, he looked back over his shoulder. The first place that steel point would hit was right between his own shoulder blades. He tore himself free of her. At the same time Belle rolled off in the other direction. She should have been quicker. The guy grabbed her wrist, then began to drag her back onto the table.

Come on, she raged at herself. You have five brothers. They only started to respect you when you were big enough to dish out the black eyes. Now isn't the time to be dainty.

He gripped her wrist in his two hands as he brutally hauled her so she'd be under the descending spike. But she still had one arm free. Hauling in every atom of strength, she balled her fist, then punched as hard as she could. Her fist smacked into the center of the mottled face. With utter satisfaction she felt the pug nose flatten under her knuckles. He grunted and flinched, but didn't quit holding her. By the time she withdrew her fist from his face, he was having to duck down to avoid the steelwork descending from above him. Blood trickled from one of his nostrils to mat the stubble on his upper lip. Although his grip remained firm, his eyes had dulled. He was no longer thinking straight, or even thinking it was high time to get clear of the descending hoist. Stupidly he hung on.

OK, grip me nice and tight, Belle thought as the steel point homed in on the crook of her elbow as her arm stretched out across the tabletop. At the last second she dragged backwards so hard her vertebrae made popping sounds. A pain speared through the muscles in her armpit. She didn't stop pulling. It caught the guy by surprise. She shifted the position of his arm before he knew what she'd done.

The metal point, driven by the vehicle's weight

from above, found its fulcrum in the back of his hand. Both Belle and her attacker watched the steel point with horror-struck fascination as it bore down, depressing the flesh, wrinkling the surrounding skin, then—*pop!* The steel shaft slipped effortlessly through the man's hand to pin it to the tabletop. At last, the hoist's motor began to make a whine of protest when it couldn't lower the spike any further.

Belle backed away. The wheel runners of the hoist had stopped three feet above the table top. The spike didn't bend. But it had the guy nailed down good and hard by the hand. Cries of pain and disbelief began to spurt from his throat.

A grin reached Belle's face. A wild, exultant grin. "I dreamt all this," she told the guy as blood poured from his hand to drench the tabletop. "I dreamt you killed me. But I've busted the hex, because I haven't heard the chimes. And I've spiked you! Boy, I can't wait until I tell the others." She stabbed her finger at him to the rhythm of what she said next. "You . . . are . . . in . . . big . . . trouble."

Then she found the exit. A moment later she was running back through the darkness toward The Tower.

Josanne heard chimes. She heard the inrush of water, too, a violent roaring that punched her ears. But she saw nothing. All she could do was tread water there in the darkness. A couple of times she tried to find the floor so she could stand. But it had gone. There was only the swirl of ice-cold liquid beneath her bare feet now.

At the same moment Belle ran from the garage to the house with triumph blazing inside her, a blind panic surged through Josanne. The cold numbed her limbs. She could hardly breathe. *The water must be over six feet deep now.* It surged through the cellar in a turbulent mass. Already Josanne could feel the strength running out of her. She twisted in the water, trying to catch a glimmer of light. *Oh, God, I can't even be sure in which direction the stairs are. I can't see a thing.*

A second later, the top of Josanne's head buffeted against something hard. As she kept herself afloat she reached up. Just level with the top of her head, her fingertips encountered the vaulted ceiling. She was trapped in an the air pocket formed by one of the arches.

"You're going to drown," she gasped, "if you don't do something to save yourself. Come on, do it. Do it!"

Josanne forced herself to concentrate on the direction of the water's current. If the water surged out from the shattered pipes, then it must flow in the direction of the stairs that led up to ground level. *What I must do is move with its flow.* Only to do that meant swimming underwater. The cold liquid touched her lips. *No prevarication, do it!* She lifted her face up until her nose pressed against the ceiling. The air gap had shrunk to no more than two inches. With a desperate gasp she emptied her lungs as forcefully as she could to expel as much carbon dioxide as possible, then inhaled deeply to fill them with air. As soon as she closed her mouth with the air locked inside her chest, she kicked herself down through the water. Even though she was completely submerged, she could hear the muted rumble of the flood blasting through the ruptured pipes. The chimes were as metallic as ever. A piercing sharpness; golden bells tied round the necks of sacrificial victims when they're hurled into the maw of the volcano.

Icy currents tugged her through the subterranean chamber. She was a fetus in a womb of ice . . . no . . . a doomed astronaut cut adrift to tumble forever through the lightless void between the stars. Josanne's mind became disconnected from her body. She could imagine herself as a feather floating on the night air, not a pallid pajama-clad figure clawing her way beneath six feet of water where the suits of dead airmen swirled beside her. She imagined Kym's white face ghosting through the water toward her. Dull eyes stared from their sockets. *Josanne, come join me. Death is such a lonely place. Stop swimming, Josanne. Let out the air. It'll be quick. It won't hurt. I promise. . . .*

Josanne's chest did hurt. Her lungs had become two molten sacs inside her ribs. God, she needed to breathe. The pressure grew inside of her. Air spurted from her lips. She couldn't hold it in any longer. *I've got to breathe. I need to breathe. I must have air.* . . . The chimes grew louder. The rhythm became faster. In the Good Heart, the metal chime vibrated with triumph. It created a sustain of pure sound that rose in pitch and in volume. The note ascended into a scream. A cry of exultation that her oxygen starved brain could visualize as well as hear. She saw the sound as a beam of light that seared through the water, venting blue sparks that were so bright she couldn't bear to look at them.

Meanwhile the ghost Kym reached out deathly pale arms toward her. *It's all right, Josanne. You're nearly through it now. Just open your mouth.*

The arms darted through the water. Hands seized

her. Soon she wouldn't be able to bear the agony any more. Then she'd open her mouth to receive this filthy, stagnant jism of the house.

"Josanne? Josanne." A hand gripped her jaw to hold her head up. "Josanne, are you all right?"

The world of light resolved itself into steps that led up to an open doorway. Water swirled behind her, but it wasn't as fierce now. The chimes had stopped, thank God. Another hand brushed the matted hair from her eyes. With a gratitude that melted her inside, she inhaled. Cool air soothed her burning throat.

"Marko? Fisher?"

Marko stood behind Fisher as he angled a flashlight to illuminate the few steps that hadn't been engulfed by floodwater.

Her brain still swimmy from oxygen deprivation, she murmured, "Fisher. You're pulling me out of the water. How . . . how very, very apt."

Neither Marko nor Fisher commented on what to her seemed such witty words. Their concerned expressions said it all. What words they used were terse, such as, "Get her clear of the water." "She's cold as ice. She'll be suffering from exposure." "Watch her head as I lift her clear." "Now go back before the water gets any higher."

Her body was numb. Reality had retreated to a place far, far away. And no chimes. She was so grateful for that. The peace was exquisite. Her eyelids were too heavy to keep open. When she closed them, she didn't even realize Fisher was carrying her up the steps and back into the body of the house.

As Fisher bore the limp, dripping form of Josanne out of the cellar, Belle raced back to the house. It appeared to gaze broodingly down at her. A cold, hard mass of multiple hatreds. Its shell was suffused with disapproval, antipathy. The timbers oozed hostility. The very air it contained was stained with contempt for anything human. Belle sensed the evil spirit of the house as she picked her way, barefoot, across the driveway. Even so, she still felt the heat of her triumph over the madman. He was neatly pinned by the steel rod to the tabletop. Good, let the bastard squirm in agony for a while. She'd take her time telling the others what had happened to her before leading them down to the garage to view her captive. Besides, Belle was sure he knew what happened to Kym. If he was hurting badly enough, he might be inclined to indulge in confessional talk.

"Suffer, you bastard," she hissed as she pushed open the door of the house.

The lights in the corridor were lit, but not those in the entrance hall. The staircase curved way up into the darkness of the tower itself. She'd go wake Adam, then rouse the rest of them. A madman nailed by the hand to a table was something they had to see. She'd beaten him. And she'd beaten the hex.

"What do you say to that, house?" Her voice rose as she tossed her head. "I've beaten your curse, you pile of crap. I've outwitted you!" She gave a grim laugh. "So, go on, do your worst. You can't get the better of us."

As she crossed the entrance hall toward the corridor, she noticed that the doors to the Good Heart were open. Lights played on the walls as if someone had decided to view it by flashlight. It might be Fabian or one of the others. They were sick to death of the bloody chimes. Probably someone had been woken by the damn things and had decided to put paid to that clock once and for all. Well, if there was someone here, they'd be the first to hear about her adventure.

Belle stepped through the doorway into the Promenade that led to the Good Heart. Diffuse patches of light skated across the stone face of the medieval façade. She made out the little deep-set windows and the stunted doorway that appeared as if it had been designed for the local hobgoblin population, not men and women.

A rush of air blasted against her. It rippled her silk nightdress; her hair fluttered. Belle turned as the doors slammed shut behind her. How the hell had that happened? She stepped back to the door. Tried the handle. It wouldn't shift. Surely no one had locked her in here. The wind must have blown the door shut.

"Damn you," she hissed. For some reason she felt a reluctance to glance back. There had been something unearthly about the way those patches of light skated across the ancient building-within-a-building. Not so much lights playing on stonework but a witch fire pulsing outward through its walls. "Come on. Open," she whispered as she pushed at the door. Changing tack, she pulled as she twisted the handle. "Stupid door. Stupid house. Evil bloody house. I hate you." She tugged harder. The thing didn't even rattle. The handle might as well have been welded into the same position.

She slammed her hand against the wooden panel. "Adam!" Even louder she shouted, "Hello! Anyone! Can anyone hear me!" The echoes slowly faded before swelling in volume to rush at her in a distorted cry.

"Crazy house. Even the echoes are all wrong."

Belle gripped the handle again. This time it turned smoothly with only the slightest effort on her part. "Hmm. At last." Belle pulled open the door.

He stood there. The same wild nest of hair. The moon-shaped scar of gray skin on his forehead.

As her heart lurched, the chimes started. This time they were eager. The metallic clanging thrust from the air to burrow through her ears into her head. The chimes pulsed in triumph, a shimmering celebration in sound. As the chimes rang from the walls, the man stepped forward. He'd wrapped his right hand in a filthy rag. Now it glistened red with blood. In his left hand he held a knife.

Without a sound he plunged the blade into her chest. As Belle slumped, she heard the vicious clamoring of chimes. A victorious peal of metallic laughter. They hadn't sounded in the garage. Because she'd not been meant to meet her death there. This was the place where the house intended she'd die.

"But I don't want to die," she murmured as she lay on the floor in an ever-expanding tide of blood. "I don't want to die. I don't want . . ."

Chapter Thirty-two

Cantley stood in the doorway to the Good Heart. There he watched the woman in the robe of red silk die. When her last breath sighed from her lips, Cantley looked up at the façade of the ancient house-within-a-house.

"See? I'm good with a knife. Right in the lungs, right through the heart. Look, she's dead." Cantley pushed the body with the toe of his boot. "Stone dead." The lights skating along the walls contracted, than expanded, changing color as they did so, until it seemed as if purple blooms appeared on the walls. "You owe me now," he told the house. "I—I want you to take these pains outta my head. This time you gotta do it forever. D'ya hear? I've given you two women. You owe me back." Cantley closed his eyes. Purple light pulsed inside his head. The pains that had tortured him since childhood faded from his face. The old agony that would chew his spine with all the ferocity of a chainsaw morphed into a relaxing tingle. The house paid him back. It took away the pain that had made his life hell for the past thirty years. The doctors told his parents that the pains were phantom ones caused by his schizoid condition.

Yeah, they were saying I was crazy. But let one of the those smug bastards from the psych ward live for just one hour in my skin! Then they'd know the pain's real. That you can't sleep because it feel like rats are gnawing at your toes. That you can't even take a crap without being terrified that your bowels have ripped lose and are unspooling through your asshole into the john. Even the blood in my veins hurts. It's corrosive. An acid. Burning me, torturing me . . .

Now . . . this felt good. . . . So fucking good. The pain had gone. He'd given The Tower its blood sacrifice. In return it had lifted this burden of physical pain.

Cantley opened his eyes. "You know something?" he told the Good Heart with its tiny sunken windows. "I'm going to give you the rest of these people. Everyone in the house is going to be like this." Cantley pointed at the dead women as she lay on her back with her arms flung out straight. Her legs were bent at the knee. What was important were the holes in her chest, which released her life-giving blood onto the floor. The Tower could taste her now. Cantley imagined the luscious crimson fluid being drawn through the surface of the floor where a network of capillaries would draw it through every stone and timber of the house. It would give it strength. Make it powerful. A vital living beast. He'd once read that builders in ancient times would mix their mortar with chicken blood or bury the bones of a horse in the foundations. Cantley knew the wisdom of this. He'd fed the house for twenty years. Usually from the inexhaustible population of rats, sometimes pets stolen from nearby villages. Now, best of all, the men and women who trespassed here. They'd nourish this stone and mortar like no other gifts of his could.

A sound caught his ear. At first he hoped the sound came from the walls, a vocal expression of gratitude. But then the it became a furious peal of barks. He stepped back into the entrance hall. The black dog bounded along the corridor toward him. He could see its fur spiked furiously on its back.

Damn that animal. He'd have loved to be able to plunge the knife into its throat there and then, but its barks would have warned the people he was in the building. Christ knew he'd deal with that dog before the night was out.

Cantley bounded up the stairs. They took him into the darkened interior of the vast structure of the tower itself. He heard the dog's claws clatter on the bare steps as it raced up after him.

After showering, Josanne sat on the bed in fresh clothes. She'd chosen blue jeans and one of Adam's sweaters. It was far too big for her, but Fisher could see she was grateful for the way the thick material swathed her in a warm embrace.

The room was full. Adam stood by the window. Fabian paced the floor. Marko and Sterling stood alongside Fisher near the door.

"Give the girl some air, for Christ's sake," Adam told them. "Last thing she needs right now is to be interrogated."

"But I can't understand why Josanne went down into the cellar alone." Fabian turned to her. "What the hell did you think was down there?"

Josanne had recovered enough to react angrily, "I

didn't want to be there. I just opened my eyes and there I was."

"Sleepwalking? You've never walked in your sleep before."

"Hell, Fabian, I've never been through this kind of shit before."

Adam said, "Maybe we should get everyone to a higher level, if the water's flooding this dump."

Sterling shook his head. "I checked the cellar a few minutes ago. The water level's dropping."

Josanne looked up at them. "Guys, we've got to get away from this house."

"Sunrise'll be in a couple of hours," Sterling said. "It gives us time to pack everything into the van. Then we can drive out of here in the daylight."

"Suits me," she said with feeling.

"What an absolute fuck-up." Fabian shook his head. "All this planning. It took me weeks to get this place. We were going to rehearse here so we could take our songs into the studio. Now we're scuttling away like frightened mice."

Marko stared at him in surprise. "You're not suggesting we stay?"

Sterling nodded. "Yeah, what about Kym?"

Fisher looked round. "Come to that, where's Belle?"

A baffled expression clouded Adam's face. "I stumbled out here half asleep when I heard you guys shouting in the corridor. It was all I could do to pull some pants on." He shrugged. "I guess Belle must still be in bed."

Fisher began, "I think you should check that—"

"Sshh." Marko touched his arm. "Hear that?"

Fabian clicked his tongue. "It's the bloody dog

barking its stupid head off again. You should get the thing a—"

"No. Jak's going crazy at something. There must be someone at the door."

"Kym?"

Marko didn't answer. A second later he was running along the corridor in the direction of the frenzied barking. Fisher followed.

Cantley reached the top of the staircase. Here he was high in the core of the tower. He caught glimpses of the marsh with its silvered pools of water bisected by the old runway. It wouldn't be light for another couple of hours yet. If anything, the night had renewed its grip on the world outside the house. The fields and woods were patches of variegated shadows. Cloud had drowned the stars.

A pitter-patter of paws grabbed his attention. The animal had followed him upstairs as he knew it would. It wanted to attack Cantley. That was OK. He had the upper hand now. He'd wait for it. Take it by surprise. The light filtering from the entrance hall below would be enough to see the dog when it appeared. Cantley crouched down at the top of the stairs. He used the post of the balustrade to conceal himself. As soon as the dog was close enough he'd drive the point of the blade into its neck, then hook his fingers into the collar so it couldn't run. Make a good job of it. Slice through all the main arteries in the neck. If he made good progress, why not continue all the way through to the spinal cord? Then he could separate the head from the body. Cantley grinned. The Tower would enjoy that. Just think of all that sticky, sweet canine blood dribbling down the stairs. He could even daub streaks on the banister rail. What a paint job! What a fucking brilliant paint job! Cantley could barely restrain himself from chuckling.

Come on boy, come on. The click of paws grew louder. He could even hear the animal's panting breath. It must only be a few yards away. He flexed his left hand before renewing his grip on the knife handle. When he'd done that, he checked his right hand. The pain had stopped in the palm, although the rag he'd tied round the hand was saturated in blood. Jesus, a hell of wound. The woman's punch had distracted him enough to allow her to yank his hand directly under the spike. It had bored right down into the center of his palm. Gone all the way through to bury the metal point in the tabletop. That had been stupid of him. He'd let her get away too easily.

After she'd run from the garage, he'd been fortunate enough to be able to reach the car hoist control, which was on the end of a long cable. It had only taken a second to lift the hoist, despite the fact he'd parked an old car on it to add weight. The steel rod had gone all the way through between the bones of the hand, then the point had bent when it hit the table top. This formed a barb. It took some heaving downward to rip his hand free. Like trying to pull a nail out of a block of wood without a claw hammer. Such pain would have felled any other man. But he'd experienced far worse over the years. Agony had been the background to his life. It never stopped playing until he'd learned that he could do a little trade with the house. Blood for analgesia. How cool was that?

He flexed his hand. In his mind's eye, he could see

the gory dime-sized wound in his palm where the steel rod had punched clean through. The wound would be full of shitty red stuff as the blood congealed. But his fingers worked. There was no pain. Only a pleasant buzz. The Tower was being good to him, so he'd be good to it.

Cantley smiled. *Here comes the dog. I raise the knife.*

Fisher followed Marko along the corridor at a run. They could no longer hear Jak's barks, but figured he must be close by. The instant they reached the entrance hall, Fisher noticed that the twin doors that led to the Good Heart lay open.

"Oh, God." Marko had seen something else too.

They both froze. Their eyes were locked on the figure in the red robe that lay just inside the doors. More red of a similar shade formed a glistening pool around it. Belle lay on her back, her legs bent at the knee. Bloody holes in the silk garment told their own story.

Marko found it hard to speak. "Fisher . . . I don't think she's breathing."

Fisher took a step forward to where Belle lay motionless. "Marko. Bring the others."

Cantley tensed. Another half dozen steps and the dog would reach him. He raised the knife. He needed to make a powerful downward stroke to impale the dog's neck. He'd hook it like a fish so it couldn't escape.

The dog's shadow appeared on the wall opposite him. Its ears were pricked. The sharp jackal-like point of its muzzle was raised. Three more steps. Two. One! He lunged forward, swinging the blade downward.

He anticipated the crunch of the pointed blade as it penetrated the skin, then the slower but oh-so-satisfying passage of the blade through canine neck muscle.

The dog flashed by, a missile of fur and shadow. Damn it to hell, it knew he was there all along. The dog skirted wide at the top of the staircase, way beyond his reach. Momentum still carried his arm downward. The knife point clattered against the parquetry floor. Cantley anticipated that the dog would make a U-turn to attack him from behind as he still crouched there. In a second he was on his feet with the knife ready. But damn that dog. . . . It had vanished into the shadows. *When I get my hands on you . . . Just you wait . . . Just you friggin' wait!*

Fabian was matter-of-fact. "She's dead."

Josanne bit her knuckle as she stared at the corpse of Belle.

Fabian crouched down to conduct a cursory examination. "Shot or stabbed. It's not possible to tell without—"

"Don't touch her." Fisher held out his hand to stop Fabian. "This is murder. You can't disturb the body. The police will need to examine everything as it is."

Fabian nodded, then stood up.

Josanne shuddered. "Body . . . examine? This is Belle you're talking about. Look at her."

Adam had frozen in shock. At last he managed to speak. "We should cover her. It doesn't look right to leave her lying with blood all . . ." Grimacing, he turned away.

Fisher shook his head. "We've got leave her as she is. There can't be any contamination of evidence."

Fabian said, "Fisher's right. We've got to leave everything as we found it."

"It!" Josanne snapped. "Her name is Belle."

"I'm sorry." Fabian's voice softened. "Everyone wants the bastard caught—and we want him convicted."

As they stepped back into the entrance hall, Fisher closed one door while Fabian took care of the other. The doors slowly cut off the view of Belle lying there in the pool of blood. Fisher had wanted to straighten her legs. They looked so uncomfortably awkward, the way they'd bent at the knees. Not that she feels any pain now, he told himself.

"I can't get my head round this," Marko said. A tremor ran through this body as though he were wired to a power grid.

Sterling clenched his fists. "What kind of bastard would do a thing like that?"

"Belle never hurt anyone." Adam murmured the words. "She never hurt anyone. Never hurt a fly. Always wanted the best for everyone. Never hurt a living soul."

Josanne's dark eyes scanned the hallway area. "I know who's responsible."

She sounded so self-assured that everyone snapped their eyes to hers.

"You know?" Fabian's voice rose in disbelief.

Marko looked round. "You saw someone?"

"No, use your noses." She sniffed. "That's engine oil and filth. You even get that greasy hair smell."

Fisher breathed in through his nostrils. "I can smell it. You know, someone in need of a shower."

Adam seemed to wake from his trance. "Shit, you bastards. That's my girlfriend lying through there, and you bastards are talking about body odor."

"It's important, Adam," she said gently. "We've smelt this before."

Fisher nodded. "The guy in the woods."

"Cantley," she said. "When Cantley got close to me this is how he smelt."

In a quieter voice, Fabian said, "Then Cantley's here. In the house."

Adam lunged for the stairs. Fabian grabbed him.

A howl rose from Adam. "Let go of me."

"No. Adam . . . no! Stay here!"

"I'm going to rip the bastard apart."

"Adam, no! He's armed."

"Get off me!"

"You saw what he did to Belle. We don't know what caused that. A knife, a gun."

"Adam. Fabian's right." Josanne tried to soothe him. "Come back to the kitchen; we've got to talk about this."

At last Adam consented to be led away. Josanne walked with her arm around him.

Fisher realized it was high time they bring the police to The Tower. *The question is, how?*

Cantley didn't waste breath trying to coax the dog from whatever room it had scurried into. The dog hated him. It wouldn't be fooled by cajoling. Not that it was Cantley's style, either. He preferred the knife to solve his problems. Now the dog was the first problem to be solved. Then the blade would deal with the rest of those trespassers downstairs. Cantley stood in the doorway should the dog decide to dash for the stairs. It was so gloomy in the room that he could barely make out the clutter of discarded furniture, old mattresses and cardboard cartons.

"Dog," he hissed. "I'm going to kill you, dog." Cantley listened. Either his threat had gone unheard, or the mutt remained perfectly still. Damn the thing. It had cunning, that was for sure. He moved on to the next room. In the darkness he could just make out dozens of old paint cans stacked on top of another. Looked like a decorating job that had never got completed. This time he tried the light switch. It clicked, but the light refused to come. The developer must have cut the power to the upper stories. No worries. He'd still find the dog. Come hell or high water.

They assembled in the kitchen.

"I'll stay at the door," Marko told them. "We don't want the lunatic taking us by surprise."

Fisher said, "See anything, you shout, OK?"

"I'll shout all right," he said, grim-faced.

Adam yanked the cutlery drawer and tipped it onto the counter, ready to spill blood.

Fabian said, "Chose a weapon you think you can handle. Don't take anything that's likely to do more harm to you than to him. Be careful of knives. If you have to use it on him, slash rather than stab. If you stab, your hands are apt to slip from the handle and you'll end up carving your own fingers on the blade." He followed his own advice, choosing a hammer that lay on a shelf. Adam grabbed a carving knife, then headed back to the door. The light in his eye was murderous. He was out for revenge.

Josanne called to him. "Adam, wait until everyone's got a weapon."

"I'm killing the rat—that's all there is to it."

Fabian held up his hand. "Don't rush this. We

don't know what he's armed himself with. It might be a gun."

"We didn't hear any shots," Marko pointed out.

"That's good enough for me," Adam said.

"No. Wait. There's something else," Fisher told him. "Adam . . . wait just a minute."

"Why? So he can get away?"

"No." Fisher's heart beat hard in his chest as he looked at their drawn faces. Belle's death had hit them hard. Now he had to go and hit them even harder. Only this time it was with the truth. "Take a minute to listen to me. Marko? Can you hear me?"

Marko leaned back through the door. "I hear you."

"Good, because there's certain facts we've got understand here. Belle saw what would happen to her. . . ."

Adam snarled, "You bastard, not this."

"When she fell asleep in the car—" Fisher pushed on regardless "—when she fell asleep in the car, she dreamt that she was stabbed to death by a man who she described. Scruffy, messy hair. A scar on his forehead. Adam, don't walk away. She was describing Cantley."

Fabian spoke through gritted teeth. "Save the philosophical discussions for later, Fisher."

"This isn't philosophy. I'm talking about us surviving. Listen. Kym described how she'd had a nightmare where this machine came down on her with a spike. It went straight through her chest. She told me she really believed she'd died. When it happened, she heard the clock chiming."

Josanne spoke in flat voice. "When I was drowning in the cellar . . . nearly drowning, I heard the chimes, too."

"The guy I met on the runway." Fisher forced himself to speak clearly. "Blaxton explained how this worked. I told you in the ballroom. Now I'm telling you again. People who stay in this house have a dream or some kind of hallucination. They're given a vision of their own death. It's accompanied by the sound of the clock chimes. They wake up. They say, thank God, it was only a nightmare. Then later—whether hours or years later—shazzam! The vision becomes reality. They die just like they saw in the dream. They die hearing the chimes." Fisher's heart thudded. A bead of perspiration crawled down his face. They'd listened to him. Great God in heaven, they'd listened.

"But I beat the house," Josanne said at last. "I was trapped in the cellar. It was full of water. I heard the chimes. But I got out."

"Fisher got you out," Marko told her. "He saved you."

Sterling rubbed his jaw. "Does that break the curse, if someone else rescues you?"

Fisher shook his head. "I don't know. All I know is the sequence of the 'death dream,' as Blaxton called it. That you're hit with the vision. Then it happens." A stillness settled on everyone in the room. "I don't know why it happens. Evil doesn't always have a motive. People grow up with the idea that Satan is this guy with a pitchfork, that he's always plotting his evil acts. But I think of evil as being as intelligent as an earthquake or a famine that wipes out ten thousand people. Evil is a blind, mindless force that drifts along until it happens across an opportunity to hurt you. If I stick my neck out here, I'd say there's a force connected to this house. It's conducted through the walls like electricity runs through a wire. It's found some quality in us that it can use ... or that it needs. Whether it's fear, or even the terror of people dying a violent death—who knows? But a long time ago, hundreds or thousands of years ago, it hit upon a process where it can harvest from us this ingredient that it wants." The effort to relay his thoughts dried his mouth so much that it felt as if he'd bitten into a handful of dust.

A breeze stirred the bushes outside. Branches hissed as if some enormous presence released a heartfelt sigh. The breeze quickened. It elicited a thin-sounding cry as it ran through gaps in the window frame. Suddenly the room grew cold. A deep shudder ran through Josanne.

Fisher licked his dry lips. "The question that is important to our survival is this: who else has dreamt their own death?" He looked round. The faces were grim.

Josanne spoke first. "For me it was water. I dreamt my room was flooded. OK, the setting turned out to be different, but it was still a deluge of stinking swamp water."

Fisher added his own experience as a prompt. "I saw the walls and the ceiling close in to crush me. Anyone else?"

Sterling said, "I dreamt I had something in my mouth. I couldn't breathe. What it was I don't know, but I remember knowing in the dream that I blacked out and then I died."

"You heard chimes?"

"Yes. I heard the bloody chimes."

Marko grunted as he stood there in the doorway. "For me it was burning. No details. Just fire. Lots of pain. Yeah, the chimes went with it, too."

Adam blinked as if images flickered before his eyes. "Tonight when I went to bed . . . the moment I closed my eyes I was convinced that I was suspended in darkness. Like I was floating out in space."

Fisher turned to Fabian. "What did you see?"

"Nothing."

"You've not had the dream?"

"No. Maybe this old house doesn't see anything inside me it wants." He gave a grim smile. "Story of my life, huh?"

Sterling watched Fabian's face as if trying to assess whether the man told the truth. "Then maybe you're the only one of us who's immune?"

"Maybe."

The breeze hissed through the bushes again, this time a sinister sound. After this long night, there was an impression that close by something was stirring.

Marko spoke up. "Best take a look at this."

Adam gripped the knife so tightly his knuckles whitened. "He's there?"

Marko stepped through the door with the words, "Grab your weapons. We might need them."

Fabian had the hammer. The others chose sharp kitchen knives, while Fisher picked up a screwdriver that tapered to a lethal point. He handed Sterling a flashlight and chose one for himself.

"Easy now," Marko told them as they moved from the kitchen into the corridor. "Don't startle him."

They looked in the direction Marko pointed. There, in the entrance hall at the end of the corridor, they saw Jak. He stood at the bottom of the stairs poised ready to attack.

"Jak's pointing the way for us," Marko whispered. "Let's go find our man."

Chapter Thirty-three

Blast the dog. He'd slice its throat open, then watch it slowly bleed. He'd gloat over the animal's death throes. *Damn it. Damn, damn, damn.* These hot, poisonous thoughts spurted through Cantley's mind as he shuffled to where the stairs opened out onto the fifth floor at the top of the tower. He'd thought he'd blocked the dog's escape. Yet as he walked into the last room on this floor—the only room where the dog could still be hiding—it darted through the legs of a bunch of old chairs that had been stored there. Cantley furiously slashed at the mutt's head with his knife.

The dog moved like a black ghost. It was swift, silent. It could run almost in a crouch so that its body skimmed the floor. And once more the only thing the blade cut was air. Hell, he hated the animal. At school years ago, he'd seen photographs of the black jackal that guarded Tutankhamen's tomb. This dog looked exactly like it. He remembered the way it lay on its belly outside the coffin chamber, with its head upright, the ears pricked, its eyes always watchful. Now that supernatural jackal appeared to have moved into The Tower with those kids. He didn't fear them, not for one bloody minute. But the dog? That was another matter. It didn't even seem to be made out of fur and bone. The damn thing was a spirit.

One of the pains returned. It felt like a long thin needle being slowly inserted into his eyeball. He winced. Before the night was out he'd have to complete his deal with the house. The lives of everyone here in exchange for the rest of his life without pain. He moved closer to the staircase. He half expected the dog to rush back up to attack him. Then we'll see who's a spirit dog or not, he thought as he tightened his grip on the knife. Do spirits bleed? Let's find out, shall we, boys and girls?

What he saw made him flinch back. Coming slowly but purposefully up the stairs were the trespassers. He counted five guys and a girl. Some carried flashlights that they used to dispel the darkness in front of them. He didn't fail to notice that they'd armed themselves with knives and hammers. One-on-one they wouldn't be a problem. But six of them? What's more, the dog led the way.

He heard the girl's voice echo up the staircase. "There. You can smell it again. Stale sweat. Motor oil. That's Cantley."

Another said, "Remember what he did to Belle. When I get hold of him, nobody stop me from ripping his head off, OK?"

Cantley murmured to himself, "So you've figured it out, eh? You know it was me." His voice came out a faint whisper. But he'd barely finished speaking when the dog's head jerked up. Its amber eyes locked on his. Don't believe for a moment that dogs are handicapped by poor eyesight. The animal saw him, alright, even though it was still three floors below him. It immediately unleashed a volley of savage barks. They sounded as loud as gunfire echoing up the grand sweep of the staircase. In a second the kids had their flashlights locked onto him. Cantley scowled against the glare.

The woman shouted, "See him! Right at the top of the stairs!"

They moved faster now. The brilliant lights were trained on him. Another disadvantage. He was too dazzled to see his enemy properly. From the sound of the eager barks, the dog was racing toward him.

Fisher ran upstairs behind the dog. The others were close behind him.

Marko called out, "Jak . . . Jak! Stay with us, boy."

The dog held formation with his human pack. He knew better than to rush ahead alone. Fisher's heart beat hard. It wasn't purely exertion, it was the excitement of the manhunt. Something primeval flared up inside of him. From the way Adam's eyes blazed, he guessed Belle's death wouldn't be the only one tonight. Adam lusted for revenge. So be it . . .

When they reached the final flight of stairs, they slowed to approach it more warily. Jak stopped to raise one paw, tucking it back into his body as he leaned forward, staring in the direction of where Cantley must have been hiding. The classic "pointer" response of a dog. For the moment he was showing the way rather than attacking.

"OK, nice and easy," Fabian said. "Make sure he doesn't have a gun before you make a move on him."

As they climbed the remaining steps to the top floor, a cold breeze reached them.

Josanne hissed, "Feel that draft. He's opened a window."

"I hope the bastard falls," Sterling said with feeling.

Adam grunted. "He better not. I want him to suffer." He dashed toward the room from where the cold air flowed. Fisher followed with the flashlight held high so that he could direct the beams over Adam's shoulder. What they saw was the sash window yawning wide open. Cold air gushed through the aperture as if the house sucked oxygen into its stone lungs. Fisher made it to the window the same time as Adam.

"There's a fire escape," Fisher called back. "He's gone."

Adam began to climb out through the window. Fisher grabbed his arm. "You're not going to catch him that way."

Adam shrugged himself free. "We'll follow the dog. He'll find him for us."

"We need to get the other flashlights," Marko told them. "Everyone needs one."

"And see if there's any rope. We might need to tie him up."

Adam spoke with a dark passion. "After I've finished with him, he won't need tying up."

"No!" Josanne stood in the doorway to block their exit. "Listen. Nobody's chasing after Cantley."

"You think we should let him get away? Did you see what he did to Belle?"

"I know what he did." Josanne stood her ground. "No, don't push by me, Adam. Stop . . . you've got to listen to this. OK, we took Cantley by surprise. From what I saw, he didn't have a gun. But if he has access to one, that's where he'll be going now."

"He doesn't frighten me." Adam was so revved up that he was ready to rip Cantley's face from his skull.

"I know," Josanne told him, "but that doesn't alter the fact that if he has a gun, one or more of us will wind up being shot."

Adam's veins stood out in his neck. "Let him try."

Fabian nodded. "Josanne's got a point, Adam. It'd be crazy to take on the guy if he's got a firearm."

Adam kept his jaw clenched. He didn't want to hear this.

Sterling sighed as if logic now got the upper hand over the passion for revenge. "She's right, and we all know it. Cantley's on home ground. He's got the advantage."

Fisher sensed the bloodlust fade into thin air. "All we've got are kitchen knives and a hammer. Cantley could pick us off one by one."

"It's got to be the police," Fabian told them. "They'll handle this."

Adam rubbed his forehead. "Haven't we been through this before? We've no phones. Cell phones can't pick up a signal. Roads are flooded."

"All of them won't be flooded. We'll find a way through somehow." Josanne squeezed Adam's forearm gently. "Listen, we'll find a phone this time. We'll call the police. They'll soon have Cantley."

"We can take Belle with us, can't we?"

Fabian shook his head. "We can't, Adam. We have to leave her exactly where she is. The police have got to . . . you know . . ."

"Yeah, sure." Adam sounded beaten now. The girl

he loved lay dead in a pool of her own blood. The poor guy couldn't even cover her face.

"OK." Marko's voice was gentle. "What's the plan now?"

Fisher expected Fabian to speak first, but the guy seemed to have something else on his mind. Fisher decided to take the lead. "First we make sure we don't split up. We stay together at all times. We collect the keys to the van. You've got them in your room, haven't you, Sterling?"

Sterling nodded.

Fisher continued, "Then we all get in the van. We drive out of here. OK?"

Adam voice was shaky now. "I . . . It's best if I stay here. Someone should be with Belle. . . ."

"I'm sorry, Adam. We all go. If Cantley returns with a gun . . . you know what I mean?"

Adam gave a single nod of his head. His eyes bled a naked pain.

"All right. Everyone ready?" Fisher looked at each in turn as they muttered an affirmative. "Keep the flashlights ready. Cantley shouldn't have had time to grab a gun yet. . . ." His voice adopted a grimmer tone. "But I wouldn't want to stake my life on it."

Josanne stood aside. When they descended the staircase, Fisher went first. His flashlight swept through the shadows below. He was watching for that first telltale movement. But if they were attacked, what happened then? God alone knew.

Within eight minutes they'd climbed into the van. It was ten to five on a cold March morning. Dawn hadn't even begun to break yet. Josanne sensed the pressure of the darkness here, as if it had the power to crush her. The Tower loomed over them, a thousand tons of icy stone. It stood against the night sky, a menacing rock face that harbored a loathing for anything human. At least now they were leaving. Fisher was at the wheel. Fabian sat beside him up front. In the back, sitting on a blanket, were Marko, Sterling, a gray-faced Adam and herself. Jak stood by the rear doors. The dog appeared on edge. He couldn't relax yet.

There was plenty of room: the band had elected to leave their gear behind in the ballroom. They'd collect it once the police had taken care of Cantley. The clock on the dash scrolled forward to 4:52. Eight minutes to five. Just eight more minutes before the blind clock in the Good Heart struck five chimes. *And I don't want to be sat here when they strike.* She shivered when she imagined those five grave notes ghosting through the night air to the van. *We've got to get away from here . . . right away.*

A sudden anxiety gripped her. "What's wrong? Why aren't we going?"

The battery's dead. When Fisher turned to her, those were the words she was sure he'd utter. "There's a problem," he said *I knew it!* "I've told Fabian there isn't time, but—"

"Listen to me," Fabian interrupted. "I'm not leaving the songs here. I've worked too hard to abandon them."

"Abandon them?" Fisher echoed in disbelief. "Fabian, they're not human beings. They're pieces of paper."

Josanne intervened. "You've got copies at home."

"I revised them on the way here. They're the only copies in that form."

"Hell's bells, Fabian." Marko couldn't believe it. "The songs will be there when you get back."

Josanne put her hand on Fabian's shoulder. "We've got to leave. . . . I don't want to be here when the chimes sound again."

Fabian glared. "It's a bloody clock."

"Maybe you're immune to what it can do, but if you'd heard the chimes when the house screws with your head, then you wouldn't say that."

"Listen to yourself, Josanne."

"Please, I just want to get away before the clock strikes five. If we're here when it does . . . Look what happened to Belle. Something bad will happen to us if we're here when the chimes sound."

The clock on the dash rolled forward to 4:54. Six minutes until the metal hammer fell on the chime bar somewhere deep inside that house-within-a-house. In her mind's eye she could glide over the corpse of Belle lying on the floor to that evil-looking tomb of a house. There the medieval façade would stand in defiance of time and in contempt of humanity. A mass of skull-like stones, with gloomy apertures for windows, the stunted doorway, a stone mouth with a gluttonous appetite for human misery and fear.

Then, thank God, Fisher started the motor.

4:55.

Josanne could imagine the striker cranked up with all the dark promise of an executioner's axe. In five brutally short minutes, the hammer would fall. She could sense the resonance building before the strike—an impossible resonance, a grave full of echoes waiting to burst forth and release its deadly power on them.

Fabian opened the van door. "I'm going for the songs."

Ignoring shouts of, "No! Leave them!" he swung his legs out of the van. Fisher leaned sideways over the passenger seat as Fabian exited. Whether he was going to yell at Fabian or even haul the man back into the vehicle Josanne would never know: Fabian slammed the door back with a powerful sweep of his arm. There wasn't a metallic crash; instead the concussion came as a thud. Fisher's face immediately deformed into a snarl of pain.

"Hell, Fabian!" Marko shouted. "You shut the door on Fisher's hand. Fabian, hey, Fabian!"

Fabian ran across the driveway, through the twin doors, and into the house. Fisher straightened up in the seat behind the wheel. He cursed as he clutched his injured hand in the other.

"What an idiot," Josanne hissed. "Fabian doesn't care about anyone but himself. Fisher, are you all right?"

Fisher grimaced. When he tried to flex his hand, sheer agony brought a spasm to his face. "It caught me across the fingers. . . ." He grimaced again. "Marko, you drive. When he gets back, floor it. Just get us away from here."

As Marko climbed out through the rear doors to dart to the front of the van, Josanne watched the relentless progress of the clock. 4:56. Four minutes before the chimes rang out. Dear God, she knew something dreadful would happen if they were here when they did. Either Cantley would step out of the bushes with a shotgun, or it would be something worse. Something only the house could throw at them. She remembered only too clearly how the water had thundered through those ruptured pipes.

A moment later, Fisher joined them in the back of

the van. A grunt burst from his lips as he leaned back against the metal panel, cradling his injured hand. Jak gently nuzzled his forearm. Meanwhile Marko sat behind the wheel with the engine idling. He'd already switched on the vehicle's headlights so they cut a dazzling swath through the darkness. Hawthorn bushes twitched restlessly as a breeze passed through their branches.

"What's keeping the guy?" Sterling hissed.

Everyone stared at the house. They willed Fabian to appear. But what if Cantley had been lying in wait? Might Fabian lie dying in a pool of his own blood? Josanne bit her lip. Four minutes to five. What if the dashboard clock was slow? Four minutes slow. Any second now she'd hear the tolling of the chimes. They'd fly into her heart like bullets. The sound was death. Make no bones about it. The chimes announced when it was your time to die. Her heart quickened. Perspiration forced itself through her skin. She found herself staring at the clock. The numerals hypnotized her. 4:56. Tension constricted her chest. She found it difficult to breathe. The metal hammer of the clock would be fully raised by now. Changes in tension would occur within the mechanism. Its power would be increasing as it readied itself for the first blow against the striker. And in the buildup of that mechanical tension would be another form of tension. The dark power that suffused The Tower's stonework would be tensing now, ready to leap out at the first chime of the clock. 4:57. Her eyes were watering, but she couldn't blink. She had to watch those numerals. She realized she no longer inhaled. Her breath was locked tight inside her aching lungs.

The clock blinked. 4:58. At that moment a crash shook the van. A cry shot from her mouth with shocking power.

"Got them!" Fabian bounced into the passenger seat. He showed them the leather briefcase that contained his precious music.

Fisher slammed his good hand against the panel of the van. "Marko! Drive!"

Fabian was still closing the door as Marko crushed the gas pedal to the floor. The van lurched forward, its tires spinning, flinging gravel up against the wheel arches with the sound of machine gun bullets striking the metal.

Josanne watched the headlights sweep over the hawthorn as the van careened in a loop, then tore down the driveway. Trees flashed by, gaunt skeleton creatures at this time of night. The engine howled. Potholes buffeted the vehicle. The jarring made Fisher clench his teeth as he tried to protect his injured hand.

The clock on the dashboard said 4:59.

One minute . . . just one minute left. The words echoed inside Josanne's head. *One minute. Then the clock strikes five.*

She could feel the house reach out to her. Its toxic power crept into her flesh. A cold touch snaked down her back. It would reach into the motor. That malignant energy would infect the wiring. Every weakness was something to be exploited by the grim deity that dwelt in the core of the house. The van's motor would fail.

Josanne's eyes fixed on the clock. 4:59. Any second now.

At that moment Marko struggled to hold the van as

it cornered a bend in the drive. The vehicle careened off the gravel to run on soft earth. The slushing sound of its tires told her that the house hadn't been beaten yet. The speedometer had been touching forty. Quickly it fell to thirty, then twenty, then with aching finality it dropped to ten. The machine made slow progress through the mud. She could see The Tower through a stream of mud that the rear tires threw up. The rear lights appeared to turn it a bloody red. Branches struck the van. They could be bony hands fighting to hold the vehicle back until the blind clock struck five.

"Come on, come on," Marko urged. The engine screamed. Sliding and lurching, the van crept back onto the drive. Then the tread bit deep. Seconds later the van cannoned from the driveway onto the road. Marko pushed the van's motor to bursting point. It roared as he accelerated away. Trees blurred by. The speedometer nudged seventy. When the dashboard clock at last rolled forward to read 5:00, Josanne heard no chimes. There was only the sound of the motor and the tires on the road. She looked back through the rear windows. The dark block of the house shrank into the distance. Then a moment later The Tower was gone.

Chapter Thirty-four

In the back of the van, Fisher cradled his left hand on his lap. The door had cracked across the second joint of his fingers and they hurt like hell. Pains shot up his forearm directly, it seemed, into the center of his head. Although a milky glow on the horizon told him dawn had begun its debut, it was still too dark to examine his hand properly. In the gloom it looked like a claw. The fingers curled inward, although the little finger kinked outward.

That's a break if I ever saw one, he told himself while shooting a smoldering glance at Fabian in the front seat. The jerk. He jeopardized all our lives for the sake of his songbook.

Everyone rode without talking. Jak sat by the back doors. His head swayed to the motion of the vehicle. Marko's driving wasn't so frenzied now. The dog allowed his eyes to close.

Eventually Sterling asked, "How long to the ferry?"

Marko slowed the van to a crawl. "We're not going to the ferry."

"What?"

"Take a look out front."

Fisher knelt up so he could see between Fabian and Marko. Josanne and Sterling did the same. Adam roused himself, too. His face was still blanched with grief.

Marko said, "The road's flooded. Is this the same stretch that stopped you, Adam?"

Adam's voice sounded dead. "Yeah, I can see the rails. There's a bridge somewhere under there."

Fabian spoke up. "Clearly we can't make it any further this way."

Marko didn't want to be beaten. "I could wade across."

"Don't even think about it," Josanne told him. "You don't know how deep it is."

"Look how fast the current is." Fisher grimaced. It hurt his hand even to talk. "It'd sweep you away."

For a second everyone stared through the windshield. The van's headlights illuminated an ugly stretch of brown water that swallowed the road. Branches rushed by as a current swept them down to join the river.

"There's no crossing that," Josanne told them firmly. "So no one even think of trying, OK?"

Marko grunted. "I'm not grabbed by the notion of returning to the house."

Josanne echoed the heartfelt grunt. "Neither am I. Nor do we need to. We passed a road branching off a couple of miles back. If we follow that, it should take us east in line with the river. We've got to reach a town before long."

"Even a farmhouse would do," Fabian muttered. "Anywhere with a bloody phone that works."

Marko pulled a U-turn. Soon the floodwater receded into the gloom. Moments later Josanne pointed out the right. At least it was a paved road, not a dirt track. Fisher gazed out the back window as a faint streak of red appeared above the tree line. Just when you were beginning think that the night would last forever, he told himself. He steadied himself with both hands and grunted with pain as Marko took a bend. That blow across the hand had been a bitch. Jak made a small *yip* sound in the back of his throat. Fisher accepted that as a note of sympathy.

"Hi there, boy. You get my vote for the hero of the hour." The dog regarded him with its amber eyes. Their dark pupils moved just a touch from side to side as if Jak read the expression on his face. Smiling, Fisher stroked the dog's head. He heard the thump of the wagging tail as it struck the side of the van. Once more Fisher glanced through the rear windows. Now it was a little brighter, he could just make out an object—a series of objects, in fact, that caught his eye.

"See the telegraph poles? There's a wire, too." His smile broadened. "If there's a telephone cable, then it must reach a telephone at some point."

Five minutes later Marko braked sharply.

"Not another flood?" Josanne sounded anxious.

"No."

"Seeing as there's been no traffic since we left the house, I was beginning to wonder."

Marko looked back with a grin. "How's a garage and a motel for you?"

"Really?"

Josanne's pleasure at a pair of mundane conveniences of the twenty-first century made Fisher smile again.

Marko said, "We can drive on or stop here."

"Stop here, for God sakes." Fabian's clipped, lordly diction had returned at long last. "We'll phone the police from the garage."

As soon as Marko pulled up in the forecourt, they all tumbled out into the fresh morning air to stretch their limbs. Now the chill felt good. Even better was the light creeping over the fields. Of course it revealed nothing but trees and plowed earth, but it was God-given light. It chased all the night shadows away.

Fisher stood there supporting his left hand in his right. The fingers had become bulbous across the knuckles where they'd begun to swell. Fabian's slamming the door across his hand like that had been an accident, but that didn't stop Fisher from aching to kick the guy in the rear. He was sure the little finger was broken. That meant his bass playing would be curtailed for the next couple of weeks at least. Thanks a lot, Fabian, you self-centered great—

"Garage is shut," Sterling announced.

"It can't be."

"There's only the security light on inside. The pumps are dead."

Fisher felt as insignificant as a fly in the midst of that vast tract of land. They'd gone through hell. The Tower was miles behind them. Now they'd reached a gas station complete with snacks, candy stripe awning, three gas pumps standing smartly to attention, and yet . . . and yet the damn thing was shut.

Josanne asked, "Any sign of life?"

Sterling and Marko checked. They shielded their eyes so they could peer through the windows.

"Not a bean," Marko said as he rattled the door. "Locked up tight."

Fisher winced with every step he took. The pain throbbed to the same rhythm as his pace. He found a card wedged into the bottom corner of the frame behind the glass. "Opening times," he read. "Weekdays seven AM."

Sterling shrugged. "Today's Wednesday."

"What time is it?"

"Twenty-five minutes to six." Fabian used his best pedantic tones. "Another hour at least before our pump jockey rides in."

"Marvelous, bloody marvelous." Adam's voice was as dark and as flat as before.

"Any sign of a pay phone?" Fisher asked.

"There's one inside the store." Sterling nodded at the window. "There's some pretty hefty rocks round the front. We could put one through the glass."

Josanne clicked her tongue. "Of course, we could just take a walk across to the motel."

Fisher followed the others. The dog trotted quickly to keep up. Josanne's answer appeared to be the smart one, but the entire facility looked deserted. Not a single car occupied a space in the lot. The drapes on the motel windows were all open. So unless anyone had walked here . . .

"I don't believe it," she said, kicking the door. "This is locked, too."

Fisher checked the telephone cable again. He saw the black licorice whip of wire that ran from a wooden pole to a cleat that fastened it to the motel fascia board, then the cable ran into the building through a drilled hole.

"There are phones inside."

"I know." Josanne seethed with irritation. "There's probably a phone in every bloody room. It's just they're in there and we're out here!"

"Breaking in's going to be a difficult option," Sterling said. "See those steel bars over the windows?"

"Surely the motel can't be closed, too."

Fisher stepped closer to the bright yellow doors. In one window was a notice. "It's the equivalent of a vending machine," he said. "I've stopped in one before. Look, it's all automatic."

"You mean they don't have staff?"

"They do during the day. But if you arrive at night, you just use your credit card like a key. See the slot?"

Fabian pulled out his wallet. "Stand back. I'll get us in." He moved in that waspish way of his, a controlled speed that got the job done fast. He inserted the credit card. After a moment the door buzzed. A green light flashed above the card slot as the door locks disengaged with a click. The door admitted them into a small hallway where there was something like an ATM. Fabian had to insert the card again, tap his code into the keypad, and then follow more instructions on a touch screen.

"I'll order two rooms," he said. Then, with a rare flash of humor, he added, "It says no dogs allowed . . . but they can go to hell."

As he cradled his throbbing fingers, Fisher prayed that the machine wouldn't swallow the card or declare it invalid. If recent events were to go by, anything could happen. He even glanced out to the road, awash with early morning light. He half expected to see Cantley loping toward them with a shotgun in his hands.

Fabian prodded at the key pad. It bleeped monotonously as he answered yet more questions. Hell, this was taking forever.

Then, at last, a square of paper slid out from a slot. "Door code numbers," Fabian announced. He retrieved the credit card, then held up the slip so he could read the code. As he did so, the second door gave a metallic *thunk*. Fabian pushed it open to admit them into a reception area with plastic benches in that same banana yellow. Artificial flowers in light vases adorned the room. A shutter had been locked down across the reception counter with the words CLOSED UNTIL 8 AM printed across it.

"Open sesame," Fabian declaimed as he keyed numbers from the slip into a numeric pad beside a third door. "You might want to freshen up while we wait for the police." He pulled open the door to a corridor lined with bright yellow doors. "We've got rooms one and two, so it looks as if we're the only guests." He clicked his tongue to encourage Jak through into the corridor. "You'll be able to make coffee, too." He reached the first door and tapped the number into the pad. After the lock clicked, he pushed it open. *"Yes!"* A note of triumph raised his voice. "At last we have a telephone." He stood back. "Guys, you use this one. Josanne take the next. I'll make the call, then let you know what's happening. Jak? Where do you want to go, Jak? Looks as if you've got company, Josanne."

Fisher stood back as Sterling, Marko and Adam filed into the room. Fabian went to the next door and tapped in the door code to unlock it, then he pushed open the door for Josanne. She paused to let Jak in, then she called back in the most cheerful voice he'd heard in hours. "A motel room. A bed, a TV, a phone. Who could believe it's heaven on earth?"

Fisher nodded. Right now this place did seem like heaven. This wasn't the kind of place to be haunted by chimes from an ancient clock. A clock buried in its lair in a medieval house within a house.

Fabian walked back to room number one with a terse, "OK. I'll phone."

Fisher followed Fabian into the room. Marko and Sterling sat on the king-size bed. Adam slumped into an armchair by the TV. Shock had left him in a detached state. He stared without being aware of the people with him or where he was. Fabian strode to where a telephone sat on desk. Right now it was the key to their dilemma, their savior angel, and their magic carpet out of here rolled into one.

Fabian picked up the handset and began to dial.

Cantley had watched the van leave The Tower. It had barreled furiously down the driveway. Gravel spewed from its spinning tires. The motor had roared. Its headlights had blazed against the trees. Then it had screeched through the gates onto the roadway before it hurtled away into the night. He'd seen everything. All six—five men and a woman—had gotten into the van. The black dog had gone with them.

Whistling, his fists pushed deep into the pockets of his jacket, Cantley walked up to the front doors that had been left open by the trespassers in their rush to escape. Now, he told himself, it's time to wait.

Fisher went to stand by the motel window as Fabian dialed. In moments the crime would be reported to the police. Fisher imagined a line of police cars with their sirens whooping as they raced up the driveway to the godforsaken mausoleum of a building that was

The Tower. Now the early morning sun broke through the clouds on the horizon. Shafts of red light struck fields and bushes. A jet trail drew an orange line across the sky as the rising sun illuminated it. A passenger jet full of people being served coffee by the smiling cabin crew. Across the parking lot, a white Audi pulled up beside the filling station. This must be the proprietor arriving to open before the rest of the staff arrived. On the road a yellow school bus ambled by. No doubt it had to make an early start to collect the schoolchildren from whatever rural backwaters they inhabited. Adam was still slumped in the armchair. Sterling and Marko sat on the edge of the bed. Their heads hung wearily. Now that their escape from The Tower was over, they began to relax. Fisher glanced at his wristwatch. Six o'clock.

At the other side of the room, Fabian spoke into the phone, his tone businesslike: "I need to report a crime. . . ."

A scream—a piercing one—a scream powered by anger and shock with a searing undercurrent of disbelief.

Fabian dropped the phone. "That's Josanne!"

Following the scream came a volley of furious barks from Jak. Fabian ran to the door. In a split second he'd wrenched it open and disappeared into the motel corridor.

Cantley! The madman must have followed us here. The thought sped through Fisher's head as he followed Fabian through the yellow door into the corridor with its corporate carpeting and branded décor that led directly into . . .

. . . into the cellar of The Tower. Fisher stopped so hard his feet skidded across the slime covered brick floor. The old Hoovers, furniture and moldy blankets lay scattered in heaps where the receding floodwaters had left them. He stared about him in that cold gloomy vault.

When he hissed the words, "No . . . you can't do this to us," his breath peeled from his lips in clouds of white vapor. For a moment all sound was sucked from the air. There was a silence that went beyond mere silence. A profound absence of noise. The silence of a tomb that had lain undisturbed for a thousand years.

Then it broke. In shimmering notes, as ice cold metal struck ice cold metal, the chimes ghosted down through the walls—not only through the fabric of the building, but through the fabric of time itself, as if an ancient voice vented its cold fury on him. The instant the chimes began their toll, he heard the arched vaults above him groan.

Chapter Thirty-five

Fabian heard the single chime as he ran out of the motel room. There was no resonance. The vibration was abruptly cut; it sounded as if what had started as a clock chime ended as a *clunk!* He registered the sound in the back of his mind, but his priority was Josanne. He, too, had thought one name when he heard the scream. Cantley.

In seconds he raced from the room, flinging aside the telephone, to the one where they'd left Josanne just moments before, from where he'd heard her scream and the dog's barks. Her room was empty. There were no signs of commotion. A depression showed on the bed where she must have lain for a moment.

"She's gone," he shouted back to the others. "The dog, too."

When there was no reply, he looked back. Marko, Fisher and Sterling had been following from the motel room. He was sure of it. Only the corridor was de-

Simon Clark

serted. A rush of cold flooded him as he returned to the room he'd exited just seconds ago.

"Fisher? Adam?"

The bright yellow door yawned wide open. Beyond it, room number one held no human occupants. The four men had gone.

The volume of the chimes made Fisher grimace. Not only were they loud, but the metallic notes vibrated on his eardrums with such an intensity that they itched. Fisher craved to drive his fingers into his ears to scratch at the sensitive skin. In the light falling through the doorway at the top of the cellar steps, he saw pools of stagnant water on the floor. The walls bore streaks of black silt from the flood that had nearly claimed Josanne's life. Pond weed hung in vivid green strands from where it had snagged on shelves. It even clung to upended Hoovers in shaggy pelts that still dripped water. Even though the sound disoriented Fisher, he found himself thinking, a minute ago I was in the motel. I heard Josanne scream. I ran out of the room into the motel corridor. So how come I'm back here in The Tower? How on earth can it have brought me back?

Above the chimes, Fisher heard the bricks groan as they chafed against one another in the ceiling vaults. Pieces of mortar crumbled away to fall with a pitter-patter on the floor. The movement of the bricks became more pronounced. Now they appeared more like the scales of a monstrous reptile that shrugged its body to produce ripples in its skin. The brickwork bulged. The walls deformed as a colossal force pressed inward from the other side. Now the nightmare came back to him with a power that was nothing less than caustic. He flinched as he recalled lying in his room as its walls and ceiling bulged in at him.

You've had the dream—the death dream—now the chimes, Fisher told himself. This is when the vision becomes reality. Images of himself lying crushed beneath the masonry struck him with a force that made him gasp. The image of his mutilated head. How the eyeballs had been pressed back into the skull to be replaced by twin pools of glistening crimson. A brick worked itself from the ceiling to fall so close it brushed his arm. The movement required him to raise his arm to shield his head; instantly it brought a jag of pain to his injured hand. Pain skewered through it like a jet of flame. It hurt enough to shock Fisher out of standing there like a slab of wood. As the bricks worked loose from the bucking ceiling, he ran for the stairs. Bricks slipped from their mortared joints with a grating sound. All around him they crashed down to shatter in a splash of red dust. One struck his shoulder hard enough to make him curse. Busted fingers or not, he held both hands above his head to protect his skull from the tumbling blocks.

And all the while, clock chimes beat through the air and through his skull into the center of his brain where they echoed with a savage power. When he reached the stairs, a brick ejected from the wall to strike him on the forehead. He stumbled. The next second he was on his hands and knees. More bricks struck his back. The chimes rose in pitch. A note of triumph. The house celebrated his fall into the filth. It exulted at his pain. More bricks cascaded. One landed an inch from his broken finger.

Fisher! If you don't damn well move, you're going to be buried under a pile of the things!

Gritting his teeth, he let out a yell of fury. Then he used that rage to fuel his scramble up the stairs. The moment he crashed the cellar door shut behind him, the chimes stopped.

The chimes. Adam didn't know whether they came from inside his head or outside the motel. An ice cream truck out here? In the middle of nowhere? He'd looked up from where he sat in the armchair when he heard the scream. Fabian and the others had rushed to the motel room door. Thoughts of Belle dominated. Grief at her murder overwhelmed him. All he could see in his mind's eye was her bloody body lying in that monstrous house. Josanne's scream, however, roused him. Adam ran after the others from the room into . . . into . . . *into* . . . *onto* . . .

Onto the concrete runway. Mist swirled about him. Turning round and around, he saw acres of swamp. The pools of viscous mud that looked like molten tar in the dawn light. Adam heard the chimes from the house. He turned to gaze at it. The huge bleak building, with the central tower that was like a fist raised to shake its fury at the world of man. Its windows had the dull quality of dead eyes, while at its base was the bristling barrier of a hawthorn. The botanical version of razor wire. Keeping people out? Keeping people in? That depended on the circumstances . . . whatever the house wanted.

Come to that, whatever The Tower wants, The Tower gets. That's why a minute ago I was in a motel miles away—and now I'm here. The chimes came tolling down the meadow with all the measured gravity of a funeral bell. Fog rolled in from the swamp. The pools of stagnant water began to vanish into murky gray.

312

"Find the others," Adam murmured to himself. "They're back, too." He was sure of it. He wouldn't be the only one. As he walked along the center of the concrete runway, he looked for the dry land that would take him back to the house. The chimes continued. They shape-shifted on the cold dawn air. One moment a thin, brittle sound, the same as ice cracking beneath your feet on a frozen lake; then they would descend into deep shimmering bass notes that appeared to roll from the ground. The measured pounding of dead hands from behind the tomb door. Adam didn't know whether the sound was in his head or was some weird distorting effect of the topography of the landscape. Maybe his mind was being torn loose of its moorings as he wrestled with the concepts of Belle's slaughter, the panicky dash from the house, and finding that he'd been flung by supernatural forces back here to the runway that lay beneath the brooding presence of The Tower.

"It scared you, didn't it?"

The voice had a cracking quality to it as it floated through the mist. Adam's eyes roved over the marsh as he searched for the speaker of the words. He saw hundreds of yards of water, liquid mud, tussocks of grass. . . .

"It's the house. It did that." The voice sounded pleased. "The house makes it seem like the chimes are coming outta your head." The voice changed into cracked laughter. "It scared you, didn't it? You should've seen your face!"

Now the chimes had returned to their steady brassy rhythm. Adam figured the voice came from his left, out in the swamp itself. He walked to the edge of the runway that formed the linear man-made island.

"The house can do anything. It can make you fly back here. You didn't know that, but you do now! From anywhere in the world, it can just pull you back. You can never escape it!"

Adam sang out, "The house wants, the house gets?"

"You understand how it works now, eh? Better late than never."

As Adam moved slowly toward the edge of the runway, he saw a figure out in the swamp. It stood so still that for a moment he began to question whether it was a man or simply a post poking upright from the grassy tussocks. The chimes changed. They'd quickened. They sounded like breaking glass. He could only take one more step closer. The edge of the runway was in line with the toes of his shoes. Just a couple of inches away was one of the stagnant pools of water streaked with bright green veins of weed. For some reason it reminded him of a vast discolored eyeball without a pupil or iris. Perhaps the eye of a man who'd lain dead for a dozen years. A ruin of moss and decay.

The figure took two steps forward. "You can see me now, can't you?"

Adam recognized him now. *"Cantley."* The man was perhaps a hundred feet from him. He stood on grassy mounds that poked just inches above the slick surface of the noxious silt. The mist thinned enough for Adam to take in the scruffy mass of hair. Above the coldly gleaming eyes that stared back at him was the distinctive crescent of scar tissue. Cantley wore a dull green jacket that had had frayed into wisps of loose fibers. The jeans weren't in better shape. Holes at the knees revealed grimy skin.

"You should have listened to The Tower talk. You'd have understood it would give you what you wanted."

"Cantley? Did you kill Belle? The woman with blond hair?"

"You have to give something in return. You don't get something for nothing, do you?"

Adam's eyes took in the malnourished form. He might have been armed with a handgun or a knife. But if he was, why didn't he show them? Maybe he'd caught the guy without a weapon. A plan began to form in Adam's mind.

"And there was another girl?" Adam followed the line of grass tussocks that formed something like a raised spine through the marsh. "Did you see her?"

"I was born with pain in my body," Cantley's voice cracked. "When I came here, the house sometimes made the pain stop."

"Did you kill Kym?"

"I only had to pay the price."

"Listen to me. *Did you kill Kym?*"

"Of course I did. What do you think I gave to the house? Cow shit?"

The line of grass tussocks formed tiny islands. They ranged in size from a dinner plate to a tabletop. The sight of Cantley gloating at him was too much. Cantley had killed both Kym and Belle. That knowledge was a big sweet candy bar to the madman. He sucked on it with pleasure.

He knows that I know that he knows. . . . That's how it goes, doesn't it?

Adam took a step forward onto a clump of grass. It squelched under his feet but was firm enough. The chimes continued. Six o'clock was long gone. They were faster now. An urgency drove them.

Cantley raised both hands with the fingers splayed outwards. As if to say: *Look at these hands. These hands*

Simon Clark

held the knife that stabbed the woman until she bled to death. Take a look at these hands, a good, long hard look. These hands killed two women.

With a bellow of fury, Adam ran along the line of grassy islets. His feet made the earth yield a little, but the matted vegetation held his weight. The clock chimes beat louder. The sound worked deep into his ears to irritate the sensitive skin. But he wasn't about to stop now. Cantley was just fifty feet away. He didn't appear to have anywhere to run. He wasn't armed. Adam bunched his fists. He'd pound the guy until the bones of his face snapped beneath his knuckles.

The mist thickened. It didn't matter. Adam was only paces away from the murderer. His scrawniness and pinched sick-looking face told Adam that Cantley lacked the muscle for a fistfight. Adam's eyes flicked down to make sure he didn't stray off those tiny islands of marsh grass. Cantley was ten paces away when he took three steps to the right. *Trying to get away, huh?*

Adam turned right to stop his escape. Immediately his foot splashed down into a substance that offered no resistance to his weight. Momentum carried him forward until both feet were in the liquid. He tried to step forward. The liquid was mud, a loose silt that had the consistency of something like yogurt. It couldn't hold him; he sank down into its cold grip, which stank of wet leaves that had spent the winter rotting beneath a tree.

From a half a dozen paces away, Cantley looked down at him. "Didn't I tell you it wasn't safe? Or did it slip my mind?" He nodded with satisfaction, then put his hand to one ear as he fixed the staring eyes on Adam. "What do you hear?"

"Damn you!"

Adam wasn't going to give the madman the satisfaction of knowing what he heard. It was the raucous chiming of the clock. It sounded like someone abandoning themselves to peals of deranged laughter. The ice-cold liquid had reached his chest by the time he struck out for the nearest tussock of grass. It formed a grassy dome that rose about four inches out of the liquid mud at its highest. If only . . .

Adam strained forward to reach it. The grass was wiry. If he could grip it he was sure he could haul himself out. Then Cantley would experience pain like he'd never felt before. The brown slop reached Adam's shoulders. His arms were smeared with the stuff. He could feel it sucking him down. Meanwhile, the chimes had speeded to a *ding-ding-ding-ding!*

A shape moved above him against a background of mist. That cracked voice said, "Hey, idiot. Did you ever think I'd let you catch me?"

Adam snarled, "Damn you, Cantley. When you die, you're going to hell!"

"I'm going to hell, you say?" Cantley smiled. His misshapen teeth were a sickly yellow. "You're wrong. We're already there."

He reached out with his boot and rested the muddy sole on Adam's head. Adam screamed at him. Cantley took no notice, but shifted his balance so he could press down on the man's head. The extra weight made the inevitable come more quickly.

Adam felt the tide of muck rise up over his neck to his chin. It was bitingly cold. Unlike treading water, being neck-deep in mud is a crushing force. Even before it reached his lips, the pressure against his stomach was so great he could no longer inhale. By the time the moist filth crept over his mouth, the compression of his torso caused what air remained in his lungs to whisper out through his nostrils. All he could do was roll his eyeballs upward to see the grinning man press down with his foot. The weight on his skull hurt so much he longed to cry out, but the flood of silt into his mouth made screaming impossible. Somehow he knew he screamed with his eyes. He knew they'd be bright with pain as they bulged from his skull. His hair, which Belle loved so much, was coated in mud.

Adam could still hear the chimes. They were deafening. Like the peal of cathedral bells inside his skull. As his head passed from the world of air and life into this liquid world of choking mud, the chimes changed again. This time they sounded like the roar of aircraft engines. Only they rose in pitch as if the engines ran out of control to shake themselves to pieces. From those whirling propellers in his mind's eye, sparks of purple and red sprayed out into eternity . . . forever and ever.

In the motel room, Josanne had heard the clock chimes strike with such power that it felt like a blow against the side of her head. Jak heard them, too. As he'd barked, she'd stumbled toward the motel corridor with the intention of finding Fabian. Josanne knew she was screaming. Part of her detested the cries she made—they were a sign of weakness and panic—but dear God, the pain from that sound was phenomenal. Only she never stepped into the corridor. With her eyes three-quarters shut from the pain, she'd staggered past the bright yellow plastic door to find herself in a cold void. Perfect darkness. Not a glimmer of light. She couldn't see a thing.

The chimes receded to a faint metallic hum that swelled before falling away. The sound made her think of the silvery lungs of some nightmare machine. A robot sound . . . Strange thoughts . . . They didn't stop there. She recalled what Fisher had told her about the house returning Blaxton to its grounds so it could finally make his death dream come true.

So it's brought me back, Josanne told herself. I was in the motel; now I'm back here.

"Hello."

The chimes shaped her echo into a metallic snarl, then hurled it back at her. *Hello!* It could have been the house throwing out a sarcastic, "Hello yourself."

"Fisher? Is anyone there?"

Fisher! Is anyone there! The mutant sound roared back at her. Its harsh resonance set her teeth on edge, the sound less pleasant than a knife screeching across a plate.

"Are you there?"

Are you there!

Josanne stepped forward. Her hands swam through the darkness, trying to find a wall.

"Fabian? Marko? Fisher?"

Fabian! Marko-ohh! Fish-urrrr! The chimes deformed her echo into a maelstrom that spun around her head. *Damn. I've got to find a light. I can't bear that sound. . . .*

It seemed to read her mind. The chimes fused into a scream that ascended in pitch until she thought her skull would shatter. Josanne had to keep moving forward. Where she was going in the dark she didn't know. But she couldn't stop here. That wasn't an option. But where was here? This icy darkness suggested that she was back in the cellar. Thoughts of the flood sped through her mind. She recalled how it had tumbled her on its currents like a rag doll. A soft form pressed against her thigh. Gulping with shock, she reached down to push it away. Her mind's eye supplied an image of Cantley creeping out of the darkness to grasp her. Josanne's fingers encountered fur.

"Jak?"

The dog came up next to her. She felt the gentle thump of his tail against her thigh; then he nuzzled her hand with his nose.

"Jak. Stay close to me, boy."

The dog had found her in the darkness. Knowing she was no longer alone prevented the all-consuming panic. Suddenly the chimes didn't seem as harsh. They continued, but they settled into a rhythmic pulse of metal on metal. She bent down to hook a finger in Jak's collar. The moment she did so, he began to walk. *Just hope to God he's leading me out of here.* The darkness began to change. Instead of the black fog that pressed against her wideopen eyes, a gray patch appeared to her left. It brightened. A moment later, she realized she was looking at the medieval façade of the Good Heart.

So it's brought me back into the center of The Tower. I'm walking along the Promenade.

The chimes became blossoms of sound; there was a sense of opening, of unfolding. Each bell-like note began as a ringing tone before mutating into a shimmering rush of sound that ghosted through the air. To her left the ancient wall glowed. She could see the stones, the deep-set windows, the carved animal above the doorway; the door itself, a stunted thing that most would have to stoop to enter. Inside the house-within-a-house had been a mass of shadows. Now an illumination grew there, a sickly yellow light that revealed the interior. Through those windows she saw figures. They were silhouettes of people dressed in archaic clothes; she glimpsed the outline of oddly bulbous hats and women in long dresses. At first she thought they were playing a game, but then she saw that some of the silhouettes wielded swords that they used to hack off the heads of the other figures. The house was showing her a massacre that occurred there centuries before. Blood ran in thick crimson rivulets through the doorway. Above the grim rhythm of chimes, she heard the dying screams of women and children.

"Get me out of here!" she whispered to Jak as she broke into a run. In front of her, a man knelt on the ground. He wore a flying suit and a yellow life vest. His shoulders shook as he wept.

Don't look at him. The house is showing you what happened in the past. It's not happening now. It's an echo, nothing but a fucking echo.

But Josanne couldn't stop herself. As she ran past, she glanced down at him. He wore tinted flying goggles, so she couldn't see his eyes. The black muzzle of the pistol slipped through his lips to touch the roof of his mouth. When he squeezed the trigger, cordite smoke jetted from his mouth, his head jerked, and the flying goggles filled with blood; but she didn't hear a gun shot. Instead one of the clock chimes swelled into a metallic clash that was so loud it slammed the air from her lungs. Jak yelped in pain.

"Keep going!" she shouted. Ahead she could see Belle in the weird custard yellow light. Belle still lay in the same position with her legs awkwardly bent at the knee. Her dead eyes stared at the ceiling. Her spilt blood had congealed on the floor.

Josanne gritted her teeth as she raced for the twin doors.

Marko's smooth transition from the motel to The Tower was like the rest. As the chimes started, he simply was no longer in the motel room with its TV and yellow décor. He opened his eyes to find himself lying on a hard, lumpy surface. A protrusion dug into his spine. He looked up at a white-painted ceiling. The chimes rang loudly. Instantly he knew the score. Fisher had repeated it often enough. *You dream your own death. Then it happens to you.* Marko's nightmare had been fire, a consuming furnace. He rolled to one side as he heard a hiss, smelled cooking gas, then heard the pop of it igniting. The back of his neck smarted as heat seared the skin. Now instead of the gas smell, there was the acrid stink of singed hair.

Marko rolled sideways off his lumpy platform to fall three feet onto a tiled floor. In a second he was on his feet slapping at his scorched clothes.

"Yeah, you tried your best," he told the house. "You dumped old Marko on the stove to fry."

It was a big old iron range in the main kitchen, intended to cook food for a hundred people. Six pairs of gas burners ran along its length. One of the gas jets had been the unyielding lump that pressed into his spine. When he was satisfied his clothes and his hair weren't on fire, he turned to watch the jets hiss with a bright blue flame.

The chimes stopped dead. It was as good as a

prompt. He turned the knobs on the front of the stove to kill the flames.

That done, Marko stood back to glare up at the ceiling. "Nice try, house! You didn't get me that time!"

Sterling never achieved full consciousness. In a dreamlike state, he heard the clock chime. It wasn't the regulation six for six o'clock. They went on and on. He realized he sat on a chair. He knew that the dimensions of the room were different from the motel room that he'd occupied moments before. Cold air touched his skin. No light reached his eyes. In the darkness there was no air to breathe. His death burst on him with the suddenness of a lightning flash.

Chapter Thirty-six

Fisher had told him often enough in the past few hours, yet Fabian had played the modern man. Blinkered by the digitized, computerized trappings of modern technology, he'd refused to admit the truth: The Tower was evil. It wouldn't let them go. Only for some reason the house hadn't been able to get its hooks into one of its visitors. And that visitor was Fabian. The Tower had taken the others back into itself. Belle had been murdered. Kym had most likely suffered the same fate.

Now Josanne and the others had been snatched back there. Fabian knew he had get back there as fast as he could. As he ran from the motel, the proprietor of the garage was mopping the area around the gas pumps from a steaming pail. Fabian didn't know if the guy looked his way in surprise as he raced like a lunatic to the van. He didn't care. He had to find Josanne. God alone knew what had happened to her back at that evil heap of stones. Within moments

Fabian had turned the ignition key. The motor howled as he floored the gas pedal to send the van rocketing across the lot to the road. It would take twenty minutes to return to The Tower. Already a sick feeling crept into Fabian's throat as he anticipated what he would find there.

They found Sterling in the ballroom. He sat on the sofa with the audiotape spools and cassettes that Fisher had found in the cellar arranged around his feet. Sterling had slumped low enough down into the sofa for his head to be held upright by the backrest. Fisher had entered the ballroom, tying a handkerchief around his injured hand so as to protect the broken little finger from further damage. What he saw there stopped him in his tracks. As it did Marko and Josanne when they joined him.

Sterling slouched back as if taking a nap, only his mouth was wide open. Running from the man's mouth were dark brown lines of audiotape. They spilled from his overstretched jaws to the cassettes and spools lying on the floor at his feet, where yet more of the tape was still wrapped around the spindles. Sterling's mouth had been packed tight with the tape. It formed a compacted mass of shiny plastic ribbon. A trickle of blood ran from his nose to drip from the end of his chin onto his shirt.

Marko started forward. "Sterling . . . Sterling?"

Fisher spoke bluntly, "He's dead."

Marko looked back at him with pain filled eyes. "Fisher, how can you be sure?"

"Look how swollen his throat is. The tape's been forced into his throat. There's so much it's stretched his windpipe." He grimaced as he finished tying the handkerchief around his hand. "It probably fills his lungs, too."

"Cantley did this?" Josanne's voice rose in horror. "How on earth could he—"

"The Tower brought us back here from the motel." To Fisher's ears his voice sounded brutally matter-of-fact. "The moment it dumped us back here, it tried to kill us. With Sterling it succeeded." He slowly approached his friend. It looked as if Sterling was in the process of vomiting a dozen strands of magnetic tape. Fisher was surprised at himself for not being felled by grief—he'd known Sterling for years. Only there wasn't time for grieving now. What they did in the next couple of hours would determine whether they lived or died. Sorrow would come later. If they made it.

"Hell," Marko breathed. "Why did it do that to Sterling?"

"Because it could," Josanne said.

Fisher nodded. "And it wants whoever survives its attacks to know what it's capable of."

"But how could it force so much tape into his mouth that he suffocated? I mean, the mechanics of it?"

Josanne's face was grim. "How did the house yank us back here from miles away?" She crouched down to put her arm round Jak as he sat beside her, a gesture to bring comfort to her as much as the dog. "If you can answer that one, you've got an answer to how it can choke a man with tape."

Fisher grimaced. "We know it's not going to pull any punches. It's not even content with killing us." He looked up at the ceiling. "You want to put us through hell first, don't you, house? You want to mess us up so badly that we haven't the guts to put up a fight." His voice echoed back at him. And the echo changed slightly, so that the reverberation was out of sync with his speech. When he spoke next, the echo even preceded the words as he spoke them. Just another example of the house toying with them. *Call it Jack*—"Call it Jack the Ripper Syndrome"—*the Ripper Syndrome. See you're* . . .

"See, you're doing it now. You're aiming to screw with our heads."

Screw with our heads . . . The echo shimmered, a ghostly sound that chilled them to the bone.

Instead of allowing the confused welter of echo to throw him, Fisher pushed on. "I'm calling it Jack the Ripper Syndrome, because when the killer struck in Whitechapel over a hundred years ago, he wanted to show off." *Wanted* . . . *show off* . . . "He wanted to prove to the police that he not only could slaughter defenseless women without being caught, but he also butchered them. He cut out their wombs and slashed their faces. Finicky little crosscuts on their skin. Frivolous patterns carved on their flesh, just so he could say, 'Aren't I a clever boy?' But hear this, you ugly pile of stones, Jack the Ripper was a coward—and so are you!"

The echoes fused into a thunderous roll of sound that quickly died away to silence.

Josanne took a deep breath. "The Tower sure as hell heard you, Fisher. And it didn't like what it heard."

"Good. Because if we're going to make it out of here, we're going to have to start fighting back."

Fabian pushed the van hard. He hurtled round corners. Tires screamed. More than once, he wound up leaving the blacktop to fishtail across the grass at the side of the road.

"Just don't put the fucking thing in a ditch," he hissed to himself.

As Fabian neared The Tower, the mist thickened. Soon he couldn't see the rising sun. It became gloomier. He could even feel fingers of damp reaching in through the vehicle to touch his skin. Within a hundred yards, visibility had dropped to all but zero. All he could see were gloomy, formless shadows that must have been trees. A sense of danger crackled through him. Any second now he might power the van into a tractor or a bus. He saw himself flying through the windshield to crash against the ground. Fabian stomped the brake. The van slithered to a crawl. With the speedometer touching ten miles an hour he rumbled forward.

Hell, this was a fog, alright. The king of fogs. He couldn't even see the white lines on the road when he switched on the lights. It was only as he passed the entrance gates that he realized he'd missed the turn in the murk. Quickly he reversed the van, then advanced along the gravel driveway.

Huh. Back so soon. Fabian thought he'd left the place for good. Now, with a dark, irresistible gravity all of its own, The Tower pulled him back.

They quit the ballroom for the little kitchen they'd used during happier times to prepare their meals. Fisher glanced round at the exhausted, battered people gathered there. Josanne had dark rings etched beneath her eyes. Marko: he appeared only semiconscious from the shock of Sterling's death. Then there was Jak. He appeared the most alert of all and stood between them and the kitchen door. The animal kept his guard up. Fisher felt a surge of gratitude that Jak was with them. No bones about it, he was a source of strength to the beleaguered group.

Fisher took a breath. The question had to be asked. "So we all experienced it?"

Josanne nodded. "We heard the chimes in the motel, then *pfft*. A second later we were all back here."

"What happened when it hauled you back?"

Josanne explained that she'd been subjected to a psychological attack in the Good Heart. The house had replayed an ancient massacre, then she'd seen a revenant of an airman blowing his brains out with a handgun. "The house was trying to make me crack," she said. "I'm sure of it. The chimes were going crazy."

Marko said, "I found myself lying across the gas stove in the big kitchen. It tried to set fire to me. See the singe marks on my hair at the back?"

"Your clothes are scorched, too." Fisher pointed out, then he told them what happened to him, his manifestation in the cellar followed by the brick ceiling falling in on him.

"Yeah," Marko said. "You've got the wounds to prove it, too. Do they hurt?"

Fisher found the graze on his forehead with the fingertips of his good hand. "With the speed of everything, I hadn't got round to noticing." Then he added grimly, "I'll live."

"It's going to pull this stunt again, isn't it?" Not so much a question from Marko but a statement.

Josanne rubbed a hand along her forearm. "So what happened to Adam?"

* * *

Cantley returned to the house. Once more he climbed the central staircase into The Tower. In his hands he carried a steel rod that was as thick as his thumb and almost as tall as he was. He'd filed the rod to a point that was as thin as a needle at its tip. And, oh, he knew the trespassers were back in The Tower. He knew also The Tower had pulled them back from wherever they'd fled to. Cantley had seen this happen before. He'd seen them when he'd peeked in through the windows into the ballroom. One of their number lay dead on the sofa. And the tall one had vanished into the swamp, his descent aided by Cantley's boot pushing down on his beautiful hair. So how many did that leave alive? Four plus the dog? Although he'd only seen three living people with the corpse. *So . . . one of their number's unaccounted for.*

Not that it mattered. They were doomed to die. As simple as that. The only question now was: Did the house plan to kill them all by itself? Or would it permit its faithful servant, Cantley, to have some bloody fun, too?

Fabian roared up the driveway in the van. So dense was the mist that he didn't even see the house until he'd nearly smashed into it. He braked hard, and the tires skidded through the gravel. Even before the vehicle had stopped, he'd leapt from it, then raced through the twin doors of the house.

Hell, you smell the same. You even stink of evil.

Chapter Thirty-seven

If Jak hadn't wagged his tail when the footfalls sounded in the corridor, Fisher would have hurled the heavy iron pan into the face of whoever walked through the door. Jittery? Ye gods, he was convinced it would be the murderer Cantley.

"Josanne!" Fabian crashed through the door, then embraced the woman so fiercely Fisher thought her ribs would crack.

Fisher and Marko slapped him on the back.

"What the hell happened to you?" Fisher demanded. "Where did it put you?"

"The house? It didn't put me anywhere. I drove back from the motel."

They were all talking at once. Josanne told him about finding Sterling dead in the ballroom. Marko pulled knives from the drawer while calling out they had to arm themselves in case they ran into Cantley. Fisher said, "Fabian, you must be immune from the house. It can't get its hooks into you."

"You might be right," Fabian agreed as he unpeeled his arms from a trembling Josanne. "But I'd wager good money it's still going to try its hardest to hit me in some way. Any sign of Adam?"

Marko shook his head. "We were hoping he'd just show up like you."

Fabian was wired. His eyes darted round the kitchen. "We all know that running away isn't an option. It won't let you."

"There's nothing to stop you," Fisher pointed out.

"There's no way I'm leaving without you all."

Josanne took a deep breath to steady her nerve. "It may come to that, Fabian."

"No way. I'm staying until we've beaten this crock of shit." He clenched his fists. "Listen. I've been figuring this out. We've got to fight back."

Marko frowned. "How?"

"Yeah," Josanne said nervously. "This place can do what it likes to us."

"No, it can't." He picked the heavy iron pan that Fisher had contemplated hurling at him until Jak had signaled that the visitor was friendly. "The house did its best to drown you, Josanne, but it failed. This place isn't all-powerful. It's got limitations." He crossed the kitchen to the window and swung the iron pan at a pane. It bounced back with a clang. He tried again. Same result. The pan struck the glass. Bounced off.

Fisher pointed out dryly, "If it has limitations, we haven't found them yet."

Marko grabbed a chair. "Here! Let me try." He hurled the chair at the window. It bounced back, forcing him to dodge it.

Josanne's voice came as a frightened gulp. "It won't let you damage it."

"There's a way!" Fisher shouted. "We'll find a way to hurt it so badly that it'll be glad to be rid of us."

Marko rubbed his jaw. "But if we can't even break one of its damn windows . . ."

"How are we going to trash the place?" Josanne added. "Besides, it hears what we say. It knows what we're trying to do."

Fabian clenched his fists. "Remember what Fisher told us about evil? About the nature of evil? Evil is opportunistic. It drifts along in an aimless way until it gets the chance to cause hurt. Evil needs a victim. If there aren't any victims, then it can't inflict damage."

"That's like saying if there wasn't gravity, then we couldn't fall down," Marko said. "It's a fact: there is gravity, and there are victims. They don't chose to be victims. People don't invite murderers to kill them."

"The point is," Fabian said, "we've got to act like we aren't victims. We've got to be brave, so overwhelmingly brave that we beat this thing through sheer willpower." His voice rose. "Tell yourself that the house can't hurt you. Convince yourself that if we choose to do so, we can rip down the walls with our bare hands." He still held the heavy-duty pan. Without any warning he slammed it back against the wall with so much force that it became mangled out of shape. "There!" He pointed. "There's your proof!"

Fisher looked at where Fabian pointed at the wall. "There's a dent. A small one, but he's marked the paint."

Fabian eyes blazed. He was ready for a fight. "OK. Let's throw a party."

"A party?" Josanne's expression suggested that she thought her lover had gone crazy.

Simon Clark

"A party," he repeated. "It's to celebrate the impending destruction of the house!"

A metallic shimmer sounded on the air. A cold steel sound. Fisher didn't think Fabian heard it. The rest did. They looked about anxiously. The house knew what Fabian said. Its reaction was something like the warning growl in a tiger's throat.

"Come on, we're going to the ballroom. We're going to play music."

"Music? Hell, man, you're crazy." Marko's face flushed red. "Didn't you hear what we told you about Sterling?"

"I know. That's why we're doing this. We're going to find out where the house is weak. When we've found its Achilles heel, that's when we'll strike." Fabian swept toward the door. "Come on. Music! That's what we're magnificent at!"

They ran along the corridor to the ballroom. Jak raced alongside them. He barked as he picked up on their mood, which had become nothing less than electric.

Or have we gone mad? Fisher thought. Has the house won? Has it sent us crazy? Because I don't feel terrified anymore. I feel as if my nerve endings are on fire. I feel so up that I'm never going to come down.

Sterling still lay on the sofa. That made them all pause, with the exception of Fabian, who raced across to the keyboard. He shouted back, "We're doing this for Sterling as well. And for Belle and for Kym! This is payback!" He thumped the power button on the keyboard, then ran to the amps to switch on each one in turn. "All the way up to ten, guys!" He cranked the volume. Speakers buzzed like a swarm of angry bees. "Marko! Fisher! You can do it!" Fabian played a run on the electric keyboard. As if in defiance of the clock chimes, he set the electronic voice to mimic bells. The notes rang in the air at such volume that the dog flinched.

"Are we really doing this?" Marko asked. "Or are we sitting in a padded room hallucinating like crazy?"

Fisher felt a wild grin reach his mouth. "Either way. We go with the flow." He picked up his bass guitar from the stand and plugged in. Instantly it came to life in his hands. He sensed the power running through its circuits. Fisher loosened the handkerchief from his injured left hand. The little finger still jutted out at an odd angle. Strangely, however, it didn't hurt anymore. Neither could he feel pain in the swollen fingers. If he didn't try and force the little finger to perform, he could still use the other digits to depress the strings against the fret board while the fingers of his good hand did the plucking.

Marko sat on the drum stool. Looking up at the ceiling, he cried out. "Keith Moon! If you can hear me, guide my hands! And give me strength to raise bloody hell!" He gave a savage laugh. It wasn't because he was amused by his spontaneous prayer to the patron saint of rock drummers. This wild rush of energy crackled through him, too. Seizing his sticks, he flailed at the drums in a mighty roll that sounded as if thunder crashed inside the ballroom. Fisher played a vicious rhythm on the bass. At the same moment Fabian struck keys on a laptop connected to the keyboard. His prerecorded synthesizer lines swirled through the air. He stepped back from the keyboard as it obeyed the presets to play a stabbing salvo of notes.

"Keep playing," he shouted over the wall of noise.

"This might not kill the house but it might give it a headache . . . enough to distract it."

A weird logic began to emerge from this. Fisher realized that The Tower frightened people by its repeated use of the clock chimes. If it knew that sound had the power to frighten, then might it be susceptible to sound, too? Fisher imagined the vibrations of the deafening music running through the fabric of the building to assault the foundations.

Marko must have been thinking along similar lines, because he yelled, "Walls of Jericho! Walls of Jericho!"

Then trumpets brought the walls tumbling down. Fabian gestured to Josanne to bring a newspaper. It lay on the floor by the sofa that still held the body of Sterling Pound. She didn't hesitate. With a determined expression, she ran to pick it up as Fabian went to the windows. He pulled the drape from the wall with one hand as he delved into his pocket for his lighter with the other. He thumbed the button to produce a narrow blue flame. Josanne realized what he intended. She held the newspaper over the flame. It caught in a second. Fabian held the drape out to the orange flame that consumed the paper. He stayed like that for thirty seconds until the flames threatened to scorch Josanne's fingers. Then he shook his head and gestured to her to drop the burning newspaper.

Fisher realized that his and Marko's music had faltered.

Fabian ran across the ballroom floor. Both his hands were outstretched as he made a lifting gesture. He was urging them to keep playing.

"I couldn't get the material to burn," he shouted. "It's stopping the flame from touching it somehow. But don't stop playing. Keep the tempo up. Play faster! We're not beaten yet!" As he crossed the floor again, the chimes sounded for eight o'clock. Immediately Fabian dashed to the keyboard and began hitting buttons. Then he straightened a microphone stalk so it pointed into the air. That done, he tapped more keys. As the chimes of eight o'clock died away, he pressed another key. The chimes returned through the speakers. Only this time they weren't The Tower's doing. Fabian had digitally recorded the sound. Now he replayed the chimes. He teased the sound using the synthesizer's modulators. He tortured the notes into new shapes, adding overlays, altering the pitch and the tempo—as far as the house was concerned, an unholy racket.

"Fight fire with fire!" he shouted over the wash of electronic harmonics. "It might only piss the house off . . . but we can try to hurt the bastard." He made adjustments to the keyboard controls, then stepped away from the instrument as the repeat function kicked in. Now it recycled the same sequence of sampled chimes over and over. Fisher and Marko fell in line to play their instruments as a backing to Fabian's cloned chimes.

Fabian beckoned Josanne. As he headed for the door, he turned round to shout through cupped hands, "If it works, it's going to distract this thing, whatever's been trying to hurt us. Josanne and I are going to attack the underbelly while it's not looking." He gave Fisher and Marko the thumbs up. "OK, guys. Play your hearts out!"

Fisher watched the pair of them leave the ballroom. This is it, he told himself, we're fighting back.

Chapter Thirty-eight

Josanne followed Fabian out of the ballroom and into the corridor. Jak came, too. The volume of the music was immense. It didn't sound any less volcanic away from the ballroom, either. Fisher played an elemental bass pattern while Marko flailed the skins like a demon drummer. The electronic keyboard maintained a cycle of repeated notes. They were a mixture of horn sounds and the sampled clock chimes that pulsed through the air in great beats of sound that made Josanne picture enormous temple bells of shining gold.

With the decibel level so high, they couldn't communicate by speech. Fabian pointed to the kitchen door and mouthed, "In there." She nodded. When they were inside the kitchen with the door closed behind them, they could at last talk.

"Some racket we're making, eh?" Fabian gave a grim smile. "If you ask me, our old friend The Tower doesn't like this. We're playing on a nerve."

"Then watch your back," she told him. "It's bound to try something."

He picked up the claw hammer from the counter. "We best arm ourselves."

"Human attackers might not be the problem."

"The house is weakening. Can't you feel it? OK, it's pulled off some spectacular stunts in the last few days, but my guess is it's only got a limited reservoir of energy. Once that's depleted, it could take years to rebuild to the levels we've encountered."

"Dear God, I hope you're right, Fabian."

"Another thing." He lightly tapped the steel head of the hammer into his palm. "Cantley. He and the house are in this together. If we can take him out of the picture, the house is going to lose an ally. OK, it might not be a body blow, but it might knock some fight out of it."

"Then we've got to find Cantley. How are we going to do that?"

Fabian's eyes settled on Jak. "I'm sure he's got some bloodhound in him. Let's put it to the test."

"We'll start with the buildings in the wood. That's where I saw Cantley first."

"Grab a knife. He's not going to give up without a fight."

The words chilled her as she selected a carving knife from the drawer. Before heading to the kitchen door, she glanced back through the window. Outside, a thick fog pressed through the hawthorn to encircle the house. It occurred to her that Cantley might have a gun after all. She was going to ask Fabian, what then? But what could they do? Their only option was to outmaneuver him. This is the bottom line, she told herself. It's a fight to the death. The only question—whose?

The second they entered the corridor, they were swamped by the torrent of music. In those hypnotic rhythms a power crackled through the notes. Music can energize you. It can make you tap your toe or want to dance. It makes you feel strong. That has to count for something, Josanne told herself. If music can make you believe you can triumph over the destructive forces that threaten you in your day-to-day life, then right now music can become a silver bullet that kills the monster.

They'd planned to exit through the main doors, then race through the mist to the outbuildings in the wood. However, they were still a dozen paces from the entrance hall when Jak froze. His hackles rose as his ears pricked. The animal's amber eyes locked on the staircase.

"He's here!" Fabian hissed.

"Jak," Josanne whispered. "Stay with us. Don't go—"

But the dog sprinted at the stairs. His volley of furious barks cut through the music thundering from the ballroom.

"Jak," she shouted. "Stay, Jak! Stay!"

Jak was beyond listening. He'd scented his prey. Now he locked every sense onto the task of finding the killer.

Fabian called out, "Fetch the others!" Then he ran upstairs after the dog.

Josanne glanced back. *Do as Fabian says? Or leave him to face the madman alone?* Then Josanne made her decision. She followed him up the staircase that wound itself into the shadows of the tower.

* * *

The dog came bounding up the stairs. Cantley gripped the steel rod. Although the sun had been buried by fog, enough gray light filtered through the windows to reveal more than the last time he'd tried to conceal himself here. What's more, he'd evened out the odds. Instead of the knife, he carried the sharpened steel pole. Cantley would simply harpoon the dog with it. For some reason the trespassers had decided to play thunderous music downstairs. Even so, he could still hear the mutt's furious barks. Where Cantley stood on the upper landing, he could see that the dog had reached the third floor. Below that one, he could still follow the sweep of the banister. A male hand on that told him the dog had at least one human companion. The canine was much faster, of course; it ascended the risers in a blur of black. Quickly, Cantley retreated along this floor, the fifth, to the far end of the corridor where he stepped through the door. He left it partway open, then waited.

The mutt's barks grew louder. He could hear its drumming paws on the floor. Cantley knew it didn't have to see him. It could smell his trail as if it had been a blazing flare guiding in an aircraft. A second later the dog sped through the door. How tempting to see the mutt pierced on the pole—squirming, yelping, bleeding, dying. However, there was no time for such pleasures at the moment. The momentum of the dog carried it into the unfurnished room. When it tried to stop, it slid across the bare linoleum floor. Cantley twisted round the door, then slammed it shut behind him. He heard the dog charge at the door to snarl at it. Furious scraping came through the woodwork as it tried to claw it open.

"There, you blasted devil," he hissed. "See if you can get out of that one!"

Its human companion wouldn't be far behind. Time for Cantley's second part of the plan. He ran back to where the stairs opened onto the landing. He could hear the thump of drums. Good, the trespassers had gone mad. With their wits scattered, it'd be easier for him to pick them off one by one. He stopped just short of the stairs; instead of descending them, he swung open another door to reveal a narrow staircase. This was made of bare wood; purely utilitarian, there were no adornments or carpet. He raced up it to a door as narrow as a coffin lid. The moment he pushed it open, he was engulfed by cold, damp air. Cantley blinked. It seemed bright out here after the confines of the house. He glanced round at the flat roof with chimneys that protruded from the leadwork. He'd been outside here before. Normally he would have been able to see miles of countryside. Now when he looked over the edge he could barely see the ground. It was like peering down into a misty white ocean where clumps of hawthorn showed as little spiky islands.

Cantley scuttled around the far side of the little protrusion of stonework that housed the top of the staircase and exit door. The music was faint up here. He'd hear footsteps when whoever followed him up the stairs emerged onto the roof.

Chapter Thirty-nine

Josanne stepped out onto the roof to find Fabian lying there bleeding. The man she recognized as Cantley had driven a steep spike into his chest. Fabian had dropped the hammer. He used both hands to grip the steel spike, as tall as its wielder, from being plunged any deeper.

Through a grimace of pain, Fabian cried, "Josanne! Get the others!"

Josanne had expected to find Jak cornering the madman or even tearing hunks out of him. But even though they'd heard the dog as they climbed the narrow staircase to the roof, she couldn't see him now.

"Josanne—" Fabian's shout ended in a grunt as Cantley stomped his boot down on her lover's head. Then using both hands—one of which was bloodily bandaged—he twisted the spike so the steel, as thick as a man's thumb, turned in Fabian's ribs. He screamed.

"Stick around." Cantley grinned. "You're next."

Josanne backed across the roof. Her heel caught

one of the raised seams that welded the lead water-proofing sheets together. She stumbled back to land on her rump.

"Clumsy!" Cantley snapped. "Gotta be careful up here. It's a long drop."

She scrambled on all fours to the door. If only she could warn Marko and Fisher. In the distance she could hear their manic playing. Had they gone mad? Or did they really believe that music could weaken the house?

If she'd expected Cantley to be content to stand there with one foot on Fabian's head while he bore down on the pole, she was going to be disappointed. Cantley saw the direction she scrambled. Taking a moment to draw the steel spike from Fabian's chest, he ran across the roof to block her way. The creep stood there with her boyfriend's blood running a glistening crimson down the pole to trickle in sticky rivulets across his fingers.

"You're not going." He spoke matter-of-factly, like a parent telling a child it couldn't step away from the dining room table just yet. Not until it had finished its greens.

"Marko! Fisher!"

"You really think they're going to hear when they're making that racket?" He glanced at Fabian, who clutched both hands over the upper part of his chest as he lay on the lead flashing. Blood streamed from him into the gutters. "And do you really think he can save you?"

Josanne lifted the carving knife to eye level. It didn't even slow the man down. He slashed the long pole sideways against the knife blade. She winced with pain as he knocked it effortlessly from her grasp.

"You've got the choice between jumping . . . or dancing your funny little dance on the end of this." He jerked the bloody point of the spike. "'S'only about a drop of seventy feet." He chuckled. "Either way we've got you. Me and the house. You're for keeps, sweetheart."

Joanne had to back away as he advanced. As he did, so he made little jabbing motions with the spike. She glanced round as she moved. There was no barrier at the edge of the roof. It simply ended. Beyond that, there was a misty gulf of seventy deadly feet between her and the ground. The roof of the tower was little bigger than a tennis court. It was featureless, too, with the exception of a couple of stunted chimney stacks and the cuboid protrusion that formed the exit onto the roof.

What can I do? There's nowhere I can run without him catching me. He's keeping between me and the entrance to the stairs.

When she shouted, she knew she was wasting her breath, but what else could she do? "Marko! Fisher! Help!"

As he played the bass guitar, Fisher sensed the change. It was as if the fabric of the building had twitched. He felt the single pulse of vibration run up from the floor, through the soles of his feet, and into his legs. He glanced across at Marko, who slowed the drumbeat. He was looking round in surprise. He felt it, too. Fisher didn't know what it was exactly, but maybe sheer intuition—or was it the spirit of his dead father?—whispered the suggestion into the folds of his brain. With the bass still plugged in, he ran at the ballroom window until the lead was in danger of being yanked from the amp. But there was just enough cable for him to grip the guitar by the body and swing the instrument so the machine head stabbed at the glass. The moment it struck, the windowpane shattered into a thousand crystals.

"Marko!" he yelled. "It's weakening. It can't stop us from damaging it. Look!" He plunged the neck of the guitar through another pane. It broke like any regular glass in any regular house.

Marko shouted above the loop of keyboard notes that fired back the reformed chimes at the house, "Find Fabian! Tell him! And if he wants to burn the fucker down, let him!" He gave a huge triumphant drumroll as Fisher ran to the corridor.

Fisher wasn't sure where Fabian and Josanne had gone. He prayed it wasn't far. When he reached the bottom of the stairs, a muffled barking gave him a clue where they were. It didn't take more than a moment to realize the furious barks came from above. Fisher raced up the stairs two at a time. The barking grew louder as Marko's drumming became more muffled.

"Jak? Jak!" Fisher paused as the dog's barks returned with renewed power. "Jak, here, boy!"

But why didn't the dog appear? And where were Josanne and Fabian? He ran hard now as he homed in on the sound. When he reached the top of the staircase, he saw a smaller one behind the door. He'd already taken three paces through the door to the narrow flight of stairs when he realized the barking was coming from up there. Fisher returned to the landing. Listened. The barks were a relentless volley of fury. There were only a few doors off this landing; most were open. Logic dictated he try the closed one at the end. He loped across the landing to push open the door. The second he did so, Jak exploded from it in a blur of black.

"Jak . . . Hey, Jak, come here, boy!"

The dog didn't listen. He raced across the landing to the narrow staircase, then vanished up it.

Sucking in a deep lungful of air, Fisher followed.

Josanne couldn't retreat any farther. Even though they hadn't touched her, Cantley's relentless jabs had driven her to the corner of the roof. Now there was a misty drop to the ground on one side or down two stories to the steeply sloping roof of the wing of the house on the other. To fall either way wasn't survivable.

"You're going to jump, aren't you?" Cantley cracked a smile that revealed his rotting teeth. "Be my guest."

Josanne glanced across to where Fabian lay on his back. He was so weak that he couldn't raise his head, although he had rolled it to one side so he could see her.

"I'm sorry," she called out to him. "I did my best. I love you, Fabian!"

"Love." Cantley spat in disgust.

Then she saw it. She didn't recognize its shape. To her it appeared as a bundle of shadows cutting through the wraiths of fog that drifted across the roof. Only at the last second did she see the blazing amber eyes.

Jak didn't snarl or bark. He simply sank every shred of energy into running full tilt into the man's back. At the thud of the collision, Cantley's expression registered pure shock. The guy must have been convinced he'd been shot. He staggered forward as he looked back at what had struck him. Jak didn't hesitate, he leapt at the man to sink his teeth into the wrist. Cantley squealed. But even as he did so, he tried to reposition the spike so he could drive the point into the dog. Josanne lunged forward to try and wrest the weapon from the man's hands. The shaft was slippery with Fabian's blood. Josanne couldn't grip it, but she could make it difficult for the madman. Especially now that Jak clamped his jaws together with so much force that Cantley's blood began to stain the animal's teeth a brilliant red.

I can't let go, she told herself as she grabbed the spike. I've got to hang on until—

Then another concussion struck Cantley. Fisher had appeared through the fog. He was panting with exertion, but he summoned enough strength to fire a volley of punches at the man's head. Instead of fighting, Cantley tried to flee. Jak, however, had no intention of quitting the attack. In the melee Josanne saw that Cantley wrenched back from all three: the dog, Fisher and herself. At first she thought he'd ducked to avoid them, but then she saw he'd stepped back from the tower. As he plunged downward, his legs kicking back into the cold morning air, he bent his torso forward so it slammed against the roof. Both his hands were outstretched. One hand found one of the lead flashing seams, so he had a good grip. She could see his top half lying forward on the roof. He didn't appear in imminent peril.

But Cantley looked at her in surprise. He tilted his head to one side, listening. She turned her head, too, and heard nothing but Fisher's labored breathing. Even Jak stood there beside them, perfectly still, as he stared at the madman who tilted his head from one side, then to the other.

With a surge of emotion, Josanne said, "You hear them, don't you?"

"Hear them?" he cried in terror. "I don't hear nothing!"

Fisher looked round. "Hear what?"

"Cantley can hear the chimes," she panted. "Isn't that true, Cantley? You can hear the clock chiming."

"No, I don't," he protested, his face blotching red. "I can't hear them. I can't!"

"You hear the chimes," Josanne shouted. "You know what that means!"

"Please! Help me back onto the roof! You've got to."

A rumble sounded in the dog's throat.

"No, Jak. Stay there!"

The animal lunged forward, his mouth yawning wide. Fisher leapt to grab the collar to pull him back. But the dog locked his jaws onto Cantley's face. Jak worried at it as though shaking a rat. And although the lower half of the man's face was obscured by the dog's jaws, with the bared teeth sinking into his skin, his eyes were in plain view. They bulged in horror as Cantley screamed. When he tried to force himself away from the dog, he only pushed himself back into space. Instantly Jak released him. He watched dispassionately as the man fell seventy feet to crash to earth amid the hawthorn.

Cantley's physical body died dead the second it struck the ground. But some part of his mind detached itself from his shattered skull. His heart had stopped. His blood halted in his veins. But he could still hear the chimes. They rang out in hard peals like the sound of a vast subterranean bell. What some might describe as his spirit separated from his cooling flesh to descend into the earth. The two faces that looked down at him from the roof seventy feet above faded as his conscious self sank down through the soil that formed a brown mist all around him. Beneath the foundations of the building, a purple stain spread through the subterranean clay. Cantley didn't hear any words, but he sensed another's overwhelming anger at his failure. The power that had been known by many names through the ages swam through the cold soil toward him. Anger. Fury. Contempt. In a moment its rage at the man's failure would burst with devastating force.

Cantley's mind was no longer housed in flesh, yet when he felt the first searing touch of that elemental power, he understood that his torment wasn't over yet.

In the moments before his eternal agony began, he realized this truth: *To die in The Tower is no release. It is the beginning of all nightmare.*

And when, at last, Cantley began to scream, he knew he was far beyond the help of any mortal hand.

Chapter Forty

Marko helped Fisher bring Fabian downstairs to the entrance hall. Sunlight streamed through the open doors.

Marko asked, "Do you think the house is really going to let us leave?"

Fabian grimaced as he clutched a bloody towel to his chest. "Can't you feel it? The atmosphere—the ambience—it's different." He grimaced. "Easy, boys. I feel like I've just been turned into a walking shish kebab."

Josanne followed them with Jak at her side. She said, "Before we leave, we should wreck that damn clock once and for all."

Fabian managed a grim smile. "We'd be damn fools if we did. We've fought to win a cease fire with the place. That's enough. We don't need any more."

Marko looked back into the shadowed vault of the tower. "But is it going to let us go?"

Fisher grunted, "There's only one way to find out."

After easing Fabian into the back of the van,

Josanne and Jak climbed in with him. Marko leapt in behind the wheel to fire up the motor. Fisher chose to sit in the back, too. He nursed his injured hand on his lap as it started to throb. Missing from the vehicle were four of their number: Kym, Belle, Adam and Sterling. Fisher longed to search for the missing, but that would require the services of professionals now.

"Here goes." Marko crossed himself. Then he drove them away from The Tower.

They crossed the river without incident. The ferry had been on time. Despite the rain, the height of the river was falling. As they drove along one of the narrow roads that had brought them to this remote corner of England just a few days before, Jak stood up in the back of the van and ran to its back doors. He scratched furiously at them as he made a whining noise.

"I guess someone needs a rest stop," Fabian observed through a grimace of pain. The towel he pressed to the wound was slickly bloody. It was Fabian's opinion that the wound wasn't life-threatening, but then again no one wanted to delay in getting the guy medical help.

There was no other traffic as Marko pulled over to the side of the road. The moment Josanne opened the door, Jak shot out of the vehicle to sit on the grass.

Fisher's skin tingled as the realization crept over him. "You know something? This is where we picked Jak up on the way down here."

Marko opened his door so he could lean out and call to the dog. "Hurry up, Jak. Do what needs to be done. We can't hang around."

As Jak sat there in the morning sunlight, he regarded them with those calm amber eyes.

"Jak?" Marko whistled.

Josanne called him, too. Fisher heard anxiety creep into her voice. But in the end it was the still-bleeding Fabian who had to state the obvious.

"Jak's not coming with us."

Marko shook his head. "We can't just leave him here."

"Don't you get it?" Fabian gave a tired smile. "Jak's waiting for the next sorry bunch of human strays in need of his protection."

Josanne clenched her fist. "You can't know that."

"Listen to what your hearts tell you. . . . Go on, look at Jak, then hear your intuition. It's over, people. The Tower's letting us go. We know it. Jak knows it. We don't need him anymore."

Fisher found himself wishing that Jak would jump back into the van, but he found himself saying, "Fabian's right. Jak wants to stay here."

Marko's eyes glittered. "I've got room for Jak at home. He'd like it there."

"No. Jak's made up his mind." Fabian grimaced as the pain bit into his punctured ribs. "If you don't mind, guys. I don't want to debate this right now. Just get me to a hospital . . . please."

Without another word, Marko pulled away. They left the back doors of the van open in case Jak should change his mind and come racing after them to leap into the back of the vehicle. Jak, however, sat there and let them go. He remained watchful, his ears pricked. Fisher lifted his good hand in farewell. For some reason that was impossible for him to explain, he couldn't manage to release the word that fixed itself deep inside of him. Only as they rounded a corner and Jak's bright eyes vanished from sight did it reach his lips.

"Good-bye."

SIMON CLARK

THIS RAGE OF ECHOES

The future looked good for Mason until the night he was attacked…by someone who looked exactly like him. Soon he will understand that something monstrous is happening—something that transforms ordinary people into replicas of him, duplicates driven by irresistible bloodlust.

As the body count rises, Mason fights to keep one step ahead of the Echomen, the duplicates who hunt not only him but also his family and friends, and who perform gruesome experiments on their own kind. But the attacks are not as mindless as they seem. The killers have an unimaginable agenda, one straight from a fevered nightmare.

ISBN 10: 0-8439-5494-9
ISBN 13: 978-0-8439-5494-4

COVENANT

WINNER OF THE BRAM STOKER AWARD!

The cliffs of Terrel's Peak are a deadly place, an evil place where terrible things happen. Like a series of mysterious teen suicides over the years, all on the same date. Or other deaths, usually reported as accidents. Could it be a coincidence? Or is there more to it?

Reporter Joe Kieran is determined to find the truth.

Kieran will uncover rumors and whispered legends—including the legend of the evil entity that lives and waits in the caves below Terrel's Peak....

JOHN EVERSON

ISBN 13: 978-0-8439-6018-1

SARAH PINBOROUGH

The quiet New England town of Tower Hill sits perched on high cliffs, removed from the outside world. At its heart lie a small college…and a very old church. There are secrets buried in Tower Hill, artifacts hidden centuries ago and long forgotten. But they are about to be unearthed.…

A charismatic new priest has come to Tower Hill. A handsome new professor is teaching at the college. And a nightmare has settled over the town. A girl is found dead and mutilated—by her own hand. Another has slashed her face with scissors. Have the residents of Tower Hill all gone mad? Or has something worse…something unholy…taken over?

TOWER HILL

ISBN 13: 978-0-8439-6052-5

GRAHAM MASTERTON

A new and powerful crime alliance holds Los Angeles in a grip of terror. Anyone who opposes them suffers a horrible fate…but not by human hands. Bizarre accidents, sudden illnesses, inexplicable and gruesome deaths, all eliminate the alliance's enemies and render the crime bosses unstoppable. Every deadly step of the way, their constant companions are four mysterious women, four shadowy figures who wield more power than the crime bosses could ever dream of. But at the heart of the nightmare lies the final puzzle, the secret of…

THE
5TH WITCH

ISBN 13: 978-0-8439-5790-7

GARY A.
BRAUNBECK

COFFIN
COUNTY

The small town of Cedar Hill is no stranger to tragedy and terror. Nearly two centuries ago, when the area was first settled, a gruesome mass murder baptized the town with blood. More recently there was the Great Fire, the notorious night the casket factory burned down, taking an entire neighborhood with it. But no one in Cedar Hill can be prepared for what is to come—shocking murders that grow more horrendous with each victim, and a trail of taunting clues that point to the past…and to an old, abandoned graveyard.

ISBN 13: 978-0-8439-6050-1

☐ YES!

Sign me up for the Leisure Horror Book Club and send
my FREE BOOKS! If I choose to stay in the club, I will
pay only $8.50* each month, a savings of $7.48!

NAME: _____

ADDRESS: _____

TELEPHONE: _____

EMAIL: _____

☐ I want to pay by credit card.

☐ **VISA**   ☐ **MasterCard**   ☐ **DISCOVER**

ACCOUNT #: _____

EXPIRATION DATE: _____

SIGNATURE: _____

Mail this page along with $2.00 shipping and handling to:
Leisure Horror Book Club
PO Box 6640
Wayne, PA 19087
Or fax (must include credit card information) to:
610-995-9274

You can also sign up online at **www.dorchesterpub.com**.
*Plus $2.00 for shipping. Offer open to residents of the U.S. and Canada only.
Canadian residents please call 1-800-481-9191 for pricing information.
If under 18, a parent or guardian must sign. Terms, prices and conditions subject to
change. Subscription subject to acceptance. Dorchester Publishing reserves the right
to reject any order or cancel any subscription.